Please return or renew this item by the last date shown. You may return items to any East Sussex Library. You may renew books by telephone or the internet.

East Sussex
County Council

0345 60 80 195 for renewals

0345 60 80 196 for enquiries

Library and Information Services
eastsussex.gov.uk/libraries

HERE'S Looking At You

MHAIRI McFARLANE

AVON

AVON

A division of HarperCollins*Publishers*
77–85 Fulham Palace Road,
London W6 8JB

www.harpercollins.co.uk

A Paperback Original 2013

1

First published in Great Britain by
HarperCollins*Publishers* 2013

A catalogue record for this book is
available from the British Library

ISBN-13: 978-0-00-748806-3

Set in Bembo by Ben Gardiner

Printed and bound in Great Britain by
Clays Ltd, St Ives plc

ACKNOWLEDGEMENTS

Oof, prepare for a long one, as Count De Vici might (should) say. Firstly, thanks unbound to Ali Gunn and Doug Kean at Gunn Media – you're both an agenting dream team and a great night out.

Hugest thanks to my talented editor Helen Bolton for all her hard work and patience during the very steep learning curve that is the second one, and everyone at Avon and HarperCollins for their enthusiasm and skill. Keshini Naidoo, you're an additional marvel who made HLAY all the better.

My loyal first draft readers – my brother Ewan, and friends Sean Hewitt, Tara and Katie de Cozar (who in no way resemble the Alessi sisters) and Tim Lee – thanks so much for your encouragement. I'd give up without it.

Special thanks to the brilliant historian Lucy Inglis – forgive me for calling you 'historian' – for the Theodora show pointers. Gratitude also owed to Jeremy Fazal for Barking intel, and my father Craig for the Italian vocab. Sorry for the swearing in the rest of the book, Dad. Oh, and my film agent Mark Casarotto has to be thanked or else he sulks.

Funny people who've had their witticisms thefted and/ or adapted include: Jenny Howe, Alex Wright, Martyn Wells, Natalie Jones, Matt Southall, Rob Hyde and Sam Metcalf. Sorry dudes. Lawyer up or do fewer lols.

I am lucky enough to have met some amazing people in recent years, and for inspiration and great company, particular knee-squeezing thank yous to Bim Adewumni, Tom Bennett, Sarah Ditum, James Donaghy, David Carrol, Dan Gilson, James Trimbee, Andy Welch and Jennifer Whitehead.

I have an extended family of in-laws and friends who are always supportive and please know I thank you greatly and sincerely, without having space to list you all here.

Biggest thanks go to Alex and Mr Miffy. You put up with a *lot*.

And thank you if you bought this book. It still seems a miracle, one I don't take for granted.

For Helen
A school friend who's more like a sister

PROLOGUE

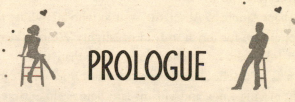

'Ladies and gentlemen. Mr Elton John!'

Gavin Jukes, in huge pipe-cleaner spectacles and a duck costume, strode out to deafening cheers. Well, strode out as well you can in canary yellow foam feet: a jaunty waddle. He sat down at the keyboard – with some difficulty due to the padded tail – and started bashing noiselessly at a keyboard, carolling along with 'Are You Ready For Love'.

Standing in the stage wings, Aureliana adjusted the sash on her 1970s peach polyester maternity gown with knife-pleat skirt, and touched a hand to her hair-sprayed bouffant.

She took a deep, shaky breath, inhaling that school sports hall odour of tennis shoe rubber, Impulse body spray and ripe adolescent hormones.

The leavers' Mock Rock was a simple but wildly successful formula: dress up as a pop star, the sillier the outfit the better, and mime along to an old hit.

And thank God, the crowd loved Gavin.

1

According to all witless graffiti that tackled the topic of Gavin Jukes, he was 'a massive gayer'. And yet he'd fearlessly chosen to impersonate a flamboyant homosexual singer, to this rapturous reception?

Perhaps Aureliana Alessi, the weirdo who ate whiffy lasagne in Tupperware for lunch instead of Mighty White sandwiches, might also finally be laughed with, rather than at.

It was as if school had been a pantomime, with everyone merely playing roles, and villains and heroes alike came on to take their bows together at the end.

Even Lindsay and Cara, Aureliana's most committed antagonists, dressed in minis and platform boots as Agnetha and Anni-Frid from ABBA, had studiously left her alone today.

Their coven members were swigging contraband 'Minkoff' brand vodka from bottles of Happy Shopper cola and watching her with their heavily Rimmelled eyes, but keeping their distance. Aureliana wouldn't have minded a nip of something herself.

Maybe the Mock Rock magic came from the fact that popular older kids were already like rock stars to the younger. Apart from James Fraser. He was like a rock star to *everyone*. Aureliana glanced over at him and told herself again that this would be fine because she'd be on stage with James Fraser.

James Fraser. The mere music of saying his name made her stomach lining dissolve.

She'd been skiving PE in the library a week ago, re-reading a *Sweet Valley High* book, when he'd approached her.

'Hi Aureliana. Aren't you meant to be in PE?'

It was the most extraordinary moment.

James Fraser, God of Rise Park, was for the first time

speaking to her. *To her.*

He knew her name. Not just the 'Italian Galleon' or 'Pavagrotty' ones.

He knew her timetable?

He smiled a lazy smile. Aureliana had never seen him this close up before.

It was like meeting your idol – all those hours spent obsessing over their every detail and suddenly confronted with them in the walking, talking flesh. And what flesh. That incredible white lit-from-within skin, like a church candle flame burning low and glowing through the wax. The oil-spill shiny black hair and the purple-blue eyes.

She'd actually tried to draw him in her *Forever Friends* diary once, using felt tips. It didn't work, he ended up a ringer for Shakin' Stevens. She reverted back to the usual hearts and flowers doodles, and the legend 'AA 4 JF 4EVA'.

'Don't blame you. PE's such crap.'

Aureliana made a sort of disbelieving honk noise and nodded vigorously. Sporty James secretly hated PE too?! This was proof. They were meant to be.

'I was wondering, the Mock Rock. I thought doing Freddie Mercury and the opera singer could be funny? A duet, me and you? Fancy it?'

Aureliana nodded. He'd used the phrase 'me and you'. Fantasies had become reality. Right then he could've said *I'm planning on jumping out of that window. Doesn't look a long way down, me and you, fancy it?* and she'd have followed.

It was only in the days after that she pondered the wisdom of going on stage as one of Rise Park's most fat, foreign and bullied, next to its sex god pin-up. What if all the worst bitches crucified her for it? But, she'd reasoned she'd never see any of them again after today, and they wouldn't wreck James Fraser's big moment.

She thought James might want to rehearse but he'd never suggested it, and she didn't want to look pushy. He knew what he was doing, he always did.

Perhaps they should've conferred on wardrobe though. Aureliana thought the deal was that they went all out. She'd backcombed her hair into something approximating a soprano's coif and plastered her face with pan stick. James, from what she could see, had only drawn on a cad's pencil moustache. But then she didn't know what she expected – he was unlikely to do a frontless leotard and stick-on chest wig.

Gavin was taking his bows. Oh, God. This was it. Here goes. James ambled over to her side and she'd never felt more important or special.

The Mock Rock's MC, Mr Towers, cued the music. Dry ice gushed out with a soft hiss, and the opening bars of the 'Barcelona' track swelled.

They walked onto the stage to deafening cheers and applause. Aureliana gazed at the gallery of delighted faces, getting an exhilarating glimpse into what it was like to be James Fraser. To feel that much excitement and goodwill reflected back at the very sight of you.

She turned to him, to exchange a nervous grin of solidarity before the singing started, but James was giving her a funny smirk and backing away into the wings again.

It was a green Praline Triangle that got her first, glancing off her cheek and arcing onto the stage floor. She felt a small pain in her stomach as another missile hit its target, like a rubber band being snapped against her body. A purple one with the hazelnut sailed past her head and she ducked out of the way, only to catch a toffee penny on the chin.

And then came a hurricane of Quality Street, as the air filled with a blizzard of shiny, multi-coloured shrapnel. Mr Towers turned the music off and started shouting to try to restore order, but all in vain.

Aureliana looked over in desperation at James. He was bent nearly double with laughter. His friend Laurence had one arm slung round his best mate's head, the other arm busy with a fist-pumping triumphal gesture.

Lindsay and Cara had tears of mirth streaming down their maquillaged faces, holding on to each other for support.

It took a moment for Aureliana to accept what was happening.

That this had been planned from the start. That someone had gone to the trouble of buying dozens of those big tins of sweets and handed them round the audience. That they had been given a cue to start lobbing them, and for everyone else, this was the extra helping of mock in the grand finale.

Slowly, it dawned on her that her crush might not have been as secret as she thought. This she found even more humiliating than being at the centre of the confectionery tornado.

She could see Gavin trying to remonstrate with them all from underneath his duck bill hat.

James Fraser was clapping and he uttered a three-syllable, single word, as he looked at her, enunciating clearly. *Elephant*.

Aureliana had long ago steeled herself not to cry under pressure. Not only did she not want to give her tormentors the satisfaction, she'd figured out the less reaction you gave bullies, the faster they lost interest. She saw no reason to break that rule now and start weeping in front of a vast and hostile audience.

Unfortunately, at that moment of dignified resolve, she was hit with a Coconut Éclair in the left eye, and they both started streaming anyway.

Anna stepped out of the stark autumn chill and squeezed into the steamy warmth of the restaurant. It was buzzing with conversations and pounding music, set at *the weekend has started* pitch.

'Table for two please!' Anna bellowed, feeling that flutter of nerves and anticipation, tinged with scepticism. When it came to crap dates, she had her proficiency badge.

Thanks to practice, Anna knew to choose lively and not-overtly-romantic venues to take the pressure off. And the trend for sharer plates that arrived at different times was a gift. With the traditional three courses, there was nothing worse than a date going badly, and knowing you were locked in the deadening back-and-forth of *really* and *where are you from originally* until the *just an espresso for me, please*.

Of course, you could simply go for a drink and cut out the dining. However, Anna vetoed alcohol and no food since an incident where she woke up at the end of the Central Line with only a patchy memory of how she got there, holding a plastic pineapple ice-bucket and a phone bearing eleven texts of increasing incoherence and pornography.

The intimidatingly young and cool waitress took her name and ushered her down into the dark basement.

Anna stood in the three-deep crush at the bar among the mouthy straight-from-work suits, wondering if tonight would be the night.

By 'the night', she meant the one she fantasised would be mentioned in the best man's speech in the splendour of The Old Rectory, as he stood in a shaft of sunshine splintered through mullioned windows.

For those of you that don't know, Neil met Anna on an internet date. I'm told he was attracted to her sparkling sense of humour and the fact she'd got him a drink without being asked. (Pause for weak laughter.)

She eventually part-screeched and part-semaphored an order for herself and her date, and found a corner to loiter in.

Honestly, she remonstrated with herself, an internet date is basically an interview for a shag. Isn't that pressure enough without mentally spooling forward to imaginary nuptials? Anna wasn't at all obsessed with getting married, per se; she was simply keen to find the person who mattered. She was thirty-two and the bastard was taking his time. So much so that she suspected he'd got lost en route and accidentally married someone else.

She scanned the throng for a ghostly echo of the face she'd seen in the pictures. Not only was it dark, but Anna was used to a disconnect between the profile photographs and reality. In her online profile, she'd tried to balance out a few flattering snaps against a realistic sample to avoid the horrific prospect of her date's face dropping when she arrived. Men, she guessed, thought more pragmatically: once they had you in the room, their charisma could take over.

'Hello, are you Anna?'

She managed to turn ninety degrees to see a cheerful, inoffensive-looking man with thinning brown hair grinning at her delightedly in the murk. He was wearing a Berghaus jacket. Fell-walking wear on someone who wasn't fell walking. Hmmm.

On first impressions, Anna wasn't too sure about Neil's dress sense. I'm pleased to say she chose his outfit today, or he'd probably have said his vows in Gore-Tex …

He looked approachable and trustworthy, however, smiling his gap-toothed smile. Not a problem for her; Anna was not the slightest bit fussed about pretty boys. In fact, she was positively suspicious of them.

'I'm Neil,' he said, shaking her hand and going for a peck on the cheek.

Anna proffered the spare Negroni she was holding.

'What's that?' Neil said.

'It's gin and Campari. A favourite drink from my homeland.'

'I'm a beer man, I'm afraid.'

'Oh,' Anna withdrew it and felt foolish.

Chrissake, wouldn't you drink it to be polite? she thought. Then: maybe this is something we'll laugh about eventually.

Apparently Anna was shocked to discover Neil didn't drink cocktails and he made a great first impression by disappearing off in pursuit of a beer. Start as you mean to go on eh, Neil? (Pause for more weak laughter.)

Anna knocked back her Negroni and quickly made inroads with the second. At that moment, as '80s Madonna hammered in her ears, she was Singlehood In London, distilled. It was all too familiar a feeling for her, experiencing intense loneliness in a room so crowded it must be nearing a fire regulation risk, feeling as if life was happening elsewhere. Right when she was supposedly in the beating heart at the centre of everything.

No! Positive thinking. Anna repeated the mantra she'd rehearsed a thousand times: how many happy couples trot out a dinner party origins tale about how they didn't fancy each other at first? Or even *like* each other?

She didn't want to be that woman bearing a checklist, always finding that suitors fell short in some respect or another. As if you were measuring space for a new fridge and moaning about the compromise in the dimensions of the ice-box.

Plus, it hadn't taken her many internet dates to realise that the *There You Are* thunderbolt she'd so craved simply didn't exist. As her mum always said, you have to rub the sticks to get the spark.

'Sorry, a few of those and I'd be out for the count. Falling-down juice,' Neil said, returning with his Birra Moretti. Anna wanted him to be nice and this to be fun with every fibre of her being.

'Yes, I'll probably wish I'd followed your example tomorrow,' Anna shouted, over the music, and Neil smiled, making Anna feel she could make this work through sheer force of will.

Neil was a writer for a business and technology magazine

and seemed, as per their previous communications, the kind of decent, personable and reliable sort who you'd fully expect to have a wife, kids and a shed.

They'd spoken only briefly online. Anna had banned the prolonged woo-by-electronic-*billet-doux* since the hugely painful disappointment of Scottish Tom the author, whose wit, charm and literary allusions she fell hard for, over a course of months. She'd started to live for the ping of the new message alert. She was halfway to in love by the time they finally planned to meet up, when he apologetically disclosed a) a spell in Rampton Secure Hospital and b) a 'sort of wife'. After that, Anna changed her sort of Gmail address.

As the alcohol took effect, she found herself laughing at Neil's tales about the 'rubber chicken' speaker circuit and shyster make-a-million industry gurus.

By the time they got to the table and over-ordered soak-up-the-booze-mattresses like meatballs, calamari and pizza, Anna was telling herself that maybe Neil was exactly the kind of solidly plausible candidate she needed to take a chance on.

'Anna isn't a very Italian name?' Neil asked, as they both prodded battered hoops of squid and dragged them through a small pot of aioli.

'It's short for Aureliana. I changed it after school. Too … flowery, I suppose,' she said, cupping a hand underneath her fork as the squid made a late bid to get back to the sea. 'I'm not very flowery really.'

'Hah no. I can see that,' Neil said, which seemed a trifle presumptuous.

Her free hand involuntarily moved to her hair, which was in the usual messy knot. Perhaps she should've done more with it. And added make-up beyond reddish tinted lip balm, applied in haste while on the Tube. Start as you mean to go on, she always reasoned. No point pretending to be a dolly-bird type and disappointing him later.

'The pork and fennel meatballs are the best variety, by the way,' Anna said. 'I've tried them all and can confirm.'

'Have you been here a lot?' Neil said mildly, and Anna squirmed a little.

'A fair amount. With friends as well as dates.'

'It's OK. We're in our thirties. You don't need to pretend to be the blushing ingénue with me,' he said, and Anna found something rather dislikeable in his pointing out her discomfort. Although maybe it was merely a slightly inept attempt to put her at ease.

Conversation stalled amid a loud Prince track, one of the ones where he went squeaky and frantic about wanting to filth a lady.

'I'm actually poly,' Neil said.

He's actually Polly?! 'Sorry?' Anna leaned in sharply against the noise, fork in mid-air.

'As in polygamous. Multiple partners who all know about each other,' he added.

'Ah yes. I see!'

'Is that a problem?'

'Of course not!' Anna said, perhaps too enthusiastically, fussing with what was left on her plate, thinking: *I don't know.*

'I don't believe monogamy is our natural state but I realise that's what a lot of people are looking for. I'm willing to give it a try for the right person though,' he smiled.

'Ah.' Good of you.

'And perhaps I should say that I'm into mild sub and dom. All hetero, but I'm not vanilla.'

Anna gave a grimace-smile and debated whether to say: 'I'm sorry, I don't speak kink.'

What was she supposed to do with this information? Blind dating fast-tracked the personal stuff, that was for sure.

'I mean, I'm not that *out there* in the scene,' Neil continued. 'I've tried figging. But we're not in the realms of the Shaved Gorilla though, hahaha.'

He was invoking shaving and animals in the boudoir. And figs, if that was what figging involved. Anna wasn't disappointed anymore. Disappointment was a motorway junction ago. She was passing through into severe bewilderment and at this rate she was likely to take the next exit into a Welcome Break.

'You?' Neil said.

'What?'

'Anything your "thing"?'

Anna opened her mouth to reply and faltered. She'd usually go with 'none of your business', but they were on a date and it putatively was his business. 'Uh … uhm. Usual sex.'

'Usual sex.' Oh God. She was underprepared and over-re-freshed. This was like that temp job in a cinema one summer where, during the fun selection process, she'd been asked: 'If your personality was a sandwich filling, which would it be?' She got brain-blankness and said: 'Cheese.' 'Just cheese?' 'Just cheese.' 'Because …?' 'It's normal.' Normal cheese and usual sex. She shouldn't even be on the internet.

Neil surveyed her over the rim of his water glass.

'Oh. OK. From your profile I thought you presented as heteronormative but might be genderqueer, for some reason.'

Anna didn't want to admit she didn't know what the key parts of that sentence meant.

'Sorry if this is quite confronting,' Neil continued. 'I'm a big believer in honesty. I think most relationships fail because of lying and hypocrisy and pretending to be something you're not. Much better to say This Is Who I Am and be completely open than for you to say on our fourth date, woah.' Neil held his hands up and beamed reassuringly, 'You like piss play?'

So ladies and gentlemen, I ask you to charge your glasses and raise a toast to the happy couple, Neil and Anna. And to the blushing bride, bottoms-up. You'll want a full bladder for later. (Applause.)

2

'Right, I've got Inspector Google on this Shaved Gorilla bull-shit,' Michelle said, squinting at her iPhone screen, Marlboro Light aloft in the other hand, smoke curling upwards in the empty dining room.

Anna couldn't have coped with so many bad dates without the prospect of her friends to flee to at the end of the evening. Fortunately they worked hours that made them ideally suited to nightcaps rather than nights out.

Michelle's 'traditional British cooking with a twist' was served at The Pantry, just off Upper Street in Islington. It was Grade II listed, with antique chandeliers, potted palms and buttercream wooden panelling. The kind of place where you have wartime affairs with men called Freddy in BBC dramas, and use phrases like 'it was a horrid business'.

Daniel, Michelle's long-standing front of house, was one of those semi-famous maître d's who got mentioned in *Time Out* for being a 'character'. The word character could be a euphemism for 'tiresome git', but Daniel had genuine charm and authentic eccentricity.

It was partly his appearance: a sweep of thick sandy hair, a bushy beard and high-magnification glasses which gave him cartoon eyes. He looked like a *Looney Tunes* lion crossed with an Open University professor. He dressed like Toad of Toad Hall in vintage tweed suits and spoke with an arch, old-fashioned cadence, like a junior Alan Bennett.

The three of them often met for drinks once Michelle had closed up, draped across the waiting area sofas, as the stubby candles guttered on the tables. Michelle was businesslike in her chef's whites and kitchen-only Crocs. Her short, shiny bob, dyed exactly the same red you found in curry houses on tandoori chicken, was worn tucked behind her ears. She had ginormous hazelnut-coloured eyes, a generous painterly mouth, and a statuesque figure that flowed from a prow of a bosom. A supermodel, but out of time. She was instead stuck in an era where people would call her a beauty but a 'big girl'.

'Maybe it's not deviant,' Daniel said from across the room, where he was sweeping up. 'Maybe everyone else but us is doing the shaved gorilla and the funky chicken and the … jugged hare.'

'I've had jugged hare on the menu and I can assure you it's nothing you want to be a sexual euphemism, given the amount of blood involved,' Michelle said, still peering at her phone.

Daniel set his broom down and joined them.

'Someone asked me why I wasn't wearing a hair net today,' he said vaguely, as he poured out a port from the cluster of bottles on the low-slung table.

'What? Who? Did you say "Do you think you're in Pork Farms"?' Michelle asked.

'Your head hair, but not your beard?' Anna asked.

'No, they said that was unhygienic too.'

'A beard net? Because there'd be nothing more reassuring than someone serving you food in a surgeon's mask,' Michelle said. 'Hang on. Who asked you this? Was it table five who had the vegan, the wheat intolerant and the one who subbed the cheese for more salad in the Stilton and walnut salad?'

'Yep.'

'How did I know? A band of pleasure dodgers.'

'Subbed the cheese?' Anna asked. She could've applied her brain to it, but she was by now pretty drunk.

'Americanism. Infuriating trend. Act as if they're in a sandwich bar saying *hold the mayo, extra pickle*,' Michelle said.

'We're firmly in the era of the fussy fuck I'm afraid and there's nothing we can do about it,' Daniel said.

His Yorkshire-accented lisp pronounced it more as *futhy fug*, so it sounded like it could safely be uttered on a Radio 4 panel show. This was Daniel's secret in defusing problems, Anna thought: whatever the words, the expression was gentle.

Michelle ran her index finger up her phone screen.

'Gotcha! The Shaved Gorilla … oh my,' she said, as she read. 'I'm not sure our grandfathers died for this.'

'He did say this is what he *isn't* into?' Daniel said.

'Dan, get with it. Classic grooming technique to float it as a joke first,' Michelle said, shaking her head. 'Brace yourself, it's something gruesome with jism.' She turned her phone screen to Anna, who squinted, read it and grimaced.

'Want me to try figging?' Michelle asked.

'No! I never want to try figging! I want to meet a nice man who wants to have standard sex with *just me*. Has that really gone so far out of fashion?'

'If something's never been in fashion it can never go out,' Daniel said, tweaking his own lapels, as Anna weakly shoulder-punched him.

3

'I mean, where's the romance and mystery?' Anna continued, holding up her glass for a refill. 'Mr Darcy said *you must allow me to tell you how ardently I admire and love you*. Not, you must allow me to tell you I'm into this spunk-throwing thing.'

'We don't live in the right era for an Anna,' Michelle agreed. 'Not much formality and wooing. But, you know. If you lived in Jane Austen time you'd have teeth like Sugar Puffs and seven kids with no pain relief. Swings and roundabouts. What appealed about this Neil's profile, before you met him?'

'Uhm. He seemed sane and pleasant enough,' Anna shrugged.

Michelle flicked her fag into the Illy coffee cup that was performing ashtray duties. She was constantly giving up, then falling off the wagon.

Anna and Michelle had met in their early twenties at WeightWatchers. Anna had passed with flying colours, Michelle had flunked. One day, their bouncy cult leader was barking: 'Strong minds need healthy bodies!' and Michelle had said loudly, in her West Country lilt: 'That's Stephen Hawking told, by Jet from Gladiators,' and then, into the shocked silence,

'Fuck this, I'm off for a boneless bucket.' That week, Anna missed her weigh-in and made a best mate.

'"Sane and pleasant enough" is aiming a bit low? I've hired staff that had more going for them than that.'

'I dunno. I just spent an evening with a man who talked about weeing on people as a leisure activity and demanded to know what I like in bed. So in the face of that, I'll take sane and pleasant. Try internet dating, and your expectations would tumble too.'

Michelle had people she called when she fancied a tumble. She'd had her heart broken by a married man and insisted she was not interested in looking for further disappointment.

'But you make my point for me, my love. That was someone "safe", so why not take a risk on Mr Exciting?'

'Even if they agreed to a date, I don't want to handle Mr Exciting's disappointment when he turns up and meets *me*.'

There was a brief pause while Frank Sinatra bellowed his way through 'Strangers in the Night', from the stereo held together with duct tape underneath the till.

'Are we going to say it?' Michelle said, looking to Daniel. 'Fuck it, I'm going to say it. Anna, there's modesty, which is a lovely quality. Then there's underrating yourself to a self-harming degree. You are bloody brilliant. What disappointment are you talking about?'

Anna sighed and leaned back against the sofa.

'Hah, well. I'm not though, am I? Or I wouldn't have been single forever.'

Anna's British gran Maude had a dreadful saying about the lonely folly of romantic ideas above your station: '*She wouldn't have a walker and the riders didn't stop*'.

It had given eleven-year-old Anna the chills. 'What does

that mean?'

'Some women think they're too good for those who want them, but when they're not good enough for the men *they* want, they end up alone.'

Maude had been an utter misery-tits about everything. But a misery-tits could be right, several times a day.

'When did you get this idea you're in some way not good enough?' Michelle said.

'That'd be school.'

A pause. Michelle and Daniel knew the stories of course, right up to the Mock Rock. And they knew about The Thing That Happened After. There was a tense pause, as much as anything could be tense when they were supine with alcohol at knocking one in the morning.

Michelle sensitively turned the focus, for a moment.

'I'm not sure hanging round with us two does you good. We're no help. I'm perma-single and Dan's … settled down.'

There was another pause as Michelle used the phrase 'settled down' with some sceptical reluctance.

Daniel had been with the somewhat droopy Penny for nearly a year. She was a singer in fiddle-folk band The Unsaid Things and sufferer of ME. Michelle was deeply sceptical of the ME, and claimed Penny was in fact a sufferer of POOR ME syndrome. Daniel met Penny when she'd waitressed at The Pantry and been sacked for being useless, so Michelle felt she had some rights to an opinion. An unflattering one.

'You are a help. you're helping right now,' Anna said.

'By the way,' Michelle waved at a bowl on the table, 'you've heard of Omelette Arnold Bennett. Well these are Homemade Scotch Eggs from Arnold's buffet. Dig in.'

For all her tough talking, Michelle was kind and generous to a fault, and had supplied food for a former customer's funeral earlier in the day.

'I've been eyeing them like a wolf for the last hour, but I feel guilty eating a dead man's eggs,' Daniel said.

'They're from the wake, Daniel,' Michelle said. 'No one goes to their own wake. Ergo, they're not Arnold's.'

'Oh yeah,' Daniel said. 'Egg-scused. Eggs-culpated.' He picked up an egg, and started eating it like an apple.

'Arnold's brother dropped them off. He told me what Arnold's last words were. Well, strictly speaking, his penultimate words. His final-final words were *not the cloudy lemonade, Ros* but that wasn't as profound. Are you ready? It's a bit of a choker.'

Anna looked at her with glassy eyes and nodded.

Michelle tapped her cigarette. 'He said he wished he hadn't wasted so much time being scared.'

'Of what?' Anna said.

Michelle shrugged.

'Didn't say. Life terrors, I guess. We're scared of all sorts of things that won't kill us, aren't we? The things we live our lives around avoiding. Then we realise when we get to the end that what we should've been afraid of was a life lived by avoiding things.'

'Fear of fear itself,' Daniel said, wiping breadcrumbs out of his beard.

Anna thought about this. What was she scared of? Being alone? Not really. It was her natural state, given that she'd been single almost all of her adult life. She was scared of never being in love, she supposed. Hang on, no – that wasn't fear, exactly. More disappointment, or sadness. So what was the fear she was living around? Hah. As if she didn't know the answer.

It was the fear of ever being that girl again.

She thought of the email that had dropped into her inbox a week ago, which had coated her in a sheen of unseasonal sweat as soon as she saw it.

'Some fears are justified,' Anna said, 'like my fear of heights.'

'Or my fear of bald cats,' Daniel said.

'How is that rational?' Michelle said.

'Cats keep all their secrets in their fur. Don't trust one with nothing to lose.'

'Or my fear of going to my school reunion next Thursday,' Anna said.

'What?' Michelle said. 'That does NOT count. You have to go!'

'Why would I do that?'

'To say, screw you all, look at me now. You didn't break me. You could slay the demon forever, this way. Wouldn't that feel good?'

'I don't care what they think of me now,' Anna said, with feeling.

'Actually going proves it.'

'No it doesn't. It looks like I'm arsed.'

'Not true. And look, if *he's* there …'

'He won't be,' Anna cut in, feeling a little breathless at the thought. 'No way would he go. It would be a million miles beneath him.'

'Then there's even less reason to avoid it. Do you ever want to be Arnold, wondering what life would've been like if you'd not wasted time being scared? This school show, the *Glee* thing where they were vile. You've never seen them since that day, right?'

'Yeah.'

'Then it's a loose end. An unfaced thing. That's why it's still got a hold over you.'

'Great Crom!' Daniel said, sitting up, looking in the direction of the restaurant's picture windows.

Anna and Michelle turned in their seats to see a thirty-something man hooting with laughter. His trousers and pants were at half mast, while he looked over his shoulder at people beyond.

'He's flashing us!' Anna said.

'That's the king and the privy council,' Daniel agreed.

They stared some more and saw the lights of a crowd in the distance, the firefly blink of camera phones going off.

'I think he's mooning his mates and we're getting the nasty by-product,' Michelle said.

The man lost his balance and staggered forwards, landing with a soft but significant thud against the glass.

'Woah, woah, woah!' Michelle was fast on her feet and over to him, rapping her knuckles against the glass. 'These windows cost five grand, mate! Five grand!'

A moment of slapstick comedy followed as a pissed man with his chap hanging out realised that there was a woman on the other side of the window. He screamed and ran away, trying to pull his jeans up as he went.

Anna and Daniel, weakened by alcohol, were left senseless with laughter.

Michelle returned, flopping down on the sofa and clicking at a fresh cigarette with her lighter.

'Tell these fuckers what you think of them, Anna. Seriously. Show them you're not scared and they didn't get the better of you. Why not? If you avoid them, you're wasting time being scared of nothing. Don't let fear win.'

'I don't think I can,' Anna said, laughter subsiding. 'I really don't think I can.'

'And that's exactly why you have to do it.'

4

In the merciful hush of the empty office, James was nasally assaulted by the sticky, urinary smell of lager spill.

The odour was rising from the detritus of last night's riotous session of beer pong. The cleaner had started fighting back against the mess generated by freewheeling urban hipster creatives, tacitly making it clear what was within her jurisdiction. Alcoholic games popularised by North American college students clearly fell outside.

Just as soon as James felt irritated about her work-to-rule, the emotion was superseded by guilt. Office manager Harris got stuck into arguing with the cleaner whenever their paths crossed and James didn't know how he could do it. She's your mum's age, wears saggy leggings and dusts your desk for a living. All you should do is mumble thanks and leave her a Lindt reindeer and twenty quid at Christmas, or you're an utter bastard. Mind you, on all the evidence, Harris *was* an utter bastard.

For about the last six months at Parlez, James had really wished someone would come in and shout at his colleagues. Not him, obviously. Someone else.

When he'd first arrived here – a multi-channel digital

partner offering bespoke, dynamic strategies to bring your brand to life – he thought he'd found some kind of Valhalla in EC1. It was the kind of place careers advisors would've told sixteen-year-olds didn't exist.

Music blared above a din of chatter, trendily dressed acquaintances drifted in and out, colleagues had spontaneous notions that they needed to try Navy strength Gimlets and did runs to the local shops.

Work got done, somewhere, in all the bouts of watching YouTube clips of skateboarding kittens in bow-ties, playing Subbuteo and discussing that new American sci-fi crime drama everyone was illegally downloading.

Then, all of a sudden, like flipping a switch, the enlivening chaos became sweet torture to James. The conversation was inane, the music distracting, the flotsam of fashionable passers-through an infuriating interruption. And he'd finally accepted the immutable law that lunchtime drinking = teatime headache. Sometimes it was all James could do not to get to his feet and bellow 'Look, don't you all have jobs or homes to go to? Because this is a PLACE OF WORK.'

He felt like a teenager whose parents had left him to run the house to teach him a lesson, and he well and truly wanted them back from holiday, shooing out the louts and getting the dinner on.

He thought he'd kept his feelings masked but lately, Harris – the man who put the party into party whip – had started to needle him, with that school bully's antennae for a drift in loyalty. When Ramona, the punky Scottish girl with pink hair and a belly-button ring who wore midriff tops year-round, was squeezing Harris's shoulders and making him shriek, he caught

James wincing.

'Stop, stop, you're making James hate us!' he called out. 'You hate us really, don't you? Admit it. You. Hate. Us.'

James didn't want to sound homophobic, but working with Harris, he thought the stereotype of the bitchy queen had possibly become a stereotype for a reason.

And the humdrum petty annoyances of office life were still there, whether they were in a basement in Shoreditch with table football or not. The fridge door was cluttered with magnets holding 'Can You PLEASE …' snippy notes. The plastic milk bottles had owners' names marker-penned on them. People actually got arsey about others using 'their' mug. James felt like putting a note up of his own: *If you have a special cup, check your age. You may be protected by child labour laws.*

James told himself to enjoy the rare interregnum of quiet before they all arrived. The sense of calm lasted as long as it took for his laptop wallpaper to flash up.

He knew it was slightly appalling to have a scrolling album of photos of your beautiful wife on a device you took to work. He'd mixed the odd one of the cat in there but really, he wasn't fooling anyone. It was life bragging, plain and simple.

And when that wife left you, it was a carousel of hubris, mockery and pain. James could change it, but he hadn't told anyone they'd separated and didn't want to alert suspicion.

He'd turn away for a conversation, turn back, and there would be another perfect Eva Kodak moment. White sunglasses and a ponytail with children's hair slides at Glastonbury, in front of a Winnebago. Platinum curls and a slash of vermillion lipstick, her white teeth nipping a lobster tail on a birthday date at J Sheekey.

Rumpled bed-head, perched on a windowsill in the Park Hyatt Tokyo at sunrise, in American Apparel vest and pants, recreating *Lost in Translation*. Classic Eva – raving vanity played as knowing joke.

And of course, the 'just engaged' photo with James. A blisteringly hot day, Fortnum's picnic at the Serpentine and, buried in the hamper, a Love Hearts candy ring saying Be Mine in a tiny blue Tiffany gift box (she chose the real article later).

Eva was wearing a halo of Heidi plaits, and they squeezed into the frame together, flushed with champagne and triumph. James gazed at his grinning face next to her and thought what a stupid, hopeful idiot he looked.

There was that sensation, as if the soft tissue in his chest and throat had suddenly hardened, the same one he'd had when she'd sat him down and said *things weren't working for her* and she *needed some space* and *maybe they'd rushed into it*.

He sighed, checking he had all his tablets of Apple hardware of varying size about him. He was probably worth about three and a half grand to a mugger.

His mobile rang; Laurence.

'Jimmy! What's happening?'

Hmmm. Jimmy wasn't good. Jimmy was a jaunty alter ego that Loz only conjured into existence when he wanted something.

'This school reunion tonight.'

'Yep?'

'Going?'

'Why would I do that?'

'Because your best mate begged you to go and promised to buy you beers all night, and said we could get gone by nine?'

'Sorry, no. The thought gives me a prolapse of the soul.'

'That's a bit deep.'

'You realise that at our age everyone will be doing that competitive thing about their kids? It'll be all about Amalfi Lemon's "imaginative play". Brrrr.'

'Think you've forgotten our school. More like "Tyson Biggie is out on parole."'

'Why do you want to go?' James said.

'Naked curiosity.'

'Curiosity about whether there's anyone you'd like to see naked.'

'Don't you want to know if Lindsay Bright's still hot?' Laurence asked.

'Yurgh, no. Bet she looks like a Surrey Tory.'

'But a dirty one, like Louise Mensch. Come on, what else are you doing on a Thursday, now you're on your own? Watching *Takeshi's Castle* in your Y-fronts?'

James winced. His Brabantia bin was crammed with Waitrose meals-for-one packaging.

'Why would my telly be in my pants?' he parried, sounding as limp as he felt.

'Wap waaah.'

James's phone pipped with a waiting call. Eva.

'Loz, I've got a call. We'll continue "me saying no" in a minute.'

He clicked to end one call and start another.

'Hi. How're you?' she said.

James did a sarcastic impression of her breezy tone. 'How'd ya think?'

Sigh.

'I've got some ear drops for Luther. I need to bring them

round and show you how to give them to him.'

'Do you drop them in his ear?' James hadn't necessarily decided relentless bitterness was his best tactic, but unfortunately the words always left his mouth before he'd put them through any security checks.

'Can I come round tonight?'

'Ah, I can't tonight. Busy.'

'With what?'

'Sorry, is that your business?'

'It's just the tone you're taking with me, James, makes me think you *might* be being needlessly obstructive.'

'It's a school reunion.'

'A school reunion?' Eva repeated, incredulous. 'I wouldn't have thought that was your sort of thing.'

'Full of surprises. So we'll have to find another night for Luther.'

After they'd rung off, James allowed himself the sour pleasure of having won a tiny battle in the war. The satisfaction lasted a good three seconds before James realised that now he was going to have to go to this school reunion.

He could lie, but no. This merited some small stray reference on social media as incidental proof – a check in, a photo, a 'good to see you too' to some new Facebook addition – to let Eva know she didn't know him as well as she thought she did.

'Morning!' Ramona unwound sheep face ear-muffs from her head. 'Och, why did I drink on a Wednesday? I am *dying*, so I am.'

'Hah,' James said, which meant, please don't tell me about it.

Naturally, he spent the next quarter of an hour hearing about it, then she repeated the tale to each new arrival. Wine served in plastic pint beakers got you pissed, who knew.

5

Anna tapped 'Gavin Jukes' into Facebook, hoping his name was rare enough to make him easily flush-outable. She wasn't completely sure why she was looking him up. She wanted one person she could safely say hello to, should he appear.

And there was his profile, second down – she recognised the long nose and chin. She clicked his page, the photo a family portrait. Wife, three kids. Turned out his own gender was not his thing. Lives: Perth, Australia.

Good for you, Gavin. When it came to Rise Park, she could see the appeal in going so far away that if you went any further, you were getting nearer again.

The phone on her desk rang.

'Parcel for you!' trilled cheery Jeff on reception.

Anna put the phone down and bounded down the stairs. Jeff was resting the delivery on the counter, a wide, shallow black box with glossy embossed letters, tied up with wide satin ribbon. It subtly but unmistakably trumpeted *I have spent more money than I needed to.*

'Something nice?' Jeff said, then muttered 'none of my business, of course,' flushed at the evident thought it could be

Agent Provocateur-style rutting wear, the sort of thing with frilly apertures and straps with buckles dangling from it.

Even though it wasn't, Anna went warm in the face too, knowing she couldn't correct it without making the suspicion stronger. It was like using the toilet stall with the foul smell and then not being able to warn the next person without them thinking you were trying a poo double bluff.

'A dress,' she said, hurriedly, 'for an … event.'

'Ah,' said Jeff, 'that's nice,' avoiding her eyes. In his head, she was obviously already in an *Eyes Wide Shut*, pointy nose opera mask, grinding away to Aphex Twin's 'Windowlicker'.

She carried the box up the stairs, back to her office on the flats of her palms, like a pizza. The University College London history department was spread over a row of Georgian townhouses, with high ceilings and huge sash windows.

It was a magical place to work. In her more sentimental moments, Anna felt it was a spiritual reward for schooldays – the dream after the nightmare. The building had that lovely old-fashioned carpety smell and yellow light from large round pendant lamps, as if you were living inside a warm memory.

Anna pushed her office door open with her back, pleased that no one had spied her. She'd feel self-conscious at any cries of *ooh let's see it on then*.

Anna might've lost her schoolgirl weight and become a perfectly standard dress size, but it didn't mean she thought and acted like the person she now was. She retained an intense dislike of clothes shops. The advent of online shopping had been a revelation. She would much, much rather use her office as a dressing room.

So when she realised the reunion needed a dress – no, not

merely a dress but something truly flash, that would raise two fingers to them all in the form of fabric – she'd gone straight to an expensive designer website and spent the cost of a nice weekend away.

She dislodged the lid, rustling through the layers of tissue paper. There the exorbitant dress lay. Not a lot of material for … well, she wasn't going to dwell on it.

Anna laid it carefully over a chair and checked the office door was locked, then wriggled out of her shapeless Zara smock, swapping it for the evening gown. She twisted it into place with forefingers and thumbs very carefully, as if it was gossamer, and pulled up a reassuringly chunky zip, with only a little breathing in.

Hmmm. She turned this way and that in front of the mirror. Not *quite* the transformation she'd hoped for. A black dress is a black dress. She flapped her arms up and down and watched the diaphanous chiffon sleeves waft in the breeze. She heard 'The Birdie Song' in her head.

On the website's mannequin, with its blank white Isaac Asimov robot face, the black Prada shift had looked 'Rita Hayworth during Happy Hour at the Waldorf Astoria' chic. Now it was on her, Anna wondered if it was in fact rather blowsy. Like a cruise ship singer who would launch into 'Unbreak My Heart' while everyone enjoyed their main of breadcrumbed veal with sautéed potatoes.

Inevitably, as she stared at herself, she remembered that other day, that other dress. And that other girl.

Eventually she picked up her phone.

'Michelle. I'm not going to the reunion. It's rank madness and the dress makes me look like Professor Snape.'

'Yes you are. After you've been, you'll experience an incredible sense of lightness. Like a colon cleanse. Barry! Prep that squid and stop playing *Fingermouse* with it! Sorry, that last bit wasn't for you.'

'I can't, Michelle. What if they all laugh at me?'

'They won't. But even if they did – doesn't part of you want a chance to live that moment again, but this time, you tell them all to go to hell?'

Anna didn't want to admit what she was thinking. What if she crumbled, cried and had to face that she was still Aureliana? Aureliana, holding more exam certificates and carrying less weight.

'Do I look alright in this dress you can't see?'

'Is it the Prada one you sent me the link to? BARRY! Get that off that sausage! Do you think you're working for Aardman fucking Animations? There's no way you won't look good. Your problem is going to be you'll look so good no one will be looking at anyone else.'

'Knock knock! Permission to enter the bat cave!' Patrick sing-songed through the door.

'Michelle, I've got to go.'

'You're right. You have *got to go*.'

Anna half laughed, half groaned.

'Come in!' Anna called. Cave was a reasonable adjective for Anna's sinfully messy space on the second floor.

As a lecturer, expert in the Byzantine period, she was allowed some stereotypical nutty professor licence. When it came to housekeeping, she took it. Books were piled on folders piled on more books. The disarray was an insult to a lovely room though, and Anna felt some guilt about it.

Patrick lived down the hall, teaching the wool trade in the Tudor period. They'd started at UCL at a similar time and shared a passion for their work, as well as an ability to laugh at it and talk about something else entirely. This wasn't to be underestimated in academia. Many of their colleagues were incredibly earnest. Something about experiencing life on an exalted plane of 'clever' could lead to malfunctions on the everyday level. As Patrick put it, they were people with brains the size of planets who couldn't boil an egg.

Patrick often began his day by bringing Anna a cup of tea, drinking his while sitting on the bright blue office supplies chair, once he'd moved a pile of box folders, Anna's coat and sundry items of course. Anna usually sat at her desk, scanning her emails and gossiping.

Patrick passed Anna her cup.

'Goodness me, new frock?' he said, watching Anna set her tea down.

'Ah, yeah.' She turned back and stood with her hands on her hips and legs slightly apart, as if she was a plumber about to give her price for addressing a particularly capricious combi-boiler.

'Is it for the Theodora show? I thought that hadn't kicked off yet?' Patrick added.

'No, I wish. School reunion tonight. Not sure if I should go. I had a molto horrifico time at school.'

Patrick squinted. 'Oh. Right. So why are you going?'

'My friend said it would be a defiant gesture. She's mad, isn't she? I don't think I can do it. It's a stupid plan. Oh, and do us a favour while you're over there, and top Boris up?' Anna said, nodding towards the large, beleaguered-looking cheese plant, and a scummy-looking milk bottle of water on the windowsill.

'I'm thinking Prada and spillages don't mix.'

He obligingly tipped an inch of greyish fluid into Boris's soil.

Patrick had very neatly-cut auburn hair and the quivery, undernourished look of someone who had been shucked from a shell, rather than woman-born.

His uniform was fine knit V-necks and a mustard-coloured cord jacket with leather elbow patches. He claimed it had become such an academic cliché it had gone right through cliché and come out the other side as original.

He looked up at a portrait on Anna's office wall.

'Ask yourself this. What would your heroine Empress Theodora do?'

'Have them all killed?'

'Then second best; knock 'em dead,' Patrick said.

6

Anna stood on the stairwell in front of a Blu-tacked sign in a distinctly ungentrified pub in East London with two stark options spelled out in Comic Sans.

Beth's Leaving Do→
←Rise Park reunion

Damn, she wished she knew Beth. It was a young name. Probably off to travel the world. She could hear a very bad karaoke rendition of Take That's 'Patience' drifting from Beth's party HQ.

Anna felt the vodka and oranges she'd had for Dutch courage sizzle acidly in her gut and trudged up the creaking, threadbare stairs and along the musty-smelling corridor to the appointed door. She had the pulse-in-the-neck trepidation of someone navigating the Ghost House at a funfair, her whole body tensed for surprise. Underneath the Milanese chiffon, she was clammy.

Another, deeper breath. She remembered what Michelle had said, that this was a demonstration of strength. She opened the door and stepped into the room. It was near-empty. A few people she didn't recognise glanced over, returned to their conversations. In her many, many rehearsals in her head, a gallery of familiar faces turned towards her, accompanied by a needle scratch noise on a record. But no, nothing.

The worst of them weren't even here yet, if they were going to turn up at all. Was she relieved, or disappointed? Weirdly, she was both.

A sagging banner above the bar announced a school reunion: *16 YEARS SINCE WE WERE 16!!!!!!* Oh dear, multiple exclamation marks. Like having someone with ADD shaking maracas in your face.

Anna got herself a glass of bathwater-warm Stowells of Chelsea white wine and retreated to a wallflower location on the left hand side of the room. She judged that everyone was only one alcohol unit away from circulating more freely, and she would be approached. She'd throw this drink down and get gone. There, she'd put her head in the lion's jaws. Done. Extra points for doing it alone. She wasn't quite sure why that felt so necessary, but it did. Like when the action hero growled: 'This is something I have to do for myself.'

It was an anti-climax, but wasn't it always going to be? What did she expect, that everyone would be queuing up to make their apologies?

The wall opposite held a collage of pictures on large coloured sheets of sugar paper, with childish bubble letters spelling out *Class of '97* above it. Anna knew she wasn't on it. No one would've asked her to squeeze – squeeze being the operative word – into the disposable camera snaps.

Below the display was a congealing finger buffet that

sensibly, no one was touching. When everyone was pissed enough, a few dead things in pastry might get snarfed, but the crudités were strictly for decoration.

The room filled steadily. Every so often there'd be some ghostly reminders – no one that prominent, but the odd aged version of a face Anna faintly recognised from groups in the lunch hall, or the playground, or the sports field. There was one semi-significant: Becky Morris, a chubby girl who'd made Anna's life a misery in the third year, to make it clear they were nothing alike. She still looked like a malevolent piece of work, Anna noted, just a more tired one.

It was a strange thing, but their flat ordinariness felt diminishing to Anna, rather than wickedly triumphal.

She'd let such people bring her so low? The banality of evil, the pedalling wizard behind the curtain in Oz. By comparison, Anna felt as if she was an inversion of a Halloween mask, moving among these people as one of them, a normal visage concealing the comic horror beneath the surface.

Hang on … was that … could it be? NO. Yes. *It was.*

Huddled in the far corner were Lindsay Bright and Cara Taylor. It was so strange looking at them. They were instantly recognisable, and yet all the vibrancy of her memories had leached away, like photographs that had lost their colour.

Present Lindsay's long blonde hair was now mid-length and slightly mousey, with roots that needed doing. Her middle had thickened, though her tight dress displayed fake-tanned legs that went on forever. The teenage hauteur had set as lines, giving her once-pretty face a set-in scowl. Anna could close her eyes and see Past Lindsay in a hockey skirt, chewing Hubba Bubba with a casual, glamorous menace.

Cara's dark hair was short, and she had the unmistakable sallow, pinched complexion of a behind-the-bike-sheds smoker who hadn't stopped. She used to hit Anna on the back of her legs with a ruler and call her a lezzer.

So this was the revelation that was supposed to make her feel better. They weren't terrifying, glittering ice princesses anymore. They were slightly beaten, early middle-aged women who you wouldn't notice pushing a trolley past you in Asda. Anna didn't know how she felt. She was entitled to gloat, she guessed. But she didn't want to. It didn't change anything.

They both looked over at Anna. Her heart hammered. What would she say to them? Why hadn't she prepared something? And what do you say to your former tormentors? *Did you ever think about me? Did you ever feel bad? How could you do it?*

But there was no light bulb of recognition in return. Lindsay and Cara's eyes slid over her and they carried on chatting. Anna realised they were probably looking at the only other dressed-up woman in the room.

And then, as time ticked by, Anna had a realisation. *No one* knew who she was. That's why they weren't speaking to her. She was so changed she was anonymous. They weren't going to risk admitting they'd forgotten her to her face.

The door to the function room opened again. Two men walked in, both wearing an air that suggested they thought the cavalry had arrived, and the cavalry wasn't much pleased with what it saw.

As their faces turned towards her, she had one of those funny moments where your breath catches in your throat, your heart high-fives your ribcage and all sound seems distant.

7

James really had to ask himself who he'd become if he'd put himself through this to score a tiny point against Eva.

Stuck in a windowless function room upstairs in a dingy boozer, pear-shaped pairs of semi-shrivelled balloons were dotted about the place, like garish testes. As always with forced gaiety, it came off as the very antimatter of fun. There was textured wallpaper painted the colour of liver below a dado rail, and the stale musk of old, pre-smoking ban tobacco. These were the kind of pubs he never went in.

Against one wall stood a trestle table with paper tablecloth and plates of mini Babybels, bowls of crisps and wizened cocktail sausages. In a nod to nutritional balance, there were withered batons of cucumber, celery and carrots arrayed in a sunburst formation around tubs of supermarket guacamole, bubblegum-pink taramasalata and garlic and onion dip. Only a sociopath would eat garlic and onion dip at a social event, James thought.

The room was sparsely populated and had divided broadly into two groups, each single sex, as if they had rewound to pubescent years of the genders not mixing. There were the men, many of whom he recognised, their features softening, melting and slipping. Hair migrating south, from scalps to chins.

James felt a shiver of schadenfreude at still looking more or less the way he did when he was a fifth-former, albeit a good few pounds heavier.

Everyone had given him quick, hard, appraising stares, and he knew why. If he'd gone to seed, it'd be the talk of the evening.

And hah — he'd said hello at the bar, and Lindsay Bright had actually blanked him! She may be an ex-sort-of-girlfriend, but surely she didn't still have the hump about things that happened seventeen years ago? I mean, they could have a kid doing A–levels by now. Perish the thought.

Returning with two pints of Fosters, Laurence nodded back towards where Lindsay stood.

'Blimey, she's not aged like fine wine,' Laurence muttered. 'Made of lips and arse now, like a cheap burger. Shame.'

'So can we go?' James said, under his breath. Bloody Laurence and his bloody schemes to meet women. These were even women he'd met already. 'I don't think there's anything here for you.'

'Yeeeaah … No. Wait. Holy moly. Who the hell is that?'

James followed Laurence's line of sight, towards a woman standing on her own. James realised he'd overlooked her numerous times but it wasn't because she wasn't worth looking at. She was dark: black hair, olive skin, black clothes, so much so that she had disappeared into the background like a shadow.

Mysterious Woman was done up to the nines in something that he thought looked a bit '*Eastenders* trattoria owner throws a divorce party'. He could imagine Eva telling him it was doing things the male mind was too crude to appreciate.

She radiated a kind of European art house film or espresso-maker advert beauty. Heavily lashed, vaguely melancholy brown eyes, thick eyebrows like calligraphic sweeps of a fountain pen, big knot of inky hair in an unwinding bundle at the crown of her head. All in all, it wasn't especially his thing, but he could certainly see the appeal. Particularly in these drab surroundings.

'Oh, we *have got* to say hi. I am appalled that she must've done an exchange programme and we didn't introduce her to our country's customs,' Laurence said.

'You realise you're getting to the age where this is grotesque?'

'You're not the slightest bit curious about who she is?'

James glanced over again. Her body language was that of someone desperate to be left alone, the arm holding her glass clamped tight to her body. It was a puzzle who she was, and why she'd come here. If James was on his own, he might approach her, given she was the only point of intrigue in the room. He didn't want to spectate a Laurence seduction attempt, however.

'I know who she is, she's the wife of the guy who's going to punch you in about fifteen minutes,' he said, brusquely.

'Plus one?' Laurence asked.

'Of course she's a plus one.'

James knew without question this woman was an exotic outsider. She hadn't gone to his school. No way his libidinous adolescent radar wouldn't have picked up the slightest incoming blip. Obviously some trophy wife, dragged along reluctantly. And the women here clearly didn't know her, bolstering the theory.

'Whatever her marital status, she's gorgeous.'

'Not that hot and not my type,' James snapped, hoping

to shut Laurence down. As James spoke, she glanced over. Mysterious Woman swigged the last of her drink and shouldered her handbag.

'Shit no, Penélope Cruz is leaving? I'm going in,' Laurence said.

8

In her twenties, Anna had a few fantasies about running into James Fraser again, and constructed elaborate imaginary verbal takedowns. Bitter excoriations in front of his wife and kids and co-workers about what a completely vicious conceited bastard he was, which usually ended with everyone applauding.

Now here he was. Over there. The man himself.

Anna could stride over and say anything she wanted to him. And all she could think was: *yuck. I never want to share the same carpet square with you ever again.*

He'd kept his looks, she'd give him that. Still the obsidian black hair, now worn artfully mussed, instead of those silly floppy curtains all boys had in the 1990s. And the shaving advert jaw line was hard as ever, no doubt much like his heart. It was a type of 'stock model in a water filter infomercial' handsome that didn't move her in the slightest now.

He was in a very thirty-something trendy combination of plaid shirt, buttoned up to the collar, grey cardigan and desert boots. What was with this thing of dressing like a grandpa, lately? Anna did a young fogey job but she didn't go around in orthopaedic sandals.

The youthful smirk had been replaced with an ingrained look of distaste. Exactly as she anticipated – he was surveying the company with the expression of a Royal being shown the pig scraps bins at the back of a chippy. Why deign to turn up, if he thought he was so far above the company? Wanted to reassure himself he was still top of the heap, perhaps.

And God, he was still with that lanky Laurence, court jester to James's king. Laconic Laurence, who once fired off machine-gun-like rounds of quick fire ridicule at her. She felt their eyes move to her. But unlike everyone else's, their gaze didn't move on. In fact, when she risked looking back their way, she got the distinct impression she was being discussed.

A self-conscious warmth started creeping up her neck, like a snood of shame. Had they recognised her …?

The thought sparked great comets of stomach acid, making her hands tremble. She suddenly felt as if she was nude in the middle of a crowded space, an anxiety dream made reality.

And at that exact moment, she could perfectly lip-read James Fraser's words.

'*Not that hot. And not my type.*'

Amazing. She'd come all this way, and he still found her wanting. Only this time, he could go to hell.

She chugged her drink and headed to the door. She was intercepted by Laurence, cutting right across her path.

'Tell me you're not leaving,' he said.

'Er …' once again, Anna felt her lack of a script. 'Yes.'

'Put us out of our agony and at least tell us who you are. My associate and I have been completely *foxed*.'

Laurence put a caddish emphasis on the last word, making it clear this was a chat-up.

Anna glanced over at James, who didn't look like he wanted to speak to her at all.

'Anna,' she said, dumbly, as she frantically calculated how to play this. She knew what happened next if she answered him honestly. He'd whoop with disbelief, say patronising, oleaginous things about how she was looking fantastic.

Then he'd call others over: *Hey everyone, this is Aureliana! Remember her?* As if she was so stupid she wouldn't decode the *Bloody hell, how did this happen?* And she'd feel like something in a zoo. They always did treat her like a separate species. She should never have come.

'Anna? Anna …?' Laurence shook his head and waited for the surname.

Mercifully, magically, letters in Comic Sans came back into her head.

'… I'm supposed to be at Beth's leaving do, next door. I wasn't sure if I was in the right place, I don't know many of the other guests. I was trying to finish my drink and slip out before anyone noticed.'

A wolfish grin spread across Laurence's face and she could see he was delighted at having a conversational opening.

'The whole SCHOOL REUNION banner thing didn't tip you off?'

'I … uhm. Usually wear glasses, the words were fuzzy.'

'Well, you've just settled a bet with my friend,' Laurence said, calling out: 'You were right! She's not from Rise Park. We were agreeing there's simply no way we wouldn't have remembered you.'

And before Anna could stop him, he'd beckoned James Fraser to join them.

'James, this is Anna. Anna, James.'

'Hi,' James put his hand out to shake hers. It was chilly and slightly damp. She gave him a look that was simultaneously intense and unreadable.

'Anna here is actually meant to be in Beth's leaving do in the next room. But lucky old us, she stumbled in here by mistake.'

Anna looked awkward and James tried to convey with his eyes that he wasn't encouraging or condoning Loz's hitting on her.

'Who is Beth and to where is she departing?' Laurence asked.

'Uhm. She's my cousin,' Anna said.

'And …?' Laurence made a 'tell us more' circling gesture with his hand.

'And …' Anna's line of sight cast around the room, as if looking for escape. 'She works at Specsavers. She's travelling round Australia. Flying to Perth.'

Poor Anna was clearly dying to be released to Beth from Specsavers' karaoke song murdering party. James was wishing very hard he'd reminded Laurence that striding over and introducing yourself to sultry strangers rarely went well. Not that it would have stopped him.

'Wait, wait. Are you saying you came in here without your specs, but you literally *shoulda* gone to Specsavers?' Laurence hooted.

Anna waited for him to finish laughing. James rolled his eyes in what he hoped came off as tacit apology.

'Anyway. Australia!' Laurence said. 'Always quite fancied the Outback. James here says Oz is the choice of boring uncultured beer monsters, but I disagree.'

Oh my God, we're playing good cop, bad cop now? You utter … James was going to have some words for Laurence when they left, not all pre-watershed.

'Not exactly,' James said.

Anna looked at him with burgeoning hostility.

'James here works for a digital agency, lots of big impressive clients. And I'm in sales. Pharmaceutical sales. So if you're fresh out of Anusol, I'm your man.'

'Loz, how about we let Anna get to the right party?' James said, hoping to redeem himself and halt the haemorrhoids chat. She scowled at him, as if he was trying to get rid of her.

'I've got a better idea. Given this reunion has all the atmosphere of a Quaker quilting party, how about you smuggle us in to Beth's do, and we buy you drinks by way of thank you?'

'Loz!' James said, sharply, writhing with embarrassment.

'I think Beth might mind,' Anna said.

'Nah. Sounds like there's karaoke in there? I do a belting "Summer of '69". Come on. Don't you think it'd be a laugh?'

'Nope,' Anna said, smiling. 'Bye.'

She slipped away through the door and Loz let out a low

whistle. 'Was that a second or third degree burn?'

'You can't hustle a woman you've never met before into drinking with you, without her exerting her free will to tell you to sod off,' James said, shaking his head.

Laurence gazed at the door, as if Anna might come back through it.

'Do you think that was a hint for us to follow her?'

'No, Loz. Now can we go?'

Laurence shrugged, scanned the room and necked the last of his pint.

Minutes later, debating 'more beer or kebabs' on the pavement outside, Laurence prodded James's arm. He urgently gestured down the street.

There, a few yards away, was the Mysterious Anna, climbing into a cab.

'Can you believe it? The lying …'

'Haha!' James liked her style.

'If she wasn't really going to that leaving do, why was she in ours?'

'She was left so depressed by one encounter with you, she couldn't face any more socialising?' James said.

'No. This is officially weird. Maybe she did go to our school and didn't want to say.'

They watched the cab turn the corner and then set off down the street in the stinging chill, chins angled down into coat collars.

'Do you remember any Spanish-looking girls at our school?' James said.

'Nope. You know, her whole story was off. How could you not read a banner that big? You'd need to be Stevie Wonder.'

'OK, try this for an explanation. Someone from school is a suspected terrorist and she's an MI5 spook. The suspect's gone to ground and the whole reunion was a herd and trap ruse by the British secret services to lure the target out. This Anna is their top woman, on secondment from Barcelona. But crucially, they forgot that to pass muster undercover as an ex-pupil of Rise Park, you need a KFC-zinger-tower-and-twenty-a-day complexion.'

James glanced over at Laurence and started laughing.

'What?' Loz said.

'Oh, just the fact you were actually considering that as more likely than an attractive woman not wanting to talk to you.'

10

'So, how did the reunion go?' Patrick asked, as Anna put down a cup of tea on his desk.

Patrick's office was as forensically neat as his clothing and, unlike Anna, he didn't use chairs as receptacles for overflow from his shelves.

'It was … peculiar.'

Anna debated saying no one recognised her but she realised that would involve pulling worms out of cans like streamers.

'Didn't run into any old flames?'

Patrick was a 'committed' – read: resigned – bachelor. His terror that Anna might betray singles club by finally meeting someone was only matched in scale by her equal certainty that she never would. She sipped from her own cup of tea and hovered.

'You must be kidding. No old flames at Rise Park, more scorch marks.' She wanted to talk about something else. 'How's The Guild doing?'

'Good thanks. Spent the weekend disciplining wayward teenage Danish warlocks and facerolling our way through the current wave of raid progression.'

'Much like here then. You're still a panda?'

Patrick always knew he could discuss his hobby without fear of judgement from Anna. She might not be a gamer herself but there was a geek solidarity.

'In Pandaria. Only temporarily. I used to be a female orc. A shaman.'

'Ah.'

Patrick was mostly into what Anna had learned to call 'immersive' games like World of Warcraft. He always tried to persuade Anna to give it a go, but she was dubious, especially when she found out he wore a headset microphone.

'Still, glad you went to the reunion, all told?' Patrick said.

Anna pondered this. She was more perplexed by it than anything.

'It was a useful reminder of everything and everyone I don't have to put up with anymore, put it like that. Like a vaccine shot of aversion therapy in the buttock. After that, I appreciate every single little thing about work today.'

She beamed and Patrick beamed back, perfectly in tune.

'Oh woe, I have first years at ten a.m. I challenge you to appreciate them,' Patrick said. 'I think this lot are the worst yet.'

'We say that every year.'

'I know, I know … but were we ever this bad?'

'We did go on to become batshit old lecturers ourselves, so we're hardly typical.'

'I suppose so.' Patrick swilled his tea. 'I had one last week who sat there and said "Henry VII was brilliant, just brilliant." As if you can skip the set texts and get your pom poms out and *cheerlead* instead. And I said "Brilliant how?" and he said' – Patrick mimed a blank stoner face – '"Just … brilliant." Roll over Simon Schama, there's a new guy in town. Another of them thought parsimony had something to do with income from parsnips. They should get a TV show together, *Bill and Ted's Excellent Historical Adventure.*'

Anna laughed. ''Fraid I can't say the same in return. My freshers are eager beavers. Plus, Operation Theodora Show kicks off this week.'

'Well done you. Can't wait to see it. Feather in your cap with poison Challis, too.'

'Hope so.' Victoria Challis was their head of department. She didn't have a warm and inviting demeanour, it had often been noted. She did, however, have the keys to the research funds and promotions cabinet.

'Lunch later?' Patrick said.

'Yes! My shout. It'll take my mind off having to go wedding shopping with my sister tonight.' Anna picked up a folder on Patrick's filing cabinet and lightly batted it against her forehead.

'Ah. Choosing flowers and trying different flavours of sponges and so on?'

'She's looking for her wedding gown— no, NO sentiment,' Anna held up a finger as Patrick formed a soppy face. 'There's the "aww" factor and also the "argh". If Aggy finds The Dress and it's huge, I'll have to follow the showy theme as a bridesmaid. It'll be tangerine or canary yellow shot silk with a zebra print fur trim, like some "Santa Baby" swingy thing. My sister's taste is very "Miami". She has already uttered the bowel-freezing phrase "seen something in the Ashley and Cheryl Cole wedding". Given they've divorced, it might even be the actual thing on eBay.'

'Ah. Well. I am sure you'd look marvellous in a refuse sack.'

Anna made her umpteenth face of gratitude. 'Thanks. See you later.'

Patrick beamed, doing a little wave as she exited.

Returning to her office and sitting down to her computer, Anna saw a name she didn't recognise in her email and realised it was Neil from Friday. She could see from the preview window that this said rather more than she required; it used the word 'lovers'. And an emoticon. Christ's fuzzy clackers.

She opened and read it, feeling her piss steadily boiling as she did so.

Dear Anna,

I am sorry you didn't feel our date had the required 'spark.' I enjoyed it very much. If you will allow me to give you some feedback in return, I think you may be more likely to discover this elusive 'spark' if you are more open in your attitude. I found it difficult to get you to enter into a real conversation and our topics rarely strayed from the superficial. In fact, I got the sense you found honesty positively intimidating. I require a little more confidence in my lovers. And in general, I am tired of women over thirty who claim to want to meet an available man, then play the game of 'catch me if you can' once they know he's interested. This rigmarole is not for those of us not in the first flush of youth ☺

However, having said this, I'd be prepared to try a second date if you persuade me it is worthwhile.

Best wishes,
Neil

Anna wrestled the temptation to craft a stinging riposte. She should resist. Ah, sod it. She opened a reply.

Dear Neil,

I'm not playing any game, I'm simply saying no thanks to another date. Maybe you'd have had more luck if you didn't make presumptuous and egotistical judgements like this about women you don't know. Or make rude observations about their age. Or quiz them on their sexual preferences on the basis of a half hour acquaintance.

Best,
Anna

She hit send and took an angry swig of cooling tea.

Online dating could turn the most spangled romantic into a grizzled cynic. Wasn't the internet supposed to herald a new era of ease and democracy in such matters? Instead it made the league tables, and winners and losers of the game, even more explicit.

Here was its stark reality: seeing that the person who hadn't replied to your days-old message had logged in mere hours ago. Or noticing that the exciting entrepreneur who told you he was moving to Amsterdam, and thus sadly not free for a date, appeared to be very much still in the UK and available to other women.

Spotting that for all the 'I want fascinating conversation' claims, the site's most popular of either sex were always the conspicuously beauteous. It was really 'Am I Hot Or Not', with some bullshit tacked on about how you liked crunchy peanut butter and the cool side of the pillow.

Oh, and men still tended to date five years younger than their own age.

Some people imagined Anna was grandly holding auditions, enjoying testing her market value. Or gadding round as if life was some Nora Ephron film, the world bristling with potential suitors you'd bump into while holding a brown paper bag with a baguette sticking out of it.

No, Anna was searching for a soulmate who probably didn't exist, in a place where he almost certainly wasn't.

Well-meaning types would say: 'You're the last person you'd expect to still be single! The world's gone mad!'

Anna had to disagree there. For her, the world had always been this way.

11

There wasn't really the conventional phraseology to describe what had happened to Anna, in terms of her physical transformation. If she said something understated like *'I used to be heavier'* or *'I blossomed after university'* or *'I was a bit of a duckling'* people nodded and said *'oh me too, I didn't really come into my own until my mid-twenties'*, or similar.

But to end up looking like a completely different person, one born to a radically different genetic fortune? *That* journey was so rare as to only usually feature in saccharine films with makeover montages. Bonsai supermodels 'disguised' in dungarees, ready to remove the specs and shake their glossy Coke can-sized curls out of a barrette.

Anna had not been a plain child. Plain suggested unremarkable, average, easy to miss. She was very eye-catching. A combination of her inflatable size, oily complexion, orthodontics, heavy metal singer mop of untamed black curly hair and homemade outsize clothes (God how Anna came to hate her mother's Singer sewing machine), made her stand out.

Seeing any glamorous potential in her future would've been deemed blind optimism, emphasis on the blind. Anna was, as her Rise Park peers often reminded her, fat and ugly.

She lost the weight when she was twenty-two. 'The weight' as opposed to just 'weight' seemed the right term, as her size had become a thing, an entity. Because Anna was A Big Girl. The fact followed her around and defined her. It was the monkey on her back that tipped the scales at an extra four stone.

The process of changing had been kick-started by a simple thought, after coming home in tears from a 'Oy, Ozzy Osbourne – who ate all the bats' heckle from a white van not long after she'd started her PhD.

She was intelligent and capable, and ran every other part of her life with rationalism and success. So why did adjusting the 'calories in/calories used' ratio to achieve an average BMI defeat her?

Like a lot of people who were overweight in childhood, by the time Anna fully awoke to the fact she was larger than other girls, it seemed incontrovertible.

Her younger sister Aggy was a whippet-thin livewire like their mother. Anna, they all said, was built like her dad. Their father Oliviero was a Central Casting roly-poly 'baddabing geddoudamah kitchen' Italian paterfamilias with a big broom of a moustache who advertisers would use to sell olive oil.

Anna's mum made his native cuisine in trencherman portions as an apology to her father for not being in his sunny homeland, even though he had left under his own steam in 1973. And while he loved Tuscany and often complained about London, he never expressed any serious desire to return.

She extended the policy of indulgence to Anna and her sister, who managed to combine the most fattening elements of two cuisines. Cheese, pasta, ragus as nod to their Italian roots, Oompa Loompa orange chicken nuggets and oven chips in nod to their Barking surroundings. Plus Somerfield's Neapolitan ice cream to notionally combine the two.

Anna was ten stone by the time she was ten years old.

Slimming was both mind-bendingly simple and psychologically complicated, all at once. Anna realised that seeing off a whole Marks and Spencer's tiramisu in one sitting was not her reward for being exiled from the world of the normal-sized, it was what was keeping her there. She swapped the stodgy carbs for fish and salads, and began running, pounding the streets in flapping old tracksuit trousers.

And Anna joined WeightWatchers. She didn't do it expecting results, she did it in the spirit of testing the hypothesis she was born to be hefty. If it didn't work, she could cross 'ever being slender' off the Bucket List.

As she lost pounds, then stones, her former identity melted away and a strange thing happened. She discovered she was pretty. The possibility had never occurred to her and, she was fairly sure, anyone else.

Previously, her expressive dark eyes, neat nose and sardonically amused Cupid's bow of a mouth had been completely lost in a pillowy face, like raisins and fruit peel in dough. But as her bones sharpened, indistinct features were revealed as the regular ones of the conventionally attractive.

'Aureliana looks like an actress!' trilled her aunty, on the first Boxing Day where Anna was not doing the 'roast potato challenge' with her Uncle Ted. For once in her life, when Anna pasted on a shaky smile, then ran away and cried, it was with happiness.

Initially, the wonders didn't cease. Anna learned there was

a whole secret world of coded glances and special treatment from the opposite sex that she never knew existed before. It was like joining the Masons, with arse-pinching in place of handshakes.

Even now, ten years on, when a student was sitting slightly too closely as she leafed through their work, or she got her coffee loyalty card peppered with stamps after one drink, she had to remind herself: *they're flirting with you.*

Some larger people could never adjust to being smaller, kept picking up Brobdingnagian trousers and getting halfway to the till before they realised they weren't the width of a doorway anymore. Anna suffered the same perception shortfall. She couldn't get used to being thought attractive. 'Gorgeous and insecure, the chauvinist's dream,' Michelle said.

Having assumed she would only ever have the pick of serious young men of the kind she dated at Cambridge, with huge IQs, dour expressions and well-ironed shirts, suddenly, the doors to a kingdom of choice had swung open.

So who did she want? It turned out, she didn't know.

At first, out of a sense of loyalty to her tribe and in some confusion, she dated the same kind of quiet, studious men as before, when she was bigger. These failed experiments had a pattern. At the start, she was worshipped like a goddess, as if they couldn't believe their luck. Eventually, they decided they definitely didn't believe it and the relationship collapsed, eroded by corrosive suspicion and buckling under the pressure of extreme possessiveness.

Anna had been completely committed to clever Joseph, her only long-term boyfriend to date, who understood jet propulsion but didn't understand how it was possible for Anna to spend an evening out that wasn't a hunt for his successor.

As for good-looking, confident men who sought a similar woman to be their matching bookend: Anna was too sardonic, too aware of their machinations to be suited as a partner. She bristled at any sense that it was beauty rather than her brain that had piqued their interest, and it manifested in prickly defensiveness.

And there were some negative consequences with women, too. There were rules of engagement when you were a 'looker' that she was very late to learning.

She didn't recognise the signs of jealousy when they flared, and rush to douse them with buckets of self-deprecation. Or join in when females were enthusiastically listing their flaws, which had occasionally been taken to mean she didn't think she had any. Anna had never needed to itemise her shortcomings, as it had always been done for her.

She never felt she *fitted in*, the same way she hadn't before.

Anna was unusual, a one off, an awkward oddity, and thus finding what people blithely called their 'other half', someone who tessellated, seemed impossible.

It was no coincidence her best friends were Michelle and Daniel, two people for whom image meant little.

And as desperately as Anna didn't want to be defined by those terrible younger years, she still felt much more like the girl who got called a hairy beast, than the woman who was wolf-whistled.

12

James knew the moment of reckoning would arrive eventually, and arrive it did, at 11 a.m., after Spandau Ballet's greatest hits had left him feeling destitute.

'Guys, just confirming we're still on for the big night out for the company's fifth birthday. I'll email the itinerary soon,' Harris said to the room. He was in his ironic t-shirt that said BOB MARLEY under an image of Jimi Hendrix and a pair of tartan drainpipes. 'We all good?'

James had turned the options over already. He could play for time and simply say yes, he and Eva were still coming.

But the deposit was £100. He'd need a reason for Eva's no-show. Something gastric, or a family crisis. James would be telling the kind of fibs that tie you in knots, bind your legs together and trip you over, face down onto a hard surface.

So far, failing to tell them he and Eva had split up was a lie of omission, navigating little semantic slalom courses when someone asked what he'd been up to at the weekend.

This would require active untruths – doctor's appointments and non-transferable flights to Stockholm and remembering who'd done what, and to whom he'd told it. And when the

truth of her absence was finally revealed, they'd work backwards and work it out. He could picture Harris, in one of
his Playdoh-bright tank-tops, holding a hand up and saying:
'OMFG, dudes. *That* was why she didn't come to the five bash?
I always thought the cancerous nephew was a crock of plop.'

The pity would be all the greater, mixed with derision. It
was bad enough they had to know; James couldn't bear them
knowing he minded them knowing.

'Uh. Actually, change my plus one. Eva and I have split up.'

Harris goggled at him. Ramona's jaw dropped almost as
far as her Tatty Devine *MONA* plastic nameplate necklace. A
hush fell over the room, a hush punctuated by the squeak of
half a dozen people turning in their chairs at once. Lexie, the
pretty new copywriter, audibly gasped. Charlie, the only other
married member of staff, who still dressed like he'd wandered
off a skate park, mumbled a *sorry mate*.

'Seriously?' Ramona said, always ready with the wrong
word.

No, she danced off in clown shoes squirting a custard gun.

'Seriously.'

'Why …?'

James mustered every last scrap of nonchalance he didn't
possess.

'Wasn't working out. It's pretty friendly, it's fine.'

He sensed Ramona's desperation to ask who–dumped–who,
but even her level of crass shrank from it. For now.

'OK … well, I'll put you down for one place then?' Harris
said.

James wrestled with the stigma of *divorcing loser*. Wrestled
with it for only seconds.

'Actually I was going to bring someone else. If that's OK?'

Ramona's jaw clunked open again.

'Someone …? There's someone new already? Oh. Is that why …'

James felt totally, completely justified in having not told them the truth. This was agony.

'It didn't help,' he said, in a brusque, heartbreaker manner.

James turned back to his screen and congratulated himself on a job done, if not a job well done. He'd take plenty of time getting his lunchtime sandwich so that the analysis would be done by the time he returned.

So all he needed now for the birthday party was a one-night-hire-only girlfriend. Sounded like the kind of thing Laurence could help with.

13

'Welcome to Sleeping Beauty. I am Sue and I can make your fairytale dreams come true!' the boutique owner chirruped, which Anna thought was a fairly mental claim. Wasn't Sleeping Beauty in a persistent vegetative state for a century?

Sue looked like a backbench MP in a skirt suit and pearls and Anna guessed her sales techniques would be brisk, despite all the wispy pouffiness around them.

Aggy and their mother's eyes shone at her words, and Anna knew she was a lone cynic in the realm of true believers. It was an enchanted grotto for those who wanted to walk down the aisle looking like a Best Actress Oscar nominee.

The salon was softly lit by peachy bulbs. It had a deep, spotless cream shag pile and lavender wallpaper with a dragonfly print, and rococo oval dressing-room mirrors – the sort wicked queens consulted.

The air was heavy with a sweet freesia scent, like some kind of sedative love gas. Michael Bublé crooned from hidden speakers, no doubt using subliminal hypnosis techniques.

Promise me your heart, give me your hand … and the long number on the front … now the expiry date, yeah baby.

There were racks of giant gowns, stiff and sticky-outy with net and bustles and laced corsets and an 'aristocrat before the French Revolution' attitude to making a bit of a show of yourself.

Sleeping Beauty could have been called *Go Big Or Go Home*. It was one big Pavlovian memory-trigger to Disney fantasies, in a world where the magic wand tap was the swipe of the Visa card.

Brides-to-be disappeared into a changing room through a crystal beaded curtain, to reappear transformed. Anna tried to imagine uttering the words 'something simple' in here, and failed.

'You must be my bride,' Sue said to Aggy. 'I can tell you're going to suit everything. Some fresh-faced young women simply make natural brides. And a sample size ten; the world's your oyster when it comes to choosing a style.'

Anna itched to say: 'What happens to the old broiler chickens then? Do you not flog them stuff?'

Aggy near-gurgled at the flattery. Physically, Aggy was a more angular, shorter version of her sister, but what she lacked in height and width she made up for in noise.

Aggy worked in PR, specialising in event management, and she was superbly suited to the job. She'd been organising things to her liking since she was very small, and her wheedle power was second to none. You wouldn't mistake Aggy for an academic: today she was in a puffa coat, high-heeled boots and carrying a Mulberry Alexa. She lived life in caps lock. GETTING MARRIED LOL!

There were two years between the sisters, and in some ways, a chasm of difference.

'This must be the beautiful mother of the beautiful bride,' Sue said, speaking to their mum as if she was serving her a soft-boiled egg in an assisted living facility. 'And this is the gorgeous sister and chief bridesmaid.'

'Judy' and 'Anna', they said in turn, as Sue clasped their hands and gazed at them with expression set to 'purest bliss'.

Aggy had booked an hour-long private appointment, and whilst Anna hated a stalking sales presence, Aggy revelled in the attention.

Anna shrugged her grey duffle coat off. Her family characterised her as a tomboy in contrast to her sister's girly-girliness, but she felt it was a simplification. She liked *some* girly things. Romance – in art if not in life, so far – and dresses and shoes and fizzy wine.

She just didn't like the full range of girly things that Aggy did. Such as nights spent on the sofa with *Vogue*, toe separators, Essie polish, spoon wedged in Ben & Jerry's *Peanut Butter Me Up*, white iPhone welded to her ear on the gossip grapevine. Instead of Cinderella's pumpkin coach, Aggy travelled in a Fiat 500 with rubber eyelashes on the headlamps and a bumper sticker revealing the worrying news for Saudi oil barons that it was *Powered by Fairy Dust*.

Anna was glad she liked Aggy's intended. Aggy was capable of marrying lots of men Anna wouldn't like, but luckily it was the affable, laddish Chris, a painter-decorator from Hornsey. He sincerely loved her sister and also knew when to say, 'That's henshit, Ags.'

They were tying the knot in the splendour of the Langham Hilton ballroom this Christmas.

Since the family dinner where Aggy arrived wearing a

diamond solitaire the size of a glass brick and her sister and her mum did lots of squealing, Anna had felt the tiniest bit nervous.

The one thing Aggy couldn't successfully manage was her own expectations. Anna was pretty sure the way the wedding was being organised was thus: Aggy choosing exactly what she fancied (which was usually at the top price point), and finding a way to pay for it afterwards.

Chris looked increasingly hangdog each time Anna saw him. Chris would've been happy with an Iceland party platters buffet at the Fox & Grapes, driving them to the venue in his company van, furry trapper's hat sat on head, ear flaps flapping, singing along very loudly to Smooth Radio.

At this rate, Anna feared her sister might end up adjusting her priorities too late to save causing damage to sanity, relationship and credit rating.

'Bubbles before we start!' Sue said, pointing to a silver tray with three flutes and a bottle on the marble-topped coffee table, next to a pile of glossy bridal magazines and a bowl of water with floating lotus flower candles.

Aggy was only a mouthful through hers when Sue cried, 'Let's get you into the first dress!'

Aggy and Sue disappeared through the beaded curtain and Anna and her mother exchanged smiles and tapped their feet.

'Do you think Aggy's in for the long haul here?' Anna said eventually, scanning the scores of lampshade skirts.

'Of course she is, Aureliana! It's till death do you part.'

'No, I meant ...'

'*Dum dum de dum!*' Sue sing-songed, holding the beads back for Aggy to re-enter, unsteady on cream satin bridal shop stilettos. She was in a halterneck gown with a simple A-line skirt and lots of Swarovski sparkle.

'Oh, lovely!' Judy said.

'Anna?' Aggy asked, uncertain.

'Your collarbones look nice. I'm not sure about the cowgirl rhinestones though. Could be worse. I give it three enchanted slippers out of five,' Anna said. 'It's … cut quite revealingly around your ta-ta's, too.'

'The modern way is to show slightly more skin,' Sue said, through a taut smile. Then reassuringly to their mum: 'Nothing tacky. Merely a hint of what lies beneath.'

Anna tipped her head to one side. 'Hmmm. I'm getting significant side boob, with the promise of full udder swing if she leans down to kiss a flower girl.'

'Ah no way, I don't want some rancid randy vicar being all "to have and to hold".' Aggy did a Rocky Horror pelvic thrust.

'Agata, the vicar will not be randy!' Judy exclaimed. 'Stop this!'

'We can tighten it,' said Sue, shooting Anna a look that suggested Sue was already doing some tightening of her own.

'Er mer GERD.' This was Aggy's latest expression. 'Did I ever tell you what happened to Clare from work? Strapless dress, bridesmaid trod on the train walking down the aisle, pulled it right down,' Aggy indicated waist level. 'But Clare said she didn't mind because she'd dropped five grand on saline implants in the Czech Republic. She was like,' Aggy pointed at her chest with both her index fingers, 'Feast your eyes, it's a banquet.'

'Surely a properly fitted dress couldn't be pulled down that far?' Judy said. 'That's a failure of the boning.'

Anna and Aggy exchanged a look.

'Maybe like Aggy said, she was an exhibitionist. Maybe she'd *booby-trapped* it,' Anna said, making a 'winding a handle' movement and a whirring noise.

'Possible, she was quite a rowdy skanger when she got a drink in her. Marianne said Clare with wine was like a Gremlin with water,' Aggy said. 'She used to show clients her bikini-line tattoo that said *mama is forever* in Sanskrit and our boss had to tell her to stop because the older ones haven't heard of vajazzling yet and she could upset them.'

'What does *mama is forever* mean?' Anna asked.

'Her mum died of an aneurysm in Bluewater. It was a tribute.'

'A tribute in the form of writing on her fanny? Who wants that? Mum, would you like me to get RIP JUDY down there?' said Anna.

'I can't say how I'd feel if I'd died,' her mum said. 'I think I'd rather have a memorial fig tree at St Andrew's.'

'So that's a pass to this one?' Sue interjected, desperately.

Anna felt a whisper of remorse that Judy wasn't sitting next to someone who'd do firework show gasps of 'ooh' and 'ahh' at the gowns, but to some extent you played the role that fell to you in a family. There was no question Anna had pulled the *voice of reason* straw in hers.

People often reacted with disbelief that Judy was their mother, firstly because she was youthful-looking and expensively blonde-streaked for her fifty-something years. And secondly, what with coming from Surbiton, entirely un-Italian looking. She was inordinately proud of her daughters' continental heritage and made a point of using their full names.

Their father, funnily enough, was less of a fan, pronouncing Aureliana and Agata as 'not traditional'.

'Your mother goes and registers these fooling names behind my back, saying it was her hormones! She does this twice! Can you believe it?'

Anna certainly could believe it. It was also very like her dad to let her mum have her way.

'Mum. How is Aggy paying for all of this?' Anna said in a low voice.

'She has a good salary. And savings. And Chris has money.'

'Not that much money. Do you not think this might be getting out of hand?'

'You only do it once. I know it's not *your* sort of thing, but it's her special day.'

Anna bit her tongue. She'd have a quiet word with her dad instead. The family had two distinct factions: Anna and her father's more sober self-containment, and her mother and Aggy's silliness. As Aggy changed again, Anna feared Sleeping Beauty was the start of a very long hike around London's upscale dress shops.

There was a loud shriek from the changing rooms.

'Has her false leg fallen off?' Anna said.

Sue appeared, only her head poking through the brothel curtain, wreathed in stagy drama.

'We've got something rather special here,' which Anna took to mean, *I think she's about to buy this, so stay on bloody message, bitches.*

Aggy walked out wearing a sheepish smile and what was obviously The Dress. It had a full Tinkerbell skirt in glistening layers of raggy tulle and a strapless, thimble-sized bodice, which Anna wouldn't have been able to wrestle her ribcage inside.

Aggy looked like she should be onstage in a ballet, and rather wonderful.

'Oh Agata!' Judy said, bursting into tears and jumping up to hug her.

'S'amazing, Mum,' Aggy sniffled. 'I feel like a princess.'

Anna stayed put and let her mum's raptures subside while she poured the last dregs of the cava into her glass.

'Don't you like it?' Aggy called to Anna.

'I do. I'm toasting a job well done. You look like you're really getting married in that. And only the second dress. Good going. Honestly, you look beautiful. It's "big wedding" but it's tasteful.'

Aggy twirled and pinched at layers of the skirt, letting them drift back down. 'You know how they say when you meet The One, you know? I've just met the one.'

After sufficient cooing, sighing and ogling had taken place, and an elated Sue had dashed off to find the paperwork, Anna asked how much it was.

'Three,' Aggy said.

Anna's mouth made an 'O'.

'And a half,' Aggy added. 'And another 250. It's £3,750. Veil not included.'

'Gordon's alive, Aggy! Four grand on something you're going to wear once?'

'Don't you like it?' Aggy pouted.

'I think you look amazing, I think you could look amazing for half that though. A large proportion of the amazing is you. Like Sue said, you'd look lovely in most things.'

'Hmmm,' Aggy twirled again. 'Mum?'

'You look like Audrey Hepburn! Or Darcey Bussell in *The*

Nutcracker!'

'Soon you'll need to be a safe cracker.'

Aggy giggled.

Anna was in a bind. If she counselled against the expense of this dress any further, they'd simply question her motives. She'd be accused of letting bitter spinster wrath wreck Aggy's happiness. Nevertheless, Anna genuinely felt no unsisterly envy. She'd need to want to marry someone before she could seriously covet a wedding. She couldn't put the gown before the groom.

'I'm going to make sure single men come to the wedding. For you,' Aggy said, as if her mind was running along similar lines.

'Yes. You should get out and see people, Aureliana,' their mum said, as if this was the moment to finally address her elder daughter's agoraphobia.

'I meet people!' Anna said.

Aggy was twisting her hair into a chignon and pouting, angled towards a mirror. Judy bustled off for a confab with Sue.

'I went to a school reunion,' Anna said.

'Did you?!' Aggy said, hand slipping from hair and jaw falling open, reflection momentarily forgotten. 'Why?'

'Thought I'd face my fear. It was pointless, as it turns out that fear didn't know my face. Seriously Ags, not one of them twigged who I was. I don't know whether to be pleased or not. Michelle says it's proof I've left it behind for good.'

'Did you see … any of them?' Aggy said.

'Er … oh. James Fraser?' Anna said, with a hollow little laugh.

'James Fraser?! What did he say?'

'Nothing. He didn't know who I was either. Still so far up himself it's unbelievable. I felt like saying to him, you know you

were only a hero when you were sixteen? Now you're nobody.'
Anna surprised herself with the vehemence in her voice.

'Real talk. Is he still totes bangable?'

'Depends on whether you like cardigans and cancer of the personality.'

'Aw, does he look like Elmer Fudd now? No way!' Aggy placed a hand on her hip and turned, with difficulty in the fantasy dress.

Anna smiled.

'He remains vile and arrogant but also still good-looking, which is all that matters, obviously.'

'I simply need to take a deposit!' Sue said, emerging again, triumphant, their mother in tow. Aggy demanded their mum bring her Alexa handbag.

They left, showered in Sue's love, with Anna feeling distinct unease at her sister's spendthriftery.

After hasty goodbyes outside in the miserable weather, with their mum having to rush to catch her bus to Barking, Anna tried to reason with Aggy.

'You can get a dressmaker to recreate that design for loads less, you know.'

'Marianne did that, and it never looks as good, honestly. You spend the whole day thinking about the other dress.'

'If you spend the whole day thinking about a dress, something has gone wrong anyway.'

Aggy tuned out remarks like that.

'Your dress next, Anna! We'll make a day of it, go for lunch.'

'OK. Nothing ridiculous, promise me.'

'Ridick! You're going to look the best you've ever looked in your whole life.'

'Setting the bar quite low,' Anna grinned.

Aggy looked as if she was hesitating about saying something, which was rare.

'I never knew what they were going to do, you know. At the Mock Rock. I was telling them to stop.'

'Oh God, I know. Don't worry about it.' Anna felt a familiar and severe twinge of pain and shame. No matter how many times she reassured Aggy she didn't blame her for being in the audience, this always came up.

Aggy's eyes welled and Anna patted her shoulder. It was typical Aggy that in trying to console Anna, Anna ended up consoling her.

'And when Mr Towers made us clean up the Quality Street,' she said, tears coming in a stream, 'I didn't eat any *on principle*.'

14

An hour before Eva was due to arrive at the home they once shared, James showered and got into his running gear. He wanted to show her he was active, virile and not at all pining or depressed.

As much as part of him fancied doing the takeaway cartons strewn around, dark-shadowed eyes, whisky-on-the-breath suffering pose, he feared it might be self-defeating. He reasoned that only by showing what a stupid thing it was to pass him up, was he going to win her back. Eva was never one to love a loser.

It was still a humiliating piece of theatre though and as he laced up his trainers with more force than was necessary, James tried not to think about it too much.

It was two months since Eva had dropped her bombshell that she was leaving, after only ten months of married life and virtually no signs of discontent that James could pinpoint, other than her seeming slightly distracted. It was like as soon as they finished decorating the house, she ran out of things to keep her occupied.

Now he was in this mortgaged-up-to-the-eyeballs millstone, deep in Farrow & Ball front-doored, Bugaboo-and-babyccino country, where he'd thought they'd start a family.

Eva was coming round to 'pick up a few things' again. She'd potter about and clank in the cupboards, as if life was normal. As if she hadn't recently sat him down on a Saturday morning, punched her fist into his chest cavity, taken out his still-beating heart and minced it into something fit for a pouch of Whiskas Senior.

Speaking of the other inconvenient, costly responsibility he inherited.

Luther was a Persian Blue, one of those pedigree breeds that looked unreal and toy-like enough to be sold in Hamleys. A football of fag-ash-coloured fluff with spooky little vivid yellow pebbles for eyes and a permanent frown, or a criminal forehead – James couldn't decide which. Eva had taken the breeder very seriously when they'd said it wasn't safe to allow him out, so the cat was also captive.

Luther had been named after their first dance song, Luther Vandross's 'Never Too Much.' Nicely ironic, as it turned out a year would have been too much. Given Luther was entirely an Eva-driven acquisition, James had been astonished – and not a little disgruntled – to find she wanted to leave him behind in the separation. *He knows this house, I don't have the space at Sara's for now, it would be selfish of me to have him.*

But then, if Eva could abandon a husband, he guessed a cat was small beer.

The doorbell sounded. James tried to greet Eva with an expression that wasn't set into cement-like hostility, but wasn't a fake smile either.

He didn't know how Eva could still do this to him – three years now since they first met – but every time he saw her, he was struck by how breathtaking she was in the flesh. It was as if the full impact of her beauty simply had to be seen to be believed. It was a physical sensation as much as an intellectual appreciation of proportion and symmetry.

That heart-shaped face, and generous mouth that he'd initially thought might be too wide, and seconds later, realised was the best mouth he'd ever seen. Her slanted eyes, dimples and her hair; naturally dazzling Timotei white-blonde.

If she wanted something and turned on the charm, she'd let her hair fall across her face, then delicately pick a strand between forefinger and thumb and draw it back carefully across her ear while keeping her gaze fixed on you, lips slightly apart.

Early on in their courtship, James thought she had no idea how madly seductive this was. Then, on a mini-break, they'd inadvertently landed themselves with a gigantic restaurant bill in Paris. The prices were already set at dialysis levels and they'd bungled the conversion to sterling with the wine list. James had nearly fainted at the final figure.

'I'll explain,' Eva said, summoning the head waiter, speaking in halting pidgin French — even though she was fluent — and using that look, while James watched his then-girlfriend's machinations in awe.

With pinwheel eyes, this man, a snobby Parisian no less, had fallen into a trance and for no reason other than he was being asked to, agreed to halve the cost of a dusty bottle of *Château D'Oh My Christ I Missed the Last Zero*.

If Eva hadn't been an art teacher, then hostage negotiator or shampoo model could've been equally plausible options.

Standing at the door now, she looked daisy-fresh, sylph-like and about twenty-five in a dove-grey belted cape coat and skinny indigo jeans. Resentful as he was, James ached, just ached, for her to say 'What on earth was that all about? I'm such an idiot!' – and fall back into his arms.

'Hi. Are you about to go out?'

James looked down at his clothes, forgetting what he'd put on.

'Oh, no. Well, yeah. Once you're gone.'

'You can leave me alone in here, James, I'm not going to steal your DVD player. Is that a beard? Is it staying?'

James's hand went to his chin. 'Maybe. Why?'

He was ready to be snappish about this – *it's no longer any of your business* – but he'd already lost her attention.

'Oooh! Hello you!'

Great. Wild excitement at seeing a sullen in-bred feline, after a greeting with her husband that could be measured with a spirit level.

Eva danced round James to the spot where Luther was hovering on the stairs, picking him up and nuzzling his blankly uncomprehending, angry-looking face.

'Aw! How's my best happy hair baby?'

James was starting to really hate the happy hair baby. 'Happy'? How could you tell, when you're dealing with something that looked like a tubby dictator in a mohair onesie?

'And how've you been?' she asked, as an afterthought.

He hated Eva asking this. She knew full well the honest answer was more than his pride could take, and the alternatives let her off the hook.

'Same. You?'

'Good, thanks. This year's intake seem a cute bunch. They really behave for me.'

'No doubt.'

Eva worked at a redbrick private school in Bayswater and her miraculous crowd control was not unconnected to her aesthetic appeal.

Every so often, she'd come home with some smitten pupil's unsubtle daubing of a full-lipped blonde, possibly floating Ophelia-like in water. It was usually a stealthy excuse to paint Miss in the scud. James had been irritated at being expected to look at this febrile fan-fic pinned to the fridge door.

'Here are the ear drops for Luther,' she dumped her bag on the table and rummaged for the packet. 'Twice a day and some brownish discharge is normal.'

'Fantastic. Looking forward.'

'I'm going to get some more clothes from the spare room.'

'Knock yourself out.'

'There's no need to speak in such a … diminishing way, all the time.'

James rolled his eyes.

Eva stalked upstairs and Luther padded off to the kitchen, with a flick of his tail to express his disgust at James's inability to keep a woman.

After she had rifled through it for the ear drops, Eva's tan shoulder bag gaped open enticingly in front of him. James could see a folded piece of paper and made out a name, 'Finn Hutchinson, 2013' with multiple kisses. Pupils were painting her this early in the term? He peered more closely. If he acted like a jealous spurned lover, that's because he was one.

Listening to her moving about on the floor above, James pulled the drawing out. It was textured, thick cartridge paper, the sort you get in art supply shops.

He unfolded it and stared at a charcoal outline of his naked wife, legs hooked over the arm of a sofa, arms thrown back, staring at him unrepentantly from heavy lidded eyes, hair pooled in serpents behind her head.

This could, of course, be another Eva tribute. Nevertheless, something told James this had been sketched from real life, notably the accuracy of the detail.

For as long as he'd known her, Eva had favoured a bikini wax that left only a vertical, cigar-shaped strip of hair. The small smudgy line between the thighs was a sure sign that the artist was gifted with first-hand knowledge. The smoking gun pubes.

James left the portrait unfolded on the table and leaned against the wall, breathed out, and folded his arms.

Feeling nauseous, deathly cold and yet in control, he measured each minute she remained upstairs as an eternity.

15

When Eva walked in, James took savage pleasure in the moment of grisly silence as she pieced the scene together.

'You went through my things?!' she blurted. There it was. If any doubt remained that this was a memento from her new man, her reaction sealed it.

'You left your bag open. What is it?' James asked, dully.

'It's a drawing. You've seen them before.'

'You're going to lie to me? Even in the face of this?'

'How am I lying?'

'Because this isn't from anyone's imagination, Eva, it's you. Do you think I can't recognise my own wife?'

A pause. Her face dropped, her shoulders heaved and she started to weep. Frustratingly, James felt automatic guilt at making her cry. He knew he was being manipulated and his fury broke.

'No, don't cry! You don't get to cry. You've done this to me, to us! How the fuck do you think I feel? Do you think I deserve to find out you're having an affair via a doodle of your tits?'

'I'm not having an affair!' she said, blearily.

'What word would you prefer?'

'I knew you'd make this about Finn when it's not.'

'Oh I think it's a bit about Finn now you're shagging him, don't you? How long has it been going on?'

When they first split, he'd asked her if there was anyone else and it was *no, no, no – absolutely not.*

Eva shook her head. 'Nothing happened until we'd separated.'

'Hah. Right. You obviously finished things to start this. Thanks for the Bill Clinton definition of honesty.'

Eva shook her head vigorously. 'No.'

'Is that too straightforward for you? Does trashing our marriage have to be about higher, spiritual needs than you being into someone else? That would be so *ordinary*, wouldn't it? And make you in the wrong. Heaven forbid we call it something as shitty as you CHEATING.'

James had built up to shouting and Eva was wiping at her cheeks, head bent, hair falling forward over her eyes. It wasn't remorse, it was a tactic to make James the villain of the piece and he wasn't having it.

'Who is he?'

'He did some life class modelling. We've become closer recently …'

'How close? This close?' James gestured with his hands apart. 'Or let me guess. *This* close,' he put his palms together.

Eva shook her head and sniffled.

Wait. Finn. Life modelling. She'd talked about him. She'd met him at a launch, with her restaurant PR friend, Hatty. He'd offered to model for her students and she'd said they couldn't afford him.

Then a few weeks later there'd been a giggly, supposedly

84

disparaging tale about how this 'Abercrombie & Fitch type' had swaggered into school to pose, dropping his robe and flirting with the blushing A-level students.

James remembered saying, 'What, flirted while flopped out? I have to admire his confidence.'

Eva had demurred with talk of strategically placed towels, and said something about how he was an up-and-coming who was signed with a major modelling agency.

James realised now that cocky Finn had made rather a big gesture in working pro bono.

Eva had gaily wondered which of her sixth formers might have a fling with him. James now detected the sleight of hand, with hindsight: it was Eva he'd met, before he posed. It was a gesture to impress her.

'How old is he, Eva?'

'Twenty-three.'

James put a hand over his forehead. 'Twenty-three? What the— ? You're into kids now? *Harold and Maude*?'

'Oh that's right, start running him down and making your James jokes. Let's not discuss this in a mature way.'

'How do you expect me to behave? Did you think I'd be calm and reasonable in the face of finding out you're sleeping with someone else?'

He nearly said *how would you feel if the situation was reversed*, then realised that question might not do him any favours.

She shook her head in a patronising way, as if it was James who had something to be ashamed of.

It was at this point that Luther decided to interrupt, the treacherous scruff-sack making distressed yowling sounds at Eva's feet. She scooped him up and made extravagantly soothing noises, as if it was James breaking up happy homes and cat's hearts.

'I'm not having sex with him,' Eva said, without much conviction, over Luther's giant feather duster of a squirrelly tail.

He shook his head in disbelief.

'Put that thing down, will you.'

Eva bent and dropped him.

'We meet for coffee. I've only been to his flat once. To pose for him. He's interested in art.'

'What the …? I'm supposed to believe that you then put your thong back on and shared Muller Corners? And by the way, tell him not to give up the day job. You look like Richard Branson in that sketch.'

'Posing is not a big deal for me. That's a British hang-up, sexualising nudity.'

'And Finn's Scandinavian is he? No? British and male and heterosexual? Ah right. So you're telling me nothing happened after that?'

'Not … I told you.'

Her hesitation about how to categorise their activities was worse for James than an outright confession of Biblical knowledge. She might as well take a knife, slice a flap in his stomach, and tuck in with a chilled spoon.

'If you've done things with him that would get you arrested if you did them in public, Eva, you're sleeping with him. Sorry to be so old-fashioned. It's just with me being your husband, I get terribly hung up on the detail.'

There was a pause where Eva didn't demur.

'Is it serious?'

'I don't know.'

'All this for "I don't know."' James put his hands on his

head. 'I'd prefer it if you said yeah, he's the love of my life, it had to be done.'

He wouldn't. James was picturing this Finn's eyes, hands and possibly tongue on Eva and trying not to cry, vomit or punch a wall.

'Maybe your inability to comprehend that this isn't about someone else is the kind of attitude that put a distance between us.'

'What the fuck's *that* meant to mean?'

'It means that the fact I could feel anything for Finn shows something wasn't right with us.'

James swallowed hard. His Adam's apple had apparently swollen. 'I think you've got this back to front,' he said, struggling to keep his voice even. 'The whole point of being married is you resist the temptation of other people.'

Eva picked up her bag, eyes downcast.

'Since we got married, things haven't been the same. More routine, perhaps. I can't explain it.'

'There will be some routine in a marriage, that's how it works. We have a home, and jobs.'

Eva looked at him contemptuously, as if to say *is that it? That's all you got?*

'Am I supposed to wait this out, while you decide if you're gone for good or not?' James said, though with less fire than before.

'I'm not asking you to do anything, James.'

She was composed now, contrition over. That was Eva. Maddening, supremely self-assured Eva, who he was inconveniently hopelessly in love with.

James had no idea what more to say, or what to do. Any

threats were bluffing. When someone took a shit on your heart like this, they either lost you, or discovered they had all the power.

'When you've calmed down, we can talk.' She let herself out, and left James slumped on the sofa.

Was it true? Had he trapped Eva like a schoolboy with a butterfly in a jam jar, and watched her wither? No, bollocks to that. Eva was no fluttering helpless creature, and North London had plenty of oxygen.

She'd spoken as if their life together was something he'd designed, and sealed her inside. They both wanted this, didn't they? Looking at the house, it was Eva-ish in every detail, bar his PlayStation 4.

But he was boring. Life with him was boring. How did you fix that? How did you make your essence interesting to some-one again? He did want to fix it.

Whilst he hated Eva right now, and she was making him utterly miserable, he felt more addicted to her than ever.

When James was eight and his parents had sat him down and told him they were separating, he'd not understood why his dad couldn't be around for some of the time. Surely to go from living together to nothing at all made no sense? Stay for weekends, he'd said. Or Wednesdays. Wednesdays were good, *Teenage Mutant Ninja Turtles* was on and they had pasta bow-ties with the red sauce.

They'd both smiled sadly and indulgently. Now here he was with his own marriage falling apart, and although he now understood why they couldn't be saved by scaling back their hours, he wasn't sure he understood them any better either.

And yet again, Eva hadn't mentioned the 'D' word. Knowing

her, she'd probably stick it on a text. *'Got Luther something 4 his tickly cough. PS Decree Nisi on way 2 U.'*

James tried to push the bad thought away, the worst thought, even worse than her being scuttled by some idiot with a Smurf hat and no belt in his jeans. *If she does come back, how are you ever going to feel sure of her again?*

He closed his eyes. When he opened them again, Luther was in front of him on the rug, staring at James with an accusatory menace, breathing like Darth Vader.

'C'mere, you grumpy git.'

James picked the cat up and held him to his face, letting his thick fur absorb the tears as he sobbed. Luther smelt of her perfume.

16

When she was eight years old, on a trip to see the Italian family, Anna's dad had taken her to see the Ravenna mosaics. While her mother, with a trainee consumerist in Aggy, had done the rounds of the boutiques, Anna was stood with cricked neck in the saintly hush of the Basilica of San Vitale. Her father told a sketchy outline of the story of Byzantine Emperor Justinian and his consort Theodora.

It was enough to get her hooked. She was utterly lost in the story of the daughter of the bear-keeper of Constantinople's hippodrome who became an actress, prostitute – her dad had gone with 'she made money from her adventures' but Anna wasn't stupid – and Empress of the Roman Empire. She stared at the regal beauty depicted in those tiny glittering tiles and felt as if those lamp-like dark eyes were staring directly into her own, communicating across the distance of centuries.

It was as close as she might come to a religious experience; the sense of finding something you were looking for, being transformed in a moment. Anna's family weren't religious, but in some ways, Theodora became a deity for Anna. Here was an inspirational woman who'd travelled very far from her beginnings, who demonstrated that the start point need not define you. She was a heroine, a role model. Well, there had been some fairly wild activity in the process of making a name for herself, involving all the orifices, and Anna wasn't going to try that. But in general.

Her parents had tried to slake her newfound thirst for knowledge by buying her one of those hardback *A Brief History of All the History There's Ever Been* books, with lots of pictures. She devoured it in days and wanted more. Eventually her mum let her have free run of a library card and Anna was able to get to the good stuff, proper detailed lurid biography.

Books showed Anna other universes, promising her there was a big world beyond Rise Park. It might not be overstating it to say books saved her life. She never understood why some of her friends thought history was dry and dusty. Young Theodora was getting up to shit a sight more colourful in AD 500 than any of them in the twentieth century, whatever Jennifer Pritchard was claiming went on in Mayesbrook Park.

Some went into teaching because they loved imparting knowledge, or more often, bossing people about. Once Anna overcame her fear of standing up in front of an audience – through therapy and practice, and in the early days, a gin miniature – Anna enjoyed lectures and tutorials well enough. But for her the raw thrills were in research.

It was the 'eureka' moments – where she felt like the first detective on the scene, finding the vital clue. Then she wasn't merely consuming historical fact, she was adding to its sum.

It felt like some kind of full circle, punch-the-air joy when lovely John Herbert, curator of Byzantine history at the British Museum, had got in touch and asked if she would help him put together an exhibition on Theodora. Her inner child, who'd stared up at that gilded, domed ceiling and been transported to another time, was dancing a jig.

Anna was translating texts and helping to choose and caption the exhibits. She couldn't think of anything more wonderful than getting to fiddle around with bits of the past, to raise the dead in some small way. Anna had only assisted with the odd aspect of exhibitions before, a good excuse to poke around at the British Museum.

This was the first time she'd been a behind-the-scenes driving creative force. She'd worked late for months to prep for it, willingly.

As she tripped off for her first meeting about Operation Theodora, she enjoyed every second of the walk through Bloomsbury, even beaming foolishly at passing strangers. This was a chocolate-box pretty part of the capital, the London of films and TV. Peaceful, wide streets, the green space of Russell Square, red phone boxes that were now historical monuments themselves, existing only for overseas tourists' photographs, ransom demand calls and massage parlour business cards.

She arrived at the back entrance of the museum, like a VIP. She signed in, with a nod of familiarity from the reception desk, and made her way to the meeting room. It was a blazing brilliant modern white, with desks arranged in a horseshoe, as if they were having a table read for a drama. Anna would've much preferred something full of careworn wood and leather that was reassuringly cluttered, dust motes dancing in cidery-yellow autumnal light. Order and fluoro-lighting reminded her too much of classrooms.

John smiled benevolently at the sight of her.

'Ah, the woman of the hour. Everyone, this is Anna Alessi from UCL. She's our academic liaison and resident expert. You might think *I'm* the resident expert. However, I'm a glorified shopkeeper. She sources the products, checks what's fit for purpose for sale, as it were …'

As he spoke, Anna scanned the room, smiling and nodding hellos in turn, until her eyes met James Fraser's.

She almost physically started with surprise, and couldn't be entirely sure whether she made a noise.

Her bouncy cheerfulness stopped so abruptly it almost had a sound effect. She knew her face was a mask of repulsion but it was too late to rearrange it. *What. The. Fuuuuccckkkkkkk …?*

James looked very disconcerted, if not quite as ruffled as she did.

John was still talking: '… So this is James from our digital helpers over at Parlez. James is the project leader, and his colleague who handles the technical design and development, Parker …'

Anna mumbled a vague greeting at a skinny twenty-something with asymmetric hair, and dropped with a thud into her seat.

She fussed with getting the notes out of her bag as a way of not having to meet the eyes in the room. Her heart was making a ker-plunking noise. She could hear the valves pulsing, as if they were amplified.

How in the hell had this happened? What sort of grotesque prank was being played on her this time?

As conversation continued and John outlined the themes of the exhibition, Anna joined the dots; John joking about the necessity of having 'the digital johnnies' as well as marketing and comms people at the initial get together to discuss the exhibition.

At the reunion, Laurence saying of James '... *digital agency, lots of big impressive clients.'*

It was a gruesome turn of events. And it wasn't lost on Anna that if she'd swerved the reunion, she'd have the upper hand. He'd still have no idea who she was.

So much for enlivening ideas about facing your demons. How long had that taken to bite her on the arse? Those demons weren't meant to pitch up a few days later in navy John Smedley cardigans in professional interactions. Only this time, unlike the reunion, she'd been introduced with her surname. Would he realise who she was?

Oh God, she hoped not. It was impossible to know if he'd figured anything out. All she could do was to try to look aloof, dignified and glacially in control.

Conversation moved on, with John doing most of the talking. He concluded, 'And now I should hand over to

James, who will take us through plans for the exhibition's multi-channel strategy ...'

The academics in the room looked politely blank while Parker put both hands on his hair and shaped it into a quiff.

'Erm, yeah, thanks ...' James said, clearing his throat. 'Obviously, the principal thing we'll be designing is the official exhibition app for iOS and Android devices and so on. This is key in giving the show a higher profile and will help with media coverage.'

He looked round the room and Anna thought sourly, *hardly any need for this pitch spiel, when you've already been hired*. She sensed he was nervous but she had no interest in empathising.

'The app will include a lot of imagery from the show, and text from yourselves. Rather than merely transpose the material from the exhibition, we want to make the app hold real unique value, with original content. We were thinking of some talking heads ...'

'That's experts, talking, not Talking Heads the old music,' Parker said, tucking his pen behind his ear and grinning widely.

'Old,' John Herbert chuckled.

'Yes. Thanks, Parker,' James said, eyes narrowing. 'And we want to build an A.R. layer for the exhibition, with digital versions of the artefacts we don't have or can't move here. What we thought we'd do is take personalities from the mosaics, and use actors in costume to film recreations of interactions. We can have them walking about the space. A virtual Theodora and Justinian and so on.'

Anna's nerves overcame her and she spoke before she could stop herself.

'It's not going to be all rotating 3D scans of people's heads, like "Wooh, heads"' – she made a gesture with her hands, thinking, I have no idea what I'm on about either, but I sound a bit angry so people won't dare laugh – 'And no text, is it?'

There was usually a small tension between academics and designers over such issues and Anna was minded to make it a larger one.

'We'll have space for captions with each artefact. Written by yourselves,' James said, making an 'I am taking you very seriously' business face.

'How many words?'

'Around 150 or so.'

'That's not a lot.'

'I think people have a limit for how much information they can take in per artefact.'

'We were thinking the show might attract quite a few "readers",' Anna said, caustically.

'Our research suggests people start skimming after 150,' James said, tapping his pen on his pad.

'Well, what does actors titting about really add? Do people need reminding what people look like? We haven't evolved significantly since Theodora and Justinian. They didn't have prehensile features.'

James blinked.

'It's a way of making the artefacts more vivid. The emphasis with what we do is on the experiential.'

Experiential. These people always brought their made-up words.

'No, I mean it'll get in the way of looking at the mosaics, which are the point of the thing aren't they?' Anna said. 'Won't it mean visitors spend their time playing on video games, instead of looking at the exhibits?'

James put his head on one side and made a 'trying to find a respectful way to answer a question I think is stupid' face.

'It's an "as well as" not an "instead of". To help people visualise the world and bring the scene alive. We'll tag the videos to objects so people can choose to watch the sequences if they're interested.' James paused. 'It's a modern way of engaging visitors.'

'Ah, that's the thing about history. *It's not modern.*'

'But the people going to see this are. Are you doing without electricity as well?'

James only half-phrased this as a joke and all the backs in the room stiffened. Except for Parker's.

'The point of the app is that it's something different to the exhibition itself, something that complements it,' James said, aiming for an air of finality.

'I don't understand why the emphasis is on recreating stuff that isn't there, to distract people from stuff that *is* there. It's as if the artefacts aren't interesting enough in themselves.'

'It's about narrative. People are principally going to be interested in Theodora as a person, right? She's the focus of the exhibition. Along with Justinian. They're the story.' James was matching Anna in vigour now. It was that kind of terse politeness that strained at the leash to romp into full-blown rude.

'Yes but that's not to turn the show into a Ye Olde Posh and Becks power couple.'

'Justinian Bieber,' Parker said, guffawing. Everyone in the room dead-eyed him.

'We're coming at this from different angles but our aims are the same,' John intervened. 'Wait until you see it, Anna. The Royal Manuscripts app was really something, I'll get James to show it to you.'

James nodded. Anna simmered.

'We're drawing up some questions on the themes of the exhibition, to help us develop our side in line with your vision for the key messages of the show.'

Key messages! Like it was an ad campaign. *Buy Zantium!* That's all these digital gits were, Anna thought. Advertisers, with a big shiny social media sheen pasted over the top. Might as well be flogging chamois leathers as the artefacts of the sixth century. James Fraser did look like Don Draper from *Mad Men.*

James cleared his throat. 'We were playing around with a "medieval bling" theme for the digital pre-launch presence …'

'*Bling*?' Anna said, her intonation holding the word between finger and thumb, at arm's length.

'Yes . . .' James said, but this time had the decency to look embarrassed.

'You know, bling, like, big rocks, baller ass, fly, dope …' Parker began.

'We were thinking it was an accessible way to represent the wealth of the period,' James cut in, desperately. 'Obviously we can work on this in tandem with you.'

'The "whore" angle is strong for grabbing attention, but causes problems with your younger, school age demographic,' Parker said, in a solemn tone that made it sound as if he was quoting someone else.

School. Anna's throat tightened.

'We've been throwing ideas around, nothing's set in stone,' James said.

'Not sure about the use of the word "whore" really,' John the curator said, mildly. 'It's a bit of a value judgement about a female.'

'Yes. It's not as if you'd ever call a show *Genghis Khan: Mongol Warlord, Massive Shagger*,' Anna said.

Parker looked as if he might be about to try to answer a rhetorical question.

'We want to stress that Theodora was an amazing, ambitious woman. Not some … hooker who got lucky with the right husband,' Anna continued. 'It was more burlesque dancing anyway. She was an entertainer …'

This was pushing it. Theodora's sex life was pretty darn rococo. But Anna wasn't going to have her beloved heroine casually slut-shamed by a man wearing an Acid House smiley earring, named after a Thunderbird.

'Oh right. I was going by her Wikipedia page, and there was something on there about a party trick with barley on her … down there, and geese pecking it off? Quite rad,' Parker said.

James rubbed his eyes in a way that might have been an attempt to put his face in his hands.

'Oh well, I bow to the knowledge of someone who's been on Wikipedia,' Anna said to Parker. The tension in the room reached snapping point.

'If we could meet up to film a Q and A soon, that'd be helpful,' James said, stony faced, with a near-sarcastic emphasis on 'helpful'.

'Yes I think it'd help, Anna, if you and James touched base over a coffee soon,' John said, nervously. 'Make sure we're all happy with the direction. I have a feeling this is going to turn out to be a very fruitful collaboration.'

Anna gave James a look that said she'd rather touch his prostate than his base, and the meeting was over.

18

Anna flew back to UCL as if she had the wind at her heels. But this time she wasn't buoyed by joy, but borne aloft by the kinetic energy of outrage.

Had James Fraser recognised her? It was impossible to tell. Her instincts said not – there was no dawning of the light writ across his features at any point. But that didn't mean much.

Now he had her surname *and* he'd seen her at the reunion. If the penny hadn't dropped yet, it would soon. It was teetering, wobbling, right about to roll. *Alessi.* She might be Anna not Aureliana, but her full name was unusual. It alliterated, it was memorable. No doubt about it, the bells would soon chime.

He'd have a look of triumphal malignity on his face at their next encounter, and conclude by saying: 'It's come back to me, I *do* know you ...'

Technically, of course, it didn't matter. It wasn't as if he could use that information in any way that harmed her professionally, beyond embarrassing gossiping with the exhibition team. It was hard to explain why it felt so catastrophic.

She had dealt with school by moving forward and never looking back. She boxed her inappropriately titled *Forever Friends* diaries and banished all reminders to the loft. She changed her forename. And eventually, she'd changed her appearance.

She'd walked into the reunion knowing she could walk out again at any time she chose. And she'd never imagined he'd be there in the first place.

This turn of events felt like a taunt from above at her audacity. God saying: *if you want to mess with the order of things, I'll mess with you right back.*

To have the monster tear through the paper screen like this, someone who knew who she used to be – and *him*, of all people – working with her in the present? It was a merging of realities she never, ever thought she'd have to face. She was near-tearful at how she could be so improbably unlucky. *Of all the gin joints in all the world …*

'Faster than a speeding bullet!' Patrick called after Anna as she stomped through reception.

She felt pathetically, overwhelmingly grateful for the sight of him. Someone who would never judge her, never snicker, never betray and ridicule her. These were *her* kind of people. This was a safe haven, where you were assessed only on your brainpower. Only your essays got marked. Not your circumference, or your income, or your cool, or your clothes.

'Meeting go well? Eager to get stuck straight into exploring Dora?'

'Patrick, I've had a complete nightmare,' she said, trying not to sound wobbly, and not entirely succeeding.

'Are you OK?' he said, instantly concerned, hand on her arm.

Anna glanced over at Jan the receptionist. She had ears the size of cabbage leaves for scandal.

'Time for a quick coffee? Walk in Russell Square?'

Patrick checked his wristwatch. 'For you. Any time.'

'Thank you so much,' Anna said, and Patrick looked gratified at the extravagant emotion over a latte. 'I don't mean to sound dramatic.'

Once they were settled on a park bench with takeout coffees, Anna began. 'You know I said I had a bad time at school? Guess who the lead from the digital company working on the Theodora show is? Only a thundering anus who bullied me.'

'He *bullied* you?' Patrick fiddled with his sugar packet.

'Yes. I saw him at the reunion. It was worse … he was worse to me than I explained. In the past, I mean.'

'Oh dear, Anna. Did he …? Were you …?' Patrick avoided her eyes. Anna realised he might've misconstrued what she was going to reveal.

'Oh no, I left that school when I was sixteen, I wasn't … I was a …'

Anna felt herself colour and Patrick nodded, relieved, and put his hand on her arm.

'I was different at school,' she said, taking a deep breath. 'I was … a lot bigger.'

Patrick's face was one set in extreme concern. She'd forgotten his hugely protective streak. A streak in the same way the M1 had a middle lane streak.

'This man was particularly cruel to me. He tricked me into appearing on stage with him and then half the school pelted me with sweets and called me names.'

'Good grief,' Patrick said.

'He didn't recognise me at the reunion. But now he knows my surname. Patrick, I'm dreading having to see him again. He's going to bring it up and I'm going to end up crying. And work's always been a safe place where I didn't have to deal with that stuff, you know. I don't want to be too dramatic about having a new identity, but … I do feel like someone in witness protection who's had the mobsters show up.'

'This is awful.' Patrick paused. 'And terribly odd timing. Do you think it's got anything to do with you going to the reunion?'

'Oh, no. It's complete coincidence. Imagine. What a one-two punch. Not had to see this idiot for sixteen years and then twice in two weeks.'

Anna made a 'huh' noise and sipped coffee.

'Part of me thinks I should resign from the Theodora show. But I so want to be part of it, and I can't think of a plausible excuse.'

'Oh you *must* work on it, Anna. You told me it was the greatest moment of your career so far. You can't let this dick-head ruin it for you. And, like we said. It's potentially going to do you a lot of good round here.'

A pause.

'Why not get him moved off it?' Patrick asked.

'How? I can hardly go to John Herbert and say: "He was nasty to me at school."'

'What if he was nasty to you now?'

'How do you mean?'

'You think he might say something when you next meet?'

'Yes. I think he's snide by nature and I've not helped myself by annoying him in this meeting.'

'Then encourage it. Get him to goad you. Then take it to John and say you can't work with him for these personal reasons, and someone else from that agency should take over.'

'Oh. Wow. Yes, I *suppose* that could work … depending on what he said.'

'Look on it as insurance. If he says nothing too dreadful, then you can cope. If he taunts you, he's sealing his own fate.'

Anna thought about this. The idea of taking the lead and giving him attitude emboldened her. A psychological layer of armour.

'Thanks. This is brilliant advice.'

'One tries one's best.' Patrick patted her arm again.

'You're my furry Pandarian hero,' Anna said, grinning.

Patrick beamed.

Anna wasn't confrontational by nature. While Patrick had the odd spluttering fit at idle students, Anna always tried to empathise. You never knew anyone's full story. She played the 'what if' game. *What if they have money worries … what if they have an illness?* ('Like Lazy Bones?' Patrick said.)

But being unpleasant to James Fraser? She reckoned she was up to that.

19

At the end of a long week, Anna found herself, her coat, bag and her glass of red wine a seat in the basement café-bar of the Soho Curzon cinema. She didn't want to do a meerkat at every man who walked in and hoped Grant would recognise her.

He was quarter of an hour late, although Anna didn't mind. She knew some women were very concerned with the respect implied by strict punctuality and chairs being pulled out and generally Walter Raleighing about, but she really wasn't. As long as he seemed respectful and didn't swear at her for not getting all the drinks in, Anna was easy-going. Dating was difficult enough without sweating the detail.

She liked it in here and often ducked in, even when she wasn't seeing a film, to people watch over a hot chocolate. It was a little oasis of cerebral calm when the city upstairs felt frenetic.

Unlike Anna, Michelle wasn't from London, having moved here from the West Country when she went to catering college, and saw it with outsider's eyes. She said London was one of the worst places to have a bad day and one of the best to have a good day.

Anna knew what she meant. She'd left for that meeting at the British Museum with a Beach Boys soundtrack in her head, and walked back to Joy Division.

When Anna had a particularly terrible time at school, she used to take a book to Mayesbrook Park and walk, and read, and walk some more. She learned that sitting in her bedroom, brooding on what the next day might bring, was unhealthy.

So she had intended to wait longer after the Pied Piper of Piss incident to go on another of these dates, but she recognised her need not to dwell. Plus Grant had messaged his extreme enthusiasm. Everyone on dating sites was available for a limited period only. If you turned them down, they went to the next on the list, a person who might take them out of circulation.

Anna could miss the love of her life if she hung back. Grant could be the one for her and she'd have let BDSM Neil and *James Fraser* ruin it for them. Imagine that! Yep, it was the lottery logic again. And what were your odds for winning that, and getting yourself the gated mansion and the bull mastiffs called Pucci and Gucci?

Her Granny Maude said anyone single after thirty had a 'problem'. It was up to you to find out what that was. 'And if you don't see what the problem is at first,' she said, pausing for effect, 'you'll find out what it is, soon enough.'

Aggy inhaled the anthrax spores of their gran's wisdom with wide eyes. Late teenage Anna, in her CND symbol-Tippexed Doc Martens, with an aubergine streak in her hair, had started to question the older generation.

'What if you're a widower and that's why you're single? What if that's the problem?'

'Yes. And who'd want someone who wanted someone else

and couldn't have them? You'd always be second-best.'

What was Anna's problem, in that case? Granny Maude had died, so, probably mercifully, she'd never get her opinion.

'Hello, Anna?'

She'd been deep in thought, leafing through the Curzon's programme of forthcoming events.

'Hello! Grant?'

'Are you OK for a drink?'

'Yes, thank you,' Anna said.

'Right, give me a sec …' Grant said, shrugging a trench coat off and flinging a briefcase down by the chair legs.

Cor. Hang on. He was quite dashing. Mid-blond hair tucked behind his ears, strong nose, tall, broad shouldered, looked like he might win boat races or get a small role as a philanderer with Velcro mutton chops in *Downton Abbey*.

She'd thought he was attractive in the photos, but as always, deferred excitement until meeting in the flesh. He had an impressive job, communications director for a big charity. Anna felt a shiver of anticipation and adjusted her skirt over her woolly tights. After Neil's 'not flowery' remark, she'd done her hair in a coiled, plaited bun, put more make-up on and bought a tighter dress than usual. It wasn't difficult – everything in Topshop was like a tourniquet.

Grant set a pint of Kronenbourg down.

'Sorry I'm late, got something dumped on me as I was leaving work.'

'Ah, I know that feeling.' Pause. 'Do you enjoy it? What you do?' Anna asked.

'Most days. Now my last manager, Ruth, has left. She was

the hardest taskmaster you've ever met, honestly. In the end me and a few colleagues made a formal complaint. She didn't leave but there was a disciplinary and then after that she was even worse. We were asking, is it even worth making a complaint … What are HR for? Ruth had no idea how to assess us, she'd never even done the job and it was all— ' Grant made an Emu-style talking hand pincer, '"Wah, wah, do it like this." And we were like, OK, whatever. She's in Doncaster now.'

'Oh dear …' Anna said, wondering why Ruth had got so much airtime. Maybe the memory was raw.

'How did you get into comms?'

'Comms? Good question, I did pharmacology for my degree. At Newcastle. It was the right degree for me at the time and I got a 2:1 but then I was like, do I want to go into this? It's a good discipline to have you know, don't get me wrong, but in essence I'm a communicator, I like talking to people.'

AT PEOPLE, Anna thought, and tried to silence her rebellious inner voice.

'So then I moved to London and at first, my brother's in IT, and I was like – is IT for me? I temped at his place and it was, you know, OK, and he was all "You're good at it, you can have a job" and I was like, hmmm. Maybe there's more for me, you know? Then I went to Indonesia with my girlfriend … Haha, my ex-girlfriend, I should say …'

Grant leaned over and squeezed Anna's arm, reassuringly, and some would say, over confidently.

'That took my perspective and shifted it. Amazing place. Have you been?'

Anna shook her head, biting the insides of her cheeks, as she realised they were about to spend a year in Indonesia as a result of this answer. Grant indeed embarked on Indonesia, its topography, customs, cuisine. Its … SHOES? The kind of *shoes* people wore? Oh boy.

Anna's mind boggled. Whatever topic was introduced, Grant had absolutely no filter. It was like turning a tap on. Ask him something, get an information flood, until the room was ankle-deep and you were calling Dyno-Rod.

At first it was perturbing, then infuriating, then blackly comic, then very, very boring.

An hour later, Anna no longer knew how to arrange her face so it didn't look like one you might see filling the porthole window of a crashing plane.

She could've embarked on monologues of her own by way of retaliation, but what was the point? Grant wasn't sufficiently interested to ask any questions and Anna was sure that unless he produced documentation to prove he had Yapping On Disorder and she was legally obliged to give him a second date, she was never seeing him again.

Grant was now on Indonesia's critically endangered Sumatran Orang-utans and the attack he suffered at their long-fingered hands. It was a topic with the potential to be interesting, but for the fact they were working backwards, covering every inch of his travel arrangements to get him face time with the primates. From the Greggs cheese and onion lattice at Gatwick onwards.

Anna started to cut the moorings and drift away. While Grant was narratively hacking through the jungle, she was mentally writing her supermarket shopping list and drafting two work emails.

'Another?' Grant said, second drink finished. Anna had

been willing the last two inches of his beer to disappear for a long time.

'No, sorry, ' – she checked her watch – 'I've got to meet my friends.'

'Ah,' Grant said, clearly thinking: *invite me?*

Anna felt bad for him and hated herself for being so weak that she felt bad for everyone, constantly, even when their level of sensitivity was 'endangered rhino hide'.

The farewell outside involved Anna keeping a pointed distance. She didn't see how Grant could possibly think this had gone well enough to warrant kissing, but then she didn't understand a lot of things about Grant.

'We should do this again,' Grant said.

'Erm …'

Anna stuck her hand out for Grant to shake. He obliged, slightly blank.

'Thanks. I've had a lovely time. I think my dating odyssey continues though.'

'Oh. Uh, OK …' Grant smoothed his hair, 'Is that a "I don't want to see you again"?'

'I don't think we sparked,' Anna said. The spark thing again. A word to cover a thousand sins.

'What does that mean?' Grant said.

'The – rapport,' Anna said, gesturing with a palm on her chest, then flapping at the air between them. 'Between us.'

'I thought conversation flowed!'

Conversation. If you went to a lecture on climate change, did you come away thinking you'd had a great chat with Al Gore? Anna wrestled with kindness versus cruelty, and frustration and cheap red plonk edged her into 'cruelty'.

'You talked a lot more than I did.' As she said it, she felt how sad and undignified this was, standing in the street, telling someone why they didn't measure up as company.

'You asked a lot of questions,' Grant said, frowning.

'I suppose I did,' Anna said, wanting desperately to be gone now, hoping Michelle would ring with their location rather than text, and save her from this post mortem. 'Sorry.'

There was no nice way to say, and no point in saying: we're not on the same wavelength and never will be and the fact that you can't see that proves the wavelength point beyond all doubt.

Her phone rang.

She loved Michelle anyway, but at that moment, she loved her more than sunshine, cake, or the orang-utan called Hercules that had slapped Grant on the forehead.

20

In the purple of the evening light, Anna made out Michelle, scuffing her feet on the street outside Gelupo, puffing on a smokeless e-cigarette that looked like a tampon holder.

'Can't you smoke those inside?' Anna said, when she reached her.

'Penny's here,' Michelle said, grimacing.

'Ah.'

'We've already had a barney. She made a big thing of giving a fiver to some guy sat in a doorway, then went on about how she doesn't understand people who only give a quid and how she always gives them enough to get a hot square meal. I said "a hot square meal of HEROIN" and then it was *stereotyping the poor mweh mweh mweh.*' Michelle did the rodent-like meeping noise that she used to impersonate Penny. 'I wouldn't mind the sanctimony if she was some aid worker who stood a chance of being blown up, but it'll be bloody Daniel's fiver. Why are bleeding-heart hippies always the most selfish people you could meet?'

Anna laughed. She knew Michelle's Penny rants well.

'Don't make me go back inside,' Michelle laid her head on Anna's shoulder.

'How about the ice cream though?'

Michelle sagged.

'Count the number of seconds it takes for her to say something rude or gloaty to you. Just count them.'

Inside Gelupo's warmly lit, sailboat blue-and-white interior, Anna ordered chocolate and espresso granitas for herself and Michelle and felt guilty at Penny's enthusiastic waving at her across the room. There were wafer cones the size of wizard hats on the counter but Anna opted for scoops in tubs, the calorie calculator in her never completely switched off.

'How did the date go?' Penny said, flicking her long straight hair out of her own pink ice cream, as they sat down. She had a moon-shaped face, a large fringe that seemed to start very far back on her head and a tinkly voice. Like Daniel, it made it seem as if the content couldn't be harsh. But unlike Daniel, it could be.

'Cataclysmic. So boring I felt as if I could bend space and time and see into the future.'

'You're so unlucky with your dates. I wonder why it is?'

Michelle checked her watch, in Anna's eye line.

'It's not easy to find, somebody who is just your kind, to quote a song,' Daniel said to her, drawing the back of a spoon out of his mouth.

'Do you ever think you might be too choosy?' Penny said, with her head cocked to one side.

Across the table, Michelle swiped a finger in the air to make an imaginary 'one' score.

'Whenever you've been single for a while people always say that. I'm not sitting there being picky about near-misses, I promise you. More "a mile wide of the marks",' Anna said.

113

'Yeah, plus it's the sort of analysis only single people get. You'd never say to couples: "Do you think you weren't choosy enough?"' Michelle said, smiling broadly.

'I mean, how much can you really tell from one date?' Penny said. 'Who did you meet tonight?' she persisted.

'Grant.'

'OK. Maybe right now he's thinking oh gosh darnit!' Anna had forgotten Penny liked to use the language and mannerisms of a 1920s Southern Belle. 'I sure wish I could have another date with that Anna, but I blew it.'

Penny did a click of the fingers with swinging hand motion. Anna looked blank.

'But maybe if you went on a second date, it'd be like, magic click!' Penny said, clicking fingers on both hands, with a glittery laugh.

It was generally Michelle who lost patience with Penny, but tonight it was Anna's turn.

'I don't have time left to date everyone who I don't like twice, while looking for someone I do. And maybe that does mean I'll miss Mr Right. Frankly there's a good chance that if he ever existed, I missed him years ago. We were waiting side by side for the same late train in 2002 at King's Cross and at the last minute he walked further up the platform and we never spoke. Now he's in Kuala Lumpur up to his nuts in his new bride and I'm only looking for Mr Happens to Be Available at the Right Time. But I don't see why that condemns me to waste nights of my life with Mr TripAdvisor to prove it's not me being picky. Maybe it looks like a romantic adventure from the perspective of a relationship, but it's a grind. A grind that makes you sad. You start off thinking "this could be the one" with every date and you soon realise it won't ever be the one. You're lucky to get "half decent" or "not a nutter".'

'Oooh! Calm down,' Penny said, patting Anna's arm, while Anna glowered at the table and tried not to bite her.

'Fuckin' well said,' Michelle said. 'Which is why I don't date at all.'

'I'm giving it a rest for a while,' Anna agreed, glumly.

'Be careful that you two don't end up a pair of old grump-ies! You're like Marge's sisters on *The Simpsons*!' Penny giggled, while Anna and Michelle exchanged a look of disbelief. Self-styled 'nice' people were truly dangerous.

Daniel, polishing off the last of his ice cream, seemed oblivious to Penny's misdemeanours.

'If you don't mind sharing,' Daniel said. 'I can go Mormon if you like, and save you all.'

Michelle did one of her 'Nyaaah' filthy laughs and peace was restored.

'I have some more madness for you,' Anna said. 'Guess who was in my first British Museum meeting. Evil James Fraser from school who I saw at the reunion.'

'What? The one who ...?' Michelle broke off, in deference to Anna not wanting it hauled over in front of Penny. 'How come?'

'He's one of the digital people doing the app and whatever. Emphasis on the whatever.'

'Does he know who you are now? Did he apologise?'

'Don't think so and no. I decided to go on the attack, and if he has a go at me I'll get him moved off the project.'

Anna feared more questions from Penny about how it was possible that someone from school didn't recognise her. She was grateful to Michelle possibly sussing this and saying, 'And more identity surprises, remember the cock and balls flasher the other night? He came and introduced himself because he's running a burger van opposite. Now, what's the one thing you wouldn't say he was?'

'Shy?' Daniel said.

'Posh! He's posh! "Guy"! Apologising for the flashing like he was Hugh Grant after the prostitute on the chat show. *We had taken drink ... lot of high jinks ... shenanigans ... tomfoolery. Waffle coughle.*'

'Nice of him to say sorry?'

'I think he didn't want me phoning the police and ruining his pop-up burger racket. They've called it "Meat Cute". The burger is "Beefy The Hunger Slayer". There's not one menu item without massive smug as the main ingredient. I give it a month.'

'I've tried one. Absolutely delish,' Daniel said.

'Dan! Can I have some bloody loyalty? My front of house giving money to the competition?'

'We've got to check it out. And actually he gave it to me free.'

'Oh marvellous, now we're in debt to them.'

'He asked a lot about you, actually.'

'I bet he did. Why not just show him our books, eh? Next time you put that traitorous meat in your mouth, remember Guy's soft danglies squashed against my window and have some respect.'

'If I ever put his danglies in my mouth, do I have to think of his burgers?' Daniel said.

Michelle guffawed and Penny squealed.

Anna laughed and scraped out the rest of her ice cream. When it came to dating's sour moments, what would she do without her friends to take the taste away? Even if Penny came as an unwanted side dish.

'Are you two coming to my gig?' Penny said, frowning. 'You know The Unsaids are playing?'

Penny phrased this not as if it was the first mention, but as if a) the offer of the gig had already been made and accepted and b) Anna and Michelle were now letting her down with a refusal. Classic Penny.

'I probably have things to do in the restaurant,' Michelle said, finishing her ice cream.

'Oh no, I made sure it was when the restaurant's closed so Dan can come. Anna, will you be free?'

Anna opened her mouth.

'I can confirm she will be,' Michelle cut in.

21

'Hate to say it, mate, but I'm not remotely surprised,' Laurence said, not sounding like he was hating it at all.

'Why?' said James, not wanting to ask.

They fell briefly silent as the waitress set two tumblers down in front of them, cracking the ring pulls on Dixie beer and pouring two inches into the bottom of each glass.

'I'll be back in a moment to see what you guys fancy eating,' she said. 'The Red Rice is real good.'

'Real good?' James said, when she'd left. 'If London likes America so much, why doesn't it go live there?'

Laurence and James had a routine of meeting once a week for dinner out. The rule was that they never went to the same place twice, with the exception of Tayyabs, which was mandatory with a hangover.

Laurence usually chose the venue and this time it was somewhere serving authentic New Orleans po-boys. With authentic Louisiana beverages. In Soho. The main thing was, it was one of the currently talked-about places, and now they could talk about it.

Laurence tipped the liquid in the glass, sniffed it gingerly.

'It was this or root beer, which tastes like dentist's mouthwash,'

Laurence said, sipping. 'Cheers. I'm not surprised Eva's seeing someone else, because there's always someone else. Very few people can be bothered to walk out on a solid thing for nothing. A Laurence Law of Life. She wasn't doing it for the love of the view from her friend Sara's spare room, was she?'

'Why didn't you say so?'

'Sorry you're cut up your wife's left you, I bet there's a wanger involved? That'd have gone well.'

'Hmmm,' James studied the mains. '*Fully dressed with all the fixins*. God don't you hate it when menus talk folksy to you. There best not be any mention of Tommy K sauce.'

The waitress returned and they ordered giant sandwiches with gravy. Despite the dazzling array of proteins that could be stuffed inside these bready behemoths, James had a strong suspicion they all tasted alike by the time they were 'fully dressed' with all the 'fixins'. Fully dressed. He thought of Eva in that drawing, and his appetite waned.

'What I can't get over is how cold it was to leave me to find that picture. Imagine it, Loz.'

'I wouldn't have to imagine it if you'd had the presence of mind to take a phone snap,' he said, and James laughed, hollowly.

'Having to see that, and think of the lovebirds sketching, like that scene in *Titanic*. Only one notch down from finding sexting photos. And he draws like a five-year-old child ...'

James shook his head, as if Finn's artistic talent was the worst of it.

'He virtually is a child. Twenty-three. Sheesh,' Laurence said. 'I dated a twenty-four-year-old last year. Her favourite music was "skronk". She'd never heard of John Major. I said, who do you think was running the country between Margaret

Thatcher and Tony Blair? She said "Was it Michael Parkinson?" I knew then it was over. Shame, because in the sack we were like a pair of drowning cats.'

James squinted. 'Ah now I feel better. Cheers mate!'

'Oh yeah. Sorry. You said they're not doing it though?'

'Supposedly.'

Once again James was forced to contemplate what this boy had done with his wife – or rather, was plotting to do to his wife. *Weren't sleeping together*. Exactly how narrow a definition was that, these days?

It was so incredibly cruel of Eva to let him find out like that. When was she going to tell him? Aside from Loz, James wouldn't be sharing this with any of his friends and family, if he could help it. He didn't want them to think badly of Eva. This was the thing about relationships; someone could fire you, and you'd still do their PR.

By this point, James had lost his appetite altogether.

And right on cue, their po-boys arrived, sliced in half and surrounded by not-needed deep-fried extras. The waitress performed the ceremony of ladling gravy over the top of each, departing with: 'Tuck in, guys!'

'Look. The age thing. The fact this Finn's a minor means he is minor. It's good news.'

'Is it?' James picked at a battered onion ring. He'd have to disassemble the sandwich and make such a mess it looked like he'd eaten it. In his distant past he'd dated women who did that. 'It's humiliating.'

'Yeah. She's not seriously going to leave you for Derek Zoolander. She wants to have kids, right? She's what, thirty-three? This is a fling.'

'Guess so,' James said. 'Though who the hell knows what Eva's thinking anymore? I don't.'

'Can I give you some advice? Well there's the business class advice, which you won't take, so then there's premium economy.'

'Which is?'

'Get revenge. Have a fling of your own. There's nothing like a taste of your own bullshit to make you realise you don't like bullshit. As Martin Luther King said.'

'Hmmm. Not sure.'

'Why not? Do you realise how lucky you are? You get to have one off the meter right now. No one would blame you, and your wife especially couldn't blame you.'

'Who with?'

'Hah. Don't give me that. I'm not going to tell you that you could have anyone you want. Are you telling me if Eva came round and you were fumbling with a twenty-four-year-old, it wouldn't give her cause for pause?'

'She doesn't have a key anymore.'

'Don't be obtuse.'

James wasn't at all sure how Eva would react. He didn't want to inflict more wounds. He wanted to make everything right and good again, not destroy it completely.

'I wouldn't drag a blameless twenty-four-year-old into this mess to find out.'

'And there we differ. It's not dragging them into any mess if you don't let emotions cloud it. You're just giving them a treat. One that's so rich and indulgent it would be unhealthy for them to have too often. Bloody hell, how do you eat these things?'

Laurence gave up trying to poke an airship-sized dripping sandwich into his mouth and resorted to knife and fork.

'Thanks, but it doesn't appeal at the moment.'

'Another Laurence O'Grady Law of Life – competition focuses your mind on whether you want something or not.'

'Or *not*,' James said. 'It's a gamble.'

'How's the "do nothing" strategy going? It's giving *Finn* a chance to get your wife to suckle his Huckleberries.'

James held up a hand to say 'enough' and Laurence nodded.

'Sorry. It must be shit.'

Laurence refilled their glasses and James noted that, despite both their efforts, they still had a table full of food.

'Oh Christ, I forgot to say. You'll never guess who was in my meeting the other day. That woman you were all over at the reunion. She's a lecturer at UCL. She's on a British Museum exhibition we're doing the app for.'

'No way! Oh man, this is amazing. First she walks into the wrong room. Then this. There was something special about the Spaniard,' Laurence said.

'Italian, as it turns out.'

'Bella Italia! And a lecturer eh? I'd give her a first. And a second.'

'God, really? She blew you out. And she was a total pain again in the meeting. She was all "What's the point of you?" I felt like saying: "You hired us, remember?" Wouldn't have thought she was your business, in personality or looks,' James said, brushing his hands.

'Why not?'

'Too … dour. Too not covered in make-up. Too covered up in other respects.'

'This is where you're wrong. I'm getting bored of girls. I'm ready for a woman. You're going to have to set us up.'

'When I've got to work with her? She's probably giving me this grief because you hit on her. No chance.'

'When you're done then?'

'Huh. Maybe. Wait. What was business class advice?' James asked.

'What?'

'You said I wouldn't take your best advice.'

'Ah. That,' Laurence wiped beer foam from his mouth. 'You should end it with Eva.'

'I love her,' James said, shrugging.

'I said you wouldn't take it.'

'Wouldn't you stick with it, if you'd married the person?'

'If I ever marry someone I'll let you know.'

Laurence always said he'd only ever marry for money. 'Why sign a contract that can only potentially lose you money, otherwise?' James had long felt a mixture of admiration and repulsion for Laurence's nihilism. Right now, he positively envied it.

'Your problem is ...' Laurence whistled. 'Have I got rights to speak my mind, with no comeback, here?'

James said he had, thinking: as if you didn't plan to say this anyway.

'She's not done this for any reason that I can tell. How are you going to trust her not to do it again?'

James's very own thoughts.

'She'll know if she ever does it again, that's it, over,' James said, trying to sound resolute, knowing it sounded weak.

Laurence grimaced.

'Recipe for a lot of paranoia and grief if you ask me. Think of it as the climber who sawed his own hand off with a pen knife when he was trapped by a boulder. Ending a serious relationship is like that. A lot of pain and ugly in the short term but you have to do it to get your life back.'

'Haha. So marriage is the boulder? I should be galloping down the mountain, blood spurting from a stump, looking forward to a lifetime of trying to eat nachos with a fairground amusement game claw?'

'Imagine tenderly stroking the bum of your new woman with that claw! Good times.'

They laughed. As crude as Loz always was, James was glad he'd chosen to tell him about the drawing.

Anyone who'd have said *poor you* would've made him feel worse. He desperately needed to laugh, however emptily.

It was petty, but the notion of getting Eva back, in order to get Eva back, had given him an idea.

22

As usual, Anna woke twenty minutes after she needed to be vertical and doing something, and waited another ten, enjoying the warmth of her bed. She checked the time on her phone, groaned. It was against all that was righteous to have somewhere to be on a Sunday.

She rolled out from under her patchwork quilt. The way some people habitually grasped for their spectacles, her first act was to reach for a band to pull her hair into a giant unruly pony-tail-bun. Youthful experiments had taught her that if she cut it shorter, she ended up with a tightly curled, rounded mop, the shape of a dandelion clock, like a superannuated Orphan Annie.

Anna disliked getting up, and dearly loved her giant four-poster brass bed. She'd ignored what the tape measure told her and now she didn't so much have a bed in her flat as a flat round her bed.

'And your bed only ever has one person in it!' her sister had said, with her usual tact.

Her lecturing wages didn't buy a lot of space in Stoke Newington, to say the least. She had to make hard choices. She preferred bed to bath, and her rather-poky-but-charming galley kitchen, which opened out onto an appealing little garden, was in the end deemed more appealing than having a spare room.

The estate agent had humorously called her bathroom off the bedroom: 'en suite', Everyone else called it: 'Why have you got a shower head in the wardrobe? Oh. Fuck. It IS the shower.'

Anna folded herself into it and out of it, into yesterday's clothes, and zipped up her boots.

The journey to her parents' in Barking was the passage back to the past. It wasn't wholly pleasant, and she felt some relief when she got home again. She felt bad for her family that she felt that way. But it wasn't her fault that her childhood held so many negative connotations, either.

Anna caught the overland, then the District Line, grabbing a seat. She kept her take-out coffee from slopping out of the tracheotomy hole in the lid with practised steadiness, like someone holding the Olympic torch aloft.

The train emerged from the Underground above street level again. Ah, the sight of that mystical barrier between old and new, Anna and Aureliana – the North Circular. She was back in the scenery of her youth.

Putting her hood up in the late autumnal mizzle, she hurried past the Vicarage Field shopping centre and down the familiar streets. They were lined with pebbledash-scarred 1930s semis, satellite dishes on their roofs like jaunty fascinators. And, she was home. For as long as her parents were alive, it would always be home.

Cliché, she knew, but the house always seemed slightly smaller than it was in memory.

She rang the bell and stamped her feet. Her mum answered the door in her 'stripper body in tasselled pasties' vinyl pinny that had ceased to be funny within thirty seconds of Aggy giving it to her one birthday many years ago.

'Aureliana! I said half twelve!'

'Sorry, they're doing repairs on the Tube,' Anna lied, smoothly.

'I didn't hear of any,' Aggy said, ambling into the hallway with a cut-glass goblet of Prosecco. All of their parents' glass-ware looked distinctly '70s, the kind of vessels that should hold Blue Nun.

'That's because Chris drove you?' Anna said. 'Hi Chris!' she called.

'Hola!' he bellowed from the sitting room.

'Or because you're a big liar, nose like a church spire,' Aggy said.

'Me and Mum are going over the seating plans, want to take a look?'

'I'll get a drink first,' Anna said, heading for the kitchen.

The house smelt wonderful, of roast pork and rosemary. Anna's mum did most of the cooking, but Italian Sunday lunches were Dad's business. They had the full works – anti-pasti, primo, secondi, salad, cheese, grappa. Chris always left saying his liver had been turned into pâté.

'Hi Dad,' Anna said, finding him shredding lettuce for the salad course.

'*La mia adorata figlia maggiore!*' he said, giving her a kiss on the cheek. 'Wine's on the side.'

Anna poured herself a hefty half pint of Prosecco.

'How was your meeting? With the museum people?'

Anna's dad was incredibly proud of his daughter's job. Unlike their mother, he tried to grasp the detail.

'Oh fine, yeah,' Anna said, leaning against the fridge. She knew if it weren't for arseing James Fraser the arsehole, she'd be excitedly gabbling about it. She felt a dragging weight of resentment in her gut.

'It's coming together.'

'We will love to see it.'

Down the hallway, she could hear her mother's delighted laughter as Chris told an anecdote in his bassy voice.

Anna suspected it'd be the only chance she'd get to speak to her dad alone. Pushing the kitchen door closed, she said in a low voice: 'Dad. Are they . . .' she jerked her head to indicate she meant the intended couple, 'OK for money?'

He rearranged the tea towel over his shoulder and started potato peeling curls of carrot into the salad.

'I said to Chris, come to me if you need to, and he said they were fine.'

Anna should feel reassured by this, but she didn't. Her parents lived on her dad's pension and what her mum had inherited. It was enough, although it wasn't lots. And Chris was not in the driving seat with this wedding.

'Aggy chose a dress costing *four grand* the other day,' she mouthed the figure.

She expected her dad to look perturbed. He shrugged. 'You know your sister, she likes …' It wasn't often his English failed him, after four decades. 'Foof?'

'Dad! No!' Anna shrieked.

'What? Frouf. Foffy faff,' her dad pulled at an imaginary full skirt, pursed his lips under his moustache and did a little dance, potato peeler held aloft.

'Foof is a rude word. Stick with faff. Or foffy, whatever that is. Never foof.'

'Ah. They sound so close. What does foof mean?'

'Er … it's something precious to a lady. Never mind.'

'Your sister will know the cost of things when she is still paying it off in a year. You know how she is, you cannot tell her. She has to find out herself.'

'I guess so.'

Anna took a sip of her drink and considered she'd done all she could. She wished she could share her father's good-natured complacency on this.

'Want a hand with anything?'

'It is fine.' He handed her the salad bowl. 'Put this on the table and say hello. They want to talk to you about the wedding.'

'No way! I wondered when Aggy was going to mention it,' Anna said, eye rolling as she took the bowl, and her dad smiled.

As Anna entered the sitting room, Aggy said, 'Can I confirm for definite you're not bringing anyone?'

'Confirmed,' Anna sighed. 'Though I'd like to remind you that we all die alone.'

Chris was on the sofa with a beer. Aggy and her mum were crouched over sheets of paper strewn across the carpet, covered in circles drawn round the base of a water glass. Anna held her Prosecco against her chest and peered at the annotations on the page: 'AUNTY BEV: NOT NEAR DAD OR UNCLE MARTIN???!!'

'Aunty Bev can't be near anyone with much success.'

'Look at the theme, sister-in-law-to-be,' Chris winked at Anna.

Anna held strands of her hair out of the way and read the table titles aloud. 'Havana … Manzanillo … Santa Clara …'

'Because we got engaged in Cuba,' Aggy said, looking up. Anna looked at Chris, nonplussed. 'Nice …?'

'Keep reading,' he said.

'Aggy!' Anna cried. 'Guantanamo?!'

Chris hooted with laughter. It was very Chris-ish to not tell Aggy, so he could enjoy the joke for longer.

'It's a city in Cuba!'

'A city in Cuba kind of inextricably linked with a massive US naval base-slash-torture prison.'

'That's not Cuba's fault!' Aggy said. 'Why is everything about politics these days?' She scribbled out Guantanamo in irritation and her mum rubbed her back, supportively.

'I reckon, go for broke, do a famous prisons theme instead,' Chris said. 'Abu Ghraib. Barlinnie. Broadmoor.'

'One for Aunty Bev at a distance, called Alcatraz,' Anna said.

'There must be other Cuban places,. Aggy started hammering at her iPhone. Pause. 'Has anything ever happened in the Bay of Pigs?'

23

Aggy's enthusiasm for her wedding planning carried them through cold meats, olives and bruschetta, porcini ravioli, the pork and roast potatoes, the salad course, and was threatening to continue into the cheese. Anna had never known a wedding had so many discussion points.

Or that gift lists could feature something as pointless as Tiffany solid silver Stilton spoons. The sentence 'Have you by any chance got a dedicated spoon for this blue-veined king of cheeses?' was a phrase that had been uttered by no one, ever.

'Why black tie? I don't have a tuxedo,' their dad said.

'It looks so glamorous and smart. Otherwise everyone wears what they want,' Aggy said.

'Imagine that, people wearing what they want,' Anna said. 'Hired tuxes smell like goat's pockets, according to colleagues who've worn them for Royal Society stuff.'

'We'll buy one!' Judy said to Oliviero, adding, 'You'd have to buy a new suit anyway.'

'When will I wear it again?' their dad grumbled.

'Anna's wedding,' Aggy said.

'By the time of my wedding, people will no longer need

clothes. They will float naked and hairless in cots of saline water and download their consciousnesses to a virtual ceremony,' Anna said.

'Shush. You need to stop trying to be clever with men and just be yourself,' their mum said, which caused much amusement.

'Not clever. Yourself,' Chris said, pointing his knife and then shearing off another lump of Grana Padano.

'My daughter is the cleverest girl in London,' Anna's dad said, raising his glass to her.

'Yes but men don't like that, they like to relax,' Judy replied.

'You haven't met all men, Mum,' Anna sighed.

Conversations with her mother and Aggy sometimes made her feel that the women's rights movement had been a largely wasted effort.

'Now you've finished eating, we've got a surprise,' Aggy said. 'Chris and I are writing our own vows. And we wanted to try them out on you. An exclusive preview of coming attractions.'

Anna put her glass down with a bump.

'Aren't you meant to say these for the first time to each other on the day?'

'I'm not leaving that to chance! What if his are rubbish?' Aggy said.

'For better, for worse,' Anna said.

Too late, Aggy was producing notepaper from her bag. Anna groaned.

'Chris, don't be bullied by my mad sister. We don't have to hear them.'

'Are you kidding? I stayed up until one this morning writing these, on your sister's orders. You're hearing them!' Chris said.

'OK, so. Me first,' Aggy said. Anna looked round the crowded dining-room table. Her mum looked delighted and expectant, her dad neutral. Anna wanted the pistachio-coloured Wilton-covered floor to swallow her up. Sometimes, despite her and Aggy's evident physical similarities, she felt like a foundling in this family.

'Christopher. When I first met you I was afraid. I was petrified— '

'*Bwahahahaha!*' Anna burst out laughing. 'Isn't this "I Will Survive"?'

'Mum!' Aggy said, stamping her foot. 'Tell her!'

'Aureliana, not everything has to be a joke, you know,' their mum said.

There was some shuffling, coughing and pouting, and Aggy returned to her notes.

'… Of opening my heart to love again. You have taught me what it is to love. You see into special secret places inside of me …'

'Ahahaha!' Anna burst out laughing again and the table erupted; their mum chiding, Aggy squealing, Chris and their dad doing some begrudging laughter.

'He sees what?!' Anna said. 'There are going to be children at this ceremony, remember.'

'Mum, tell her!' Aggy said, in mock-and-real indignation.

'Aureliana. One more word out of you and you will be sent to the sitting room.'

'Please, please send me out!'

Aggy composed herself again.

'You are my hero, my soulmate, my prince. I promise to always make your favourite calzone with sausage and to stop nagging about Sky Sports, especially as you say, it is part of the monthly TV bundle we chose together.' Aggy looked up. 'The Write Your Own Vows site on the internet said to make particular promises,' she said.

Anna held her napkin over her mouth, wheezing silently.

'When you are ill, I promise to cut your toenails …'

'What?' Anna said, removing the napkin. 'Since when do you cut the toenails of an ill person? That isn't a thing.'

'Remember when Chris broke his leg playing football and he was in the plaster cast? He was getting proper hobgoblin Catweazle feet.'

'I wouldn't invoke toenails in a wedding speech. It's the least romantic part of the body.'

'Not to foot fetishists,' Chris said. 'Google the name of any actress, any of them, and it auto completes with "feet". Sicko stuff.'

'Google actresses a lot, Chris?' Anna said, and he threw a piece of breadstick at her.

'Mum! Now Anna's got us talking about celebrity sex feet!' Aggy barked.

'Aureliana, quiet!' Judy said, her own auto complete phrase.

Aggy went back to her paper. 'I promise to honour you, cherish you, obey you …'

'Now we're talking turkey!' Chris said, and drummed his palms on the table.

'Obey?!' Anna said. 'Are we in the nineteenth century?'

'What are the chances of your sister doing this?' Oliviero said, and Anna had to concede his point there.

'From this day forward, I will love you forever. My special man … my Chris bear … my best … one.' She looked round the table, eyes shining.

'Oh Agata!' their mum said, wiping her eyes.

Anna shared a smile with her dad.

'So, Chris. Your turn!' Aggy squealed and hugged herself.

Chris wiped his mouth with his napkin and opened the paper he'd taken from his pocket.

'Agata. You look so beautiful today, like a dream— ' He broke off. 'Not today, obviously. When I see her, then.'

Aggy rolled her eyes. Anna clapped.

'When I asked you to marry me, I wasn't sure if you would say yes. Surely you could do better. But I'm so glad you said yes. And now here we are.'

There was a pause. Chris re-folded the paper.

'What?! Is that it?' Aggy shrieked.

Chris looked befuddled. 'Yeah?'

'Thanks for turning up, OK, nice one?'

Anna couldn't believe she hadn't wanted the vows to be read. This was the most fun ever.

'I can add more!' Chris said, acting stung.

'You better do.'

'Aggy, personal vows. *Personal*. Prince Chris Bear's choice,' Anna said.

'Yes and he best choose more personal words,' Aggy said.

Once they'd cleared away from lunch, Chris offered Anna a lift. He and Aggy lived in Tottenham and they often dropped Anna home.

This weekend, Anna saw an opportunity and decided to exhume the unexploded bomb of her box of school diaries from the loft. The reunion had set her thinking about a clear out. She always feared them being opened by some third party, some day. Time to dispose of them once and for all. Would Anna read through them? She wasn't sure she could stand it. She knew the ending.

As they were loading the box and a lumpy bag of odds and ends into the back of the van, Anna had a few seconds to speak to Chris out of Aggy's earshot.

'Don't be steamrollered by her, you know. This wedding has to be about you, too. Your vows are fine.'

'Oh, they're not my vows. I was winding her up. Like I'm going to read them now. They can be a surprise,' he winked and Anna laughed.

Aggy was spending what she called 'mad stacks' on this wedding, Anna thought, but she already had Chris.

She hoped her sister could sort the things worth their weight in gold from the solid silver Stilton spoons.

24

James found the room at UCL on the site plan easily enough, wrenching open the doors to the empty lecture theatre with a sense of foreboding he'd not felt since his own degree when finals were looming. (Psychology, Exeter — as much use as Luther in a Lambeth dog fight.)

Anna, sitting in a seat at the front, raised her hand in greeting. She made the acknowledgement without a smile and James nodded, with a weak upward tweak of the mouth, which wasn't much but was better than her nothing.

He adjusted the weight of his messenger bag as he descended the stairs and felt lead in his belly at having to spend an hour with this woman. For God's sake, why did some people have to bring such an attitude to work?

It wasn't his fault if she and her boyfriend were arguing or a supervisor was bullying her or her kitchen extension had gone over-budget. Just, be civil, you know?

'Hi. I see all the tech's sorted,' he said, gesturing at the video camera tripod pointing at the lectern, and the microphone clipped to Anna's dress. Given that she was going to be on film, she didn't look particularly smart.

Her mass of curly hair was again drawn off her face with an elastic band, into a bundle that looked like it was on the verge of collapsing. She was in a black cobwebby jumper with pieces of silver sparkle threaded through it, the sort of shapeless thing that probably cost loads from the Toast catalogue. Eva sometimes used to get 'scruffy Sundays' clothes from there.

Why did academics always look so messy and schlumpy? Did they want to make the point that their minds were on higher things than tailoring and ironing?

Ah well. Her funeral. Which she was dressed for.

'My colleague Patrick's on audio visual stuff,' Anna said, gesturing up at the glass-fronted booth at the back of the auditorium, where a figure lurked.

James's eyes moved to the plate she was setting down next to her. It was strewn with the remnants of something egg-based and strange, with a smear of dark brown HP sauce.

'What *is* that?' he blurted before he could help himself.

'An omelette in a bap. It's the canteen speciality here.'

'Ah,' James said, not wanting to offend. Thank goodness he'd eaten.

'Can I confirm that "doctor" is your title?' James said. 'Dr Anna Alessi?'

'Yes that's right,' she said, stiffly.

There was something familiar in her name, it had niggled him. He suddenly realised, Alessi was that make of trendy homeware. He had an Alessi bottle opener somewhere.

Best not ask if she was part of the Alessi kitchen plastics dynasty and have her throw some equal opps racism thing at him, accusing him of trivialising her ethnic heritage.

'So I'll ask you questions as prompts, and you talk about

any points of interest. We're looking for one- or two-minute soundbites for the app.'

Anna nodded and sipped from a cup that had been at her feet, which had a pink-ish teabag and a Twinings label hanging out of it. *Of course* she drank herbal tea.

'Also,' James turned from his screen again, 'I wanted to take this chance to apologise if we got off on the wrong foot when you'd stumbled into that godawful reunion. My friend Laurence isn't backward in coming forward with women. I did tell him not to bother you, but— ' he shrugged, 'that's Laurence.'

'Sure, forget about it,' Anna said, quickly.

James had expected something more – a dressing down, perhaps, but instead there was simply an expectant silence.

'Uhm. OK. The designers have a particular question they'd like me to run past you, first off,' he called up an image on his laptop screen. 'They're keen to make a reconstruction of Theodora's headdress here a major feature and wonder if they could check the detailing with you.'

Anna put her head on one side.

'The crown? I can describe fragments of the originals but we'd need to use imagination for a full-scale reconstruction and I'm reluctant to make things up. It's a bit of a no-no in my field, you know, someone else comes along and contradicts you. I'd prefer to use artefacts where we know we're getting it exactly right if that's OK.'

'Such as?' James was sighing inwardly. Nothing was going to be easy.

'The girdle we're getting on loan from the Met in New York is amazing. It's pure gold and very heavy. It would've been worn in state ceremonies and events and it's just as important as any crown.'

'OK. Hmmm. Anticipating what they'll say … I think the crown has that familiarity factor? People know what they're looking at. A girdle will be slightly more awkward as a defining single image.'

'The girdle has the "being a fascinating and complete historical artefact where we're not bodging it" factor though.'

Oh for God's sake. 'The designers were very keen on the crown idea.'

'The designers aren't historical experts. I'm guessing they only want it to look pretty. You're asking me for my opinion and I'm giving it to you.'

Yes. Yes, you are, James thought. 'I'll feed that back to them and maybe they can deal with you direct.' *Lucky old them.*

'So if you can look at a point around about here while you're talking,' James said, standing up and walking to a position on the right of Anna.

'Not straight into the camera?'

'That could look slightly bossy. Think conversational tone. It's not a lecture. I can stay here, if it's useful.'

'I can remember which direction to point my eyes without that, I think.'

Good grief. James dropped into one of the seats.

'Imagine we've seen an image of Justinian and Theodora in the mosaic. How much do we know about how and where they met? Repeat the question back at the top of the answer for context. "We know that when they met …" etc.'

Anna was slightly creaky at first but as the questions got going, her natural enthusiasm for her subject took over and she became animated, almost infectiously so.

It was pretty interesting, James had to admit. This was proper bloody *Game of Thrones* history, not broken pottery and feudal taxes. By the end of the session, James knew they had some good material. Even if they hadn't had a good time.

'I can show you some examples on our website of previous apps if you'd like? Might give you more of an idea of how we'll use this,' he said, hoping to win her round.

Anna nodded and James turned to the laptop, angling the screen on the seat so she could see the Parlez homepage. Navigating the site, he accidentally brought up the *About Us* section.

'What are those pictures, next to your names?' Anna squinted at the thumbnails.

James suppressed a cringe.

'Ah. Food.'

'Food?'

'Yeah, like. Everyone's favourite food.'

She looked at him as if he'd said they all talked like pirates on a Tuesday.

'What's that?' She pointed at Harris's photo.

'Uhm. A dessert … Bananas Foster.'

James squirmed, and thought telling Anna that the rest of the office had had a non-PC snigger about camp Harris loving Bananas Foster probably wouldn't help matters.

'What's yours?' she asked, scanning down.

James clicked away, muttering: 'A Lahmacun. It's like a Turkish pizza.'

'Yes, I know what it is,' Anna snapped.

'You can talk though, you eat omelettes in baps.'

'It's not on my profile on UCL's site. Here's Anna, she specialises in Byzantine history. She also likes omelettes in baps.'

'Just a bit of fun,' he snapped. Oh no. He'd used the phrase 'just a bit of fun'. Epic fail.

'Different world I guess.'

'Is it?' James said, not bothering to hide his exasperation. 'Everything doesn't have to be stony serious, does it?'

'I know. But "favourite food". Reminds me of old *Smash Hits* interviews. "What's your favourite colour, Kylie?"'

She smirked, and James felt a twinge of shame and dislike for having been made to look a fool.

'I hope your colleague Parker, the firm's Mac and Cheese fan, isn't going to be doing more Googling on our behalf,' she said.

James knew what the company man answer was here. An acknowledgement, a self-deprecating joke, a semi-apology. But sod that. She was being so needlessly needling.

'Parker was speaking off the cuff. We're here to present the content, not create it,' James said, voice tight.

'It doesn't seem that way when I'm having to argue my case against designers?'

'You're being rather touchy.'

'Maybe it's that "stony serious" habit of mine again. Shall I tell you my favourite dessert, lighten the mood?'

Right at that moment, James hated everything. He hated his job, he hated this superior woman, he hated himself. He hated omelettes in baps, even though he'd never tried one. He hated that his wife had left him and she was sort-of sleeping with a man called Finn. And he hated that someone was laughing at him for something that wasn't even his fault.

He puffed his cheeks out.

'OK, look. Like it or not, we have to work together for weeks on this. I don't understand why it has to be a nightmare.

You don't give two craps about what I do, fine. I get it. It's a bunch of digital twattery that didn't exist five minutes ago and now we sell it to you as essential, because unfortunately for you it is. Because everyone has smart phones and the attention span of Graham Norton after a speedball and a Red Bull, even the ones who go to museums. But this pays my mortgage and I'm alright at it, so it's what I do. Not everyone has a passion for their work like you. We're not all that lucky.

'And you think my colleagues are dicks? Guess what? So do I, with one or two exceptions. And they all seem to have surnames for forenames. But instead of sitting here trying to get a rise out of me every other minute and make it clear how moronic you think it all is, why don't we get on and work together? Then we can get the job done as painlessly as possible and we'll soon be out of each other's sight. And thank God for that.'

Silence. Shock. Mutual shock. James had never spoken in a temper to a client before. And not any old client – he'd told a clever professor woman to stick it in her pigeonhole.

She was going to make an official complaint and he'd be taken off this project. Or worse, Parlez would lose the contract over it. Word would go round other universities, they'd be blacklisted, and he'd be in deep shit.

She looked startled, but said nothing. James equivocated over apologising and reasoned it wouldn't do him any good now anyway.

Then Anna spoke, without emotion.

'Do you have enough from me?'

'More than enough, thanks,' James said, snapping his laptop shut.

25

After she'd finished a tutorial in the afternoon, Patrick popped his head round the door.

'How did it go with your nemesis?' Patrick asked. 'Did he prove himself an irretrievable mung bean?' Patrick had his own lexicon, one that could only be born of watching a lot of *Red Dwarf*. 'I made myself scarce once it was properly up and running, but from what I heard at the start you sounded tremendous.'

'Ta. It's weird, but unless he's hiding it very well, I don't think he remembers me from school at all. Strange, isn't it? Yet he loomed so large for me. The big people don't remember the little people. Even when the little people were very big.'

'I find it very hard to imagine forgetting you,' Patrick said. 'I suspect you're being hard on yourself and were merely … voluptuous.'

Anna couldn't help smiling. 'Oh no trust me, I'm not being coy. I was a proper porker. With a huge nest of Slash from Guns'n'Roses hair and a pinafore dress the size of a wardrobe.'

'Well, I'm glad there was no aggravation with him.'

'There was *some* aggro … I made a joke about his company

and he had a big rant about me thinking his work was stupid and how he thought it was too. Took me by surprise. Especially with him being the unruffled superior poser type.'

'Really?' Patrick's eyes widened, and he adjusted his weight against the door frame and scratched his chin.

'But I think, if he doesn't remember me, I can cope with dealing with him.'

'I'll send the file to you as well as this Parlez?'

'Actually, send it only to them,' Anna said, in a snap of self-consciousness, 'I don't need to see myself yammering away.'

James Fraser would no doubt take the mickey out of it with his too-cool-for-school colleagues. Let him.

Patrick nodded and made his exit, but seconds after the door closed there was a mumbled *oh dear, that's dreadful*. He knocked again, and reopened the door.

'I'm afraid someone's tampered.'

Anna followed Patrick's eyes to her name card, which had been amended with some crossings-out of letters, and the addition of a word.

Nice
Dr ~~ANNA ALESSI~~
^

'Dr Nice Ass?' Anna read out.

'Appalling that you should be disrespected. Objectified,' Patrick said, his pale skin turning livid pink at the edges, like a crabstick. 'Some people still can't cope with intelligent women. How dare they … *pass comment*,' Patrick's ire was funnier than the criminal desecration, 'on your … on your …'

'Ass niceness.'

'I'll get a replacement sorted,' Patrick said, pulling the card out.

'Thanks,' Anna said. She'd learned to let Patrick carry out his performances of conspicuous gallantry.

'I'm afraid I have a fair idea who did this,' Patrick said. 'A pair of Beavis and Buttheads in the second year who shared their appreciation of your form and asked me if I was— ' Patrick made rabbit ear quote marks in the air, '*hitting that*. I mean, really. What contentious terminology.'

Patrick went pinker and Anna started to pinken.

'It could've been worse I suppose. Could've changed it to Doctor Anal Messy,' she said.

There was a pause.

Patrick blinked. 'I'll get this changed.'

'Yep, thanks,' Anna said, retreating.

She sat down at her desk again, opened her email.

Hi Anna,

Thanks for your help earlier, looking forward to seeing the VT. Re: the artefacts. The designers are fine using the girdle. Would it be useful to go through some of the rest of them together at the British Museum? Then you can select the ones you like best.

Regards,
James

An olive branch. Anna pondered whether she'd grasp it. Being unpleasant to him was attack as form of defence, thinking he'd go on the offensive. If he wasn't ...? Hmmm.

She decided as long as James Fraser wasn't going to be mentioning the Mock Rock, they could lay down arms. It seemed incredible he still didn't recognise her. Was it possible he did remember, and was merely playing it straight? Possible, but unlikely. She saw no difference in his manner from when he and Laurence approached her at the reunion.

She'd never forgive, never forget. But given she had no choice but to be in his company, she could tough it out without antagonism. Indifference was all he deserved, anyway.

Another email pinged into her inbox. BDSM Neil again. Oh, fantastic.

Dear Anna,

It's interesting you characterise my observations as presumptuous, or egotistical – it was nothing more than honest feedback. So what does that say about your capacity to give, and receive, honesty? If I may, it was quite obvious you felt some attraction towards me during our date. Your eye contact and the way you played with your hair were classic giveaways. However, I suspect this arguing is a gambit to make me even keener to see you again …? I have to say – it's working. ☺

Best,
Neil

Anna hit the reply button with the force of someone playing whack-a-mole.

Dear Neil,

Speechless. It's obviously risky to have eyes and hair around men these days. I should've taken care to be bald and blind. It's a definite NO to a second date, thanks. If you continue to insist that I'm playing the long game then by all means, pencil some action in for the afterlife. Hell, make it an orgy – invite Marilyn Monroe, Caligula and Rod Hull. Good luck in all your future endeavours!

Anna

26

Anna was five minutes early and tossing a two pound coin into a toothless, hopeless busker's cap outside Russell Square Tube station when she realised James was also early.

'Big fan of the xylophone?' he said, as she joined him.

'It's called philanthropy,' Anna said, shirtily.

'Oh. I thought it was "Love Me Do".'

She shot him a foul look before she noticed James was smiling.

They navigated the short walk to the British Museum, making small talk about the Q and A. Once again, Anna was alert for any sign of his recollecting her, but there was nothing. Or he had the poker face of all time.

'We have to wear these gloves,' Anna passed James a cotton pair from a blue and white box, once they'd signed in. 'Or do you know that, if you've been here before?'

'Ah, I haven't,' he said, accepting them.

Anna couldn't help that even in such crappy company, she couldn't entirely contain the fizz of excitement she felt at being in the British Museum's store rooms. It was her favourite place in the whole world.

She only asked the gloves question so she could work out how much gushing she could get away with, in the guise of showing James around.

'It's like the end of *Raiders of the Lost Ark*, isn't it?' she said, as they stood in front of a vast modern warehouse of shelving units, stacked with identical manila boxes, and strewn with half-size stepladders on four wheels.

It smelt papery – the delicate musty evocative perfume of very old things interacting with oxygen. Incredible to think they were right in the middle of the throb and throng of London, in this quiet cave full of priceless treasure.

'You'll have to hope you don't dislodge the lid on the Ark of the Covenant then. Those Nazis' faces melted right off,' James said.

'You'd be OK if you closed your eyes.'

'Yeah. Never quite got the science there,' he smiled, thinly.

No, there seemed not the faintest whisper of him recalling her from school. Anna was experiencing the spiritual lightness of escaping something unpleasant. The flood of relief made her relax a little towards him.

'So, Theodora is over here,' Anna said, leading their way through the grid.

'Also reminds me of trying to find the occasional table nest you picked in Ikea,' James said.

'More fun than Ikea.'

'Haha. I'm one of those people who think anything is more fun than hiking round Ikea's Miserly Landlord furniture ranges, but yes.'

Anna thought it best not to mention how much Ikea furniture she had.

They got to the right aisle and Anna put her gloves on, pulling the first of a set of shallow drawers out, the contents set against a dark fabric lining.

'These are all earmarked for the exhibition. I'm happy to use any of them. Feel free to dig in, see if there's anything you'd particularly like and then I can find something interesting to say about it. It's gorgeous loot.'

James started to pick through the artefacts. There were delicate filigree bracelets, bangles studded with gems, rings, cameos.

Anna tried to quell the urge to gabble like a fan girl. And failed.

'The thing with Theodora is trying to choose which part of her life to highlight,' she said, in a low voice. 'There's so much to her. I mean, you can go with the traditional rags to riches tale. What's more interesting than the money and power is what she did with her position. She set up safe houses for prostitutes and outlawed pimps. She worked for women's marriage rights, anti-rape legislation. Her laws banished brothel-keepers from Constantinople. You could say she was one of the earliest recorded feminists.'

'Fit, too,' James said, looking up from a brooch, with a smile.

If he was risking jokes like this, he must think Anna had a semblance of a sense of humour. He was so relentlessly *flippant* though, she thought. Nothing ever mattered, unless he was under fire.

'Definitely. The Greek Elizabeth Taylor,' Anna obliged. 'And intelligent and spirited and courageous and all those less important things too. Justinian was no slouch either, according to the pictures.'

'Though these were times when you could be executed for an unflattering portrait,' James said, glancing up.

'True.'

'If only we had those rights with people who tag bad photos on Facebook,' James said, smiling. It seemed they were both glad not to fight.

'But if you try to make an unabashed heroine out of her, she's too slippery for that. She could be utterly ruthless and bloodthirsty towards female rivals. You had to be then, I guess, or be eaten alive. You live life in the present, you don't think of how it'll look in the future. There should be a Hollywood film.'

'Yeah … they'll probably cast Mila Kunis and Ashton Kutcher, and turn it into a gross-out comedy.'

Anna laughed. 'I only hope that the show goes well. I have a fantasy that her story will inspire a raft of new Theodora enthusiasts.' She paused. 'The later stuff, not the porny floor shows quite so much, obviously.'

James laughed. 'Wait, I thought you were scandalised by Parker calling her origins tale smutty?'

'Well, you know. I'm not judging her …'

'It's OK. This is a sign you're going to approve of our title: '*Theodora the Whorer*.'

Now Anna laughed. He was quick and witty with the comebacks at school, she remembered that. A sense of humour that ran as far as hilarious japes.

'I don't think we have anything to worry about with the show, it'll be very popular,' he said, politely, although Anna couldn't tell if he was genuine or humouring her.

'This could look fantastic in the app, actually,' James said, turning a golden cloisonné enamel brooch around in white gloved hands, like a magician with a coin trick. 'We could magnify it so you could see the detail in the illustration.'

James leaned over it and Anna found herself staring into his midnight-inky hair. Despite her best efforts, in the peaceful suspended reality of the room, she weakened and admired him.

Even if he wasn't your thing, it would be contrarian to pretend he wasn't easy on the eye, in a timeless sort of way.

Some handsomeness was the fashion of its era. Her mum thought Ryan Gosling looked like 'the result of cousins marrying, he reminds me of that Nicholas Lyndhurst', for example. But her mother – hell, even Granny Maude, when the glaucoma had really taken hold – would announce James Fraser to be *a dish*.

His face fitted age-old rules and measures and formulas for good looks, so much so, you could have dropped him into any other era with just as much success. If only they had.

And the structure was brought alive by his skin, with that ethereal, moonstone glow … wait, what was she *doing*? What had possessed her to admire this pile of man-shaped villainy in a mascara beard?

Anna remembered what she used to write about his face in her diaries, penning pages and pages of fevered adulation about what his outsides could do to her insides. And then the day she never wrote in a diary again. Yep – this was what happened with James. If there was a positive, it was swiftly followed by a negative.

'Showy stuff isn't usually my taste, but I have to concede this is beautiful. I'm finding it hard to stop gazing in wonder,' James said sincerely, looking up from under his movie star brow, giving her a jolt of embarrassment in echoing her own thoughts. Or, some of them.

27

'We can only get to you during office hours this week, I'm afraid,' said the bloodless *eat-shit-and-die-while-I-study-my-manicure* female voice on the other end of the phone line.

'Guess where I am during office hours?' James said. 'There's a clue in the question.'

'Sorry, that's all we have. Do you want the Thursday appointment?'

'I think I'll see what Foxtons can do, actually. Thanks,' James said, tartly, ringing off.

He paid for his pride: he was having to make these calls to estate agents outside on his mobile, so nosy sods in the office didn't listen in. After more inquiries, hand on phone turning to a block of ice, it was obvious that late afternoon was as good as he was going to get. He gave in and booked one for the same time and day he'd rejected two conversations ago.

Hmmm, mind you. It was welcome time out of the office. He'd claim he was getting his washing machine fixed or something. He didn't want questions about where he was moving to.

It was pretty shabby that he merely wanted to scare Eva into returning. He was trying to ignore the question, bubbling under: *and if she comes back because she doesn't want to lose the place, what sort of victory is that?*

He remembered what a surprisingly emotional trial house hunting had been and felt bad that he'd be inviting other people to imagine themselves installed at his address, when it had scant chance of becoming reality.

However, if Laurence was right and he needed to do something provocative, metaphorically flexing his muscles to sharpen Eva's attention, then the Crouch End Castle was it. He figured it was either house, cat or him. He didn't want to hold Luther hostage, nor did he want to climb into bed with someone else for the sake of it, as Laurence advised.

There was no greater passion killer than your new wife leaving you, it turned out. It was as if Eva had inflicted wounds to his head, chest and stomach, shutting off certain functions below. The thought of this notional affair, using another human being like a CPR dummy, made him feel slightly sick and sad.

Returning to the antics of his twenties now, as a broken impending-divorcee, who was liable to feel teary about his lost spouse after he'd shoved the shag-piece in a cab? *Nein danke.* This kind of misery liked no company.

James pocketed his phone, returned to his desk and flipped through his diary. He was going to have to cover this with a meeting. What could he move to a meeting at home? Not much, as it turned out.

He needed a good excuse though as Harris was on the warpath, looking for things to complain about.

Harris wasn't senior as such, but he had the ear of Parlez's owners, a luridly rich fifty-something couple, Jez and Fi (never

Jeremy or Fiona), currently making alterations to an eco-home in Umbria that had been featured on *Grand Designs*. Though given it was wildly over budget and the locals wanted to have them killed, *Grand Follies* might be more apt.

Harris was their lidless, unblinking eye and was due to give them their monthly update soon. 'Lead swingers and piss takers' were obviously going to form a reasonable part of his report and James was already on Harris's Watch List because Harris knew James couldn't stand him.

Ah, wait. The Theodora project. He had a note scribbled here that he needed to run the items they'd picked for the app past Anna thingy from UCL.

Did he want her in his house? Not really … but it should only take an hour or two, tops. And she'd been fine last time at the British Museum.

He decided to wimp out and send an email, penning an apologetic request to her to relocate to his house due to plumbing woes.

'What can you tell us about your new woman then, Jay Fray?' Harris asked, behind him. Harris adjusted his electric blue velvet fedora, complete with a feather in the hat band. It was only Harris's third worst hat.

'Hmmm?' James said, feigning absorption in his work.

'Your human woman you're bringing to the fifth do.'

'Ah. Mmmm. Early days.'

'Come on, you can tell us something …'

Harris really was a little tit. He was obviously fishing for no other reason than he'd sensed James didn't want this particular stream fished in.

'Meet her with no preconceptions!' James tried for fake friendliness.

'What's she called? How did you meet her?'

ARSE OFF, KING OF ARSES.

'Friend of a friend.'

As James was weighing up how the hell to bluster his way out of having an imaginary girlfriend, Harris's eyes lighted on something on Parker's screen and he let out a bloodcurdling howl.

'Parker, are you on Google Plus?! Who's on Google Plus? You must be talking to yourself because you are the ONLY PERSON ON GOOGLE PLUS.'

'No, your mum's on here too,' Parker said.

'Hahaha, *your* mum uses Google Plus,' Harris said. 'Create a Google hangout for your MUM. Your mum has a circle and you are in her circle.'

'Your mum uses Outlook Express at the weekends,' Parker said.

'Your mum uses Pegasus mail!' said Harris.

'Your mum has a FAX machine that she FAXES people on …'

Their delighted tones of voice revealed they thought this was a comic double act that could echo down the ages. A Pete and Dud, Morecambe and Wise standard of free banter improv.

James put headphones on.

Imagine what it must be like to work with grownups, he thought. *Imagine*. His mind returned to poring over those antiquities with Anna at the British Museum. Given how she'd reacted to the website larks, James couldn't begin to imagine her contempt if she spent an afternoon in this playpen.

The annoying thing was, as he'd conveyed in a slightly too aggressive outburst, he heartily agreed with her.

28

Anna rapped the metal knocker on the black glossed door and felt a flicker of curiosity about James Fraser's domestic arrangements. It was an ordered, quiet street of Victorian villas with white eaves, fronted by neatly clipped box privet hedges. Properties here were too expensive not to be well-kept. James's mid terrace had the mandatory blank white blinds, the front bay window ones at half mast, and tiled porch with repro gas lamp.

He answered the door in dark blue shirt sleeves, cardigan mercifully MIA. He looked less guarded and more approachable than he had done before. Inevitable on home turf, she guessed.

'Thanks for schlepping out here,' he said. 'I really appreciate it.'

'No problem. It's not far from home. I'm only in Stoke Newington. Hope the washing machine's sorted?'

'Ah. Yeah.'

Anna followed him into the dining room off the hallway. In the narrow kitchen beyond she could glimpse a black Smeg fridge, a range cooker and lots of spotless chrome. Wow. He must never come to hers. She heard an inner voice saying: *done*.

158

'Cup of tea? Coffee?'

'Tea would be nice, thanks.'

'You drink raspberry, right? I think I have some.'

'Yes, thanks,' thinking that was more observant than she expected.

A tatty, tufty throw on a stud-back leather armchair squeaked, unfurled, sat up and blinked.

'Argh!' Anna cried, before she could stop herself.

James laughed. 'Anna, Luther, Luther, Anna.'

'It's a cat? It's huge.'

'Yeah he is quite huge, isn't he? Though I suspect if you shaved all the hair off, you'd be left with Gollum.'

'Why's he looking at us like that?'

'Like what?'

'Like … he's plotting to kill us all.'

Anna was relieved that James grinned.

'He *does* look like he's plotting an extinction event doesn't he? I've been trying to sum that expression up for ages, well done. Never mind North Korea, when the nuclear mushroom plume shoots into the sky, there will be a grey paw on the red button.'

'Is it Luthor as in Lex Luthor?'

'Haha! Sadly not. Luther as in Luther Vandross.'

Anna wasn't sure if the form was to touch it or not.

'I'm not a cat person,' she said apologetically.

'I'm not smelling a lot of Doctor Doolittle here, no,' James said, folding his arms, still smiling. 'Prefer dogs?'

'No, no pets ever. Oh, other than my hamster when I was a teenager,' she said, hurriedly. 'Chervil.'

'Chervil? What, the herb?'

'Yes. It … suited him. He had big cheeks. Cheeky Chervil.'

'Bizarre. If you went for Basil it's a herb but at least it's a male name,' James said, smilingly.

'Well … thanks for the advice. He's dead now.'

'Of *shame*,' James said, and Anna laughed despite herself. 'Luther's got a lot of problems but at least we didn't call him Clary Sage.'

James leaned over to stroke the cat but it shimmied away.

'Aw Luther, we were only kidding!' James called, as Luther flumped off the chair and lolloped into the kitchen. 'He was my wife's cat,' he said.

'Ah.'

She noticed he'd used the past tense and he noticed that she'd noticed.

'Eva and I split up a few months ago.'

'I'm sorry,' Anna said. This wasn't what she'd imagined. James Fraser being single seemed unlikely. No doubt he'd frenetically nobbed a fashionable friend of hers in the toilet while high on a wrap of cocaine at Cargo in Hoxton. Or whatever heartless mid-life hipsters did these days. James wasn't wearing a wedding ring, she saw now.

He followed Luther into the kitchen and assembled the cups, flicking the kettle on.

'I'll grab the files,' he said, returning, while Anna stood awkwardly. 'Do you want me to hang your coat up?'

'Oh … thanks …' Anna handed him her grey duffle coat.

James bounded upstairs noisily on wooden stairs.

Without him there, Anna was able to have a good flagrant gawp at her surroundings. She'd never been in a home like this before, with rooms that had sprung from the pages of magazine shoots in *Living Etc.*

The wooden floorboards were molasses-dark, the Chesterfield sofa covered in rose velvet, the delicate pink of nipples in a Rosetti painting. There were curved, silvered glass lamp stands and stray splashes of colourful shabby chic, like the leather chair. A Venetian mirrored coffee table bounced light at another giant over-mantel mirror, above the original fireplace. All in all, a lot of reflective surfaces.

He didn't need to tell her they had no kids. She could imagine a toddler running through the scene with a jagged piece of glass like a lightning bolt stuck in its head.

A battered stripped dresser in the dining space displayed a forest of photos with heavy silver frames. As expected, they were a hymn to the beauty of the occupants, and extravagant holidays.

The backdrops ranged from continental cobbled streets, tropical foliage, balconies in Manhattan, to one where the estranged wife was waist-deep in steaming water, clad in a white triangle bikini top. No way would Anna have a behold-my-norks photo on display in a reception room, but then she'd never had a body like hers. Eva was lovely, of course, absurdly so. Spectacular but also toothpaste-wholesome, the kind of woman who made spirits as well as penises rise.

One photo in particular caught her eye and she stepped closer to peer at it. James was gazing into the lens, smiling over a large coffee cup at a bistro pavement table. He looked nice in it. Exceptionally nice, actually. Not handsome-nice; that was easy if you were born with the right flesh and bones. It was his expression. She'd never seen him look like that: confidential and affectionate and wryly amused. Maybe a bit post-coital.

It was the way you only stared at someone you were mad about, someone who could turn your guts to goo. For a moment, Anna was in the place of the person behind the lens. It gave her a funny pang of memory of youthful infatuation, like a shadow passing over her. She shook the feeling off.

A centrally positioned wedding day portrait showed the newlyweds in a hailstorm of confetti on registry office steps, laughing uproariously about being fabulous and in love.

James was in an ink-blue suit and floral tie, staring down at his feet, smiling, the sculpted planes of his face so photogenic. His wife was looking off to the right, at some unseen well-wisher. Her bridal gown was simple, fitted lace, designed to display narrow shoulders and a swan neck. Her hair was held off her face with a slim jewelled band, her eyes had a flick of liquid eyeliner, and there were pearl studs in her ears. The whole look was ultra-tasteful retro – *Elvis Lives, And Marries Grace Kelly*. They were perfection.

What would a couple like this do if they had an ugly baby? Fire bucket time? Anna winced at her savagery – for all she knew, they'd split up over the children issue.

There was a scratching noise in the kitchen, like mice inside a skirting board. Investigating, Anna found Luther stood beseechingly by the back door.

'Mwowh!' He put a tufted paw on the door and batted it several times to make his point. Then he went for an even more baleful: '*Mwowh.*'

'Oh, you want to go out?' Anna said, feeling glad she could make up for her ungenerous thoughts by performing a small domestic task.

There was a key with a gold tassel hung on a hook above

the work surface. Anna pushed it into the lock, turned and the door snapped open.

'There you go.'

Having bleated to go out, the cat looked unsure, loitering and staring up at her with spacey eyes, whiskers the size of porcupine quills. Anna bent down and gave him a gentle shove. It was like the daft dust ball had never seen its own back garden before.

29

They were in the middle of leafing through large floppy colour photos, Anna penning notes on the back, Roberts Radio on Classic FM softly in the background, when James did a double take in the direction of the sitting room window.

'Woah. That's weird. That cat outside looked like …' James's line of sight darted around the floor. 'Luther! Luther?'

Anna looked up in time to see a flash of grey fur move away from the pane of glass.

'Can he not get to the front garden from the back one, usually?'

'What?' James said, absently, standing up. 'Luther?'

He bounded over to the bay window and leaned on the window frame, peering out.

'Ahhh … the cat's gone. Am I going mad? That looked exactly like him …'

'Is he OK?' Anna said, startled by James's reaction.

James ducked past into the kitchen and returned, looking perturbed. 'He's not in there … maybe he's upstairs. He can't have got out …'

Anna stood up, as her stomach plummeted to her feet.

'Uh. I let him out.'

James turned to her, eyes wide. '*What?*'

A pause and he turned and darted down the hall, Anna in pursuit.

'Luther … Luther!' James called, as they burst through the front door.

'Can't he cope with outside?' Anna said, following James around the front garden, feeling very foolish and more than a little apprehensive.

'Luther can barely cope with inside,' James said, rumbling a wheelie bin forward, checking behind it.

'Why did you let him out?' he said, restraining the degree of baffled irritation in his voice quite manfully, as he glanced up. 'He doesn't go out.'

'He was scratching at the door. I just assumed … I'm so, so sorry,' Anna said.

'The little swine was trying it on. It's not your fault. Normal cats do go out,' James said, with far more graciousness than she would've expected. At this moment in time he'd have been well within his rights to flame her like a Whopper.

'Luther!'

James hopped the small wall between his property and his neighbour's, then having ascertained it was Luther-less, went into the street using their gate.

Anna did another pointless scan of the empty front garden and joined him.

'It definitely seemed as if he went in this direction,' James said.

It was rush hour and although it was a residential street, cars were passing at a steady rate.

'This is a not very nice game of trying to find him before he finds the road.'

'He wouldn't know how to cross?'

James threw her a look. 'He's never done it before. Did he strike you as a cat with its Green Cross Code? He's as thick as mince, I'm afraid.'

Anna's stomach sank even lower at his choice of words. She was about to watch a cat get turned into a hairy frittata under the wheels of a Vauxhall Zafira, and know it was entirely her fault. Oh God, this was awful …

'If I go this way, will you look that way?' James asked.

Anna nodded emphatically and struck off in the opposite direction, copying James by ducking to look under parked cars and over hedges, calling Luther's name as she went.

In the light of this development, her interference with the door seemed less charming initiative, more officious interference.

She considered how she might look through James's eyes, for the first time. Given he didn't appear to remember her from school, or know she overheard him disparaging her appeal at the reunion, he was only going by their most recent direct interactions. Judging by those alone, given he'd been polite enough, she guessed she had come across as a pretty snippy bitch. Now she was about to murder his pet.

With a start, she spotted a flash of smoky fluff emerging from behind the back wheels of a parked car opposite. With a sickening inevitability, there was the engine growl of a car approaching to Anna's left.

'Luther!' she called, glancing towards James, hoping to alert him and have him handle this, but he was momentarily out of sight.

The cat seemed as if he was crouching, not sitting – deciding when to make a dash for it, high on the excitement of new-found freedom.

'Luther, no!' she called, as if she might turn him into a small, biddable dog, who understood English. Luther shuffled another inch or two into the road, unsure.

Anna's gorge rose and her mouth went dry. She was no feline behavioural expert but she judged the chances of the animal colliding with this oncoming hatchback were fifty/fifty. It was as if Luther was using his gap of opportunity to weigh up his options, and when the car was right on him, *then* he would move.

Luther waddled forward even further and began to rock back and forth, preparing to pounce. His next movement would take him into the road.

Anna panicked and ran out in front of a car that was only 100 yards or so away, putting both her hands up, palms facing outwards.

'*Stop!*'

The middle-aged female driver, eyes wide, slammed the brakes on. It felt as if the car took ages to come to a halt, stopping just short of her.

When Anna looked down for Luther, amazingly, he was a short distance from her feet. Damn, this cat was dumb. Even the squeal of the tyres hadn't put him off. She bent and grabbed him, no longer tentative in her handling. She'd just had a crash course in cat wrangling, luckily without the crash.

She indicated her thanks to the driver with a wave of her hand, from under Luther's soft bulk. The driver's aghast expression dissolved into something more like understanding, and she put a conciliatory palm up in return to communicate: *oh I see. Phew.*

As she returned to the safety of the pavement, she saw James a short way down the street, presumably witness to the rescue.

'Luther,' Anna said unnecessarily when she reached him, gripping the squirming beast tightly.

'What in the hell were you doing? You could've been run over!'

James had one hand on his head and was noticeably pale. Anna was surprised at the idea that the risk she took might've bothered him, beyond the obvious unpleasantness of gore and paperwork.

'I felt responsible.'

'*You* felt responsible? My cat … your life. Doesn't quite equate. God almighty Anna, I thought you were heading for intensive care and I was going to be calling your parents, saying you were dying for the sake of a bad-tempered hot water bottle cover. I don't know whether to thank you or shout at you,' James said, moving his hands to his face then moving them away again so he could speak. 'I didn't make you feel that bad about letting him out, did I? You weren't to know.'

'God no! I didn't think about it.' Anna had simply seen a solution and thrown herself at it, literally. It was fairly stupid, with hindsight, to gamble everything on the brake-power in a Nissan Micra.

Anna bundled Luther over, her hand brushing James's chest briefly as she made sure he had firm hold of him. Luther's angry little face crumpled and he started quacking with annoyance that his adventure 'Operation Certain Death' had been cut short.

'That's thanks for you,' James said, and bent his head slightly towards the animal. Anna sensed he didn't want to do anything as unmanly as nuzzle him, in front of her.

She felt odd. She was awash with adrenaline, having plucked fuzzy victory from the jaws of defeat. This man she hated was behaving in a human, decent way that made him hard to hate. But he *was* hateful, she reminded herself.

'Apart from the suicidal element it was cool. *Stop!*' James held a palm up in imitation of Anna, cradling Luther in the crook of an elbow for a moment. He grinned and adjusted his hold as the cat continued to wriggle in his arms.

'Come on mate. We'll put the National Geographic channel on for you. You can pretend you're trekking through the Andes.'

Anna smiled and they trooped back into the house.

Once an irritated Luther had been becalmed with a saucer of Whiskas milk, James said, 'He's got a drink to settle his nerves, the little sod, I don't see why we shouldn't have one too. Whisky?'

'A thousand times yes,' Anna said, even though she never drank whisky.

'I think that concludes doing any work,' James said, glancing at the papers spread out over the dining room table. 'Why not have a more comfortable seat,' and gestured to the sofa.

Anna perched on the pristine shell pink Chesterfield. After rootling in a spirits cabinet at the back of the dining room, James returned with a lowball containing an inch of amber liquid. She couldn't be sure but for a moment, she thought his hand trembled when he passed it over.

'Laphroaig OK?'

'Oh is it? I might not bother then, thanks.'

James's face fell.

'Kidding!' Anna said. 'It could be Irn Bru for all I know

about whisky.'

James held the glass back for a moment. 'Oh? I'm not wasting it, in that case.'

He smiled, handing it over.

They were doing jokes? Crap ones, but still. This was a leap forward.

'Thank you. Sincerely,' he said, clinking his glass to hers. Anna mumbled *you're welcome.* The whisky tasted of peat and fire and made her mouth hot, in quite a nice way.

'Do you often make death or glory gestures for cats, given you don't like them?'

'It was instinct. Just, *nooooo …*'

'You've confirmed to yourself your instincts are incredibly noble and self-sacrificing, if crazy.'

James smiled with real warmth. Anna reminded herself this warmth was springing from the gratitude of not having half a surprised-looking cat in a leaking shoebox and a sticky call to the wife to make right now.

'Didn't your wife want to take him with her?' Anna asked, hoping this wasn't too prurient a question.

'You'd think so, wouldn't you?' James said, dropping into the leather chair. 'She's at a friend's flat at the moment and there's not much room. I guess when she finds somewhere she'll come and get him. Or, she won't. That's Eva, folks.'

He looked embarrassed at his evident bitterness. 'Nah, she's … she's something else. A force of nature, I think they say. If you marry above yourself, you have to expect some grief.'

'Is she above you?' Anna said, carefully.

'Eva's one of *those* people. You know, it's like she breathes different air.'

Odd, Anna thought. That's how I thought of you, once upon a time.

'Are you seeing anyone, settled down?' James asked.

'I'm single, and internet dating.' Anna winced.

'Oh boy, really? I might take your advice on that at some point.' James rubbed his neck. 'Have you had much luck with it?'

'You know when they embalm people, and they drain all bodily fluid out of them first? It's like that, but with hope. You do get to try a lot of recommended restaurants in *Time Out* though.'

'Oh, no. I can imagine.'

Anna smiled tightly and nodded, knowing that he was humouring her, though not in a patronising way for once.

As if someone like him ever ended up trawling online. The very notion would no doubt activate a whole social network of female sleeper agents he didn't know he knew. *Mobilise the Muswell Hill asset, James Fraser needs taking out.*

'Where are you from, assuming you didn't grow up in Stoke Newington?' he said.

'Ah, uhm. Not far from there …' She was being unmasked by degrees, fingers prying at the edge of her balaclava, anxiety levels rising.

'Mind if I use your loo before I go?' Anna said desperately, swigging the last of her whisky, needing to get out of this conversation fast.

'Oh. Sure,' James said, seeming slightly taken aback at her abruptness. 'Top of the stairs, straight in front of you.'

Anna bounded the stairs and found yet another zone of perfection. It was a dazzling all-white, with tiled walls like a sanitorium. It was, she noted, bar the kitchen, very feminine in this house.

There was a half-burned, blackberry-scented candle with a paper label on the toilet cistern, and an armoire with mirrored doors, stacked with white towels, draped with a chain of little paper lantern lights.

A magazine cover-sized photo on the windowsill showed a fair young woman asleep on her front, the upper portion of her bare back visible. It was an intimate honeymooner's portrait and Anna started to think the mistress of the house might be a little vain.

And as Anna spent a penny, another penny dropped. James's wife had left him, and he, the cat and the house were in suspense. They were waiting for her to come back.

30

Aggy told Anna she was free to choose her own bridesmaid dress.

'This is all about you and what you like and what you feel comfortable in.'

Anna insisted she wanted something high-street.

So Aggy marched into a branch of Monsoon near Oxford Circus and started authoritatively grabbing dresses and throwing them over an arm, using Anna's when hers became fully loaded.

'Uhm … my choice …?' Anna said.

'Got to get started,' Aggy said.

'Of course,' Anna suppressed a smile. It could be so much worse. Aggy might've had a phalanx of bridesmaids, but for the fact her 'bff' Marianne had only had her sister as a maid of honour at her wedding, to free up more money for her own gown. Relieved of the obligation to have Marianne in return, Aggy had followed suit.

In a changing room without space to warmly embrace a weasel, Anna struggled in and out of various options. She'd forgotten that trying on clothes could be hard work. And involved looking in mirrors and contemplating one's body a lot more than Anna liked. She got increasingly hot and dishevelled, cardboard price tags jabbing in soft body parts, hair even madder than usual. Aggy selected a pair of shoes with heels like chopsticks to accessorise. They made Anna feel foot sore and tired before she'd even walked anywhere in them. Anna periodically whipped the curtain back to reveal the results and deliver her verdict.

Electric-blue lace mini: '*Inside Soap* Awards, winner of "Best Bitch".'

Cabbage-rose floral with lavender sash: 'An Alice band away from *The 40-Year-Old Virgin.*'

Sugar-mouse pink tulip skirt, with silver embellishment: 'I have Sylvanian Families on my windowsill and kiss the McDigger Mole family good night individually.'

Each time she did this, Aggy said 'Hmmm' then nodded reluctantly in agreement.

As Anna squeezed out of dress number six and into dress number seven, Aggy said through the curtain, 'Oh, I've found you a date for my wedding. You can thank me later.'

Anna paused, mid-unzipping.

'*Thank* you? Did I say I wanted you to find me a date for your wedding?'

'You'll want this one.'

'Aggy, seriously, have you been doing "my sad single older sister" publicity on my behalf? That makes my shit itch, to use a Michelle-ism.'

'Aren't you interested?'

'No. I like to choose my dates myself.'

'And that goes SO well. How long have you been online dating? And you haven't found anyone? When was it you last went out with someone? As in a relationship?'

Anna squirmed a bit.

'Ages,' Aggy said, through the polyester curtain. 'Why not let me pick, for once? If you don't like him, it's no problem.'

'No, no pressure at all when it's your wedding!' Anna eye rolled at herself in the mirror. 'Who is it?'

'OK, so do you remember cousin Matteo?'

'Oh. Erm … yeah,' Anna said. 'The one who did that hip swivel, finger pointy dance to "When You're in Love with a Beautiful Woman" with Mum at Dad's fiftieth? And wears racer-back vests? And is our cousin? Does this get better?'

'Well this is Matteo's friend. Primo. If you say yes then I'm going to tell Matteo he can bring him as his plus one. For you.'

'Oh great, another Muscle Beach refugee. Why would he like me? Have you seen proper show pony Italian girlfriends? And Italian boys like women who can cook like Nonna, not ones like me, who float poached eggs in bowls of spaghetti hoops.'

'That's lazy stereotyping,' Aggy said.

Aggy's arm suddenly burst round the curtain, hand holding her phone, making Anna yelp in surprise.

'*Primo.*'

A ridiculously pretty boyish Italian smouldered from the iPhone screen at Anna. He had chestnut curly hair and eyes like Minstrels. Anna was half out of a crochet dress, strapless putty-coloured bra squashing her honkers like water balloons under a paving slab, and almost blushed.

'And why would he want to date me? He looks about twenty and like a member of One Direction or something. Una Direzione.'

'He's thirty-three and he's an architect.'

'Wow. Alright, point stands. But why me?'

Aggy sighed and withdrew her arm.

'Have you ever thought that it's because you act like a lonely old minger, that people treat you like one?'

'Yes that's it, that's what I sit at home thinking. *Maybe it's because I act like a lonely old minger …*'

'I'm serious! Your first reaction is no one nice would be up for it. You need to read *The Self-Esteem Repair Kit* by Oprah. I friended Primo so he had friend-of-friend rights to stalk your photos on Facebook. He says you're fit and he's well up for it.'

'Marvellous, Aggy. Perhaps you'd like to mail-order bride me to Florence and be done with it?'

'Are you saying no? I will tell him no then, what a shame.'

God, Aggy was a fearsome opponent when she wanted to be. No wonder Chris had stood no chance when it came to planning My Big Fat Itanglish Wedding.

'I'll think about it.'

'Think fast! Primos don't come along every day.'

Anna drew the zip up the side of a wiggle dress with a black crepe pencil skirt and a lace overlay bodice. After an unpleasant moment where she had thought the zip wouldn't slide past her waist, it suddenly caught the metal teeth at the top and the garment pinged into place on her body. Hmmm. Not … not bad, actually. Anna turned, looked over her shoulder, adjusting the fabric over her hips. She pulled the curtain back.

'Argentine Tango week on *Strictly Come Dancing*. Damaged prostitute with trust issues is wooed by mysterious drifter in trilby in Buenos Aires bar?'

'You look great!'

'Is it bridesmaidy enough?'

'I don't care about bridesmaidy, I care about my sister looking like a salty potato.'

'A salty potato?'

'It's from TOWIE.'

Anna checked how tight it was on her backside again. 'Sisterly love.'

'When Primo sees you in this, it'll be game over.'

Why did Anna get the feeling it didn't matter whether she said yes to Primo's presence or not because the invite had already gone out?

Aggy fiddled with Anna's hair. 'Some sort of flower clip up here … Lovely. Yes. We're buying this.'

'I'm buying this,' Anna said.

'What? Are you? Why?'

'Because you've spent enough and it's something I'll wear again.'

'Anna, you are the best sister.' Aggy hugged her. Pause. 'I was going to get you the heels as well.'

Anna stuck her tongue in the side of her mouth.

'Amazing. Heels too, then.'

Anna withdrew behind the curtain to change back into her own clothes, and mercifully, flat shoes.

'Do you know you only call first sons Primo?' she said to Aggy. 'If you translated it to English it'd be calling your first kid Firsty.'

'Yeah, don't say things like that when you meet him. It's like Mum says. Tone down your personality.'

31

Anna had just concluded a tutorial with a group of solemn third years. They were visibly sobered, if not agitated, by the prospect of their finals. She remembered that acceleration of time from her own university days. You think three years is an eternity, then discover it's nothing at all.

'Feel free to ask if you have any difficulties with that essay,' she said brightly, as they filed out.

She turned back to her inbox, the time-swallowing beast that was never fed. In the usual row of envelope icons, there was one from James Fraser. Subject line, *You're In Good Company*: *other famous Luther rescues* …

A smile pulled at the corners of her mouth. As she opened the email she laughed out loud, scrolling through three Photoshopped famous film stills.

There was Richard Gere clasping a grumpy-looking Luther to his naval whites in *An Officer and a Gentleman*, Ralph Fiennes in linen striding through the desert with Luther in *The English Patient*, and Patrick Swayze holding him aloft in the finale of *Dirty Dancing*. Somehow, using the same image of Luther each time, head turned to the camera, face scowling, tail hanging like a Ken Dodd tickle stick, made it even funnier.

The note with it read:

Thanks again for showing remarkable courage in the face of potential pedigree fatality the other week. I've found out Parlez has got a load of free tickets to that play at the Donmar Warehouse tomorrow, Friction Burns. It's got Dylan Kelly in it. Females seem to like him. Can't see the appeal myself, he's barely scraping five foot three in his stacked heels. Do you have up to two friends who'd like to go with you? Please accept as a token of my gratitude if so.

James x

An electronic kiss too? He did care about that cat. Anna drummed her fingers on her desk and dithered over how to reply. On the one hand, she didn't like to take favours from him when they had a professional relationship. Plus, he was James Fraser. On the other, their liaising over Theodora was pretty much concluded and she had to admit that from what she'd seen, the app looked great. As far as that fluffy animal went, he was being excessively gallant about her solving a problem she'd created.

She still didn't trust him. She never would.

But Aggy would kill her if she knew she had an offer of tickets to this play and didn't tell her. She was obsessed with Dylan Kelly and *Friction Burns* had sold out months ago, in a mouse's heartbeat. She could send Aggy without her. But then how would taking favours on behalf of a family member make Anna any less compromised?

It was at the Donmar Warehouse. She'd always fancied going there. What was on the agenda tomorrow evening otherwise? Microwaved soup and a whole disc of a DVD from the current box set.

She opened an email to Aggy and Michelle and told them she had come by these tickets, any takers?

Two decisive replies inside twenty minutes.

OMFG SRSLY? OMG I AM FREAKING OUT! I HEART DYLAN KELLY 4EVA. WHAT WILL I WEAR?!! Xxx

Aggy. The way theatre works is that you can see him but he can't see you. I'll take that as a yes.

Love,
Your Significantly More Sensible And Snitty Sister
x

And from Michelle:

Fuck yeah. I'll palm service off on my sous. He can't say no to me since I caught him wheel-barrowing our last commis around the dining room after hours last Christmas. CCTV's a bitch (and so am I).

M xx
Sent from my iTwat

Michelle liked to change her iPhone signature daily.

Anna enjoyed being able to spread such happiness and

180

cheerfully mailed her acceptance back to James. He replied within minutes, saying cool, he was going too and could only get his friend Laurence to accompany, *hope that's OK*.

Ah. Oh dear. Stupidly, Anna hadn't considered James might be going. Did it matter? He'd see Aggy, and vice versa. And Laurence? He'd have another opportunity to figure out who she was. It was unnecessary risk taking.

However, reason dictated that if James had still apparently failed to fit the pieces over a number of meetings in daylight, when blessed with her surname, the chances of Laurence solving the puzzle during two hours in near-darkness had to be minimal. Anna had started to think she'd never be ID'd, something that was both a relief and quite bewildering at the same time.

However, she owed Aggy and Michelle consideration on this new information, particularly her sister.

She opened an email to both, saying:

James Fraser and Laurence are going. Are you both alright with that? He still doesn't know who I am and we're being civil to each other.

If you are then I am. Plus I get to perv on him. Sorry, I know he's evil but evil men can still be fit. Like when Johnny Depp was Sweeney Todd. Aggy Xx

What she said, all parts. Michelle Xx

Anna duly RSVP'd that this was fine, then reminded her sister that if any question about where she was from came up, she was to swerve it, and say Tottenham.

Patrick rapped the door, stuck his head round.

'Permission to enter Avengers HQ?'

'Permission granted,' Anna said.

'Fancy a cup of tea?' he asked.

'Cor, yes please,' she said, eyes half on the screen.

With James's reply open, she saw the Luther photos again and giggled.

'What's that?' Patrick said. 'Student come out with another Dumb Britain? Do share, I'm thinking of compiling a list. Roger had someone spell Savonarola "Savannah" and "Roller" the other day. Presumably this was the huge wheeled machine he used to crush heretical texts.'

'Oh, no. Photoshop funnies. Remember James from Parlez?'

'The nasty schoolboy?'

'Yes. I saved his cat from being run over. He sent me a funny email about it.'

'Oh,' Patrick raised an eyebrow.

A slight, ever so slight, cool wind blew through the room.

'He's grown on you?'

'A little. A tiny little bit.'

'Remember when people like him are being charming, it's usually in pursuit of their own ends. Ends which will only become clear to you at a later date.'

Patrick's head abruptly withdrew.

Anna's smile faded, and she was left with the mild discomfort of thinking Patrick's cynicism might well prove to be justified.

An email ping. BDSM Neil. You can't keep a good man down.

Dear Anna,

My word – more sarcastic humour, your favourite weapon in attack as form of defence. You have myriad problems in relating to the opposite sex, Anna, and a greater terror of honesty than I even thought. I'll make you a prediction: you will still be online in a few months' time. And you may find yourself yearning to take up my offer of a second date … See you there. If I am still single, of course ☺

Warmest regards,
Neil xxx

32

'Thanks for doing this, pal,' Laurence said, as they nursed lagers in the squeezed environs of the Donmar bar, pints that would surely be trying to make a break from their bladders within five minutes of the curtain going up.

'No problem, I quite fancied seeing this,' James shrugged. He wasn't at all sure of the wisdom of helping Loz with a set-up.

'You liar. As if. You're back in the game, and I for one am glad of it. Who's she bringing?' Laurence said.

'Not sure,' James said, and had a shiver of apprehension about how Laurence would behave.

Actually, Loz was half right. The media fuss and star casting aside, James thought *Friction Burns* looked like an incredibly pretentious waste of time. And it was about the impossibility of romantic relationships, a topic he could live without exploring at the moment.

But the tickets were going begging and no one else who happened to be free was over thirty, or understood the point of seeing something without 3D, flying lumps of CGI or Jason Statham.

James was grumbling that letting the tickets to *Friction Burns* go to waste was ungrateful and they should at least return them to the Donmar, when a plan had formed that suited various agendas all at once. First and foremost, the *dumped James not sitting in feeling sorry for himself* agenda.

And he owed Anna for her efforts during LutherGate. It was only once they were chasing the dim bugger that he'd realised that his death would have felt like it symbolised the end of everything with Eva. Possibly literally as well as symbolically. She'd have gone *ballistic*.

He'd half wanted to warn Anna that Laurence was on the prowl, but decided against it, given that it was a trifle patronising. She was a woman in her thirties, not a teenager, and Laurence had hardly disguised his amorous interest at the school reunion. She could more than look after herself, if their interactions had been anything to go by.

A tap on his shoulder. Anna, black of hair and bright of eye in that grey students' coat, and a sight for his sore eyes after an hour of Laurence's innuendo and office gossip.

She was accompanied by a friend she introduced as Michelle, and her sister, Aggy. Michelle had generous features, an equally generous shelf of bosom, and short hair in a shade of cochineal red. Her resting expression made her look permanently poised to utter something confrontational. Michelle was not quite who James would've pegged as an Anna friend, somehow.

Anna's sister was less beautiful than her older sister, in James's opinion, albeit more dressy and made-up. She was full of that vivacious nonsensical chatterbox energy that some men found beguilingly bubbly and others found extremely wearying. He was in the latter camp.

Did he imagine both of them looked at him in a slightly hostile way?

Laurence did pop eyes behind their backs as they went to the bar and James's stomach muscles tensed. *Please don't be an arsehole.*

'Sister's another person of interest. Not sure about the other one – Maximum Baggage Allowance. Quite the upholstery. But what's that hair colour, Russ Abbot's "See You Jimmy" Scotchman?' Laurence whispered.

'*Loz,*' James hissed, face growing warmer.

Laurence laughed, clearly taking James's objection to mean that they might overhear, as opposed to embarrassed anger that he'd said it at all.

'I've got a question for you,' Laurence said to Anna, when they reassembled. 'Your cousin Beth's leaving do. How was it?'

'Oh. Er …' Anna looked startled. Her sister's brow creased and James could swear she mouthed 'Who's Beth?'

'You didn't go! You blew us out and then you legged it!'

Anna carried on looking dumbstruck whilst Laurence continued, 'But Fate has thrown us back together.'

'Or, James,' Anna said, finding her voice again.

'Well Fate had to throw you two together at work, so really he's Fate's intermediary,' Laurence said. 'He does Fate's admin. Fate's tea boy.'

James smiled tightly and thought the four letter f-word on Laurence's mind was hardly fate.

Oh my God but the play was awful. Just awful. James sank lower in his stalls seat every minute. In fact, ringside seat took on a whole new meaning, given the utter ringpiece who was centre stage.

No wonder so few people went to the theatre. He had half

a mind to call the Arts Council and complain.

The worst of it was that by arranging the tickets, he somehow felt entirely responsible for the content. As if he'd shouted *hey guys get a load of this!*

And, oh woe, the discomfiting and frequent nudity. He really would've liked a warning that Little Dylan Kelly (the even littler one) was going to make more than one appearance. James tried to gaze at the stage impassively while Dylan waved it around, so he didn't look like a prude who hated art.

He snuck a sideways glance at the row next to him. Anna's sister seemed to be oblivious to the horrors of the play, and was rapt, lips slightly apart, eyes wide, lost in every word onstage. Anna's friend looked indifferent, hand digging in her bag of wine gums. Laurence was doing his fake-intellectual concentration scowl, chin on one hand. Anna was … Anna was smiling? She must've felt his gaze on her as she turned towards him. James smiled back. James discreetly mimed gun in mouth and firing. Anna's smile widened into a grin. He turned back to the stage, feeling significantly better.

'What truth is there in love?' Dylan Kelly prowled into a spotlight, addressing the crowd, as the play rattled to its staggering conclusion that everyone and everything in life was crap.

'Love is the drug. It's an opiate, an analgesic to ease the loneliness of the human condition. And like all painkillers, it dulls the senses. Love is what we call it when we find someone else, but lose ourselves.'

Oh shut the fuck up and put some trousers on.

33

'That was very thought-provoking,' Laurence said.

'Yes, provoking the thought of how shit it was,' James said.

Anna knew James to be pitiless in his wit but she had to admit, he had a point here.

'You didn't like it?' Laurence asked, in what sounded like a telephone manner version of his real voice.

'I haven't felt that much resentment towards an Irishman screwing people since I last flew Ryanair.'

Michelle guffawed and James grinned at her. Anna was glad they seemed to have hit it off. However, Aggy's nerves seemed to have made her dafter than usual and she'd said a few things that had left James staring blankly.

Laurence had suggested a post-show drink and they'd ended up crammed into a Covent Garden pub for out-of-towners – all leaded windows, London bus red gloss paint and polished horse brasses – holding warm alcohol in cloudy glasses.

'I tell you what I learned. That Dylan Kelly is packing a kidney shifter,' Michelle said.

James and Laurence grimaced.

'Warm room,' Laurence muttered.

'He was so lush though,' Aggy said, fanning her face with her programme.

'Really, you think?' James asked, genuinely.

Aggy would usually squeal in response to a question like this, about such a subject. Instead she mumbled and fell slightly quiet and nodded. Anna thought it was amazing that James Fraser's powers could silence her sister. It created a slightly awkward pause, however.

'He looked like a pervy roofer who'd inflate his quote, flirt with your missus and eat all your good biscuits, to me.'

Anna laughed but felt a shiver at James's snobbery. Roofer? Her brother-in-law-to-be was a decorator. Not all honest toil took place on laptops, you know. *You with your Macbook Airs and graces.* Michelle asked Aggy if she fancied nipping out for a smoke, leaving Anna feeling vaguely relieved.

'What did you think of it?' Laurence asked Anna. He looked at her over the rim of his glass and she got the distinct impression this was a set-up.

'Uhm,' Anna put her head on one side. 'It was a bit … I think it tilted at these big revelatory truths and didn't deliver. I mean, why did he end up going back to the art gallery owner Eloise woman who'd treated him like crap?'

'Because we're all suckers for punishment?' Laurence said, with a rueful laugh.

'There was nothing to her though. She was so cold.'

'Sometimes it's the ones who treat you the worst that you like the most.'

'Yeah, that's fine when you're twenty-two. But this character was meant to be in his mid-thirties. I don't think you can carry on being hung up on an icicle in a push-up bra indefinitely without it saying something about you.'

She glanced at James, who was staring determinedly in the direction of the jukebox. Anna had a belated twinge that he might be making a connection with his own situation. She'd never met his ex-wife though, so how could it be personal?

'You know. There comes a point when unlikeable people having a lot of sex is just unlikeable people having a lot of sex. I wasn't sure why I was meant to care about them,' Anna concluded.

'Heartily agree,' said James.

'I'd love to write something like that, but better,' Laurence mused.

'Hahaha,' James perked up. 'About scoring with lots of women? *The Shag Wangler*. From the mind of Laurence O'Grady.'

Laurence failed to smile and seemed irritated.

'You'll be like that pick-up artist guy who wrote *The Game*. The British seaside version.'

'No need to make me sound so shallow. I do a fair bit of navel gazing.'

'Yeah, I think it's meant to be your *own* navel you're gazing at,' James said, and Anna laughed even though Laurence didn't look best pleased at this.

James's phone went and Anna tried to concentrate on Laurence's chat instead of overhearing what was an obviously tense exchange.

Well my mum wasn't to know … seriously Eva, now? I know the beast's stupid but I don't think it's going to commit suicide before I get home … oh for fu— alright, The Lamb & Flag. Yep sure bye.

He rang off, pausing Anna and Laurence's conversation.

'Erm. Eva's read something about lily pollen being poison-ous to cats and wants to go round and remove a plant my mum bought. Apparently two hours' time isn't good enough. She's coming to get the keys from me.'

Anna had a shiver of curiosity at getting to meet the ex-wife. If she really was ex — for all she knew, James and Eva were into those stormy tempestuous relationships where you split up every five weeks to keep it spicy.

'She really uses that Ewok creature to pussy whip you, doesn't she?' Laurence said. '*Pussy* whip … cat … get it? Haha.'

James grimaced.

'Hang on,' Laurence said. 'When did you tell her the house was going on the market?'

James's eyes flickered to Anna's. She knew he wasn't com-fortable discussing this in front of her.

'Today?' Laurence persisted. Anna sensed Laurence rather liked the embarrassment boot being on the other foot now.

James nodded.

'You know what she's doing, don't you? She's checking out who you're with this evening, and going back to the house to see if there's any signs of *a struggle*, if you know what I mean. Bedroom-wise.'

James looked intensely uncomfortable, shrugged. Anna looked away. Laurence was referring to him seeing someone in particular, she guessed. It didn't quite fit with the slight air of melancholy she'd scented round at his, but then, maybe he was able to nurse a broken heart and run a furious rumping schedule at the same time.

When Eva slipped through the pub doors, it looked as if prime years Debbie Harry had been given a walk-on part in a fly-on-the-wall reality show. She had Milkybar hair, high cheekbones, feline eyes, and a taut, tiny body, her legs looking like a chicken wishbone in dark denim.

'Eva, how the devil are you!' Laurence swooped in for a peck on the cheek.

'Hi Laurence,' she said, unsmiling.

Eva's voice had that diamond hard, sexy edge that came from Scandi-accented English.

James made introductions.

'Eva, this is Anna, her sister Aggy, and Michelle.'

Eva's expression implied James had introduced Crystal, Rio and Candy-Blush in Stringfellows. And in the visual sweep, did Anna imagine Eva's eyes lingered on her the longest?

'Nice to meet you,' Eva said, in a voice drained of colour.

Everyone else resumed talking while Anna pretended to listen while in fact earwigging on James and Eva as he handed her the house keys.

'If you put them under the blue plant pot when you're done.'

'I'm going to put the flowers in the bin and take the bin out.'

'Whatever you think,' James said. 'I'll tell my mum not to make such a thoughtless gesture again.'

Anna glanced over. Eva was staring at James, as if she couldn't work out whether to rise to this or not.

'It could kill Luther.'

'Yep. Got that.'

Anna was struck by how little Eva was making any concession to crashing a social occasion. She'd angled her body to cut James off from the rest of the party, her tone querulous. He looked grim.

She said: 'Nice to meet you all,' again before she went, but it had a tone of blunt challenge to it, to Anna's ears. Like a police officer saying *have a good day* when he actually meant *don't commit any crimes.*

No wonder James might've taken the *being hung up on an icicle in a bra* thing personally, what with the refrigerated wife. Bet they suit each other though, Anna thought, as she sipped her sauvignon blanc.

On the Tube on the way home, Michelle and Aggy both loyally tutted about James Fraser. His manners weren't too bad, they both said. And yes he was horribly handsome. He was so proud of himself, though. They much preferred the garrulous Laurence who, bar the laboured attempts to chat up Anna, had actually been pretty effortfully charming.

For her part, Anna felt as if James looked through her, and Laurence looked at her too much.

34

It took James some time to realise that Parker was shouting at him, over the din of Duran Duran. He'd been selecting Anna's footage for the app. She was right, it was so compelling it was a question of choosing what to leave out. As he watched, he realised she looked a fair bit like Empress Theodora herself. They had the same dark, soulful eyes.

'I saw you last night,' Parker said, once the music had been turned down.

'Oh?' James said, neck prickling slightly.

'With your girlfriend. Walking through Cov Garden?'

Lexie glanced over.

'Ah,' James said.

He was flustered. A simple mistake to make, which in turn he should simply correct. But it was convenient. 'She's not my girlfriend,' might spark more inquiries about his imaginary girlfriend, whose bio he'd yet to invent. Exploiting the confusion was too tempting. But who exactly did Parker see ...?

'You never said when we met her at the museum meeting!'

Ah.

'Uhm. No. Separating business and pleasure and all that.'

Argh, *what was he doing*? This was bad.

'She had a go at us!' Parker guffawed.

'Yeah. She's good at separating it,' James said.

'You were seeing each other then?'

'Uh. Kind of …'

What a tangled web we weave, when first we practise to deceive. Or put another way: lying is a very bad idea.

What a mess.

If James had simply toughed out that horrible power surge of curious pity after he'd told them about Eva, he wouldn't be in this predicament. He'd been weak. He'd lied and been believed and he was paying the price. It was the gift that kept on taking.

 'What's this?' Harris said, from his position at one end of the Subbuteo table. 'You've actually seen the elusive girlfriend, Parks?'

Parker nodded.

'Well well,' Harris said. He was playing table football while wearing a chequered bowler hat and a burger restaurant t-shirt saying *In'N'Out, Home Of The Double Double.* 'We'd started to think your new girlfriend was a butternut squash with a face drawn on it with a Sharpie.'

'Hey I'd never cheat with one of your butternut squash family, I know what they mean to you,' James said, limply, to a ripple of giggles.

He hated playing Harris's games, but he didn't know how else to deal with him without lapsing into open hostility. It was like being back at school.

'She's on the British Museum exhibition,' Parker added. Parker wasn't bitchy, but he was guileless, so as an informant to

Harris he could do damage inadvertently.

'*Really?*' Harris said, rattling the handles, obviously working out if there was any way he could use this to cause trouble. 'So you've been sticking to your briefs as well as sticking to the brief?'

'Oh God, Harris, yuck,' James said.

'Sorry, DAD,' Harris said, yelling, 'Goooaallllll! Mona, I am king of tiny man football! I am Lord of the Dance, said he!'

Harris did a revolting gyrating dance to this, leaving James feeling sick with dislike.

Ramona turned the music up and Harris started telling his anecdote about drop-kicking a plastic flamingo off Kensington Roof Gardens in front of Nick Grimshaw again, indicating that James's ordeal was over. For now.

He turned back to his laptop and regrouped. Parker would see Anna again at the exhibition launch party. He had two unappealing options in front of him: wait for a quiet moment with Parker and admit he made up the whole girlfriend thing, begging him not to say anything to Anna. Maybe claim he was on anti-depressants that made him briefly loopy, or something.

Yet Parker was, with all goodwill, something of a toolbox. He'd let it slip, or he'd tell a flesh-eating microbe like Harris in confidence. He could imagine Harris's *vegetable girlfriend* jokes would still be going strong in 2020. No, he might as well tell them all as tell Parker.

This put the next option up against some pretty stiff competition in the unappealing stakes. Keep Parker and Anna apart at the exhibition launch and hope to hell she never hears of this.

Yup. James was going to have to go with the high-wire Option Two.

35

It looked as if Laurence was right, never a comfortable thing to admit. James's own investigations when he got home from the theatre suggested Eva was doing some sort of on-the-spot domestic inspection.

He'd observed the pale circle left by the flower pot on the windowsill, but in order to gnaw the foliage in a death-or-glory shower of terracotta powder, Luther would've had to hurl himself at the flowers and drag them onto the floor with his teeth.

Incredible feats of athletic dexterity weren't your go-to associations with that cat. Luther often seemed surprised by his own tail. James also had a notion that he'd left the bedroom door half open, not closed, as he found it. Although Eva could be going in to pick up more of her things, he supposed.

But then Eva texted the next day to suggest they meet on the Heath for a walk and a talk that evening. It was the first time she'd shown any interest in the process of possibly reconciling with James since she left. So it seemed the 'putting the house on the market' threat had begun to work its magic. What an empty victory it felt.

It was a mild evening for the time of year and when he saw Eva waiting for him, hair split in two winsome little buns at the nape of her neck like a college kid, he felt heavy of heart, heavy of limb, and very old. Eva got straight down to business, arms folded tightly against her chest as they tramped through the park, at a speed that suggested they were going somewhere.

'Don't you think you should ask me before you put the house up for sale?'

'I have done. I told you I was getting it valued.'

'I didn't think we'd made the decision to sell it.'

'You've left. I don't need a house that size for myself.'

'Are you trying to bounce me into a decision?'

James fought to keep his temper under control. 'Shouty man in park' wasn't the role he wanted to play this evening.

'*Bounce* you? Is the deal that I sit around like an idiot, waiting for you and Finn to finish The Sofa Series in charcoal? Moving on to a whirlpool bath in watercolours? You've left me, Eva. Don't you know what that means?'

He breathed in air so cold that it hurt his throat and lungs, and waited for Eva to say it was over with Finn, it was all a mistake, she didn't want to sell the house. Why would she be here, otherwise?

She didn't say anything.

'Sara's must be feeling a little cramped. Doesn't her bloke mind?'

He looked sideways. Eva stared at the ground.

James lurched, as if he was in an old Mini with bad suspension that had gone over a speed bump.

'You're not at Sara's?'

She pursed her lips and shook her head.

His ribcage was suddenly far too small for all the organs inside it. He wanted to ask whether *that was that then* in a robust way, but his windpipe felt like it had been flattened.

They walked on.

'So much for the not sleeping together, eh? What a shocking twist,' he said eventually, hearing the misery in his voice. There were no points to be scored. He'd lost. 'Hope you'll forgive me now for calling bullshit on the stuff you called art and I called foreplay, what with me being right and everything.'

'This is it, James. All you care about is whether I've had sex. You're not interested in the reasons I left.'

'All you've said is that you were bored. I don't know what you were expecting marriage to be. We were living together anyway. Marrying is a party, a holiday, then more of the same. Are you going to make a go of the wild life with Finn, then? How's that going to work when he's clubbing and you're knocking forty?'

'Finn talks to me like an equal. Not some *hausfrau* whose opinions he finds ridiculous.'

'Oh God, Eva. As if. Are you Betty Draper with the shotgun all of a sudden?'

'I'll tell you when I knew I had to leave, James. That evening when Jack and Caron came round.'

'What? My tagine wasn't that bad.'

'You spent all night talking to Caron.'

'The civil servant?'

'And you were fascinated in everything she had to say, laughing away. You couldn't care less what I have to say. You think I'm trivial.'

'Of course I was interested in what she had to say, I had to be. It's polite, with guests.'

'And then she said private education shouldn't have charitable status, and you agreed with her!'

'She made a good case. Also, I thought you felt that way?'

'I'd be out of a job!'

James had a memory of an early date at a gastro pub in Clapham, and a conversation about how Eva was only doing her job to stockpile money so she could set up as a tutor. Then she'd take on talented cases for free as well as wealthier clients, and make the world fairer. He remembered thinking she was so giving, and the only person he'd ever met who looked wonderful in beige.

'And then my friends. What did you call them? Captain Cocksman and the low lights with highlights.'

Ach, they were awful, though. Eva's promiscuous, hairdresser friend Wolfram was the kind who'd bitch about his dying mother's lack of a cut and blow dry. And the clubbing harpies and self-appointed 'prominent creatives' who'd met at his salon were just plain frightening. Velociraptors in Kurt Geiger. James was fairly sure one of them had tried it on with him at her 'cook out' in Kew. They'd have been encouraging the Finn thing, without a doubt.

'Who were you with? At the pub the other night?' Eva carried on, as if this wasn't a non sequitur.

'I was with several people.'

'The woman with the long hair who stared at me.'

Hope glimmered. Given that couldn't be true, was Eva projecting rivalry?

'Anna? She's someone I'm working with.'

'Are you seeing her?'

James was unsure how to answer. Was it looking a gift horse in the mouth to admit to Eva she had zero cause to be jealous? He'd try for evasive bluster.

'Would you care if I was?'

'You can do what you want, James, you're a free agent. Are you seeing her?'

'So that's a no, you don't care.'

They passed another young couple on the path. They smiled at them as if they were all in Happily Coupled-Up Club.

James looked at a kid flying a kite in the middle distance, gurgling with excitement as its ribbons rippled.

Eva stopped and turned to him, nose and cheeks chilled to bright pink. Most people would look like a slab of boiled ham, but she looked like a tuck shop sugar mouse.

Time to seize the initiative.

'I'm putting the house on the market. I don't know what's happening with you and Finn but I'm going to start moving on,' James said.

'Are you seeing that woman?'

James hesitated. It was a good sign she wanted to know. Don't lie, but don't extinguish all doubt.

'We've just hit it off as friends.'

When James got home, he steeled himself to look up Finn Hutchinson's model profile online and found an entire website. He discovered he was an 'aspiring musician' – *of course you are* – who was also 'a keen surfer who's always chasing the swell'. Please do, chase it all the way to Beachy Head.

James found himself clicking through the portfolio photos, grimly hitting 'next' like a monkey with a toffee hammer.

One showed Finn in a tuxedo, tie undone, legs 'alpha male' apart in an armchair, like a 1970s brandy or Dunhill advert. *'This was a great shoot. Channelling the Rat Pack, classic tux.'*

In another one he was doing that awful *aw-shucks-me?* back of the head rub and smirk, leaning into the lens, spiky hair centre parted, in a V neck Fruit of the Loom t-shirt and silver dog-tags. *'People use words like sexy hunk but I think I'm more of a goof.'*

The next, he was sporting a ten-gallon hat and chambray shirt, chewing on a toothpick. It was captioned: *'This look is the real me, outdoorsy.'* Yes. Because obviously you do a lot of cattle ranching in Dalston.

What did it all remind him of? It reminded him of Eva. Once when James had said something uxorious about how she was always dressed so well for every occasion, she said she was like an actress. She loved playing roles. James wondered if he'd missed an awful lot of warning signs.

How had this happened? He knew he'd have to fend off rivals with Eva, but he didn't think he'd lose her while they were still shaking confetti out of their hair.

He suspected the answer lay in the same qualities he'd found so irresistible to begin with, that old cliché about growing to hate what you initially loved. She was like a shark, she could only swim forward. Or the bus in *Speed* that'd blow up if it dropped below fifty mph. He'd found Eva scarily exhilarating. He'd made the mistake of trying to settle down with scary and exhilarating.

Now he was just scared. In a crisis, there didn't seem to be enough in common between them to find the language to discuss a way out of it.

Was it possible …? Don't think it, James. Try not to think it.

He gazed at a photo of Finn leaning topless against a motor-bike with a greasy rag thrown over his shoulder, fake oil smear on cheek, in baggy denim. '*My philosophy of life? I like to be the one to create the "hell yeah!" moments.*'

Contemplating these beautiful people, James couldn't stop the ugly question forming.

Was it possible he was in love with someone he didn't like?

36

'Knock knock! Are you decent, Dr Alessi?'

'Nearly there, Patrick!' Anna called, thinking, please don't picture me in the scud.

Anna nervously did a last check of hair and make-up in her smeary mirror and adjusted the blue wool dress over her stomach.

She'd try to keep her coat on for as long as possible until she had a drink inside her. It wasn't low cut, but it was clingier than she was used to.

Not being a shopper, she'd left it until the last minute in Hobbs to throw 200 quid at the 'what to wear to Theodora launch' problem.

'Victoria's going to head over with us,' Patrick said, with that strained *we're live on air don't say fuck or bugger* tone people use when alerting a colleague that a boss was within hearing range.

'Lovely. Ready!' Anna said, opening the door. Patrick's raptures about how nice she looked were curtailed by Victoria glowering behind him.

Victoria Challis wasn't just a formidable head of department, she was also formidable-looking. She was about five foot nothing, with grey pudding basin hair that somewhat curiously had squared-off sideburns cut in. In case you didn't get the hint that she wasn't going for 'fluffy', she also wore suit trousers with a man's shirt and tie. Anna would have admired her flamboyant snook-cocking at society's sartorial rules, yet she was always too busy being scared of her.

You might stereotypically assume Victoria was same-sex orientated, yet her husband of thirty years, Frank, worked in the maths department.

'She looks more like her husband than he does,' as an ungentlemanly colleague put it.

It wasn't a long walk to the museum from UCL but it was made to feel significantly longer by Victoria firing questions at Anna about the exhibition. The tone was intimidating, even if there was nothing in them that Anna couldn't handle.

In the style of one of her heroine's contortionist sex shows, Anna knew Theodora back to front, standing on her head, with barley sprinkled in surprising places. Yet Patrick was clearly worried in case there was something she couldn't answer, and kept buffeting Victoria with statements like: 'You said John Herbert was delighted with your work, Anna?' in an unsubtle manner.

Poison Challis looked increasingly irritated and eventually barked: 'The woman has vocal cords of her own, Dr Price!' Talking to Victoria was like opening the door to a blast furnace. This was at the moment they were handing their coats to the coat check staff at the British Museum, making Anna forget to say she'd keep hold of hers.

Patrick openly boggled as Anna's coat came off. She started regretting her choice of dress. She cherished her platonic rapport with Patrick, and had no wish to disrupt it by parading tightly clad evidence of the fact she was female.

'Anna, may I say, you look *sensational*,' Patrick exclaimed, and Victoria rolled her eyes.

Anna was glad the room offered other, far more sensational things for them to look at. The British Museum's Great Court looked wonderfully dramatic by night. The centrepiece was the cylindrical reading room, its perimeter lit by a ring of bright white lights, and hung with vertical banners advertising the Theodora show. The evening sky above was carved into diamonds by the vaulted roof. Anna felt her heart lift, and a stab of excitement.

There was the echoing hubbub of guests' conversations in the stone space and waiters carrying trays of champagne flutes and breaded things on cocktail sticks, stands with the exhibition book and places to download the official app, as well as tours running in and out of the exhibition itself … well. As Aggy would say: *er mer gerd*. They were all here for Theodora. If Anna never had any children then she guessed this was the closest she'd come to the sensation of watching them collect their degree or get married.

She took a deep breath and tried what her dad had told her to do, years ago: find a way to hold on to and enjoy a quiet moment, in the middle of a melee. Quite a valuable skill when you lived with Judy and Aggy.

As she breathed deeply, for the second time in recent memory in a busy room she felt eyes on her, and saw that they belonged to James Fraser. He was looking at her with an expression of amused curiosity. Anna thought: I bet he's thinking a glamorous dress on me is a humorous juxtaposition, like paintings of dogs playing poker. She tilted her head in acknowledgement and James raised his champagne glass.

'Dr Alessi, welcome welcome! We did the old girl proud, I'd say?'

Anna turned to see the kindly John Herbert twinkling away at her.

'Oh John, I think this is the best day of my life,' Anna couldn't help but gush.

'Shall we press the flesh and tell everyone about the wonderful work you did?' he said.

After circulating, chatting, making sure the corporate sponsors' egos were suitably fluffed, the arts journalists duly briefed, and listening to a speech by the museum director, Anna felt half-cut and wildly proud.

A tap on the shoulder and Parker was stood behind her. Interesting shirt … did the tie dye actually have *bells* hanging off it?

'What did you think to the app?'

'It's wonderful,' Anna said. 'Thank you.'

Having been the scourge of Parlez at that meeting, Anna bet she was the only person who had a small weep at her desk when she watched the clip of the actors.

She'd been frightened of seeing Theodora done badly, but the woman with the aquiline nose, serene bearing and eyes the colour of coffee grounds bore a spooky resemblance.

'You know the bit on the fashions, called *Dressed To Empress*? That was mine.'

Anna smiled. 'Excellent punning.'

'So you guys can date openly, now the work's done?' Parker said.

'Sorry?'

'It's OK,' Parker said, quietly. 'I saw you. I know.'

'Saw me?'

'You and James. At the theatre. I know about you two ... y'know ...'

Parker grinned and made the world's least dignified mime of a curled fist and inserting and reinserting finger.

A deeply agitated-looking James appeared between them, looking down at Parker's hands and back at Anna's puzzled face.

'Oh no, Parker. What have you done?'

'I was saying you and Anna don't need to keep your thing on the downlow anymore! James said you were keeping business and pleasure separate and now you can be all pleasure. Wocka wocka wah wah...' Parker did a little side-to-side groin shimmy.

James rubbed his eye and looked like he wanted to evaporate.

'You think we're dating?' Anna said to Parker, and James.

'He said you were?' Parker said, looking at James.

'Uh ... I. He saw us, and ...' James was visibly sweating and grimacing and Anna found she loved it. Truth be told, she was amazed James hadn't bellowed: *Her? Ugh! No!* James Fraser, feeling ridiculous in front of her. Sweet dreams are made of this.

'You weren't supposed to tell anyone,' she said.

James's eyes widened. Long pause. 'Yeah, sorry.'

'Honestly. You try to have a highly secret fling. With literally *no one knowing about it* . . .' she added, holding James's gaze.

She was smiling, James was hardly daring to believe.

'Shouldn't have gone to Covent Garden,' Parker said. 'Should go somewhere shit that no one goes now. Like Shoreditch, hahaha. You're coming to the fifth birthday do?'

'Uhm …?' Anna looked helplessly at James now.

His mouth fell open and he spoke, with some stuttering. 'Oh, uh … yeah. I probably needed to mention that …?'

'Look, if you weren't going to invite me …' she play-acted coquettish pique to give him a moment to recover. He smiled. A smile that lit up his face with delighted gratitude. Anna melted a little bit. Obviously the effects of being sodden with champagne and goodwill. And … it was also maybe his bone structure. He really should rethink the Captain Haddock beard, though.

'No, no, no. Totally invited,' James said.

'Guys, I'm going to get off,' Parker said.

'Yeah, your work here is done,' James muttered, with a sardonic look to Anna which she found funny and charming, despite herself.

37

You leave Parker alone for ONE MINUTE … Literally, it couldn't have been much more, and he slithered off like a snake on rollerskates to Anna's side. Then of course, he just had to say something. James rued the day. (And why was Parker, having been told this was black tie, dressed in a look James could only summarise as 'Skeletal Rave Jester'?)

It was especially galling, as James had thought it'd make it easier to reintroduce Eva if his work colleagues had never met the 'girlfriend'. Although now she'd moved in with Finn, this was possibly a moot point.

'Go round and hit him,' was Laurence's expert analysis about that development. 'Make sure your Thomas Pink shirt gets torn. Women love a scrap.'

'Me and a model? That'd be an outbreak of girly slapping.'

'All the better when it's two wet blokes. Look at *Bridget Jones*.'

Instead, Parker started talking and James looked the world's largest prannock and would've signed the Dignitas waivers for death's blessed chemical kiss there and then. And yet – Anna had helicoptered him out of Saigon. That was pretty amazing.

She was quite something.

She was in a dark blue dress that revealed she had a nice figure underneath all those schlobby jumpers. Her hair was caught in a loose ponytail at the nape of her neck. Her features were emphasised with kohled eyes and dark lipstick.

He'd watched her working the room, men staring in rapt fascination with their index fingers placed on their lips as she spoke, doing academic clever person rapid nodding. He couldn't help but think *oh, bless you, Anna, you think they're all gravitating towards you because of your key research role. But no. It's the rack.*

'I expect you now want one of those fancy explanation and apologies everyone's so mad about these days,' he said, taking two champagne flutes from a passing tray. He was going to have to use plutonium-grade charm to mend this. He'd need to leave her *irradiated.*

'As you heard, Parker got the wrong end of the stick when he saw us and thought you were my new girlfriend ...'

'Isn't the woman you're actually seeing going to be cheesed off?'

'I'm not seeing anyone. I told them I was to avoid the horror of being single at the office party and endless attempts to set me up.'

'Who were you going to take?'

'I hadn't got that far.'

'Right.'

God, there was something about Anna, something in her manner, that drove him to take mad risks with the truth.

'I was considering saying I'd split up with you.'

Anna's jaw dropped and for a second James thought he'd

finally pushed his luck too far.

'Just so you didn't have to go!' he added, urgently.

'And you looked the big man! Why couldn't I have dumped you?'

'That's a very good point and more plausible. Only I haven't told them Eva was the one who left me, so again, I thought I'd try to look less loserish than I am.'

'Uh-mazing,' Anna said, into her glass, without rancour.

'Argh, I know. It makes me think I left school but I've never left school, if you know what I mean.'

This time, Anna said nothing.

'The fifth birthday do is some surprise thing on South Bank, then bowling. Uhm. Given they think you're going ... *would* you like to come with me?' James surprised himself with his own chutzpah. 'I completely understand if this sick charade is too much though, so no worries if not. It's only if you anticipate being exceptionally bored that evening. Which you probably don't.'

Oh, impressive stuff, James.

Anna sipped her drink and put her head on one side.

'As in ... with you?'

James squirmed. 'Yeah. I'm not asking you purely to cover for this nonsense. It might seriously brighten it up to have intelligent company. As I said though, feel free to throw your drink in my face. I would if I were you.'

'So we haven't "broken up"? I can't ditch you?'

James winced. 'Not unless you want to? Or I can come clean completely and confess what a sadsack I am to them.'

She raised an eyebrow. 'And how would I know if you'd done it?'

'I could ask someone to film it on my phone?'

'Hah. As if you would.'

'You hold all the cards,' James said. 'I'd do it dressed as a woman if you insisted.'

'Hmmm. I suppose a sick charade date might be more fun than my proper ones.'

'Really?'

Anna shrugged. 'Yeah.'

Wow. He really owed her.

He clinked his glass to hers. 'Well, great. And congrats on the exhibition. After a shaky start, I'm glad to have won your approval for our work.'

'I didn't think you needed it. The museum love it.'

'Your approval is the hardest to win, so the thrill is the greatest.'

She looked surprised at this.

'Oh no,' Anna said distractedly, side-stepping slightly so she was positioned more centrally in front of James, 'I think Tim McGovern saw me looking at him.'

'Who's he?'

'Tim McGovern? From the TV. I have a bad crush.'

James glanced over at a tall, thin, slickly dressed wiry man in a swirly Paul Smith jacket with a completely bald, shiny pate and designer '60s-style black-rimmed glasses. He looked back at James and Anna, and took a businesslike swig from his glass. James decoded the quick hard stare of libidinous interest fairly plainly as: *And how do I detach you, from her?*

His face rang a bell.

'Oh, is he the historian that does the BBC4 docs?' James said.

'That's him.'

'Bookish World crushes must be different to real world ones. He looks like a lecherous chickpea to me. That *is* a bad crush.'

Anna giggled. She was very tipsy, James thought. It always happened at these straight-from-work dos; champagne, hardly any food, hammered as hell by nine. He'd woken up with a few colleagues he shouldn't have, way back when, and fizzy was always to blame. It felt as if it sucked all the moisture from your eyeballs. And the caution from your body.

'Nooooo. He's amazing. He really knows his stuff.'

'Yeah, but. He's in zebra-skin loafers. Power's an aphrodisiac, it's not a roofie.'

'I could listen to him talk for hours.'

'Looks like he could listen to himself talk for hours too, you have that in common.'

They laughed simultaneously, and James realised that laughing conspiratorially with someone of the opposite sex was quite intimate. The way you held eye contact, losing control at the same time, over a shared confidence. He checked. TV Tim was still throwing wolfish glances their way.

'He's *definitely* interested. Want to reel him in?' he asked Anna.

'How do I do that?'

'Ah, so. In a moment, I'm going to whisper in your left ear. Lean in while I'm talking, smiling, like you know I'm trying it on. You're quite enjoying it, but not completely giving in. Then laugh, in a flirty sort of way, as if I said something near the knuckle. Got it?'

'Are you serious?'

'Yes. Get this right and he'll be over here introducing

himself within minutes.'

'Why?'

'Because if he thinks I'm making serious moves it'll give him a reason to make a move himself.'

'What if he just thinks we're together?'

'Men don't do this with someone they're already seeing. You can sort any couple from "man and prospective conquest" by body language. Look, I'm mates with Laurence, he's done a lot of field work. Trust me on this one. Ready?'

'Ready,' Anna said, trying to compose her expression, a half-smile on her face.

James leaned in. He could smell her perfume, both floral and salty from contact with her skin. He brushed her hair away from her ear, which he didn't plan to do, but added to the effect.

He whispered, 'I've been wanting to tell you this all night, but … Luther's constipated. I've got tablets for him but Eva went mental about how he has to have natural remedies and I should put canned pumpkin in his food. So I got some, but he wouldn't eat it. Turns out I'd bought pumpkin pie filling by accident. I've had to buy pumpkin, boil it and mash it up. Luther wolfs it down and disappears. Guess where I found him, paws-deep in orange diarrhoea? My underwear drawer, which I'd left half open. I can actually say a cat shat in my pants.'

Anna reeled back with a hand clapped over her mouth, shaking with laughter. 'Poor Luther!'

'Then he ran off with what looked like a carrot dangling from his rear end,' James leaned in and concluded, huskily, 'But the pants I'm wearing tonight have been washed, baby. We'll talk about the dangling carrot later.'

Anna shook some more and James grinned and thought, I can be a charming bastard, when I try. For a moment he was too busy enjoying the moment and Anna's expression to register it had been a complete success, and TV Tim was at his elbow.

'Hello, sorry to cut in. Are you Dr Alessi?'

'I am! Hello,' Anna said, in slight shock, composing herself and shaking his hand.

'And you are …?' TV Tim said to James, with a clear hint of NOBODY!

'Bursting for the gents, if you'll excuse me,' James said, with a smile towards Anna as he left them.

When James emerged, they were still chatting away. TV Tim glanced over at him, and James thought: *yeah yeah, you win. Only because I wasn't trying.*

As he headed towards the door, he was jostled by a pale, gingery bloke.

'Sorry,' James said, as reflex reaction.

There was no reciprocal apology. The man was staring at him with a look of unfettered loathing. It was so intense, and so designed to be *felt*, that James actually did the comedy double-take where he checked who was stood behind him to confirm he was definitely looking at him.

Odd. And even odder … That short rotund woman stood with him. Was she dressed in drag as a *man*? They were like extras from *The Hobbit*.

There were as many mad fruits here as Parlez he realised. It was Parlez with PhDs.

James made his farewells, and headed into the sobering cold of the night air, wondering if Anna's night would end the way his once did.

An hour later, he unexpectedly got an answer when he was slumped horizontal on the sofa with a foamy bag of prawn crackers ripped open on his chest. His iPhone chirruped with a text: *Anna*.

Would she be thanking him? He hoped not. He could do without the grisly confirmation. It made him feel lonely. He held the phone above him and slid the unlock bar, typed his passcode and read it.

DID YOU KNOW? You did, didn't you?

The prawn crackers slid to the floor as he typed:

Eh? What?

Buzz

ABOUT TIM

You're going to have to help me here, Anna, I'm confused …?

Buzz

HE'S GAY. HE CAME OVER BECAUSE HE FANCIED YOU.

Oh no! Sorry. Haha. The shoes were a clue, I suppose Jx PS Can I get his number?

38

'Congratulations, Oh-Really-Anna,' Patrick said, doing a little *Blackadder*-ish courtly bow as he entered Anna's office. He didn't pronounce her first name quite right – it was more Ow-Raily-Ana – but she never corrected him. 'How are we this morning? Wreathed in glory? Bathing in asses' milk?'

'Suffering,' Anna said, 'but for a good cause.'

She was on cloud nine. Theodora couldn't have gone better and now she got to imagine visitors streaming in the doors. She would sneak back and see it as another member of the public soon. That said, she was on cloud nine *and* feeling like she needed a full body blood transfusion. Blurrrggh … champagne floated like a butterfly, stung like a bee. 'Did you enjoy it?'

'Ah, yes. But had to make an early exit. Guild business,' Patrick said.

Anna nodded in understanding, though for once she wasn't sure she believed him. Patrick didn't like large groups of people or big events. Unless they were made of pixels.

'You were the belle of the ball,' Patrick said, awkwardly.

'Oh no, I wasn't all pissed and hand waving like I was when

we were discussing that theology paper on "God's penis and divine sexuality" at the history ball?'

'No, no, no. Sociable! Sparkling.'

Nevertheless, Anna felt Patrick was working up to saying something.

'Tim McGovern seemed very interested in your work,' he continued. 'I saw you deep in conversation for half an hour. Hope he's not going to whisk you away and make you his glamorous co-presenter. We'd miss you at University College, you know.'

'Don't worry, my work was definitely all he was interested in,' Anna said, with a dry laugh.

'Did you … swap numbers?'

She was a little taken aback by the starkness of the question. Anna considered that she and James had deliberately put on a performance for appearances' sake, before Tim came over. All sorts of wrong conclusions might've been drawn by spectators.

'Hah. Nope,' she said.

'I think he left with another lady, so … bit of a womaniser?'

Anna gave a cackle.

'Patrick, he's a fruitsman, as Michelle calls it. A cake boy. *He does not follow the football.*'

'What?'

'He's gay. He came over because he fancied James Fraser from Parlez. As soon as James left I started getting questions about *who the gorgeous Brandon Routh lookalike* was, and felt like a prize plum.'

'Oh that slick willy character from the digital agency was *awful,*' Patrick spat.

'Why, was he rude to you?' Anna said, slightly startled. She'd revised her opinion of James's manners and thought he didn't go around being rude. At least, not to your face. Not anymore.

'I saw him with *you*,' Patrick said, adjusting his spectacles, pale eyes blazing behind them. 'The whispering and flirting and fawning.'

Anna laughed, though gently, the laughing muscles hurt.

'Ah! It wasn't what it looked like. He obviously put on a good show though.'

'I beg your pardon, Anna, as a fellow human of the XY chromosome variety I can tell you it was exactly what it looked like.'

'I promise you, he was pretending to flirt with me so it'd help me grab Tim's interest. And it did. Sadly slightly to the left of where I was standing.'

'And why would he be motivated to help you?'

'A laugh? Because he owes me one?'

'I am sure he'd give you one. Really, be on your guard. I haven't forgotten how horrified you were to be working with him.'

Hmmm, he had her there.

'That working's safely at an end now. Patrick, I think sometimes you shade into paranoia about male wiles.' Anna rubbed her throbbing temples. God, why would she never learn to do that thing of alternating between booze and water?

'Aherm. If he doesn't have his eye on you, then I have.'

'Victoria!' Anna said, as Poison Challis appeared behind Patrick.

Victoria successfully ended Patrick's visit and although hers was also notionally to congratulate Anna on the Theodora show, Anna ended up feeling as if she'd had a mild ticking off.

As soon as Poison Challis had left, Anna checked the

raspberry rippled whites of her eyes in her compact mirror and picked up her phone.

'Michelle,' she croaked, 'I can't go to the Penny gig tonight. I broke my mechanism.'

'Oh ho ho, you are so bloody coming tonight. Take two Nurofen Plus with an Americano and a Pret ham and cheese croissant and grow some hair on your woo-woo. I can't bloody face this without you.'

39

Daniel's girlfriend Penny had few gifts, according to Michelle, but even she conceded that Penny could carry a tune.

Her band, The Unsaid Things, was fourth on the bill in a room at the back of a North London pub that specialised in live music and toilets that smelled like the devil's back waft.

Anna sipped a full-fat Coke and tried to look politely interested in a junior rock group on before The Unsaids. It was made up of thirteen-year-olds wearing unbuttoned check shirts, worn over t-shirts advertising bands that had split up before they were born.

'This next song is about a girl at school … I mean, sixth-form … who lies all the time and she thinks it makes her cool but it doesn't, it makes her a liar,' said the lead singer, through a face full of fringe. 'It's called "Sarah's Lies". We hope you enjoy it. Unless, uh. You're Sarah.'

'Guess *someone's* burned that they had their impotence broad-cast all round double geography. Is the next one going to be called "I Didn't Ask to Be Born"?' Michelle said. Anna laughed but gestured nervously towards a knot of proud parents nearby, who, frighteningly, weren't much older than they were.

Luckily the lead singer was fond of the vocal technique

called shouting, and Michelle's quip didn't carry against the squall of guitars and the thundering, tear-stained lyrics. *Fuck you Sarah you're such a bitch / You say you're emo, you shop at Jack Wills / Your boyfriend isn't twenty he's nineteen / Fuck you Sarah I don't care where you've been …*

'I think I like this Sarah,' Michelle said. 'Shall we go see if Dan needs company?'

They found him on a stool behind a trestle table full of cotton goods with smudgy transfers, reading Peter Cook's memoirs. Among the acts whose wares he was touting were Head Office and The Pungency. There wasn't a lot of consistency to the line-up – rock to thrash to whatever The Unsaids were. Michelle called them twee-folk but Anna guessed that wasn't how they self-described.

'Business slow?' Michelle said.

'You could say that, Michelle, or you could imagine the stampede will commence once the music has concluded.'

'You're a good boyfriend to do this on your night off, you know,' she said.

'Ah, well. She cooks for me on her nights off,' Daniel said, doing his big eye blink thing.

'Can we get you a beer?' Michelle said, and Daniel pointed at a half of bitter at his feet.

'Shout if you need more,' she said, and then to Anna out of the corner of her mouth as they moved away, 'Nights off from what?'

'Mind you, "Sarah's Lies" touched on a universal truth: everyone knows one person at school who IS a massive liar,' Michelle said, once they'd taken up a position. 'A boy at my school called Gary Penco said he had a Peregrine Falcon and a Ferrari Testarossa in a lock-up. And speaking of school, now the exhibition thing's done, you need never see that James again, right? You must be breathing a sigh of relief.'

'Actually ...' Anna paused. It was rather incredible, now she came to tell Michelle.

'I'm going to his works do. As his pretend date.'

Michelle coughed into her lager, blowing foam onto Anna's sleeve.

'Sorry, I think you spoke some Italian there. You're going to his what as his whatty-what?'

'His colleagues saw us together. You know, at the play? And thought I was his girlfriend and I'd plus one him at this do. As a favour to him, rather than correct them in all the confusion, I said I'd go. It's only an office party.'

Michelle frowned. 'Why are you helping him out?'

Anna shrugged. A very good question. 'You know I thought having to see him was the worst thing ever? Well, it's actually turned out OK. It proves to me he doesn't have the upper hand anymore. Things are different now.'

'He still doesn't know who you are?'

'No.'

'Are you gonna tell him?'

'No ...'

'Why not?'

'I've got no interest in dragging it all up.'

'Then how much of a new dawn is this? Are you thinking he'd be a shit to you if he knew?'

'No ...' Another good question. She imagined James would feel slight guilt and a lot of pity. In what proportions she couldn't be sure. Anna didn't want to be pitied.

'Look,' Anna said, forced into the position of pretending to be sure about something she was unsure about. 'I'm going with my gut. I feel fine. This is the new chapter you were talking about when you told me to go to the reunion.'

'That involved being yourself. I think *posing as his girlfriend* sounds weird and unhelpful. And he deserves precisely dick from you.'

'Even if it is stupid, it's only one night. Then, done.'

'Hmmm. Officially, that's my verdict on this, Anna. Hmmm.'

The Unsaids were comprised of two men and Penny, in a woollen dress with '60s-style calf-length boots. Her voice was absolutely beautiful, clear as a bell and effortlessly melodic.

Shame about the songs, which, as Michelle observed, sounded like the kind of icky ditties that were often used in adverts to sell nippy city hatchbacks to women, or make everyone feel poignant affinity with the fact a department store was open to sell you things over Christmas.

When Penny got the hand-bells out and did a little wiggling dance around the stage singing about how she liked hot coffee on cold mornings, Michelle snapped.

'Is the unsaid thing that they could give you Type 2?' she whispered into Anna's ear.

Anna made a shushing gesture at her and Michelle laughed.

'Our next is a cover of a song you probably know as a Nirvana track,' Penny said, looking out from under her eyelashes.

They launched into something that Anna recalled from the *MTV: Unplugged* session as particularly heartfelt and broken. Unfortunately, The Unsaid Things performed it as if it was twiddly fluff.

'Oh this isn't happening,' Michelle said in a hoarse whisper, to Anna. 'They're not twee folking "Where Did You Sleep Last Night?" It'll be "Rape Me", next. Only done with a lisp. Wape Meeeee ...'

'Michelle!' Anna hissed, and Dan appeared at their side. Anna did a friendly 'need a wee' type excitement face in the hope that it appeared supportive. 'Seems to be going well?'

The band launched into a very quiet, tremulous acoustic number.

Usually, Anna wasn't much good at figuring out lyrics. However, Penny's voice made every last word distinguishable.

As Anna was holding her Coke, concentrating on making a neutral face of appreciation, she noticed the words about *meeting a man / waiting tables.* She nearly turned and did a nod at Daniel, but for the fact the tenor of the song was angsty. And the chorus seemed to be a play on the word 'waiting', about waiting in vain. All in all it sounded like it added up to a *I should dump you* ballad.

There was a smattering of applause at the end and neither Michelle nor Anna could meet Daniel's eyes. When Michelle suggested another beer, Daniel demurred that he was going to help Penny pack up, and loped off.

Michelle was less restrained as they walked for the Tube.

'Fuuuuck. Was that last one about what I thought it was?' Anna said.

Michelle shook her head. 'She is something else, I tell you.'

'Why does Dan put up with it?'

'Awful lack of self-esteem when it comes to women. Deep down he must think she's all he deserves. Makes me mad.'

'Do you think he knew she was going to sing that?' Anna said.

'Nope. I think she's an aberration. You know I never told him at the time but I think she was a tip-swiper, you know.'

'How do you mean?'

'When she worked at The Pantry. We always pooled the tips. If she got a big tip, she pocketed it. I can't prove it but I've been around long enough to spot the people who won't tip, and Penny seemed to work a strangely high number of unexpectedly no-tip tables.'

'And you didn't tell Dan?'

'Didn't think I needed to, I just fired her in the end, she was rubbish. Next thing I know, they're going out. I won't make that mistake again. When friends date an idiot next time, I'll be upfront in saying so. I'll use my rights of first reaction. Be warned, if you suddenly decide Mr Too Cruel For School is viable.'

'Hah, hardly! The least likely person in the world.'

'There's nothing worse than when you lose a good person to a wanker,' Michelle said, as they reached the station. 'The day Dan told me he was with her, I was like, *man down*.'

40

As Anna approached the small trendy gaggle standing in the dark drizzle on the South Bank, she felt squirmily out of place. And she *was* out of place at a Parlez party, what with being a plus one who was here due to a mix-up.

She was somewhat rueing her decision to do this. That bloody Moet-and-Theodora high had made her feel carelessly generous. Michelle was right, Anna shouldn't forget she owed James Fraser nothing. Or rather, she owed him a bloody nose. She could simply stand him up, a sort-of revenge.

Why was she here? Covering his dignity? When he'd so brutally taken hers away, half a lifetime ago?

Curiosity, she guessed. Even after her humiliation and her indignation, she couldn't resist taking this chance to go undercover and explore. Like the reunion, it was a onetime deal. Walk in, walk out again on her own terms. She thought seeing James again at work was a taunt from God, but what if it was a useful nudge from Him Above? Go. Look upon this creature and realise that really, him and his people aren't all that.

From twenty yards away, the stench of fashion forward was strong. She'd agonised over an outfit that had enough flair not to be drab, and not enough flair to make a statement of any sort, and ended up with another black dress cliché. She hadn't quite wrapped her head around the idea of being considered fit to be James's date. His *date*? His fake date yes, but his date, nonetheless. Her younger self was watching, awestruck. Or possibly, furious.

Parlez's staff were all undercuts and buzz cuts and bowl cuts, unusual piercings, flamboyant winterwear and blocky, designer high heels. One man had a Victorian acrobat's moustache. Another woman had a hairstyle that wasn't a bun but wasn't quite a beehive either, a sort of a duck's bill on the crown of her head. Anna could hear her describing her raggedy tutu to someone else as 'steampunk courtesan'. *What the hell had she walked into?* Anna had spent so much of her life hoping her appearance *wasn't* remarked upon, she couldn't imagine courting controversy like that.

The average age was probably twenty-seven. They surveyed her with a detached curiosity.

'Hi!' Anna said, in the voice of a gauche supply teacher.

She raised her hand in a sort-of wave and was relieved that James spotted her and broke from the group.

He was in a double-breasted navy fisherman's coat, making her breathe a sigh of relief that he wasn't into extreme fashion, unless you counted the Clive Dunn granddad chic.

The cold had made him pale and bright-eyed with wind-whipped hair. He leaned over for a peck on the cheek.

Anna's traitorous infantile stomach did a forward roll, all the more pathetic given it was a stunt kiss for show. As their eyes met again, they exchanged a moment of understanding at how awkward this was.

'This is Anna. Anna, this is … everyone. Let's do names later.'

There was a desultory ripple of greeting. They all resumed their conversations, apart from a petite fair girl with a long bob and a girlish, open face. She continued staring at Anna with concentrated but not hostile fascination, with her owlish pale blue eyes. Anna thought: *aha. I recognise that look. You have the obligatory crush on James. There was always going to be someone.*

James rubbed his hands together and blew into them, saying, 'We still don't know what we're here for. Most bets are on our boss Jez having learned how to fire eat and unicycle at the same time. I for one would be happy to see him try.'

'Attention please, guys!' called a man with collar-length grey hair in a Crombie coat standing next to a strawberry-blonde woman in a fawn frock coat with a vast furry collar. They radiated monied self-satisfaction like an insulating glow.

'It's time for Fi and I to reveal how we're kicking off the evening. Champagne ride on The Eye!'

'The Eye?' James muttered in disbelief. 'Bloody hell. We're actually going to be the first people from London to go on the London Eye.'

He cast a rueful grin back at Anna and she returned it with a rictus grimace, her stomach in turmoil; turmoil that had nothing to do with James's matinee idol appearance. She hadn't even considered they might be going on the London Eye. Why hadn't she thought of it?

Giggling, chattering and clapping gloved hands together, the group moved down the South Bank. On arrival, the rich couple went into a huddle with The Eye staff.

'This has got to be about getting a freebie from a client. Total cheapskates,' James said to Anna, trying for conversation.

Anna merely nodded and smiled tightly, trying to keep a lid on her panic. She felt trapped. If she said *'I can't do this,'* she made a spectacle of herself in front of all these scary people. As she vacillated, Crombie coat man called for attention again.

'OK, OK so we have two capsules! It's been pointed out that this night–time ride is very romantic. So instead of splitting you all into two groups, why don't we let a couple ride on their own? Who fancies it?'

The response was much murmuring and no volunteers. The strawberry–blonde woman whispered something to the Crombie coat man. Looking up, his eye fell on James. 'James. How about you and your lady?'

The group turned to look at them.

'Oh. Sure?' James looked to Anna for support and she did a terse nod to indicate her agreement. *Oh my God oh my God oh my God …* there was no getting out of it now.

Mute, she followed him into the futuristic capsule. She was a matchstick figure in a bubble, about to be blown up into the air on a giant's breath. *Do Not Vomit Do Not Vomit Do Not Vomit …* She made it to the wooden bench in the centre of the floor and tried to concentrate on the sensation of the furniture beneath her fingers. The door was shut and fastened behind them. To Anna it sounded like a jailer's lock. Not that she wanted it to be loose. How long would this take? *Forever.*

'Dear oh dear. A Ferris wheel for tourists. Sorry this is so lame. At least there's drink,' James said, picking champagne out of an ice bucket. 'Want some?'

Anna, who was briefly unable to reply, shook her head.

'Are you alright?'

She nodded, but she clearly wasn't, and James kept staring.

'I have a fear of heights,' she said in a small voice, and winced as they jerked into movement.

'Really? Why didn't you say? If nothing else, it would have been a good excuse to get out of this.'

'I didn't want to make a fuss … I mean, I didn't think we'd written fear of heights into this character I'm playing.'

James looked nonplussed but gratified.

'You have a lot of heroism.' He studied her. 'You're not going to vom all over the place, are you?'

41

Anna kept her eyes closed as she felt the gentle ascent upwards and willed her gastric contents to stay where they were. When she opened them again, James was sipping from a full glass, looking concerned.

'I feel so bad, Anna. You should've said.'

'Look at the view, don't worry. I'll be fine,' she squeaked, waving her arm.

She watched as he carried his drink over to the curved window. They were quiet for a while.

'You really can't look at the view at all?' James asked eventually. 'I know I was cynical, but it's fairly amazing. Maybe the champagne's kicked in already.'

'I wish I could, but no,' Anna said, looking down at her grey-white knuckles.

'Does it help if I talk? Or is it better if I shut up?' James said.

'Talk, definitely.'

'When did you get your fear of heights?'

'Oh take my mind off it, cheers!'

They laughed.

'It was going up the Leaning Tower of Pisa as a child.'

Pause.

'Is that true? You're so dry sometimes, I can't tell when you're joking.'

'Seriously. It sounds too Italian, doesn't it? Like *"I was blinded when I got hit in the eye by a big pizza pie."* Back in the day you were allowed up the Leaning Tower and it didn't have any guard rails outside. This is way before the era of health and safety regs and ambulance chasers, obviously.

'My dad was letting me go up the steps in front of him. When we were near the top, I charged out onto one of the balconies and nearly went right over the edge. It was only because I had long hair my dad was able to grab me and pull me back. I still remember that feeling of *"oh NO!"* as the drop loomed and I realised I was about to fall. And I knew it was going to be curtains for me if I did. As much as you can do at six or whatever. It's not an age at which you should confront mortality. I haven't been able to cope with heights since then. It's like ongoing post-traumatic stress disorder. It triggers the memory.'

'Crazy how one bad experience can reverberate down the years like that, isn't it?' James said. It was so painfully apposite that Anna thought he might *know*, except he added, 'Like when my old firm persuaded me to try a client's fat-dissolving pills. What comes out of you is like margherita cheese. Papa John's delivery never looked the same again.'

Anna laughed. Another lapse in conversation.

'How's it going with the internet dating?' James said, eventually.

'Useless as ever.'

'Is it possible your profile needs another look?'

'Oh wow, cheers! "Is it possible it's your fault"?!'

'No!' James said, though with a wide grin. Anna got the

feeling not many women gave him the gyp she did, and he liked it.

'Absolutely not. Actually the thought process was more that it can *only* be something like that. Hey, why not look over your profile? I work on the internet, I do some copywriting. I also listen to Laurence's analysis of them often enough. Could help with the view from the other side?'

'Now?'

'Take your mind off the height,' James said, producing his phone and making an *indulge me* face.

'Are you going to embarrass me?' Anna said, feeling a constriction in her stomach muscles that was due to both the height and their history.

'I promise I won't. Come on, more embarrassing than the bollock I dropped at the exhibition?'

Anna laughed and put her head on one side.

'True . . .'

She didn't much like the thought of James reading her pitch to prospective partners. But she also wanted to know what he thought. OK, he was evil, but he was also bright and ... attractive. Yes. She wanted the view from the other side.

Anna gave him her name on the site and waited, tense, while James muttered about the 3G signal.

'Oh-kay, here you are.'

'No mockery!'

'No mockery. Unless you've put "enjoys the finer things in life". Now then. Nice picture. But only three of them?'

'Yes,' Anna was discomfited at revealing her thought processes, 'I don't want anything based on looks.'

'Laudable, but you have to date in the world we're in, not

the one you wish you were in. Stick some more up … Likes travel.' That's one of those one-size-fits-all statements isn't it? Since you're not nomadic it boils down to "likes holidays"?'

Anna giggled.

'I'd substitute that for something more specific … hmmm. Sporty and active. Are you? No!' James held a hand up as Anna's mouth formed an 'O' of outrage. 'Purely because sporty and active tends to be a euphemism for "boring bugger". Or, "walks to work". Unless you're a tennis pro I'd leave that one out too. They can see you don't cane the cronuts, which is all anyone's really interested in. Which goes back to my earlier point about photos: more of.'

Anna thought what a strange evening this was, stuck dangling above London with James Fraser trying to woo men on her behalf, as her Cyrano de Bergerac.

'Ah. OK. You say you're a hopeless romantic?'

Now Anna felt colour rise in her face and was glad of the low light.

'Yeah.'

'I wouldn't put that. Men read that as "will call me crying at three a.m. in week four".'

'It's saying that I'm looking for something serious. I'm not … you know … messing about.'

'Oh God, don't say "tired of playing games". That's the most frightening phrase from a woman. It translates as: "you will wake to find me licking the blade of a Sabatier knife". *I thought you weren't like all the others, James. You don't want to end up like all the others, do you, James?*'

Anna laughed and said, 'Well what should I put, smartarse?'

'It's got to be essence of Anna. Make it unapologetically

Anna-ish. And put "doesn't like cats". That's a USP right there.'

'Then I've ruled out all cat-owning men in a single swoop.'

'Be honest, have you ever met one cat-owning man you liked?'

'Thinking about it, no,' Anna said, and they grinned.

'More like, cat-owning men will be amused and intrigued. And do you really want to date Mr Liking Cats Is a Dealbreaker? He sounds like he'd listen to Noah & The Whale, eat quinoa and have erectile dysfunction.'

'Haha. Guess not. What's made you so knowledgeable then? Have you internet dated?' Anna thought hah, *as if*.

'No, but I used to date-date, and the principle I applied on the hunt was, would someone I like, like this place I am going to? Internet's the same. The more "you" you make it, the more you'll find your sort of person. Visualise who you're looking for and write it only for him.'

'Hmmm. Not sure I have any idea.'

'Have you been single for a while?' James said, pocketing his phone again.

Something about the strange circumstances made Anna risk the truth. It was pointless trying to look cool. She'd never be a steampunk courtesan.

'Since forever. I mean, not forever … Seven years or so.'

'Woah.'

'Gee, thanks.'

'No, I meant woah, seems unlikely.'

Anna acknowledged this as the polite thing to say, a platitude. She shrugged.

'I saw someone for eighteen months after uni. Joseph. We lived together for a while. He was nice. And at university I had a horrible boyfriend called Mark who used to refuse to kiss me before we did it and criticised my appearance all the time. I'm glad I don't have my nineteen-year-old attitude of "anyone's better than no one" anymore.'

Someone should do a study on the disinhibiting effect of talking at altitude, Anna thought.

'Jesus,' James said, turning. 'He sounds … bleak.'

Anna thought: *he never set me up on a stage and called me an elephant, James.*

'I don't even think I've ever been in love.'

'Lucky you,' James said. 'Gives you the upper hand.'

'That's cynical!'

'I mean it though.' James stepped over to top up his champagne, lifting the bottle from the crunchy slush of the ice bucket. 'Still none for you? Might help. Dutch courage and all that.'

'Small one?' Anna said. Groo, champagne again.

James poured a half measure and held it out. 'You don't want to let go of that seat do you?'

'Haha. No.'

'Makes sense. If this capsule became detached from The Eye and we plummeted into the Thames, you'd probably survive if you kept hold of the bench. You could paddle to the riverbank with it under you like a life float.'

'Oh *screw you*,' Anna laughed, as James planted the base of the champagne glass next to her and held it there steady, until she could find the will to let go and grab it.

She appreciated his mixture of teasing and genuine thoughtfulness. He returned to the window and she managed a quick hard swig of fizz, clashing the glass against her teeth in her haste. She had two more slugs, and it was gone.

'I mean, I've *liked* people ...' – oh no, now her chatter was being driven by alcohol and altitude. 'But I can't say I've ever had that overwhelming, whole-body sensation of all-consuming love for one person. Someone I feel like I've been waiting for my whole life. Someone who understands me and I understand him and it's like we're best friends ... who can't keep their hands off each other.'

James turned.

'Not completely sure that kind of love exists beyond rom coms. Or the first week, anyway.'

'Thanks for the encouragement,' Anna said.

'Ah, sorry. Don't ask the man whose wife is being diddled by another for views on romance.'

'She's met someone else?'

'A model. He's twenty-three. I have some insight into how the first wives of rock stars feel.'

'Is he hot?'

'No he's a hand model, he's got a head like Frank Sidebottom. Yes he's "hot", thanks, Dr Feelgood.'

They both laughed until she sensed James was thinking about his wife, and it faded. James Fraser being made to feel physically inferior was an interesting notion.

'Think you'll get back together?' Anna asked.

'Ah, I dunno. If you'd asked me that recently I'd have said a cautious yes. Now I don't know.'

'But you want to?'

'Apparently, I do. Not sure why.'

'Because you have that all-consuming rom com love for one person?'

'Because I'm a glutton for punishment.'

They lapsed into silence.

'OK, so let's recap the new Anna profile. *Historian—*'

'That makes me sound sixty-eight years old and like I use a battery-operated nasal hair trimmer.'

'*But I'm not the sort who's ancient and uses a battery-operated nasal hair trimmer. Think the kind of woman who'd fearlessly investigate a cursed mummy's tomb holding a tiki torch alongside Indiana Jones.*'

'Wouldn't that be an archaeologist?'

'Hush! Finish it with: *I'm hot. I hate cats. For brunch I like omelettes in baps. Call me.*'

'Hahahaha!' Hot? *Not that hot and not your type.* 'You're quite good at this, I guess.'

'Oh, the disbelief in your voice,' James said, smiling. 'I have a lot of responsibility you know. I run all my clients' social media accounts. One false move on HootSuite and the Scholl insoles reputation could be toast.'

And amazingly, they were back at street level.

When they stepped out of the doors, they were still laughing. Anna had forgotten they were with a group.

'Have a good ride?' a wiry little man in a bright green coat, beret and houndstooth trousers said, slightly sneerily.

Anna noticed a theme to the expressions on the faces of those waiting for them. It was something unfamiliar to her. So unfamiliar it took a moment to decode the emotion. *Envy.*

Really? James's colleagues were envying them their private trip for two? Their burgeoning pretend-romance and their secret couple jokes?

Anna thought how often envy could be completely cured by knowing the prosaic truth.

42

James hadn't expected to enjoy the bowling but when they got to the retro bar-diner in the All Star Lanes, it was actually larky fun. And despite some major last-minute, *what the hell are you doing* second thoughts on James's part, Anna's presence really made it so much more pleasurable.

She was great with everyone: relaxed, friendly, but effortful. Perhaps she started off wary, but with the help of alcohol, she became herself. And as she'd instinctively homed in on Lexie as the nicest person there, James approved of her taste.

He imagined how Eva would be right now. Listening to Harris or Ramona with her slightly-judgy-but-inscrutable Sphinx cat face on, he guessed. Then drifting back to James's side to say slighting things that would've made him feel slightly nervous, if proud that he was with the coolest girl in the room. She never made him feel good enough either, he realised.

He tried to think of a higher quality of Eva's that wasn't the sort of superficial thing that impressed you as a teenager. Kind? Pass. Considerate? Hmmm. But you know, he didn't need to date a charity worker or soup kitchen volunteer. No need to get all emo in his self-pity.

When he'd called his sister Grace to tell her about Eva leaving him, she'd said: *she always seemed a bit dismissive of you. But you like people like that.* He said: do I? *Yeah. The mean girls. And the mean boys.*

He didn't know anyone who'd pass The Grace Test in fact, but it was a test worth passing.

If Eva returned, what would his family think of her second time around? Not much, he feared. Oh well: it wasn't about what they wanted, was it? *If* he got her back. He found it hard to imagine the alternative. He'd had no practice at not getting what he wanted.

Speaking of having sufficient practice at something, he noticed that Anna could really do with some bowling lessons. She was lamentably bad, hooting with goofy laughter every time she barely grazed the pins. Eventually, James decided he couldn't watch her sling another ball uselessly down the gutter.

'Can I offer some constructive criticism?' he said, bounding up to where she stood, taking over in the guise of being an over-attentive new boyfriend.

Anna brushed her russet-black curls out of her face and looked impassive. She was teaming a cocktail dress with patterned tights and silly bowling shoes and looked very sweet.

'First of all, why are you bowling that weight? It's like a concrete cannonball. It's about half *your* body weight.'

She blushed. The ultra-sassy, smart Anna blushed at the mention of her weight. Women were bizarre sometimes.

'It … Uh. I liked the pearly colour.'

James grinned.

'Oh-kaaaay. Well, can I suggest this, which is possibly not as appealing a hue, but much better for the purposes of you knocking things down.'

He took her ball and swapped it for another, supporting it underneath with a palm as she slotted her fingers into the three holes on top.

'Swing it,' he said, demonstrating with a sweep of his arm. 'Keep your eye line fixed on where you want it to go and try not to drop the ball like a dead body down a rubbish chute. Flowing motion ...' he gestured. 'You hate me for this, don't you?'

'I think you're worse than Fred West, and own some of his knitwear,' Anna said, making James laugh loudly.

Anna swung the ball back and forth, and crashed it onto the lane from a small height. She watched it veer to the side and take out three pins before clattering out of sight.

'Better ...' James said, one hand on the back of his neck. 'Still a bit "Fling Pin". Can I make a wild guess? You were useless at sports at school?'

James smiled again and she smiled politely and yet looked mildly disconcerted. He was being pretty cheeky to her this evening, admittedly. He just wanted to make her laugh. She was sharp, and he really enjoyed sparring with her. If she was a colleague, he might look forward to going to work.

'Mind if I demonstrate? Look, you already hate me as much as a serial killer, so there's no more hate room.'

'You'd *think so*, wouldn't you?' Anna said. 'Oh, go on then.'

'Right, so, if you're like this ...' He stood behind her, and as she held the ball and swung, he guided her arm. With a lurch as she threw it, they were momentarily thrown against each other.

James felt a jolt. An undeniably male-female spark at their bodies suddenly being so close, like a key being turned in a dashboard and all the nerve-ending lights lighting up, *ding*.

He stepped back and carried on giving encouragement from a distance, thinking, well this is a surprise, because I certainly don't fancy her.

I mean, no slur on Anna, she was nice. If she *was* the kind of thing you were into, you'd go completely gaga for her. James betted she had a ravening horde after her among the boffins she worked with. Especially as a lot of the academics he'd seen looked like they were made in the Jim Henson Creature Workshop.

But even if he decided to take on a *freelance project*, Anna was definitely not someone you had 'marital break' affair sex with. She was too important and serious-minded for that. If he was going to do that, he'd do it with … a Lexie, maybe. Not an Anna. Anna he wanted to keep as a friend. She was the first person to intrigue him since forever.

In fact, he needed to figure out a way to say to her: 'I'd like to carry on seeing each other as friends' without it sounding like it implied wanting more, because he knew she didn't fancy him in the slightest either. Argh, how do you take the sex thing off the table without sounding like you assume it's on the table in the first place?

After they lost at bowling, he lost track of Anna in the melee, and half an hour later when she reappeared, it was to tell him she was leaving.

'Lexie's in a state. Drunk way too much. I'm going to put her in a taxi,' Anna said.

'Oh.' James's spirits fluttered to the floor. Anna was all that was good about this evening and he'd hoped she'd be up for the late bar, when he planned on amusing her by recounting some Parlez scandals. If she was going, he wanted to go too. 'Does Lexie need that much care?'

'She's getting that much care,' Anna said, and James wondered if he was imagining her manner had become brittle.

'I'll see you out,' James said, to her back, as she'd already turned to leave. 'I'll grab my coat.' Another bonus of a pretend-girlfriend – everyone merely nodded and winked when he said he was ducking out early.

'Is everything alright?' James said, outside, as Anna deposited a seriously indisposed Lexie on a bench while they waited for the cab.

Anna turned to face him and he could see from her expression everything was not OK.

'Laurence called me to ask me out,' she said, and James felt a flash of extreme irritation. *Can you not even stop pestering women when they're pretending to be my date …*

'He said you passed on my number?'

Oh God, why had he done that? It was lazy, Loz had been bothering him and he'd given in too easily.

'And he told me you only invited me to the theatre as a favour to him. And that you called my sister "a scientifically significant breakthrough of a living brain donor".'

James's jaw dropped, while his gut clenched in embarrassment.

'Thank you, Laurence. Both of those things have been taken out of context.'

'So you *don't* pass judgement on women you barely know in an offensive manner?' Anna said, looking Theodora-ish regal, as if she was about to order James's execution without flinching. She pulled at her hair as the wind tangled it round her face.

245

'Not usually, I hope.'

'I must've misheard you at the reunion then. I could've sworn the words "not that hot and not my type" left your mouth, about me.'

James gulped hard. Uh oh. That snipe at Laurence. She heard that? *Ouch* …

'I didn't mean … Look, Loz is shit stirring to get into your pants,' he said.

'Whereas you are a model of masculine honesty, stood here with someone you asked to pretend to be your date tonight?'

'I never said I was perfect, just not as bad as him,' James said, utterly lamely. 'Are you going on a date with Laurence?'

Anna shrugged.

'It'd be no more a bad idea than this one.'

She had her arm out, and a Hackney with a yellow light finally swung to the kerb.

'If you think Laurence is the better man, you are right through the looking glass. Trust me, Anna, he will hurt you. Don't do it.'

'I'm not interested in who you think I should date.'

'I understand that, but I'm telling you as a friend. Laurence is not a man you want to get involved with.'

'A friend,' Anna snorted.

'I thought I was.'

'For a mad moment, so did I. But I think it's best if we call it a day. Or a night,' Anna said.

After some puppetry of Lexie's floppy limbs to get her seated, Anna followed her into the taxi, banged the door hard and didn't look back as it drove away.

43

Anna was beetling around her flat, wondering if she could make enough of a lunch from half a jar of red jalapeños, a stale Warburtons toastie loaf and a lump of cheddar with blue-green speckles or if she should go to the shops, when she saw an email from James Fraser arrive on her open laptop.

On a Saturday? She didn't know what to expect when she opened the mail, but prepared herself to be angered by it. If it was any sort of apology, she guessed it'd be a bid to stop her telling anyone at Parlez she'd not been a real date.

Yet as she opened it, Anna saw the message was pretty hefty. She was surprised. James Fraser didn't strike her as someone who needed – or even wanted – women in his life who gave him grief. Apart from his wife.

She wrapped her hands around either side of her cup of tea while she read.

Dear Anna,

I apologise if this is very unwelcome, but then, you can always mark me as spam, or send me a jiggling arse cheeks gif as reply.

I wanted the opportunity to explain.

You might still hate me once you've read this, but I reason at least I'd have the comfort – cold comfort – of knowing you hate me for the truth, not Laurence's propaganda. I have to ask you to trust me that everything I say here is the truth. Quite a big ask in the circumstances I know. I keep thinking about what you must've thought of me after that call from Laurence and ... it's not nice. All I can say is, I don't come out of my version looking great either. And if I read last night's parting shot right, there's a fair chance I'll never see you again, so, why lie?

It's true that I partly invited you to the theatre because Laurence had asked me to introduce you again. He fancied you at that school reunion, as I think you might've picked up. Asking you out obliged Laurence and it suited me, because I enjoy your company. If I was doing it purely for his sake as he said, why would I go? I promise you, my commitment to Laurence getting laid, and challenging modern theatre, doesn't run that deep.

And it's true that I said I found your sister hard work. I'm sorry, it's never nice to hear anyone you love run down. I didn't dislike her, she's just such a contrast to you, I guess I was surprised. I really liked your friend Michelle. At the risk of sounding arrogant, I don't think I did anything very wrong in making a flippant remark. I'm allowed to hold unflattering opinions on people, even when they're related to friends. Loz repeated that purely to make me look crap and the cost was hurting your feelings, which I think says something about him, not me.

As for the comment I made about you at the reunion, I said that purely to try to put Laurence off pursuing you. I thought you were there with someone and I didn't want Laurence causing trouble. It was intended as meaningless discouragement to shut him down – it was laddish talk, it wasn't any considered thing. I don't know how to correct this one without going too far the other way and sounding a bit of a skeeve. I mean, it's true that broadly speaking you're not my 'type' but I'm sure this doesn't upset you in the slightest, and that the feeling's mutual.

All in all, I get to the end of this and I realise I look even worse than I thought I would. I could do some grovelling about how great I think you are, and how great you were with everyone last night. But instead I think I'm going to wheel out the really big guns. Attached is a photo of Luther looking angry while going to the toilet. He's got so much fluff, he can't fit his whole body in the litter tray, so his head pokes out the door flap while he's doing his business. Enjoy.

James x

Anna clicked to open the email attachment and let go of grudging laughter when she saw the face of a disgruntled, disembodied Luther, staring into the camera with those marmalade eyes, expression like he was licking piss off a nettle.

She read and re-read the email. It was hard to decide what she thought of this man. On the one hand, he'd taken the time to write a mostly charming confession. She gave him props for that. On the other, she disliked his natural superiority. It was so inbuilt, he wasn't even aware when it was showing. I mean, why should she care if he liked Michelle? She wasn't seeking approval of her friends and family from him. He had such self-consequence.

And the part about how she wasn't his type? Incredible! *Thanks for that data, please do give me my final ranking when you have it.* He obviously thought she felt wounded pride for not being thought attractive enough, as opposed to general dislike of men who pass judgments like that on women.

However, in general, her natural justice allowed that people said a lot of things off the cuff that they might want to retract later, her included.

Anna turned his words over and over and eventually she opened a reply.

Dear James,

While I'm prepared to accept everything you say is true, what I don't understand is this – if Laurence is such a wanker, and has treated you like this, why is he still your best friend? This is someone you've known since school? I assume he was your best man, and so on?

Anna

She got an answer within five minutes, and her ego swelled slightly at the thought James might've been hitting refresh on his email.

Good question. I don't have a good answer. I'm probably due some soul searching. Laurence is a laugh but he does have the capacity to turn round and fuck you, as he'd like you to find out.

Though I might argue that knowing him so long makes me less culpable in picking him as a friend, because your brain's only half grown back at school. By the time you see what someone's like, you're stuck with them. I say I could argue that, because I can't see your face to judge how annoyed you are and whether I could get away with it …

Loz wasn't my best man by the way. My sister Grace had that honour.

Jx

Anna fired back instantly, and knew by doing so, she was effectively forgiving him. Perhaps it was the effect of him distancing himself from choices made at school.

Your sister? Really?

Ax

Oh no, and she added a kiss?! *Anna Alessi you are apparently an utter walkover with a man who can pen a pretty email,* she thought. His response was near-instant.

Yep. I have the pictures to prove it. She's a war photographer, in Mali at the moment. It does great things for my mum's nerves. Grace got the brains, guts and talent in my family, it was well unfair. She's twenty-six and she takes absolutely no bullshit from anybody and risks stray gunfire and standing on landmines, while I'm figuring out ways to virally market probiotic yoghurt drinks.

Actually, and I'm honestly not saying this to help paddle myself out of Poo Creek, she reminds me a bit of you. Especially in her willingness to tell me when I'm being a cock-end. It'd be cool if there's ever a chance to introduce you two sometime, even if the assaults on my dignity would be terrible. She'd like you a lot.

Jx

There was James Fraser in a nutshell, Anna thought. All the warmth of wanting her to meet someone dear to him, wrapped in the tacit expectation that despite insulting her, there would be a 'sometime'.

OK, apology accepted. Btw Laurence is taking me ice-skating. Not what I'd have expected from him, somehow.

Ax

This time, it took half an hour to get a reply. Anna wondered if he didn't like her going on this date. She could see why – Laurence's information sharing hadn't gone well for James so far.

And why was she going? Laurence seemed pretty nefarious. His approach had been direct and completely disarming. Her phone had gone as she left the ladies at the All Star Lanes, and when she answered, and mentioned where she was, Laurence had said, sharply, 'You're on a *date* date with James?'

Then when she'd explained it wasn't, he'd said, *OK, well I've never done this before but here's the thing. I've never met anyone I've felt such an instant spark with as you and who I wanted to know better, and while I can imagine nothing you've seen or heard about me makes you want to date me, I want to see you. So instead of scheming and plotting, I've decided to be completely honest and simply straight out beg you for an evening together. No strings, no pressure. If you say no, I promise I won't ask again.*

Surprisingly, it was hard to say no. And then when she'd been weighing it up, boom, Laurence comes in with his: *James has been helping me out because he knows I'm mad about you, so I'm not quite sure what tonight's about. He can be rather two-faced though*

… And in curiosity, Anna had asked Laurence what he meant. Cue the unpleasant revelations.

Anna had listened to this spiel while looking over at Lexie, who was slumped, gazing at James with the un-self-consciousness of the very hammered. Lexie had told Anna at length how unbelievably kind and honourable James was at work. She took Lexie's account of his greatness with a pinch of salt, given she was smitten. And this honour didn't extend to being honest about his romantic status, she noticed.

There had been a strange moment, one she wouldn't be telling anybody about, when James was helping her bowl. He'd been pressed against her and it had felt … for a second, it felt very right. In fact, she kept replaying the sensation, imagining him holding her. Oh God, she was lonelier than she'd admitted to herself. She was going to be like someone in prison who butched up and got panther tattoos and started frotting other inmates in desperation.

Laurence and James. At the Mock Rock, who was the worse out of the two of them? James. It was James who'd lured her onstage.

And hadn't Michelle — and even James himself — said she'd been wasting her time by only going on internet dates with 'Mr Safe Bet But Dull'?

So Anna had said, 'OK, Laurence. Why not?'

You're actually going on this date with Loz? Wow. I look forward to hearing how it goes. If you're not telling the story to a courtroom via video link, using dolls. (Sorry. Don't drink anything that tastes strangely chalky though.)

Jx

44

James was Monday morning revving-the-engine dossing, emailing his sister, and started in guilty surprise when he realised he had someone right at his shoulder.

It was only Lexie, phew. She was messy on Friday, and poor girl, she still looked mole-eyed and papery-skinned today. It was possible she went out over the weekend too, of course – she wasn't an old git like James. Somehow he pictured her staying in. Lexie was a pink Blossom Hill wine, Thorntons dusted truffles, furry monster-claw slippers type of girl.

'Will you say thanks to Anna for getting me home?' she said. 'I'm so embarrassed.'

'Course, no worries. We've all got hammered when the boss is buying the drinks before, don't worry about it.'

'Did I ruin your night?'

'*My* night?'

'Yes …?'

Ohhhh. Anna took her home by herself, didn't she? He'd been relying on Lexie having a memory gap, but she obviously recalled that much. *Erk*.

'No it was fine, honestly,' he blathered. 'Did you feel a bit shabby on Saturday morning?'

'I was so sick. Like *Exorcist* head spin sick,' Lexie said. 'I was sick before we left the bowling. Anna was so kind. I wanted to stay and we were in the ladies and she heard me and said, *I know that at this moment you think you want to stay out, but if you go home now I promise you'll have nothing to regret. If you stay any longer you'll have that blackout where you can't remember what you said or did, which is the worst.* It was such a girl power thing, like something only your bestie would do.'

Yeah, Lexie definitely had a white four-poster draped in Liberty fabric bunting from Etsy, flowers in old-fashioned watering cans and the whole *True Blood* collectors' box set.

'Ah, that's nice. Yeah Anna's thoughtful, isn't she? I will let her know, Lex.'

Posh Charles had been listening in, and turned in his seat.

'If you don't mind me saying, I think she's a real catch. I didn't really get to know your ex-wife, but Anna's very … approachable. Lovely girl. And she was telling me about her work, she must be a serious bright spark.'

'Yes,' Lexie nodded, sombrely. 'Anna is so nice, definitely.'

'I never undah-stood how you und Eva ticked,' said Christabel from Germany who did the accounts and occasionally discussed her sex life in a way so matter-of-factly explicit it made James sweat. 'She voz a bit of an ice queen. You always seemed more serious around her, not ze witty James we know.'

It seemed odd to James they'd presume the 'real' James was the one at work, not the one with his wife.

'You've upgraded to the 2.0 version,' Parker said. 'Ironed out the glitches. More useability.'

Parker never meant to be a git, yet he did often achieve it.

255

James grimaced. This was odd. He'd always thought because Eva looked the part, everyone had been impressed. He hadn't thought they'd be much fussed with 'nice'. He felt a little ashamed, even chastened. He thought the Parlez people were trivial, yet here was proof how shallow he could be. He had hidden shallows.

'Yes, you're well rid of that last one,' Harris said, seizing eagerly on the chance to say something negative, as if 'that last one' was a respectful way to speak of a human you'd recently thought worthy of pledging your troth to. He'd hate to be bereaved around Harris. *You haven't lost a relative, you've pruned your card list.*

There was a chorus of muttered agreement that his chemistry with Eva was far inferior to that which he'd feigned with Anna and it left James in some discomfort.

So his successful lying left it open for them all to say what they really thought of the wife he was still in love with? And if and when they got back together, would that announcement now creak with awkwardness?

James turned to his screen, looked blankly at the amusing email to Grace, and clicked 'save to drafts'. He didn't feel very perky anymore. What was that maxim? *Cheats never prosper.*

Or, do they? An email arrived from Laurence. James didn't have the testicular fortitude to deal with him face-to-face, or on FaceTime, and had sent him a pretty blunt missive telling him he was a wanker for saying what he did to Anna.

There was something disquieting about that episode. He knew Laurence was a ruthless bastard when in hot pursuit, but James didn't usually get run over as an innocent bystander. *Maybe that's because you've never been in the way before*, a voice whispered.

James thought about the times he'd laughed with Laurence at the latest hysterical voicemail from a scorned woman, or covered for him when he'd left a venue by a fire door.

All's fair in love, war, and ten-pin bowling, Jimmy! Seriously, sorry, I didn't think you gave a shit about her, otherwise I'd have toned it down. She started fishing about you and I ran my mouth without thinking in return, big apologies. Get me back by endorsing my skills at cottaging on LinkedIn, or something.

I've finally got a date though. Dusting off my best Ciro Citterio suit and spritzing myself with Sean John's 'Implied Consent' for this one …

Loz

45

Despite being utterly useless at every sport and nearly every physical activity bar 'pottering', Anna was reasonable at ice-skating. Her dad used to take her to the local rink when she was a little girl, to avoid shopping excursions with his wife and younger daughter. He'd read a book and obligingly wave at Anna every time she completed a full circuit.

The trick was willing the belief you could do it, slicing forward and pushing your feet out in graceful swooping motions. It helped that as an amateur you didn't need to be especially lithe, you only needed balance.

Once Anna and Laurence had collected their boots from the building adjacent to Somerset House, laced them blood vessel-constrictingly tight and wobbled out onto the rink like newborn foals, she half-expected Laurence to start pulling figures of eight, screeching to a halt with showers of snow spurting behind his heels.

Instead, Laurence seemed authentically terrified, and his high centre of gravity made him particularly ungainly. He spent a lot of time gripping the rail, grim-faced. Anna couldn't work out if he knew this incompetence would be endearing or if he'd simply messed up the planning, to his advantage. He'd never been less self-assured, and Anna had never liked him more. After he waved her on, she did a few laps of the rink solo.

'You might've warned me you were good,' Laurence said, on her third pass, when he was making agonisingly slow progress behind a flotilla of tiny schoolgirls wearing *Hello Kitty* rucksacks.

'Haha, I'm not good! I've not been for years. You need to get your confidence up, is all.'

'You're one of those walk-on-water, effortlessly brilliant at everything people, aren't you? Or rather, whoosh about on frozen water.'

'I promise you I am definitely not.'

Anna adjusted her homemade chunky black scarf (the one Atelier of Judy Alessi production she still wore) over her chin, and felt girlishly pleased at the compliment, however misapplied. Wait. She was having fun, on a date? Amazing. With Laurence? Even more amazing. A man who James said was the very shit-devil in Hugo Boss. Was any sort of relationship, even a fling, even remotely possible?

Physically, Laurence's cock-of-the-walk style wasn't really Anna's bag, but she could imagine those who fancied him, fancied him hard.

When he wasn't ice-skating, he had that innate male louche 'comfortable in his own skin' appeal, the kind of confidence you hoped would rub off on you by rubbing against him. And that expressive, asymmetric face was, in its way, more compellingly attractive than perfection. Things you took a little longer to like, you liked longer, Anna had observed before.

'Do you want to hold on to me?' she asked, curious to see

how Laurence's alpha masculinity would take this offer.

'Won't I drag you down?'

'I'll take the risk.'

Laurence gingerly accepted the crook of her arm and let go of the railing. He wasn't skating so much as trying to walk in ice skates. His weight tugged on her elbow.

'Push forward,' she demonstrated with her feet. 'Think you're not going to wobble and you won't wobble.'

Laurence tried a slightly more fluid movement.

'See!' Anna said, guiding him out of the path of a gang of students, towards the centre of the rink. Being further from the comfort zone of the railing had a bad psychological effect and Laurence's weight on Anna's arm increased.

'You're OK,' she soothed. 'Skate . . .'

'*Skate*, like if you can say it, do it,' Laurence said, mock irritated.

'Sorry, true,' Anna laughed. '*Just ski* probably wouldn't help me.'

A few moments passed when she thought he was getting the hang of it, then she felt a sharp tug on her arm.

'Wait, wha-wha-wha WHOOOARGH.' Without warning, Laurence lurched back and forth and did a funny running on the spot move, before tumbling, yanking Anna to the ground with him.

Anna landed on her backside, while Laurence did the full body sprawl, frightening some elderly Japanese tourist spectators, who started taking photos as soon as they'd got over the shock.

Anna scrambled to his side.

'Oh no, are you OK? Laurence! Did you hit your head?'

He stayed lying down and stared up at her.

'Am I dead? Have I gone to heaven?'

Panic over, but adrenaline still coursing, Anna found herself laughing: proper, stomach spasm hysterics. She should've known it'd take more than that to dent Laurence's deadpanning skills.

'From all I've heard you're not going to heaven,' she choked out.

'Are you sure? You look like an angel.'

'Do you ever take a moment off from the patter?'

Laurence hauled himself to his feet, wincing.

'Let's consider this enough skating for a beginners' session,' Anna said, holding his arm, grateful no one had been near enough to skate over the fingers of Laurence's outstretched hands.

'Thank the Lord.'

'Why choose ice-skating if you don't like it?'

'I thought it would be memorable,' Laurence said. 'Honestly, putting knives on your feet on a slippy surface anyway, it's madness.'

They respectively limped and clumped back to change back to their shoes.

As evening fell, the ice rink made more sense as a date location. The glittering mammoth-scale Christmas tree, blue-green glow of the ice and the artfully up-lit majestic building made Anna feel as if she was in a scene in a romantic comedy, complete with slapstick incident. When they were settled in one of the booths overlooking the skaters, the combination of cold air and hot cider was soulful. If you were going to fall in love, the conditions were conducive.

Shame then that she was with someone doing his repertoire of honed funny anecdotes, peppered with casual references to his professional success, other females carefully airbrushed out. Eventually Anna wearied of the routine, of the sense of being an audience rather than an equal.

'Laurence,' she said, gently. 'I don't need a version of who you think I want to meet. I'd rather spend time with you. Forget I'm female for a while.'

'Not so easy,' Laurence said, with a wink. 'I'm doing it again, aren't I?' and they laughed. 'No, I do overdo it a bit when I'm nervous, you're right.'

'Nervous,' Anna said, sceptically, raising her eyebrows.

There was a short silence.

'I assume your joke about me not being headed for heaven comes from James Fraser intel?' Laurence said.

'And my own observations.'

'James is not always the easiest best mate.'

'Come on now, I don't think I can referee much more scrapping,' Anna said, with an eye roll.

'No, I don't mean because of anything he does. It's the way he is. Women flock to him. It was the same at school.'

Anna adjusted her position on her seat and chugged back the last of her drink.

'It's an assault on the ego to be stood next to Superman in his Clark Kent disguise, sometimes. You're invisible, or you're everyone's second choice to talk to. Maybe I've done the "larger than life" best friend thing to over-compensate. Know what I mean? You think, OK, I can't be that, so I'll have to be this.'

'Yes,' Anna said, 'I do.'

'Same again?' Laurence said, looking at her glass, and Anna nodded. While Laurence was at the bar, her phone buzzed with a text.

So how did it go? Jx

Still going. It's fun actually. I think Laurence has a little more to him than you think … Ax

AW HELL NO you're falling for the 'the man behind the myth' routine, aren't you? Anna that's not even a level three grift. And I thought you were all clever and so on. Are you going to see him again? Jx

If Anna didn't know this to be impossible in every respect, she'd say James was coming off as slightly jealous.

Maybe so. Ax

Right. We are going out for a drink so I can talk some sense into you. It's irrelevant whether you want to, this is an intervention and a carefrontation. We Need To Talk About Laurence. Jx

Laurence returned with the drinks, setting them down.

'Have you romanced tons of women with these tales, then, Laurence?' Anna said, after a first sip.

He grinned.

'Not *tons*. I've never met anyone special or I wouldn't be here.'

'See, you're so funny,' Anna said. 'If I was male you'd brag about hundreds. But I'm female, and you think I want to hear about how *they didn't mean anything, darling.*'

Laurence grinned even more widely and rubbed his eye. 'Don't you?'

Anna shrugged. 'If you don't regret it, why conceal it? Be yourself, I say.'

'Because of the assumptions that go with it. That you're superficial, or mess people around.'

She suspected both those things. Anna wondered about the justice of her preconceptions about who she would and wouldn't want to date. She was telling Laurence his scorecard didn't prejudice her, and it wasn't strictly true. Was that fair?

'Speaking theoretically, in general, I suppose if someone's treated people as disposable, you're more inclined to think you'll be disposed of pretty easily too,' she amended, carefully.

'Hmmm. I mean, all I think is, if you're hungry, you go out for dinner. If something looks like fun, it probably is. My motives and behaviour have always been pretty straightforward. But sooner or later you get labels like *womaniser* or *ladies' man* or whatever, and I think it's humans being human.'

Anna considered: maybe he's simply honest and I'm being judgemental. Then: is this precisely how an arch seducer works? Knocks you off balance with moral relativism, throws in some self-deprecation, a spicy cologne and some warm alcohol? Next thing you know, you aren't sure which way's up, but your knickers are off?

'I suppose I wouldn't want to be judged for my choices either,' she said.

'And what are they?'

'It's mainly involved waiting around hopelessly for someone

who matters to me.'

'I'm doing that too. I've just kept busier.'

'Are you?' Anna said.

'Yes.'

Laurence held her gaze as he sipped his drink. Anna wondered if he'd be *really good at it*, with all that practice.

'Hey, look at that,' she said, glad of the distraction, gesturing to two swishy-haired twenty-somethings in pristine white boots, twirling around on the rink. They were doing that thing of looking over their shoulder and crossing their feet as they zig-zagged backwards, almost floating. They were so fast and able they danced between the rest of the people on the rink. 'You thought I was any good. Now *they* know what they're doing.'

'You're very modest for someone with so many reasons not to be modest.' Laurence had barely glanced at them. Anna felt he was reading from a 'make her feel she's the only woman in the room' playbook.

'Oh God, please don't.'

'See? Terrible at taking compliments.'

'Believe the good and you have to take the bad seriously too.'

'It makes you even nicer, trust me. You don't meet many beautiful women without massive attitude. Or massive neuroses.'

Make explicit mention of her beauty. But make it clear she's so much more than that. James was right, Laurence should write a version of *The Game*.

Anna shook her head.

'You certainly don't have to be beautiful to be given huge neuroses.'

265

'Hah. You wouldn't know.'

Wouldn't she? She was quickly realising that it was impossible to have a proper conversation with him, he was stuck in this gear. Every line was practised, every look was carefully weighted.

And here endeth The Laurence Experiment. He wasn't for her. There were some men, she thought, for whom you'd always be quarry. And when they'd captured you, skinned you and ... er, eaten you ... OK, this was not the best analogy. When they'd done that, they'd get bored and need to go on another hunt. He didn't want to get to know Anna, he wanted to bed her. It was pointless trying to meet the real Laurence, and she doubted she would like him if she did.

'How does ice-skating compare to bowling, then?' he said.

'Not a fair fight, given I'm useless at bowling and vaguely competent at skating.'

'I more meant as a date,' Laurence said.

'What? The bowling wasn't a date.'

'I know, but ... humour me. Rate My Date Dot Com.'

'What *is it* with the pair of you?'

Anna had a flashback to James and Laurence at the Mock Rock, stood in the wings, revelling in the triumph of her complete humiliation. This was another game and once again, she was the mark.

And once again, she was participating in this set-up willingly, naively. As the mist cleared she was faintly disgusted with herself.

'Is this some sort of contest, a bet between you two? Is that why you did the whole high-stakes "I'm desperately begging you for a date" routine?'

'Come on, Anna, I didn't mean it like that about the

bowling. I was kidding . . .'

'Thanks for the drinks. I hope your arse isn't too bruised tomorrow,' she stood up to leave. 'Or your ego.'

Despite extensive protestations from Laurence that she'd completely misread a light-hearted remark, Anna insisted she was leaving.

'Laurence. Your princess is in another castle.'

'What does that mean?'

Anna hesitated.

'I don't know. My colleague Patrick says it.'

46

James Fraser hadn't immediately followed up his threat to give her a talking-to over Laurence. No doubt he'd heard Laurence had failed to close the deal and deemed it no longer necessary. Good riddance times two, Anna thought. That was until she came back from a lecture to catatonic second years a week later and found an email from James waiting on her screen. She refused to register the small pleasurable jolt it gave her.

So Anna, what about our meet up then? You can run but you can't hide. I have men everywhere. Don't quote that out of context. Jx

She'd had enough of humouring this duo. She set phasers to Major Snark and fired off:

Another evening of one of you telling me why you're better than the other one, while seeming much the same? No thanks. I think I have a toilet that needs unblocking. Ax

That'll do it, she thought, with grim satisfaction. James expected women to fall at his feet, did he? She'd enjoy his curt

bafflement in reply. His anger couldn't touch her, given she had
no interest in pleasing him.

Oooh! ***Clutches pearls*** Well, sucks to be you, sourpuss Alessi
– guess who's got an exclusive preview copy of Tim McGovern's
doc about Theodora, tying in with a certain exhibition? And was
going to offer to hold a screening? And provide booze? YES.
You're about to hastily mend your manners towards me no
doubt, you monster. Jx

    PS re: toilet-unblocking, get the stuff in the orange bottle
from Wilkinsons that goes through it like Laurence through net-
ball teams.

Anna laughed out loud and played with her pen and re-read it
and giggled again. She vacillated over how to respond. James,
with all his insouciant self-confidence, had decided they were
friends. Surrendering to it was easy. It felt nice. Plus, dammit,
she was dying to see that documentary.

'Because I am a hubristic, ageing idiot I completely misjudged
how long my run would take, so sorry,' James said, pulling a
t-shirt with a 'V' of sweat away from his body, after he'd opened
the door.

    Anna made polite murmurs about how it was no problem.
She was simply glad of there being a focus for conversation. By
all accounts they'd officially crossed the line from obligation to
tentative friendship. The date with Laurence was a one-off deal,
there were no defined guidelines here.

    'Would you think I was rude if I ran upstairs and had a very
quick shower?' James rubbed his cheek on his dark blue t-shirt

sleeve. His face was glowing with exertion and his hair was glossy with sweat. Anna could imagine Lexie passing out at the combination of Man of Steel looks and man-musk.

'No, not at all,' Anna said, sliding her coat from her back as she followed him into the front room, dropping her bag next to the pink sofa.

James brought a silver wine cooler to the dining room table, poured out a glass of white wine and put it in her hand. He placed the TV and DVD remote controls next to her.

'Cue up my fan Tim. Don't start it until I'm ready though, I don't want to miss a single trinket.'

Anna realised she was growing comfortable in James's company. She didn't truly trust him, but considering the mixture of fear and distaste that she'd once greeted him with, she increasingly felt like she knew her way around his sense of humour. She'd never had a brother, but maybe this was what it would've been like.

She played with the remote controls and couldn't get a picture on the screen. Luther waddled into the room, observing her intrusion impassively.

'Hello, Luther!' she said, politely.

'Bwaaaaaap!' he quacked.

He approached a very expensive-looking teal cushion on a footstool, clawing at it with an outstretched paw. He scowled over his fluffy neck ruff at Anna like a naughty charge left with a babysitter, daring her to object.

'Not sure you should be doing that …'

'Bwuuuurrrrp!' he pulled the cushion to the floor and started scratching at it with the enthusiasm of a child tearing the wrapping from a Christmas present.

Anna got to her feet and tried to wrest it from his clutches. He responded by digging his claws in harder. There was a nasty ripping sound and Anna stopped pulling. Was this cat determined to make her every visit a disaster? Was he doing his mistress's bidding? Luther stopped scratching.

'Thank you!' Anna said.

He arranged his rear end over it and made a face awfully like the one she'd seen in the litter box photo.

'Oh no. James!' she called.

She tried to tweak the soft furnishing out from under Luther, but the claws had sunk in again. She was not going to be blamed for this creature turding up something that cost a mint from Heals. She'd failed to check protocol before, and this time she had learned her lesson.

There was no noise from the first floor. Anna bounded up the stairs, noisily, given they were hollow-sounding wood, with only a strip of sea grass mat runner up the centre.

'James? James!' Now she'd come this far, she really had to carry on. She clambered up the last few stairs and heard the rainfall of running water. As the sound reached her ears, her eyes met a surprising sight in the bathroom at the end of the landing. James. All of James. Or all of him that could be seen with his back to her.

He had a head full of shampoo and rivers of soap coursing down his back, like some real life Diet Coke break advert.

Anna opened her mouth to speak and all that came out was a Lutherish croak. *Urgent message from her brain to her oddly sluggish feet:* James was going to turn around. Any second now he would look at her and maybe if she kept looking a moment longer she'd get a full frontal and oh my God, yes, he WAS turning round, and Anna glimpsed the merest hint of pink skin and black hair as she hurtled back down the stairs.

What was she doing? James was *married*. She was on the brink of ogling another woman's penis.

She returned to her perch on the sofa, picked up her wine, and tried to ignore the internal clamour. Her mouth was dry as she took a mouthful of wine. She needed to regroup. That had been a visual stimulus. It was merely unexpected, that was all. She waited for her heart rate, and a feeling she was going to have to call lust, to subside. Think about Boris Johnson, in a neon mankini, chest hair shaved into a giant B. OK, that was working. She felt calmer. Situation normalising.

'Cwaaarpp!' Luther squawked as he rolled himself off the mercifully smear-free cushion and crawled onto her lap. He rearranged himself awkwardly, like an arthritic old man, and settled down to snore, loudly.

Anna put her hand out and gingerly stroked his fluff.

'Phweeeeee,' he emitted an odd noise of satisfaction.

This was a weird house. A gilded palace fit for a beautiful gold-en-haired queen who'd abdicated her throne; an erotically confus-ing man who danger-showered; and a squeaky mobile Whoopee Cushion of a cat, like one of those Tribble things on *Star Trek*.

James reappeared, his calamity-creating arse now clad in jeans and his top half in a different t-shirt. He was rubbing at his clean damp hair with a white hand towel.

'Guess what, I even managed not to lock the door properly and it drifted open. I felt like a dirty old man in the park in a Pac A Mac, trying to flash you.'

Aaarggghhhh no no no, he actually mentioned it?! Anna hadn't anticipated this and went completely, instantly, smelting metal hot. Muscular buttock-pervers doom. This was her Ass-ghanistan.

47

James had been joking, but Anna's startled expression, the change in her complexion and the way she chewed air instead of speaking made it obvious she had been caught out.

He knew she was a dignified, modest kind of woman but he didn't think she was so *Lost in Austen* timid that the mere mention of an unlocked bathroom door would be enough to get this reaction.

No, she must have seen him? He twanged with embarrassment and self-consciousness but also something else. She hadn't been going to mention it or mock him … was it possible she didn't entirely hate the experience? Now he really *was* a creepy old indecent exposer, if he enjoyed the idea of her enjoying it.

'I see Luther's warming to you,' James said, to fill the awkward space.

'Seems to be,' Anna said, in a funny voice. Oh my, they needed conversation, and fast. James picked up the glass he'd left out and sploshed wine into it.

'You survived the encounter with Loz, then?'

'As if you haven't asked him how it went.'

'He only said he'd failed to convince you he was sincere.

Not surprising given he wasn't sincere and you're intelligent.'
James sat down on the armchair. There was no way he was
sharing the sofa so soon after Nob-Seeing Gaffe. God, he
hoped he'd been tensing his stomach muscles. He wasn't twenty-two anymore. And while he didn't think he had anything to
be ashamed of, he hoped Anna didn't have an ex who had one
the size of a sea cucumber.

'He wasn't sincere?' Anna said, with a smile.

'He sincerely wants to shag you, just as he has sincerely
wanted to shag lots of people.'

'Does it matter that he's shagged lots of people, if he didn't
carry on doing it if we got together?'

James pushed damp hair out of his eyes and smirked.

'Oh dear. You think you're going to be the woman who
finally makes him settle down?'

'No!' Anna said, with such force she spilled a bit of her
drink on an oblivious Luther. 'I'm not into Laurence at all but
I'm interested in why you think your best mate is such a terrible prospect because he's been around. It's not 1951.'

'His numbers aren't the issue as such, sure. You're not buying
a car.'

'Yes. I mean,' Anna began — James got the impression Anna
was chattering slightly nervously — 'Sleeping with tons of
people isn't morally wrong?'

'It's not. In theory. But massive career shaggers like Loz are
usually conniving liars. Or male ones are at least. In practice,
nobbing about is pretty much impossible to accomplish without dispensing with concern for other people's feelings and
manipulating to get what you want. The truth is the first casu-
alty and all that.'

'Laurence seems pretty upfront about it though?'

'Yeah he will be, to a point,' James sipped his drink. 'This is male brain advanced lying for expert liars. He does the he's "been a bit of a boy" spiel, but without enough gory detail to put you off. And you think, *oh he's admitting to me what he didn't tell all the others. I must mean something more.* He gives you the "maybe this time it'll be different" love-struck eyes, the definite sense that his interest in you is more than carnal. He's not actually told you any lies. But his whole method of approach has made you feel he's let his guard down. That *you* won't suddenly get the dropped calls after a couple of months of being hard at it in upscale, handily central hotels he found on last minute dot com. That he's not seeing anyone else, and you both might be falling in love. Wrong, wrong and at least fifty per cent wrong. And like all good cons, by the time you realise it was one, he'll have got what he wants and be long gone.'

James hoped Anna wasn't taking any of this to mean she was a fool to think Laurence could be interested in her. Loz would be knocking it out of the park if he pulled Anna, obviously. He didn't deserve to, nor did he appreciate her, beyond the physical. James wasn't about to let him exploit Anna's innate decency. The trouble with good people meeting bad people is they lacked the roadmap for this foreign country. James had at least visited and got a few landmarks.

'That's quite a vivid picture.'

'It's a timeless formula. So no, of course, there's nothing wrong with boffing him if you know what's what. I didn't want you to fall for anything. I've been the recipient of a few "I can't get hold of Laurence" calls from women in my time. I didn't want to sit on the sidelines and see it happen and say nothing, this time.'

She wondered at the 'this time'. Because James knew Anna?

'He said he was scarred by the effect of a lifetime living in your shadow,' she offered.

'Hahaha! He didn't? It's *my* fault! Oh, Laurence. Amazing scenes. *This is my secret inner pain, I feel so vulnerable admitting it. Stroke the pain away, Anna. No, a bit lower, just there, that's right.'*

James and Anna laughed and James fiddled with the turn-up on his jeans.

'And yet he's your best mate,' Anna said.

'I don't know about best. The friend I see the most of. The problem with male groups in general is the biggest bastard wins. Your friends are much more of a credit to you, I'm sure,' James said. 'More … quirky.'

'Quirky?! They're not pity choices!'

'No!'

The combination of wine and good company was giving James a small stomach-based glow.

'And my sister's an idiot?' Anna said.

'Oh, come on, I've said sorry for that,' James said. 'And I followed her back on Twitter.'

'What greater gesture exists? The three wise men brought gold, incense, myrrh and said unto Baby Jesus, we are Team Follow Back.'

James laughed, really laughed, from the pit of his gently glowing stomach. Anna was witty.

'Look, Aggy works in events PR …'

'Which is less sensible than what you do?'

'Oof. It's organising parties, let's be honest. She has "general funster" in her Twitter bio. It takes a lot to make me see past things like that and be the bigger man, but I'm trying. If I find out she likes The Hoosiers or something I will roll with the punch.'

Anna rolled her eyes and smiled, without any real ire.

'Shall we watch Tim, then?' he said.

Anna pressed the remote control buttons according to James's instructions, but all that appeared onscreen was monochrome snowstorm. He huffed and puffed about her being useless, only to discover when he took over that the DVD player did indeed appear to be broken.

'The problem with this streamlined modern technology is if the remote goes, you're screwed,' he tapped it on the sofa arm. 'Rubbish.'

'I think my brother-in-law has this model. There's a button if you look …' Anna crawled across the carpet and sat in front of it on her knees.

James gazed at the bundled black-brown plain chocolate shades of her wavy hair and the smaller tighter curls at the nape of her neck.

'Yeah, you need to come out of there, that's the languages menu,' he said, absently.

'Thanks for that, I was trying to select Greek because Theodora was Cypriot.'

'It's buggered. I concede defeat,' Anna said, eventually, after some ineffectual jabbing with a forefinger and pointing of remote.

'We could watch it on a laptop but it wouldn't be the same. What about you? Have you got a telly and DVD?'

'I've got two tellies and a DVD. I'm a general funster.'

James checked the clock.

'Plenty of time to cab it to yours. If you don't mind?'

Anna looked undecided.

'Has the toilet been unblocked?' James asked, doing weighing hands.

'My U-bend was always clear, as was my diary. I was insulting you.'

'Do you know, I THOUGHT so.'

48

Wine was a helluva drug. If Anna hadn't scoffed it down so fast she might well have thought better of this. Her discomfort during the taxi journey rose by steady increments. Having James Fraser in her flat wasn't a good idea at the best of times, but given they'd come straight from his *Elle Décor* home? And she'd not even had a chance to tidy up?

Even when it was organised, her place wasn't designed to be viewed. It was a messy jumble of things she needed and things she loved. It was her heart on a plate. Could she allow him over the threshold?

'Right, my flat is a tip, unlike Casa Croosh Und,' she said, with mock-posh voice, pushing her key in the flaking door.

'I've lived in lads' houses at uni and beyond, you can't shock me,' James said. 'Unless you too have rugby jockstraps drying on the radiator.'

Nevertheless, she was conscious of how cramped her hallway was, how low the ceiling felt, and how chucked together and haphazard all her furniture was by comparison.

'This is nice,' James said, pleasantly, once she'd hustled him to the sun-faded red sofa-bed and pushed wine at him.

'Haha, you kid.'

'No I don't! It's homely.'

The front room had 'cottage cheese' Artex walls and was lined with cheapo black lacquer wood bookshelves. There was a Habitat-framed print of the original Art Deco *Great Gatsby* cover over a small enamel period fireplace, and Anna lit the tea-lights in the grate whilst hoping that the gesture didn't look at all suggestive. Everything would look better lower lit, she figured.

'I might move to Stokey if I sell up. Can't afford Casa Crouch End on my wage alone,' James said, and they made polite chat about the merits of various postcodes.

It quickly became obvious that they were several shades too inebriated to concentrate on a history documentary. Anna's flat might be grubbier and more squeezed than James's, but it also made for a more relaxed mood.

She put Fleetwood Mac's *Rumours* on after James got up and examined her one row of CDs and deemed them 'the selection of a middle-aged depressed empty nester who got most of them free with the *Mail on Sunday*'. His barbs probably should offend her, she thought, but she didn't detect any ill will behind his teasing. When James delivered a jibe, or laughed at her retorts, she detected only genuine delight in a shared wavelength.

'I can't begin to imagine how unbelievably pseudy and poser your CDs on show are,' Anna said.

'I don't have CDs anymore, chucked them out along with the mangle for the washing. Favourite track?' he asked, studying the album case.

'"You Make Loving Fun". It's so hopeful.'

'It is hopeful. It's about Christine McVie having an affair with a lighting engineer with a big Burt-Reynolds-in-*Playgirl* moustache. Not the miracle I'd choose to believe in if I was going to start believing in miracles.'

'Hmph. Thank you for ruining it for me,' Anna said, sitting back down.

'Am I allowed?' James said, as he continued his perusal of the shelves, like a dinner party guest looking for conversation openers.

'I have nothing to be ashamed of!' Anna said. 'Well I do, but I'm too pished to be ashamed of it.'

'No way – Mills & *Boon*?' James said, spotting a row of slim scarlet spines in her bookcase, at eye level.

'I love Mills & Boon,' Anna said. 'And I refuse to call them a guilty pleasure.'

'Yeah, more a guilty pain,' James said.

He selected a title and turned it over in his free hand.

'*Lover to the Laird. He could take her to bed but she would never take his name!* Oof. Fucking Nora.'

'These are the Historical ones. Fucking Nora is in the more risqué Mills & Boon "Heat" series.'

'Haha. See, I don't get it. You're clever and funny. And these books are very not clever.'

'Very funny though,' Anna said.

James pulled a sceptical face. He replaced *Lover to the Laird*, put his wine glass down on the mantelpiece and plucked another out. He flicked through the pages and read aloud.

'"*Lord Haselmere's cruel eyes raked over Tara's quivering nubile form like a rake with hot coals.*" Two rakes, who edits this stuff? "*She played the coquette but she was nothing more than a sorceress!*

*He wanted to carry her away, like a marauding Viking with his loot.
But this loot was a lady, a lady whom he could never make his wife.
No matter. He must do what any red-blooded man would do when
faced with such treasure, and the pressure of his noble title and vast
inheritance"* – vast inheritance, oh aye – *"be damned. He was still
a man, with a man's needs."* I thought that said a man's knees for
a second. *"'Take off your blouse, he husked ...'"* Husked, hahaha.
How does one husk? I'll try that again. *"Take off your blouse!"'*

James said it again in a pervert's guttural mutter and Anna
laughed so hard tears squeezed out of the corners of her eyes.

'OK, that is funny. I'll give you that,' James said. 'The joke
for me would wear out long before the end though. What is
it with women and romances? Eva never liked flowers and
chocolates and all that jazz but when she was pre-menstrual
she used to watch those dreadful films where some guy chases
after a Greyhound bus in a sunset to tell a woman she makes
him his better self or whatever. What's the appeal?'

'Is that a genuine question or rhetorical?'

'Genuine. I want to understand. And then it's possible I
want to get you help.'

'If you're not going to deride ...' Anna pulled a saggy,
stained velvet cushion onto her lap and hugged it to her. 'It's
the climax – no, don't be cheap – of the big gesture scene.
That's the romance money shot. In ordinary life, no one ever
declares their passion. You get a few signals, get pissed, end up
in bed, it becomes a habit. I love the hero saying all the things
to a woman you want to hear but no one ever says.'

James nodded.

'*"Hold me, it's raining, you can't!"* That sort of thing?'

'Yes. Or, you know. Something that makes sense. It has to

be about why she's so remarkably special to him and she finally finds out all her feelings of obsession are reciprocated.'

Anna couldn't add that this desire in her probably stemmed from no one even wanting to be seen giving her the time of day, once upon a time.

'Then after this speech he enfolds her in his manly arms, kisses her, and carries her back to his castle for a proper drubbing.'

'I think the castle's a very key element in these fantasies,' James said. 'You all want Bernie Ecclestone via *Heat*'s "Torso of the Week". I don't see any titles here called *Penised by a Pauper*.'

'Third in from the right hand side,' Anna said, pointing to the shelf. 'Yes this gender-conditioning sickness is probably why I've never met anyone,' Anna continued, slightly morose. 'I have too high expectations.'

'Nah. The reason you haven't met anyone is that most men are dicks. I'd hate to be a woman or gay … That was meant to be the most New Man moment ever and it sounds really bad.'

They both giggled in drunkenness. Anna wondered if she had any food in the fridge fit for presentation.

'Er …?'

James pulled out the bookmark at the back of the Mills & Boon he was holding, a cosmetic surgery leaflet. Lest any doubt remain that it signified intent, Anna saw she'd helpfully scrawled a time and date on it. A consultation she'd later cancelled.

'Oh no! Don't look at that,' Anna barked. This should be the motherlode and fatherlode of all embarrassments, and yet Anna was twenty-five per cent embarrassed, seventy-five per cent amused at how hilariously pitiful it was. It helped that she was drunk.

James put it back in the flyleaf.

'Funny weather we've been having, isn't it?'

They both burst out laughing again.

'I'm bemoaning why I don't have a boyfriend and I have a Mills & Boon with a Transform leaflet as bookmark. Oh God …' Anna shook with weak laughter and put the cushion over her mouth. 'Next, you glimpse a bed with eleven teddy bears on it.'

'Did you get busted and need a new face to hide from the Feds?'

'I was thinking of getting a birthmark removed. A port wine stain in the shape of the words, "Sod Off James You Nosy Git".'

'Sounds like a talking point. I'd sell it to *Chat* magazine, make some money. *My very specific birthmark frightened lovers away.*'

Anna wiped under her eyes and sighed.

'If you *must* know, and now sadly you sort of do, I had a low moment a year ago and considered a … chest lift.'

James wrinkled his nose. A nose that would be permanently 'sold out' if it could be ordered from cosmetic surgery brochures.

'Why would you do that? I'm sure you're fine as you are.'

'Oh, dunno, hangover ennui. That arsehole boyfriend at uni said a few nasty things. But he said nasty things about most of me so it's not a solid rationale.'

Anna knew her childhood experiences made her highly vulnerable to dumping her insecurities into her appearance, and tried not to do it. She suspected her scruffiness was partly due to a reluctance to pay it too much attention. Yet her bust was the only part of her that hadn't emerged unscathed from being larger. When she lost weight, it deflated. Viewed side on, she worried her cans were what Aggy called 'envelope flaps'.

There was a pause.

'So you're not going to do it?' James said.

'Doubtful.'

'Good. It's completely unnecessary.'

'How do you know?'

'If you had ones like icing piping bags or whatever, you could get it sorted for free on the NHS. The fact you're paying is an admission it's vanity.'

James Fraser was criticising her for vanity? Life's journey took some very strange turns, sometimes.

'And if it's because you think men will care,' he continued, 'other than your arsehole ex, who's both an arsehole and an ex, then trust me, they don't.'

'That's sexist, assuming it's all for the male gaze. Maybe it's for me.'

'Yeah, it's not though is it? If Ryan Gosling approved them, as chairman of the board, you wouldn't bother. Hence you're doing it to suit the tastes of imaginary men in the future. And there's no need. They're definitely imaginary.'

'Oh bloody hell, thanks!'

'No! That was badly put. I mean their *preferences* are imaginary. Men are very binary. We either fancy you or we don't. It's not approval pending, like a Facebook friend request, until we've scored the bits and pieces out of ten.'

'Who died and made Ryan Gosling boob arbiter general?'

'Tell you what, show me instead then.'

'You're not serious?'

James nodded, rubbing his eyes. He folded his arms and leaned back.

'Nice try!' Anna squeal-giggled.

'Hey, this is a win-win. You either get a compliment or a cast-iron unbiased opinion from a disinterested party that surgery's the way to go. And before you say it, no, people you're paying five grand to carve them up are not unbiased.'

'Unbelievable!' Hmmm. Disinterested. Unbiased. He didn't have to hammer the binary lack of attraction element quite so hard.

'You'd be getting them out for a bunch of strangers at a clinic. I don't see this is so different.'

'Anonymous medical professionals, not pissed-up James, taking the piss.'

'Damn it. I really thought I had you there. Offer stands, anyway.'

As they laughed, it crossed Anna's mind that this evening was involving a lot more assessment of body parts than she had anticipated.

James put the book back in its place and flopped down on the sofa, eyes gazing around the room.

'What's that …? That's so strange. Hang on …' James muttered. He'd bent his neck to the left and was staring across the room at something in the corner, at the base of Anna's ancient Ikea floor lamp.

He was already on his feet and moving towards the target as Anna followed his line of sight.

If it was possible to sober up in four seconds flat, Anna did so, due to a stab of adrenaline so big it almost lifted her off the sofa in its sheer intensity.

49

The school portrait was A4-sized glass in a cheap gold frame, with a dappled studio background, supposed to resemble clouds against a blue sky. It had been taken at the height of the Aureliana agony years.

Her frizzed hair was dragged back in a plastic crocodile clasp at the crown of her head, a few curls escaping at her hairline and sticking straight up, creating a sort of Tintin effect. She'd flattened the whole thing with a gloopy gel product, but instead it looked as if she was experimenting with self-cleansing instead of shampooing, and the cleansing process had yet to kick in. It was the kind of startlingly unflattering, unhelpful style you had to be fourteen years old to attempt.

Her naan bread face was near-spherical, resembling a Cabbage Patch doll. Her forehead was speckled with teenage acne that she'd covered with a heavy pan-stick layer of Rimmel's Hide the Blemish in beige, which created a curious lunar landscape above the black smudges of her caterpillar brows, which met in the middle.

Worst of all, possibly, was her expression. Aureliana hated cameras, as much as they hated her back. Therefore she was looking into the lens with the grimace you'd give a loathed enemy. Less a smile, more the twisted mouth you might see on the disembodied head of a traitor on a spike. It flashed a hint of her train-track metal braces.

Anna thought such highly classified material had been binned or burned, with only one last school photo remaining, wrapped in brown paper, at the bottom of her mum's bedroom drawers. Anna hadn't the heart to rob her of every last one. Yet somehow, this additional grotesque reminder had slipped through the net.

As her breath came in rapid bursts, her mind raced: how had this happened? She never had any artefact from her past in her flat, let alone on show.

The answer dawned. It was poking out of the lumpy sack of bric-a-brac from the loft, the one she'd yet to unpack. It had fallen on its side and the weight of the portrait had meant it had slid from the bag and out onto the floor. She'd thought the stiff, rectangular object inside had been a school folder. Her reluctance to probe things that would remind her of the past, and slack attitude to tidying up, had well and truly caught her out.

'How on earth do you know *her*?' James said, tugging the photo out from the bag an inch further, revealing the straps of her homemade pinafore dress uniform and multiple gold chains from Argos she liked to wear under her shirt collar, for a touch of glamour.

The revelation was on its way but hadn't quite formed fully in James's mind yet.

Anna was struck mute. Then panic and horror spurred her to act.

'Stop looking at my things!' she screamed, launching herself across the room and grabbing the photo, yanking it from the bag. She turned it towards her stomach, arms clasped over it protectively. 'You've been looking through my things all night, you nosy TWAT!'

'Eh?' James said, startled by her volume and intensity. 'It was lying there. Why do you have a photo of that girl from school who – wait, she was Italian— '

His blue eyes, the rich purple-dusk blue of her Gatsby poster, widened. Eyes that Aureliana had once spent a whole chemistry lesson transfixed by, even though he was in those ridiculous spoddy safety goggles. James put a hand over his mouth and shook his head. His palm dropped from his face again, his mouth slightly open.

Anna's chest heaved.

'You aren't …? Alessi. But she was called … Ariana? Is she your sister?'

'Aureliana,' Anna said, hearing the tremor in her voice. 'My name is Aureliana.'

Making that announcement herself gave her a moment's relief. She'd asserted herself. Then the pain came rushing back as James's face contorted in disbelief, amazement … and amusement.

He laughed. He actually laughed, a snort of incredulity.

'Oh my *God*. Anna? Aureliana. You're her? *That* was you? I don't believe it.'

'You're laughing at me?'

'I'm just slightly stunned. This is the strangest thing ever. Why didn't you say …?'

'Do you remember what you did to me?'

James shrugged.

'You don't remember?' she repeated, forcefully.

The only way Anna could deal with this was to go on the attack as a form of defence, to convert the sting of shame into savage fury.

'Uh … it was a while back. Excuse me while I catch up with this, you've had longer to get your head round it than me. You're so different …'

'By different, you mean less fat? Less ugly? Less bullied? That last one might jog your memory.'

The atmosphere in Anna's front room was now nothing but confrontation and danger, and James's own instincts to defend himself had arrived. He looked uncomfortable. And aggressive.

'Sorry, where's this banshee thing come from? You're the one sneaking around, not saying who you are, acting like a nutter.'

'Nutter!' Anna shrieked. 'You're calling me more names? Fucking hell, you're no different though, are you?'

'Why are you screaming at me?' James said. 'Calm down.'

'Don't tell me to calm down!' Anna shouted. She winced at how crazy she sounded, but her emotions were not under control. 'I'll remind you what you did. You tricked me into getting on a stage in a fat person fancy dress costume and had the whole school throw things at me. While you laughed, you and Laurence stood there and laughed at me. And you called me an elephant.'

James's eyes narrowed and his lip curled.

'Uhm, OK. Do you want me to apologise for some daft kid thing that happened nearly twenty years ago?'

'Acknowledging it would be a start.'

'Have you got any idea how mental you sound? You're acting like someone else is responsible for this turn of events. You were fine with me until now.'

'*You're* responsible! I'm reacting this way because of you laughing about what you did.'

'What? I'm a big enemy all of a sudden? I was over and above worse than everyone else at school, was I?'

'You were the worst.'

'Hah. Right.'

'It's true. You did the out and out nastiest thing of all. You knew I liked you and you used it against me. No one else could've got me on that stage.'

'Stop being hysterical. It was a stupid prank.'

'The fact you can dismiss it shows what kind of person you still are.'

'Oh, for fuck's sake. Don't pin the fact you were a freak back then on me.'

'*Freak?* You bastard!' Anna spat, trembling with rage. 'You absolute, utter and complete bastard.'

James looked slightly scared. Then disgust settled across his haughty face. The sort of expression she fully expected to see, once her identity was known to him.

'I'm out of here. You're plain fuckin' mental,' James said, snatching up his coat. 'Bye.'

The front door slammed. Anna hurled the photo, face down, across the room. It bounced off the wall and landed face side up. She let go of a howl, darted forward and grabbed it, flinging it again. This time it hit a bookcase and the glass shattered, sending dozens of minuscule glittering diamond shards into the carpet. James's allegation of mentalness wasn't looking entirely unfounded.

That *bastard*. How could she, for a single moment, have kidded herself he was any better than the boy who could do a thing like that? How could she let him in here?

She sank onto the couch and sobbed. Snotty, hacking sobs that came from the lower abdomen and felt as if she was emptying her soul out through her eyes and nose.

It had been a long, slow, tortoise-and-hare pursuit, but Aureliana had finally caught up with Anna, and they were united as one in hopeless lonely misery.

On the stereo, 'You Make Loving Fun' started up.

50

'The poultice is the must-try according to *GQ*, apparently,' Laurence said, scanning the menu, as they nursed tobacco-flavoured Old Fashioneds in a tiled booth of the basement bar at the Spitalfields Hawksmoor.

'The poultice? A Victorian medicinal thing for extracting boils?'

Laurence checked again.

'… Poutine, I mean. It's from Quebec. Fries and curds and whey. Like, deconstructed cheese.'

James was doubtful and opted for the short rib that came with its own silver salver jug of French dip. Laurence's plate was awash with brown liquid.

'We are living in the Chinese year of the gravy,' James said. 'Isn't this all like a fancy chip shop order?'

'Nmmmm,' Laurence said, through a mouthful of it. 'S'well nice. You know the brass walls are from salvaged lift doors at Unilever House. Repurposed Art Deco.'

He rubbed his mouth with a napkin as his eyes followed the swingy behind of a woman cat-walking across the parquet floor. '… I like the interiors in here.'

'Curds and whey,' James said. Laurence still wasn't making eye contact with him. 'Wasn't that in a nursery rhyme? Little Miss Muffet?'

Laurence turned back.

'Tell you what, I would like to be the spider that sat down beside her.'

'Oh, no. Leave her tuffet be.'

'And her muffet, Jeeves?'

'You need bromide in your drink.'

James took a deep breath and prepared to drop the A-bomb. He'd thought of little else since that night and he very much wanted someone else to tell him he didn't need to feel the guilt that was plaguing him.

'This'll distract you. I'm going to tell you something about Anna the Italian that is going to blow your mind and beggar your belief.'

'It's not my mind I want her to blow. Wait. You haven't slept with her, have you?' Laurence said. He looked authentically pissed-off at this notion, even angry.

James was slightly taken aback.

'No. Why? Would it matter if I had?'

'Yes it bloody would matter. She's mine. I saw her first. Hands off.'

'Don't Anna's feelings matter in this hypothetical rutting? I haven't noticed her scrambling to sit atop you so far.'

'And she's not into you either, so the only way it would happen is if you put the sly moves on her. Which under this verbal contract is a clear contravention of mates' code of honour.'

James squinted.

'Right. Glad that's clear. Anyway, I'm going to tell you something that proves she's never going to be into either of us. Remember that Italian girl at school, Aureliana?'

Laurence frowned. 'Er . . .? Give me more.'

'Fat. Long curly black hair. Total loser. Everyone chucked sweets at her in the Mock Rock. We convinced her to dress up as an opera singer, remember? You came up with the Quality Street finale.'

'Oh, *her*. The Spag Hag. Probably has four massive kids she feeds up now, wears one of those flowered smocks with flip-flops. Have you ever seen continental women when they let themselves go? Brrrr.'

'That's Anna.'

'What d'you mean?'

'Anna. Aureliana. Same person. She changed her name after school. Aureliana Alessi. There was something that rang a bell in Anna Alessi that bugged me for ages.'

Laurence put his cutlery down.

'Get the fuck out of town.'

'Serious,' James took a sip of his cocktail.

'What the . . .?'

'Quite the brain-bender, isn't it?'

James considered he'd even met Anna's sister and still not twigged, though he didn't remember Aggy at all. The younger years at school were always an invisible, amorphous mass to the older.

'How is that even possible? Are you having me on?'

'No! That's why she was at the reunion. Think about it. It never made much sense her wandering into it by mistake. Can you believe we didn't know who she was? No wonder she was pissy with us.'

No wonder indeed. The more James thought about how he looked from her perspective, the worse it got. They'd waltzed up to a woman they'd once shamelessly abused, in ignorance, and Laurence had tried to pull her. They were lucky not to get glassed. She'd gradually put aside all that history and been friendly. Could he have done the same?

'What a mistake-a to make-a!' Laurence guffawed. He shook his head in wonder. 'Hardly our fault, Slim Fast doesn't usually produce results like this. I cannot believe that a two, at best, has become a solid eight or nine. There should be a whole Channel Four *Dispatches* about it.'

'Jesus, Loz. Have a bit of humanity.'

'Oh come on, you know I'm kidding.'

There was a brief silence.

'I only found out because a school photo had been left out at hers,' James said. 'She went absolutely batshit at me. I was like *woah*. You're the one who's been lying about it. Later for this shit.'

His excuse sounded very hollow, spoken aloud. James was even using Laurence lingo, a sure sign of turpitude. Yes, she'd concealed who she was. But on reflection, he had to ask, wouldn't he have done the same? Would you want to be defined by being that pariah at school, if you could leave it behind?

Aureliana was one of a handful of extreme wacky-looking oddballs that every school has. She had every qualification for being bullied bar a note from her mum for the teachers, formally requesting she be bullied. To be so much as caught talking to her could see you infected with the social equivalent of the Black Death. She was that potent. Fitting her together with the Anna of today made no physical sense whatsoever. Yet personality: he could see it. She had the acerbic perspective of an outsider.

Still, that was then.

Anna had no right to be so viciously unpleasant to him when she was found out. *Unpleasant. Then what's the word for how you were to her at school?* a voice asked.

Oh God, why did he blurt 'freak' at her? It was a defensive move, instinctual, like putting your hands up when someone made to hit you. Freak. It wasn't a word he ever used. It was as if his sixteen-year-old self had come back to haunt him, an evil spirit possession.

'Hang on, why were you round at hers?' Laurence said, sharply.

'Watching a DVD about the exhibition we worked on.'

'I mean it, Jimmy,' Laurence said, forking some curds-and-or-whey into his mouth. 'I am dead keen on this woman.'

'You were rating her out of ten a moment ago!'

'Yes, rating her a solid eight. Do not touch. Consider her lashed with crime scene tape, as far as you're concerned. I will be dusting for prints.'

James frowned. Was Loz genuinely into Anna, as much as Loz could genuinely be into anyone? They were thirty-two and Laurence had never had a lasting relationship. Maybe he'd finally decided he needed a semi-permanent, respectable some-one to make him look plausible. *My girlfriend's an academic, actually ... She's Italian ...* Yes, he could imagine Laurence liking the bragging rights of a classy choice.

'She's not your sort of thing,' James said, briskly. 'I've seen her wear flat shoes for work. And she's not rich.'

'Pffft. She's a gold-standard game-changer, a total challenge.

I'm ready for a woman with real brains. I might be falling in love.'

'You'd need a heart for that.' James glumly fiddled about in his soft roll with a knife and thought this wasn't going the way he'd imagined. He wanted Laurence to be on his side. Only he wasn't sure his side was a place anyone should be, and as ever, Loz was only on his own side.

'Oh man, this former fat girl thing is such good news.'

'Why? I can't believe I did something so harsh. We were twats and she's never going to speak to either of us again.'

'Like hell. This is why I'm in sales. Setbacks are opportunities in disguise. It's the perfect excuse for me to have another crack at her. I'm calling to say sorry. Her self-esteem will be in tatters. It's time for sympathetic Laurence to be a shoulder to cry on. And then a face to sit on.' Laurence pointed his fork. 'And do not even think about stealing this idea. It's mine. I might even tell her the Mock Rock was all your fault and I was begging you not to, if that's OK.'

'Don't you *bloody dare*,' James said.

'Aha! So you DO want to shag her! Fallen into my trap. I knew it.'

'No, I absolutely don't and I probably won't ever see her again, but I'm not proud of what we did and I don't want you upsetting her even more.'

Laurence shrugged. 'We were kids. It's so long ago it practically never happened at all.'

'She cried, Loz. We made her cry.'

'I'll make her cry out again, alright.'

James put his napkin down, and gave up. Talk about talking to a salvaged brass lift door. Laurence excused himself to the toilet and James sat playing with his phone, wondering what he could say or do to put this right. He'd humiliated Anna all the more by passing this on to Laurence. It felt ugly.

And Laurence was going to use this information to have another attempt on her? He wanted to stop him, but he didn't know how. What if she was so out-of-sorts and upset by what happened, that she did finally give in to Laurence? Then that would be on James's conscience as well? *Argh.*

Was that all he was worried about, his indirect responsibility? The notion of Laurence and Anna's unholy congress gave him a visceral reaction that went beyond reason. He had a flash image of their bare bodies together, bucking and writhing, Laurence's fingers wound in her loose hair … Nope, no thank you, no ta, delete that please, brain. His stomach clenched. He felt protective. Inevitable, when he'd brought all of this on Anna, he supposed.

Laurence slid back into the booth.

'Polly and Becca from Accenture are joining us by the way. Ah, bingo,' Laurence waved across the room at skinny women in billowing patterned dresses and spindly heels. 'Warning, Polly is so posh she calls Cambridge "Cambles". Get her to say "gastronomic", it's like she's got a mouthful of gobstoppers.'

'Thanks for checking this with me,' James hissed.

'Friends through work, no need to sprain your fanny over it,' Laurence said, adjusting a cufflink as James blanched.

James gave Polly and Becca a grimace-smile and sat numbly through Laurence's banter and their delighted twittering, avoiding meeting mascara-lashed coy glances.

He could only think about someone who wasn't there, and a few hours of his life, sixteen years ago, that until now he'd chosen to forget.

51

Anna could hear her sister saying *what if we have to break in* and decided she'd rather have Michelle and Aggy in her flat now, than tradespeople replacing her door tomorrow. Slowly, she moved towards the door and answered the knocking.

Michelle took her e-cigarette out of her mouth as she surveyed Anna.

'Woah. We may have got here too late.'

Aggy's face appeared, to the right of Michelle.

'Why are you in a baby gro?' Michelle said.

'It's a *Where the Wild Things Are* onesie. It's a wild rumpus suit and a cool cultural reference,' Anna said.

'It's a boner-killing disaster, my love,' Michelle said, bustling in with a Marks and Spencer bag for life, Aggy in tow and no invitation.

Once in the front room, they circled Anna.

'Oh my days, what's that brown thing hanging from your arse?' Michelle said.

'The tail, quite clearly.'

'It looks a bit fecal.'

'And what are you watching?!' Aggy said, looking at the TV

where the screen was freeze-framed on a fanged man.

'*Buffy.*'

Anna's guests' eyes lingered on the giant plastic wheel of half-eaten microwave paella and open packet of Kettle Chips, next to a tub of hummus. And row of Cadbury's grab bag confectionery pouches. OK, it looked bad, but Anna hadn't eaten it all today. She just hadn't cleaned up.

'We've got a Mattesson's Fridge Raider here. You eat the diet of someone who's been captured by the Germans at the best of times, but this is some next-level shit,' Michelle said.

She sat down on an armchair, while Aggy perched on the end of the sofa, gingerly. She was used to seeing her elder sister in control, and the disarray, both emotional and domestic, clearly discomfited her. Anna knew that despite the jocularity, they were worried. Ordinarily she'd put them at their ease. But now, she couldn't summon the energy: she was lower than a snake's belly in a wagon rut.

'First things first,' Michelle, rustling in the M&S bag, 'though they might be surplus to requirements, I have Percy Pigs of every variety in here. Apart from the lemon ones, they're a bit nasty. Second thing, Anna. What is going on?'

'I told you. I've been off work sick all week. Stomach bug.'

'Yeeeees. But then we call, email, text, and we either don't get answers or we get very brief replies, un Anna-ish replies. Then when we start making inquiries. Someone I am going to code name "Bee-Shell" in case you're angry with her for this, realises the last person you saw before The Ensickening was that James from schooldays. And who then calls him at work, and is told there was some sort of … fight?'

'Oh God, you spoke to James? Oh God!' Anna pulled her

onesie hood over her face.

'Are they horns?' Aggy said. 'Is that a Satan suit?'

'Ears,' Anna muttered, through the fabric. She let the hood ping back.

'I'm under serious pressure to find out what's up from your colleague, Patrick,' Michelle said.

Anna sighed.

'I've saved you from a visit from him, look at it that way. What was the fight about?' Michelle asked.

'James didn't tell you?'

'Nope. "You'll have to ask her," was all I got.'

A small flicker of respect for James's discretion burned for a second, before other memories extinguished it.

'He saw a school photo and found out who I am. He laughed at me. I lost it and screamed at him that he'd been a dreadful bastard. He told me I was psychotic and said it wasn't his fault I was a freak back then.

'It was a massive humiliating ruck and has brought back every bad memory of being at school again.'

'What a piece of work!' Michelle said. 'He called you a freak?'

'That's horrible,' Aggy said, looking as if she might cry.

'We already knew he was horrible. I just can't believe I persuaded myself he'd ever be anything else.'

'So. Suspected former bastard confirms his own continuing bastardy,' Michelle said. 'This is on him. How's it had this big an effect on you?'

It was a question that needed to be asked. Anna had been avoiding it.

'I don't know. He laughed, and in an instant we were back

at the Mock Rock. It proved to me I am that girl. I will always be that girl who no one wanted to know.'

'I wanted to know you!' Aggy said, a tear sliding down her cheek.

Anna leaned over and gave her an arm squeeze.

'Thank you. But you didn't have much choice, what with me being in your house. It was so stupid of me to hang around with such superficial, immoral people. I know who they are, why did I kid myself? They were nice to me and I let myself be flattered. It was so weak. I wanted to believe they'd changed. I wanted to think *I'd* changed. I wanted to finally be liked by the cool kids. How pathetic is that, at thirty-two?'

'You are. You could be, you're just too good for that,' Michelle said.

'No. It's like … I'm wearing a disguise. Nothing's ever real. The way I was treated then, that's the truth of what people like him think of me. And it reveals who they really are. Everything else is bullshit.'

'Then don't see these superficial people. Sorted.'

'I know,' Anna said. 'I'm waiting for emotions to agree with intellect that I have nothing to be ashamed about.'

'I never dreamt they wouldn't know who you were at the reunion, you know,' Michelle said. 'You've had all of the dragging up of the past and none of the putting it to bed. Sorry I made you go.'

'I don't blame you.' Anna adjusted her tail. 'It was me who carried on seeing James. Some part of me hoped it'd do some good, I guess.'

Well that, and you were having fun, she thought.

'But when you always say you've changed,' Michelle

303

reapplied e-fag to side of mouth, 'younger Anna was clever. Younger Anna was kind and interesting and funny. These are the things people like you for and they didn't arrive with adulthood. Yeah you look different to when you were a teenager, we all do.'

'Everyone hated me, Michelle,' Anna said, trying hard not to let the pressure in her throat turn into crying. 'They *loathed* me. I'm not sure you ever fully come back from that. The feeling you are, intrinsically … unlovable.'

Ah. There were the tears. Aggy hugged her as she wept, and Michelle got up, hugged her too and they all wept a bit more. Michelle eventually muttering, 'Your romper suit could do with a nice hot wash, I reckon.'

Anna sniffed and cleared her throat, but noticed she felt better for having uttered that terrible truth. When she saw her silly chubby face on those photos she felt so bad for that girl. She went to school keen and eager to learn and what she learned was that she was worthless.

'Given you are loved, lots, this is plainly not true,' Michelle said, as she sat back down.

'Apart from the no-boyfriends-ever thing.'

'Hang on. There are tons of men who'd like to be your boyfriend so don't try any Miss Havisham bleating.'

'This is true. I had Facebook open the other day and Phil who I work with said he'd love to have a go on you,' Aggy said.

Anna laughed weakly. 'OK. Percy Pig, please.' Michelle lobbed a packet of Phizzy Pig Tails.

'I think it's still bad because you haven't talked about it,' Aggy said. 'You don't let anybody talk about it. Mum and Dad worry they'll upset you if they ever bring it up. At the time,

304

you shut yourself in your bedroom and read books, and now you store it all up inside, and keep new people at a distance. We've never even told Chris about the thing that happened ...'

This was uncharacteristically serious and perceptive for Aggy, and Anna listened. She had to. She could feel herself welling up.

'Me and Chris have a laugh. I don't want him to think of me differently ...'

'He won't! Talking helps,' Aggy said. 'I mean, I once completely ruined things with this client I ended up in bed with and it was a nightmare – he told people stuff I'd said in bed and they laughed. And then I told the story my way and people laughed, but in a good way, and it was like, once I'd made it mine, it couldn't touch me anymore. You know? Make a school photo your Facebook profile picture or something.'

Anna pulled a face.

'OK, maybe not that. But you know what I mean. Make the Mock Rock a story. Make it one of *your* stories. You're so funny, everyone would laugh with you.'

Anna leaned over and hugged her sister's bony shoulders. When Aggy was a child, Anna used to say it felt like cuddling the Stabilo ruler in her pencil case.

'I tell you what, I don't think even this James is as self-assured as you think,' Michelle said. 'When I spoke to him, he asked if you were alright, several times. I got the impression he was embarrassed.'

'Embarrassed to know me, mainly. He should be embarrassed at the things he said but he's not the type to blame himself, I promise you that.'

'He might think on it and apologise.'

305

'Hah. Not holding my breath.'

Anna thought about how upset she was at being discovered and wondered if, had she held it together, it could've been less confrontational.

No. He'd laughed, denied all guilt and called her a freak. He'd proved all her suspicions right.

'If he has pissed off, he wasn't worth anything,' Michelle said. 'Also, you never much liked him anyway, did you?'

'Not really,' Anna said.

'Do you feel up to going back to work on Monday?'

'Yeah.'

'Good. I don't think solitude is what you need. I think remembering how much you love your job is what will help.'

'True. Granny Maude used to say: "Don't work too hard if you want to be happy. Men like fun much more than they like clever. Which means you'll be successful but lonely,"' Anna said.

'Granny Maude told me that if a man has an affair it's because he was missing something at home,' Aggy said.

'This Granny Maude you two mention. Was she happily married?' Michelle said, popping a Percy Piglet variant in her mouth.

'Not really. She was always moody and Granddad Len always had the face of a haunted ant-eater,' Anna said.

'I might stop fretting on her relationship advice then,' Michelle said, chewing stickily. 'Granny Fraud more like. What's that?'

Anna followed Michelle's line of sight.

'A box of diaries. From school. I was going to look through them.'

'*Why*, for God's sake?'

'To remember— ?' Anna shrugged tiredly, 'I don't know. After the reunion I thought, if I can't get closure that way then maybe I'll get it by facing all those memories and reading the diaries. Then I wasn't sure I could face it.'

'Bollocks, don't wallow. I have an idea,' Michelle said. 'Why don't we burn them? A pyre? Then that can be your closure. We'll dance around it making whooping sounds.'

Anna laughed and Aggy squealed.

Ten minutes later, having heaved the box into the garden, they all stood shivering, half-lit by the combination of the kitchen light and the back door security lamp.

'Don't you have a metal bin or something?' Michelle said, arms wrapped tightly round herself, shaking with cold.

'The bins are plastic,' Anna said.

'We could try microwaving the diaries?' Aggy offered.

'Microwave paper and cardboard?' Michelle said.

'And metal, the padlocks are metal,' Anna said.

'We were only going to destroy the diaries, not get rushed to hospital with no hair and make the dipshit slot on the local news,' Michelle said.

She sighed. 'You want something cooking properly, you cook it yourself. Have you got a barbecue set? And barbecue lighters?'

'Wait! Yes.'

Anna darted off into the undergrowth and hauled out a circular barbecue grill on three legs, full of ash, while Aggy ferreted around noisily in the kitchen cupboards.

Michelle got it going with liberal use of matches, and called for the first diary.

She prodded it with a barbecue fork, watching the teddy bear face warp and melt, an Alessi sister on either side, hugging her.

'Nearly done. Slice the buns and ready the ketchup. Man alive it smells rank,' Michelle said, coughing as the metal catch on the diary melted. 'Keep it away from your costume, Anna, it'll go up like a rocket. OK, Aggy, I'm ready for the 1995 diary now. Did you really have to write so much, Anna?'

As they stood in a huddle, arms linked, Anna said, 'Thank you, you two. I feel much better. I should have done this a long time ago.'

'It's time you accepted that they're the ones who have something to be ashamed of. Not you,' Michelle said.

Staring into the flickering cauldron of soot-covered diary, Anna realised for the first time how true this was.

52

James had been at a meeting with Will Wembley-Hodges, an 'artisanal cheese string producer' in the Bermondsey Arches who wanted to bring his product to the mass market.

He had to nod vigorously at a businessman in a pink straw trilby.

'So you're walking down the street, having a cheese string, but instead of processed cheese, it's Armenian sheep's milk cheese with black cumin.'

James was tempted to reply with something along the lines of *thank goodness someone's tackled the 'walking down the street with the wrong sort of cheese string' problem*, but obviously didn't.

His mind drifted during the meeting with schemes and plans of how best to apologise to Anna. He was working up to it. *Freak, what had possessed him to use the word freak?* He almost twitched with shame every time he recalled it. And then her mate Michelle had called him, and he'd felt awful when it became obvious he'd really upset her.

When he got back to the office mid-morning, the hushed room had a strange tension.

James was merely mildly perturbed until Harris passed him, carrying his vast tub of steamed chai. The look on his face was as grotesque as it was threatening: malign excitement, triumphalism, and most of all, gleeful anticipation.

'James, can I have a word?' Harris said, seating himself at his screen in the open plan office. You could have heard a pin drop.

'Uh. Yeah?' James said, sitting down.

'Over here, if you don't mind,' Harris said.

He got up and joined Harris at his desk nearby, who had the office's general inquiries email account open as full screen. He clicked to open a sound file and the graphic rippled and jumped as it started. A voice came out loud and clear, amid background rustling and movement. It was a young-ish male Londoner and James took a moment to realise that the stranger's voice was his.

'… *You don't give two craps about what I do, fine. I get it. It's a bunch of digital twattery that didn't exist five minutes ago and now we sell it to you as essential, because unfortunately for you it is. Because everyone has smart phones and the attention span of Graham Norton after a speedball and a Red Bull, even the ones who go to museums. But this pays my mortgage and I'm alright at it, so it's what I do. Not everyone has a passion for their work like you …*'

Anna. It was that time he got tetchy with her, after they'd been recording the question and answer session for the app. What else did he say? Oh God, what else did he say …

'… *And you think my colleagues are dicks, guess what? So do I, with one or two exceptions. And they all seem to have surnames for forenames. But instead of sitting here trying to get a rise out of me every other minute and make it clear just how moronic you think it all is ...'*

Harris hit pause.

'That's a nice way to talk about us all, isn't it?'

James stood motionless, trying to find a way to cope with his entire office hearing what he thought of them. It was like the experience of someone walking in behind you when you were slagging them off. But multiplied, many times. 'It's from UCL. Things going badly with the girlfriend, by any chance?'

Of course. Their fight.

Playing for time as his brain whirred, James squinted at the details of the email.

'I've already sent it to Jez and Fi,' Harris snapped, before James could come up with any sort of explanation. No surprises there. James had already sussed this was probably an employment terminator. It was nothing less than an audio resignation letter.

The email sender was an anonymous email address and the message simply read: '*It has come to our attention that a member of your staff conducted himself extremely unprofessionally during a recent project involving our university. We thought you might be interested to hear the attached file.*' The subject line was: '*Urgent from UCL. re: James Fraser.*'

James licked dry lips.

'I didn't mean it. She was being arsey and I was defending myself. That's been taken out of context.'

'Fi's in London so she's coming over at lunchtime to speak to you.'

'Fine,' James said, stalking back to his desk before Harris

could enjoy himself further. After a minute or two of swirling confusion, apprehensiveness and fury he decided to call Anna and demand an explanation.

He ducked out of the office and left a voicemail after two missed (almost certainly dropped) calls.

Jeez. So much for apologising to her. Anna didn't seem well balanced last weekend, but this was outer space monkey nuts. He didn't think she'd be that spiteful. He clearly hadn't got the measure of her at all.

To think he'd thought she was nice? Woo-ee. From now on he'd trust his first impressions.

James returned to his seat. As the minutes ticked by, conversation barely rose above a murmur. Eventually, Harris could take the exquisite tension of waiting for Fi no longer.

'Hey, James. How are you feeling, knowing you're going to be sacked like Rome?' he sneered. 'In the sack race, you're taking first place. You're back, SACK and cracked. You are in SACKcloth and ashes …'

'Yeah, hilarious, Harris, you Lord of the Lols, you,' James said. 'Can I make it clear? When I said there were one or two exceptions to the dickhead rule, I definitely didn't mean you.'

A glimmer of light in his darkest hour: there was a surprising amount of laughter at this. Harris looked like a gnome smelling a fart.

53

People often used the term 'throwing yourself into work' as if it was a negative thing; a way to avoid tackling your problems. In Anna's view though, throwing yourself into work was infinitely better than throwing yourself into a canal, under a bad man or turkey-gobbling Xanax.

Speaking of bad men, there had been one surprise interaction with a newly sympathetic Laurence, who had wanted to tell her how sorry he was about the Mock Rock. Anna was pretty sure it would be the last interaction they ever had, if she was right about the only goal Laurence was pursuing.

Michelle was right, she relished being her work-self again. Having given a pretty damn rousing lecture to her third years, she headed back across campus feeling buoyant for the first time in weeks. Torching her school diaries might've been ceremonial but it had the desired effect. She'd have cheerfully burned an effigy of James along with them.

On the walk from lecture hall to office, she thought she heard her mobile pipping in her bag and investigated the caller ID as soon as she'd put her folders down. She pulled her phone out and was disconcerted to see it was James Fraser. A voicemail message winked at her.

This was not good. Michelle might think James could find it in him to say sorry, but Anna didn't think for a moment his pride would permit it. And if it did, he'd hardly be moved to do it in the middle of a Monday morning.

She listened to the message.

'Anna. I have no idea what the hell you're playing at, but this attack really is shit behaviour on a grand scale. Can you call me back? And if you think you can dodge me by not answering my calls, I'll come and sit in your reception until you see me. Looks like I'll soon have the time on my hands to do it.' Click. Dialling tone.

Attack? Something was very, very wrong. Trying to summon up defiant courage instead of fear, she called his number. He answered on a later ring than she expected, then she sussed from the traffic in the background he'd belted out into the street.

'Hello? You wanted to speak to me?' she said. 'I'm not dodg—'

She didn't manage to finish the sentence.

'Yeah I did. Can you tell me why you think this is a proportionate response to something I did nearly two decades ago? To lose me my job? You know I have something we didn't have when we were sixteen, called a mortgage? And bills?'

'What's a proportionate response?'

'The email. With the recording.'

'I don't know what you're talking about.'

'Oh man, this is pitiful, insulting stuff. You're actually going to go through the rigmarole of pretending it wasn't you?'

Anna pushed her chair back and stood up as her heart went off like a fire alarm.

'I honestly have absolutely *no* idea what you're talking about.'

She'd spoken with enough force that there was a beat of silence.

'My company has been sent a file with a recording of me slagging off my job and the people I work with. It's from when we met to do the Q and A session that time in the lecture theatre. I was angry and shouldn't have said what I did to you, but I had no idea you'd recorded the whole thing.'

Anna was dumbstruck and a trifle nauseous.

'I didn't know that existed. And I didn't send it.'

'What, so someone else at UCL bugged our meeting, and has it in for me, a week after we've had a barney? Are there other suspects? I don't think Poirot would be rounding everyone up in the drawing room for this one.'

'No,' Anna paced her office and felt the heat of the phone on her ear. 'I thought we only recorded the Q and A. I never even had the file. You say it was emailed?'

'Yes. Marked as from UCL but from an anonymous Gmail account.'

'If I was going to send it, why would I hide it was me? As you pointed out, everyone would think it was me anyway.'

'Then who did?'

'I don't know.'

James exhaled. He didn't sound much mollified and Anna could appreciate why. He was in no less trouble, but without the satisfaction of a clear-cut enemy.

'Hang on . . .'

'What?'

'The audio was set up by my colleague, Patrick. He's the

only person I told about our conversation. He took the opposite of a shine to you at the launch. It's possible he heard the whole recording. I don't know why he'd send the file though.'

'Is he ginger?'

'Fairly.'

'I think I remember him. And he knew we'd had a bust-up?'

'No … I didn't tell him myself.' Wait – Michelle said Patrick had wanted to know what was behind Anna's absence? 'My friend Michelle might have told him.'

James sighed.

'Marvellous. Well, I have been completely done over,' James said, though slightly less angrily.

'Are you in a lot of trouble?'

'My boss Fi is coming in to deliver the bullet at lunchtime. I'll be on monster.co.uk by tomorrow no doubt. If I'm not in the pub, with my head on the bar.'

'If I speak to your boss, maybe I can help?'

'You could try but it's not going to do much when she's got the recording. Not really a he said, she said thing, is it? More of a "Everyone Heard".'

'I'm sorry, James.'

'Thanks. So am I. See you around.' He rang off.

54

Anna had to steel herself before she could embark on the short journey down the corridor to Patrick's office. She didn't know quite what she was about to find, but she was fairly sure she wasn't going to like it. Had Patrick done this? Why? How could he? And how was she going to accuse him without … accusing him?

She rapped her knuckles on the wood and walked straight in when Patrick called, 'Come in!'

'Morning! Feeling better?' Patrick said. Was she imagining he looked antsy?

'Much, thank you. What's new here?'

Anna lowered herself into a chair, perching on the edge of her bum cheeks.

'Same old, same old.'

The lack of any cups of tea and the silence that stretched between them said that this was no normal morning visit, no comfy chat. Patrick's clock on the mantel ticked heavily.

'So I've just had a strange phone call,' Anna said.

'Ah,' Patrick said.

There remained no doubt in Anna's mind that Patrick was behind sending the file to Parlez. 'Ah,' did not denote curiosity. It signalled guilt.

'Perhaps I should say here that I know your illness was psychological, not physical.'

'Oh?'

'Michelle told me of the dreadful, dreadful things that man said to you. I was disgusted …' Patrick shook his head and moved his pen on his pad two inches to the right, adjusting the papers underneath, so all the pages were in line.

'Why? You spoke to Michelle?'

'I said you'd told me about this James Fraser and she divulged his latest antics.'

Anna guessed what must've happened. Michelle had said Patrick was pestering her for the reason for her absence. Michelle wasn't careless but she was naturally honest, and no doubt Patrick had made it seem he knew all about James's backstory. Still, Patrick had no right to pry.

Anna felt the anger inching up her by steady degrees, like the volume lights on a stereo.

'And I felt someone needed to act on your behalf. No one takes care of you … and you are simply too selfless to properly take care of yourself.'

Anna merely widened her eyes at this description of herself. Patrick seemed shaky.

'… I had evidence of how he'd spoken to you on tape and I sent it to the digital agency. Let his foul behaviour impact on him and not the innocent, for once.'

Anna didn't know what fit of madness had possessed Patrick but it seemed that even he now couldn't quite believe what he'd done. Anna cleared her throat.

'You sent a secret recording of a personal conversation, without my permission or knowledge, to a professional contact, humiliated him, implicated me and cost him his job?'

Patrick's eyebrows shot up. 'He's been sacked?'

Anna's temper broke.

'Yes! Or, he might be! Patrick, how could you do this? Everyone thinks I sent it!'

'I'm sorry. I was incensed and gripped by a need to bloody do something for once.'

Patrick jutted his chin out and tried the Wikileaks freedom fighter pose on for size.

'Couldn't you have asked me?'

'You'd have considered all the ramifications, been too fair minded, and let him off the hook.'

'If the aim was striking a blow for me against James Fraser, it couldn't have backfired harder. I've had to apologise to him and vacate the moral high ground with immediate effect.'

'Why apologise?! *He's* the shit. Forgive me if I'm not going to dwell too much on any difficulties that might befall a man who once publicly crucified you.'

'Argh,' Anna put her hands to her face. 'But don't you think if anyone was going to take him to task for that, it should be me?'

'As I understand it, you did. He abused you so badly you spent a week unable to leave your house.'

Anna's breath came in quick bursts.

'I know you think you were sticking up for me, but trust me, this was not the way. I never wanted to see him again, now I'm going to have to try and sort this mess out to make up for what you've done.'

'Are you sure about that?'

'Who else is going to do it?'

'I mean, are you sure you never want to see him again? It seems from the outside that this man went from public enemy number one to somebody you were pretty pleased to spend time around.'

'I promise you, there is nothing remotely romantic going on with James.'

'What was he doing at your flat?'

Anna flapped her hands. 'Watching a documentary about Theodora. It wasn't … dear God, it wasn't a *booty call*. Is that why you overreacted, you thought he'd humped me and dumped me?'

'No. That's not why I overreacted.'

Patrick swallowed, shuffling papers on his desk again, and a long silence stretched between them.

'I'm in love with you.'

Anna almost gasped.

'No, you aren't,' she blurted dumbly, in shock.

'I believe I'm allowed to know best how I feel,' Patrick said, smiling a sad smile, full of regretful ennui.

Anna asked herself if she'd known this was coming. At some level she'd had an inkling he fancied her, of course she had. The look that lasted a little too long. The interest in her love life that had been a shade too eager. She blamed herself for not realising feelings might be building. But what could you say? Please don't like me that way? *Please don't like me so much?*

Anna rubbed her clammy hands on her dress.

'Er. I don't know what to say.'

'I'm not telling you because I expect my feelings to be reciprocated,' Patrick said, adjusting his specs. 'I know this is unrequited.'

Anna was silent, completely poleaxed.

'I just thought we were friends,' she said.

'We are,' Patrick said. 'My word, you really are entirely unaware of your effect on men, aren't you? I remember Roger saying as much at the cheese and wine do where I first met you. I thought he must be joking, you're so exceptionally lovely. But, no. Male students invent reasons to have private audiences with you, do you realise? I'm not saying your accounts of Theodora aren't spellbinding, but I know their game.

'This is why I couldn't stand by and watch this man mistreat and manipulate you, Anna. I always knew sooner or later, some flash Harry would come along and exploit your goodness and innocence. I won't have it.'

'I'm very flattered but I promise you, you've got this one wrong. There was never any risk of James trying to seduce me. Or succeeding. It's not like that.'

'Well, if he wants to know why I sent that file, he can see me. Tell him I'm in my study and ready to chat.'

'Patrick, no!'

'Why are you protecting him?'

'I'm not protecting him, I'm trying to make you see I don't need this battle fought for me.'

Anna had a funny echo of Laurence, of Patrick being the benign version of Laurence. She was a prize, she was on a pedestal. But she wanted to be equal.

Still, unlike Laurence, she felt for Patrick.

'I don't want this to change anything between us,' she said, carefully.

'Sadly, I'm sure it won't,' Patrick smiled. Anna writhed and thought they'd best give each other a wide berth for a while. Enough to let the weirdness subside, but not so much that Patrick felt shunned.

'Promise me,' Patrick said, as she made to leave, 'Promise me something. Not him. Anyone but him. He's not worthy of you.'

Anna sighed. 'I can't make you promises about who I'll date. I can promise you it's vanishingly unlikely.'

'You won't rule him out?'

'Only on principle.'

Patrick shook his head.

'You've told me all I need to know.'

First James's colleagues, now her colleagues, convinced she and James were an item. Comically far from the truth. She'd rather felch Hitler's corpse, and she betted he would too.

Anna escaped Patrick's office and bumped straight into a queue of first years waiting for a tutorial, who'd heard every word.

When she made it back to her office, her mobile had a missed call from her mother. She'd leave it till the end of the day. She could absolutely do without discussing coconut frosting and jam jar table centrepieces right now. Anna tossed her mobile in a drawer, and turned to her email.

She couldn't do much to sort this out, but she could do something.

55

Fi walked into Parlez at near-midday, by which time James thought the acid in his stomach would be enough to dissolve a dead body. She chatted with a few members of staff under her breath, leafed through some mail and then said, 'James, would you join me for a coffee?'

He swung out of his chair, tense with self-consciousness. He'd rather have been fired by Skype and never had to face any of them again. This was gruelling, but then, it was meant to be.

'Are we OK to duck into Carluccios? I've got to be across town by one,' Fi said, as James nodded and held the door for her.

He regretted choosing the seat adjacent to the wall, as a tilted mirror above reflected his embattled reflection. He didn't have much pleasure in looking at himself, these days.

'Catch you on the tenth then, Tigs. Bye bye bye …' Fi spoke these last words in a stage whisper, like an *Absolutely Fabulous* character. She often said things no one in real life said.

'… Hugs, best girl.'

Like that.

Fi pushed her diamanté-encrusted sunglasses into her salon-blonded hair, as a part-time hairband.

'Now then. I am here to demand answers.'

'Uhm, yeah. I know what I said was … extremely bad. There was context …'

'I know the context.'

'You do?'

'Yes. I had a good long chat with your – ex? – girlfriend and she supplied it all. And I was even more appalled at your utter idiocy by the end of our chinwag, let me tell you.'

Oh holy hell. Game, set and match to you, Anna. She wanted to call Fi to dig him into an even deeper hole?

'My principal question is this. What on EARTH are you doing letting this delicious dusky maiden get away?'

Fi play-slapped him and James stared dumbly.

Wait? What?

If this was a new, advanced brutality type of sacking, where you put someone at their ease and then went in for the kill, he'd never encountered it before.

'Let's get dull worky stuff out of the way first. The British Museum exhibition. We've had a hero-gram about the app from the museum, from a Victoria someone at UCL. Safe to say, Jez and I are delighted with how you handled it.'

'Oh! Great.' James needed to shift gears here without giving away the fact he had 100 per cent expected this to be a Welcome to Sackville, Population: You.

'I don't need to tell you that "digital twattery" isn't exactly how we'd like you to go around describing your occupation. However, who hasn't said something reckless to impress a new partner? When I first met Jez, I told him my favourite position was the pile driver! Hahaha! Have you ever tried it?'

James gulped and shook his head. *Christ almighty, rich people were weird.*

'Well let me tell you, you need to do a helluva lot of Bikram to even think about it. And I was thirty-nine at the time and hadn't long had India, which was a ventouse birth. Like someone putting a toilet plunger to your twinkle. Sheer madness, sweetness, to bend middle-aged legs that far, but I was in love.'

James said: 'Ah right,' in a small voice and swigged his coffee.

'No, let me tell you two things about Anna— ' Fi clicked her fingers at the waiter. 'Hot water? Marv. You're a treasure. Firstly, none of us have ever seen you as relaxed as you were at the fifth birthday party.'

'Really?' James was genuinely surprised.

'You are a fabulous boy, James, but you can look a little … tense sometimes. You positively *lit up* around her. Everyone noticed it. You wore this look where you couldn't wait to hear what she was going to say next. The James Dean pose is all very well, but laughter is important. Trust me, it's what a relationship needs, more than double-joints.

'Secondly, she is silly infatuated with you. You've not lost her yet, but be quick about it, because women like her don't stay single for long.'

Despite Fi being wrong in nearly every single respect, James was intrigued.

'You honestly think she's that into me?' he asked, not knowing if this question was acting or real. Both, he decided.

'Darling,' Fi put a Chanel nail-polished hand on his arm. 'She's utterly smit-swoo. You should've heard her on the phone to me saying that sending the file was a crime of passion, and she's normally the most level-headed woman in the world. You bring the special crazy out in her … and I *mustn't* punish you for her mistake. I said, dear heart, I thought it was funny. If we all had our pillow talk on tape, none of us would come out well.'

He felt deep gratitude towards Anna, goodwill aided by his unexpected reprieve. She might've helped incept this drama, but she'd certainly put aside her dignity to dig him out. It couldn't have been easy to say those florid things. Anna wasn't a natural fake.

'And let me tell you something else, as someone who's got twenty years of living on you …'

Arf, more like pushing thirty, James thought. Though right now he'd be prepared to agree Fi was the correct age for cheerleader try-outs.

'You don't meet many Annas. How old are you now? Thirty-two, righto. Think of it this way: if it took thirty-two years to find her, it could quite easily take another thirty-two to find someone else who measures up to her. Do you want to wait until you're in your retirement villa in Cap D'Antibes, with face lifts that make you look like you've been shot out of a cannon, or do you want to be happy now?'

As it had turned out, it actually took eleven years to find Anna, but James didn't raise this point of order. It occurred to him it might be wise to foreshadow the possible return of Eva, right about now. He realised he'd not been thinking about his ex-wife as much lately. He could at least thank work aggro for that.

'The problem was …' James said, 'it wasn't … it's not fully over with my wife.'

Fi stirred her coffee and nodded.

'I thought it might be that. Why did you separate?'

326

'Eva suffered from a spiritual disenchantment and loss of purpose that had to be eased by shagging a model. Oh and apparently I talked too much to a friend's wife at a dinner party about politics once.'

'Far be it from me to tell you what to do, darling, but if she's run off and had intercourse with another man in Year One of your marriage, it doesn't bode terribly well for the cuckolding she might be doing by Year Ten, does it? Year One for a wife should be about choosing Cole & Son wallpaper and having so much sex, she's left too bandy-legged to stop a pig in a corridor, ahahaha!'

Mad. Completely mad. James laughed uneasily. 'She was having lots of sex, just not with me.'

He paused.

'We did say for better, for worse.'

'Now, this is interesting,' Fi said, surveying him over her coffee foam. 'I was going to give you a lecture about you being too beautiful and thus afflicted with too much choice. However, someone still being loyal to the unfaithful ex-spouse? James Fraser, are you a romantic?'

'I don't know about that,' James smiled. 'Maybe too old and lazy not to be monogamous.'

It was a strange urge, given he'd come so close to disaster, to risk causing further waves.

However, James found himself sighing and barrelling on recklessly. 'Fi, I did a good job with UCL because I loved the work. Meanwhile, I spent this morning with a bloke who wants us to help him spaff his inheritance away on making flavoured cheese worms. I just can't work up much enthusiasm for the frivolous stuff lately.'

James thought Fi might fix him with steely eyes and say that frivolity was their bread and butter and cheese worms.

'I should perhaps be looking to move on instead of ungraciously whining, I guess. Sorry. *Things not to say to your boss.*' He ran his hands through his hair.

Fi looked thoughtful.

'Jez and I have been talking about making your role more focused, having a little re org. We know you're good and ambitious and we don't want to see you drift off to one of the new kids on the block, a Brand Pipe or Stuff Hammer . . .'

She went on to outline how James could have a promotion, his pick of the clients, a brief to find more prestigious accounts like UCL and even the flexibility to work from home. He tried not to lean across the table and hug Fi. Who knew honesty could be this effective?

'I'm not coming in,' Fi said, as they stood by the office doors. She leaned in to do a double air-kiss farewell. She caught his face in her hand, a move James found acutely embarrassing.

'This beard?'

'Yes?'

'Lose it, darling. It worked for Ben Affleck in *Argo*, but he was pulling all-nighters in an Iranian hostage crisis during the 1970s. We want to see more of your lovely face.'

Feeling light with relief, James knew he owed Anna a thank you. He also knew neither of them wanted another conversation. He opened an email.

What you said to Fi went over and above. You entirely saved my arse.

Sincere thanks.
Jx

Time ticked by, there was no answer. He wasn't surprised given that their most recent encounters couldn't have spelled THE END any more decisively than the last frame in a Metro-Goldwyn-Mayer cinematic epic, letters ten foot high, screen to black.

Then, as he was weighing his phone in his hand and wondering if he should simply call Anna to thank her properly, he got the message from Laurence he'd been dreading.

Great news! Allied invasion was a success, Italy has finally joined the war! ☺

A bad taste rose in his throat. He swallowed.

Laurence's plan to call Anna, apologise for the Mock Rock and wheedle his way into ... what could euphemistically could be called *her good books* had worked? This was the sort of language that Laurence only used when he'd landed a lady.

All at once, his happiness dissipated, to be replaced with a miserable tumult of uncertainty, regret and a sensation he could only call pain.

56

'Aureliana, why aren't you answering your mobile?!' her mum wailed.

'Oh, it's er. In a drawer,' Anna said, worrying that it was highly unusual for her mum to call her on the office landline.

'Have you heard from your sister?' Judy squawked.

'No, why, is— '

'The wedding is off! Aggy and Chris have split up!'

'What? Slow down, Mum …' Anna said, as she started gabbling.

With an infuriating sense of having felt it would come to pass, but none of the satisfaction of being able to say she'd done anything much to prevent it, Anna heard the full story.

How Aggy had been lying to Chris about the wedding costs, and the huge credit card debt she'd built up. Chris had opened a Visa letter marked for Aggy by mistake, seen what they were in for, and immediately called the Langham to cancel their booking. Aggy had come home, found out what he'd done and, far from being contrite, all hell had broken loose. She'd stormed out, leaving dutiful Chris to call her parents with the sorry news.

'And now she won't speak to me! She won't answer her phone! You try and talk some sense into her, Aureliana!'

Anna restrained herself from pointing out that she'd tried to warn her mum about this.

'How's Chris?'

'He's very upset. Aggy had spent fourteen thousand she hadn't told him about.'

Anna felt a little faint. '*Fourteen* thousand? How is she ever going to repay that?'

'Chris thinks there might be more. And they've lost the deposit at the Langham. Your father's gone for a lie down.'

Anna loved her father but he was, as ever, comatose in a crisis.

'We can't find her. She won't answer her phone to us.'

'She's not at her friend Marianne's? She usually goes there in times of crisis. There, or the nearest All Bar One.'

'No! No one can raise her. Oh God, what will we tell the family about the wedding …'

'Mum,' Anna finally snapped, 'isn't Aggy and Chris's relationship a bit more important than losing face in front of the likes of Aunty Bev? And as much as I love my sister, it sounds like Chris needed to stop the meter running.'

'But it's such a shame. Your sister will be in pieces. It's all she's thought about for months.'

Yes. There was a lot Anna could say to her mother about the wisdom of encouraging Aggy to be so consumed by it since day one. But now wasn't the time.

She yanked her mobile out and called Aggy, expecting to be ignored. But unexpectedly, her sister answered.

'I suppose you're going to say I told you so!' she barked.

'I want to check you're OK.'

'It's all over, Anna. With me and Chris. Completely over.'

'Don't say that. It's a fight and it can be sorted.'

'How? Have you got twenty grand? Can you get the Langham to put it all back on after Chris *cancelled it*?' Aggy wailed.

Anna couldn't entirely exonerate Chris, as much as she wanted to. He'd pulled the plug on this ruinous folly, but he should've taken a closer interest in the decisions being made to begin with.

As much as his fiancée had dug their financial hole, it needed to be agreed jointly. It was going to be a struggle to get Aggy to see reason when her beloved big day had been snatched from her.

'Let me come and meet you. Where are you?'

Anna could hear traffic noise and the whoosh of blustery street noises from Aggy's end.

'I'm going out to get hammered and enjoy being single again.'

'Come on, you're not single. You and Chris will get through this . . .'

Anna heard the off-stage murmur of a male voice.

'Who's with you?' she said. Aggy's friends were all female.

'Laurence,' Aggy said. 'Laurence is taking me out for cock-tails. I'll talk to you later, Anna. Bye!'

'Laurence?!' Anna said in a shriek, but it was too late, Aggy had already rung off.

She hit redial to Aggy, fuming. *Laurence*. What the hell? Why would he of all people be taking her out on the town? But she knew better than most that his interest in her sister would be principally crotch-based. How did he even have Aggy's number— ? James's words about Laurence's machinations with women crowded her head.

The phone you have called, has been switched off

Think, she told herself. Calm down and think. She could only imagine that Laurence had decided to move on to her sister, and she'd found out moments too late to warn Aggy that he was not a man to get blind drunk with when you were feeling vulnerable.

Oh, hell. Having gone through fluster and irritation, Anna felt herself tipping into twitchy, useless panic. This wasn't a worry she could share with her parents, either. And definitely not Chris.

Anna paced round her office. She tried Aggy again, after waiting fifteen minutes. Nope, Aggy had turned her phone off and it was likely staying that way. It didn't take her long to get drunk. She called Laurence three times. His phone was on, but it rang through to voicemail. She had the distinct feeling he wouldn't answer a call from her this evening.

There was only one option left. He was the last person she wanted to speak to, but she had no choice.

57

'Hi, James,' she said, trying to sound conciliatory, neutral and deeply dignified. 'I'm sorry to bother you. Twice in one day. Lucky you.'

He seemed mildly taken aback and equally guarded, if polite.

She went on to outline Aggy's marital and financial predicament, and her current choice of company.

'You know him best. Would he do something as low as bedding my sister? Please tell me I'm just being paranoid …' she concluded, hopelessly.

A pause.

'Uhm. I think you know what I'm going to say. I did try to warn you what he was like.'

'How did he even have Aggy's number?'

She hoped James hadn't handed it over.

'Laurence collects attractive women's numbers like most of us collect Nectar points. He'll have tapped her up for it at the theatre, I guess. Or found her online.'

'Oh, no …'

Silence. Anna appreciated he must still be pretty angry about the recording. She gritted her teeth and cursed Aggy deeply.

'Would you know where they are?' Anna said. 'I wouldn't ask but I'm out of ideas and very worried about where this could be headed, with the two personalities involved.'

'Where Laurence takes women? Wouldn't *you* have as good an idea as me?'

Anna didn't quite understand this, especially as it was said in the tone of having a swipe.

'I've tried calling him and he's not answering. He's with my sister, up to no good, so he won't. Could you try to speak to him?'

'And say what?'

'Anything that will get him to reveal his location.'

Eventually, after a long pause, James said, in a clipped voice: 'OK, I'll call you back.'

Her phone buzzed seconds later.

'Sorry, Anna, his phone's turned off.'

'Oh no. This is such a mess …' Anna couldn't speak for a moment, trying to quell the lava-bubble of frustration in her gut.

'Does Aggy know you've … er. Been out with Laurence too?'

'I didn't mention it. Which is why this is my fault. If I was a normal, relaxed sister who shared things, I'd have told her that Laurence was a cad.'

Anna could sense James's desire to finish this phone call but her need to confide in someone overtook her.

'I know what happens next. Aggy gets howling drunk, falls into bed with Laurence and ruins any chance of a reconciliation with Chris. Worst-case scenario, she even convinces herself that Laurence is a sensible person to date, before he drops her from a height in however many weeks' time.'

'You really think she'll do that? She's still engaged isn't she?'

'Technically, she's thrown the ring at Chris and called it off.'

'Look, I'll try Loz again, they're probably on the Underground.'

'James,' Anna said, pinching the bridge of her nose. 'They're not on the Tube. They've both turned their phones off so none of us can reach them while they can get on with their night out.'

Pause.

'Yeah. Does fit Laurence's MO.'

'God, I could kick myself.'

'This is up to Aggy and not you, though. If your sister doesn't want to get married you can't make her.'

'She really does want to get married though. This is all she's talked about for months.'

'But you fear she's going to spontaneously bonk Loz on her first night of freedom? Strong statement.'

'Right now she's angry and she hasn't thought it through. All this emotion will get fruity alcohol poured on top of it and she won't think straight. And then Laurence will pounce.'

Pause.

'OK, forgive me for saying this, but plan B. If she does have a lapse of judgement with Loz, does anyone else ever need to know?'

'My sister is a terrible liar. I mean, why not get the Visa bills sent to work? This'll come out too, sooner or later, especially when Chris works out that none of her friends and family know where she is tonight.'

Anna stared at a mildewed milk bottle of water next to Boris the yucca plant. 'It's like I left a gun lying around, with the safety catch off.'

'Woah there, you can't control all human interaction you know. You don't usually need to warn engaged people about the snakes in the grass. And even when you do, people make their own choices. As you know.'

'Nothing stops me from feeling responsible for having intro-duced them, I'm afraid. Well, I guess I have a fun and pointless evening of trawling Aggy's favourite haunts ahead of me, then.'

They ended the call, politely and yet stiffly. James sounded distracted, to Anna's ears. As if his mind was whirring. No doubt wondering how these chaotic, vulgar Mediterraneans ever came to be mixed up in his gleaming world.

It was an infuriating fact of life that having large things to worry about didn't manage to cancel out lesser concerns.

Her sister's loss of a wonderful fiancé, and the addition of a credit card millstone, were the biggies. The thought of Laurence chalking up her little sister as a notch on his bed post was abhorrent.

So right now, why did Anna care what James Fraser thought of her? And why did she wish so desperately that she hadn't had to lose face and ask for his help? It wasn't as if it had made any difference.

58

James was well enough acquainted with Laurence's tomcat-ting procedure that he had a shortlist of a half dozen locations where he might be.

Finding them was only job one, however. He didn't have much of a plan if he did discover them. The natives might be hostile. Well, Laurence would definitely be hostile, to a greater or lesser extent. Aggy, he couldn't tell.

Why was he doing this? He had no easy answer.

Three bars down in the hunt and he started to feel faintly absurd. Laurence was the lanky needle in London's haystack. By the time James was scanning the low-lit occupants of the rust-coloured velvet sofas at The Zetter, his fatalism had all but told him it was futile.

Somewhere in the vastness of the night-time city beyond these handsome windows, Laurence was sitting in some other anonymous bar, arm draped round Aggy's seat. Telling her the anecdote about the identical sisters in Courcheval that James was certain wasn't true. There was no such thing as twin telepathy.

He'd become so sure his mission was a lost cause, James was startled when he suddenly spotted an exuberantly drunk

Aggy. She was sprawled on a brocade armchair, dress ridden up so far you could see the gusset of her tights. She was alone, yet a drink on the other side of the table said that this wasn't for long.

James squared his shoulders and headed into battle.

Aggy sat bolt upright at the sight of him.

'James! What are you doing here? This is 'mazin'!'

Thank goodness, she was alright with him at least.

James grinned at her. Aggy's glassy, starry eyes and her enthusiastic patting of the space next to her told James she was utterly trollied.

'I've gotta bone to pick with you,' Aggy slurred. 'You called my sister a freak.'

James cringed. That's why he was here. He had arrears to pay off with Anna.

'I should never have said that,' he said. He looked at Aggy's dark curls and eyes and felt a pang at her resemblance. 'I apologise.'

'You should 'pologise to *her*,' Aggy harrumphed. She pushed her hair out of the way and, lifting her glass to her lips, let go of a small burp. 'For school too.'

'I don't think she wants to see me ever again,' James said.

'No, she doesn't,' Aggy agreed. 'She said she wished she'd never met you.'

James nodded, and swallowed hard.

'It was worse, you know,' Aggy said, sounding suddenly lucid.

James's head jerked up. 'What?'

'It was worse for her than you think.'

Aggy held his gaze and James had that spooky sense of a metaphorical shape moving in the shadows. There was something he knew he didn't know, but he couldn't work out what it might be.

At the back of the bar, Laurence appeared. His expression darkened as he saw James and came to various conclusions.

'James is here! What a co ... corin ... coinci–dunce,' Aggy said.

'Calculate the odds,' James said to Laurence. 'I think it was, ooh, one in eight?'

Laurence's eyes were no more than slits.

'Loz has got me the best cocktail, try, try!' Aggy handed James the heavy-bottomed glass tumbler. 'It's called The Flintlock. It's got Ferret Banker in it.'

'Fernet Branca,' Laurence muttered.

'The Flintlock, eh? Should be The Headlock,' he said to Laurence, whose frown deepened still further. He sipped. 'Mmm. Nice. Can't beat a bit of Ferret Banker.'

He glanced at Laurence.

'Anna says you and Chris had a fight?' James said to Aggy, setting the glass back down.

'Yeah,' Aggy's brow furrowed, and she pulled the dress over her thighs. 'Wedding's off. He's bin a wanker 'bout it.'

'You haven't been answering your phone?'

'Laurence said to turn it off,' Aggy said.

'I thought Loz might be your PR and comms man,' James said, smiling at a feral-looking Laurence. 'Anna's trying to get hold of you.'

'You talked to Anna? Is she with Chris?' Aggy said, trying to concentrate.

'No, or at least, she wasn't. How about you turn your phone on and let her know you're OK?'

'She'll only tell me off about spendin' all the money. She's mad at me, like they all are.'

'She isn't. I know that for sure. She only wants to know you're OK. Can I tell her you're here?'

'Nooooo!' Aggy's boozed eyes widened and she pointed a finger. 'Do *not* do that.'

James put both palms up in supplication. 'OK, OK.'

'I've got to go to the ladies,' Aggy said. 'Don't go anywhere,' she pointed at James, with the vehemence of a drunk person. 'Promise you'll stay.'

'I promise on Laurence's life, I'm not going anywhere,' James said, making a cross on his chest with a finger.

She backed away, tripping over a low footstool.

When Aggy was safely out of earshot, James turned to Laurence.

'She's engaged, Loz.'

'And? I didn't force her here.'

'They've had a fight and she's very drunk. But she's still engaged.'

'Her engagement is not my responsibility. Not my circus, not my monkeys.'

'Not your fiancée. So I'm going to take Aggy home.'

'She's a grown woman. Who are you to tell her what to do?'

'I'm not going to tell her what to do. I'll point out that going home might be a good idea and I'll offer to take her. If she's determined to sleep with you and insists on staying, then fine. Something tells me she's not as clear on the end game here as you are though.'

'Such chivalry. And you're doing this for nothing are you? Not looking for a gold star from her sister?'

'Nope,' James took another swig of Aggy's cocktail and winced as it hit the back of his throat.

'Yeah right. A self-interested, white knighting cockblock. Some best friend you turned out to be.'

'Oh right, we're pulling the mates card are we? Right then, I'm asking you to leave Aggy alone as a favour to me. Or does this ...' – James gestured between the two of them – 'count for nothing when a woman's involved? Every man for himself?'

'You tell me.'

'What?'

'Why did Anna hate me so much?'

'Er ... wasn't it because of everything you said and did?'

'She hated me because you positioned yourself as Mr Nicest Guy in the Room, and dripped poison in her ear about me being Mr Nasty.'

'You're going to bed her drunk sister, and you think someone else cast you as Mr Nasty?'

'Trouble with you is, you've convinced yourself that your act isn't an act. Classic case of reading your own press and it going to your head. We're no different.'

James laughed in disbelief. Laurence's self-justification was like a maze. He'd designed it and closed off all the exits: once inside his logic, you couldn't escape.

As James stared at Laurence, full of sullen antagonism, he knew that his disappointment in Laurence was vastly outweighed by disappointment in himself. What was lowering was not who Laurence was, it was who he wasn't. There was so little here, beyond cheap quips and low cunning.

And James had made him his best friend? What did that say about him? He thought Laurence suited his pragmatic cynicism; his 'no bullshit' sense of humour. Now he realised that in fact, Laurence appealed to all his worst traits. Judging, mocking, disdaining. Never caring.

James had spent his whole life thinking he was better than other people. And what had he achieved? A wife who didn't love him, a best friend who didn't like him and a cat that didn't know how to crap outdoors.

Maybe it was too late to put a lot right, but he could at least try to put this right.

'Do you want me to call Anna and make a scene? Or can we conduct this respectably and I'll take Aggy home?'

Laurence gave him a lopsided, lupine smile.

'I'm not going anywhere. Good luck with your powers of persuasion, Derren Brown.'

James debated what to do. He had a feeling that some subtlety was called for. He could call Anna and then stage a sit-in – refusing to leave until she'd arrived. But given Aggy was in a volatile mood, being babysat, and then the sudden appearance of her overwrought sibling ordering her to leave, might piss her off and completely backfire. Perhaps the softly-softly approach was safer.

Aggy reappeared and flopped onto the sofa. 'Cor I haven't eaten all day. Reckon they'd do bar snacks?'

'Great idea, want to get some food with me?' James asked.

'Or what about another drink?' Laurence added.

'Oh,' Aggy looked at the centimetre of liquid left in her glass, and from James to Laurence and back again. 'Yeah. I was going to try a Rose Petal thingy actually.'

'Marvellous idea,' Laurence said, clicking his fingers at the barman.

James turned to Aggy. He gambled on a hunch that Aggy truly didn't know who she was dealing with here.

'Laurence has booked a suite. When you're sufficiently legless, he will help you upstairs, invite you to use the minibar, then help you out of your clothes. If you want to do that, go ahead. But just as long as you know.'

'Remind us, are you her AA sponsor or her father?' Laurence said.

'Seriously?' Aggy said, looking at Laurence. 'You have a room?'

Laurence barely blinked.

'No,' he said, after a second's pause. 'Why, do you want one?'

Aggy giggled. James sensed the argument slipping away from him.

The barman arrived and Laurence ordered two cocktails and nothing for James. Inspiration struck.

'Could you put that on Laurence O'Grady's room tab, please?' James said.

'Certainly sir.'

He retreated with a nod.

'Whaddyaknow!' James said.

'He doesn't know if I have one. He's not going to query it to our faces, is he?'

'I guess we'll know when he comes back then?' James said. 'No bill, means Laurence is a big old fibber.'

'Sod off, will you?' Laurence spat. 'You're not wanted here.'

'Yeah he is!' Aggy said. 'Why would we not want him?'

Laurence glowered. He'd let his irritation at James win out. Aggy looked at Laurence in consternation. James hoped that Laurence's flash of temper had penetrated the fog of Ferret Banker.

'So what if I do have a room, anyway?' Laurence added.

'You *did* book a room?' Aggy said, tugging her dress down over her thighs and looking less certain.

'I don't. I'm saying, so what if I had? We're all adults.'

'You thought I was going to go to bed with you, just like that?' Aggy said.

'No!' Laurence rattled the ice in his glass. 'Don't listen to this one. He's playing the Good Samaritan to get into your sister's kecks.'

Aggy frowned.

'Anna doesn't want to see him.'

'What a shame,' Laurence said. 'And I wonder what sort of selfless act might change her mind?'

Laurence was misjudging this by running James down. The idea James was doing something purely to please Anna didn't offend Aggy in the same way. And Aggy looked as if she was wondering why James separating her from Laurence would make her sister so ecstatic.

'Hmmm. No sign of that bill I asked him to put on your non-existent room tab, is there?' James said, as Laurence glared and Aggy looked slightly forlorn.

James stood up. He needed to exploit this moment of being ahead.

'Aggy. How about you come with me? I reckon you'll dodge the hangover if you find a carb now.'

'OK,' Aggy said, after a second's hesitation. 'Sorry.'

'Hey, no skin off my dick, princess,' Laurence said, with real venom.

Aggy looked startled.

'Well lock that tongue up with the rest of the silverware,'

James said, tutting.

'Don't call me again,' Laurence said to James.

'Your famous catchphrase! And I didn't even have to put out to hear it.' James swigged from one of the two cocktails. 'Laurence. You have my word you won't.'

59

James briefly contemplated public transport, then assessed Aggy's level of inebriation and thought again. He didn't fancy manhandling a rag doll of a woman on and off the Tube.

She stood shivering as he fruitlessly tried to flag the cabs zooming past. He took his coat off and handed it to her.

'Are we getting Burger King?' she said. 'I feel a bit sick.' Her jaw juddered slightly.

'Maybe bed is best,' he said. 'No barfing in the cab.'

He rang Anna and offered to deliver her. '*One sister, slightly soiled but not despoiled.*' She was amazed and relieved, having just got home after her own hopeless search. It made him feel very glad he'd bothered.

A Hackney finally slowed to a stop and they got in. Aggy rested her head on his shoulder while he steadied himself, as the cab hummed and rattled its way through the city.

'What's up with you, then? Is it really over with your bloke?'

'Chris cancelled my weddin'! I will never forgive him.'

'Only because you couldn't afford it. He didn't do it to upset you. It sounds like he's done a lot of things to make you happy, but you've got to make him happy too. Spending money you don't have was clearly too much for him.'

'It was my dream though. I'd planned every last part.'

'Aggy, your wedding day isn't the be all and end all. It's the marriage part that's the important thing. I had one of those *look at us* weddings where you can reel off a checklist of all your great choices. It's not all that. Don't live life through Instagram.'

'You're jus' sayin' that. I bet your wedding was the coolest of the cool.'

'I'm not, honestly, Aggy. You get so drowned in the detail you forget that none of it matters. Absolutely no one, including you, will give a toss the next day whether you had garlic and juniper sausages for the wedding breakfast or not. Unless the sausages were off, I suppose.'

'Think you'd get married again?' Aggy asked.

'Hah. Not bloody likely, no matter who the future holds.' James paused. This wasn't helping the noble cause. 'You love Chris, right? He's the man for you?'

Aggy snuffled in assent on James's shoulder.

'What you don't realise is you're better off than most people before you start. One in three marriages has got that bit wrong. Mine included.'

'But it's such a *comedown*. I know I sound like a brat but when your heart's set on something it's like anything else is second best. I'd looked everywhere in London and the Langham was perfect.'

'Why do you have to stay in London?'

'It's where we live.'

'Yeah, but you're half-Italian, right? That's a great excuse to go abroad.'

'Yeah, but my dad's not from Milan or Rome or anywhere swish. They're halfway up a mountain.'

'Exactly. Marrying there won't be a cliché or break the bank. Hire a nice big barn in a village, get yourself some dirt cheap flights, done. It will make it a wedding to remember. How many of your friends are getting wed in …?'

'It's called Barga,' Aggy said.

'Barga. See? Special as a snowflake.'

'But who will be there?'

'Everyone you wanted to be there in London? Seriously, if they wanted to be there, they will do everything they can to make it. And if they don't, well. Exactly.'

'Mmmm. Guess so.'

The taxi engine throbbed as they sat in traffic. Looking over at Aggy, James could see the cogs seemed to be turning.

'I suppose the venue wouldn't be that much … and there's quite a few bed and breakfasts and things … What about the hen do? That was a weekend in Ibiza. Will it have to be here now?'

'What about Michelle's place? She has a restaurant. I'd love to have a mate with a restaurant.'

'Yeah …?' Aggy was sitting more upright.

'My dress though,' she sagged again. 'I can't have my dress. I've got a bonus in January but it'll be too late.'

James wrestled with how far he was going to take this soul-cleansing. Sod it. In for a penny, in for …

'How much do you need?'

'Two thousand.'

'I can lend you that.'

'Seriously?!' Aggy bit her lip. 'I should probably say no, shouldn't I? Anna would tell me to say no.'

'Well, despite your outbreaks of spendthrift hyperactivity,

you seem for the most part a sane and salaried person. You can pay me back in a few months' time?'

'I'll pay you by the end of January! Total swear-down promise.'

'Then I won't miss it and it's not a problem. I suggest we keep this between the two of us though.'

'You're 'mazin', James Fraser,' she said.

The taxi finally pulled up at Anna's.

Aggy shot the clasp on her seatbelt and returned his coat. He waved away her attempts to fumble with her purse and helped her out of the cab. He wasn't completely sure if he wanted to see Anna or not but he didn't get the chance to dodge her, as her front door opened, light spilling out over the scrubby front path.

There was much tutting and hugging and Aggy tottered into the flat, muttering about bagels with Nutella.

'Thank you,' Anna said, arms tightly wound over her chest and jumper sleeves pulled over her hands in the bitter cold. 'I've been to every All Bar One within a five-mile radius and was just about ready to start howling at the moon. Did she pay you for the cab, can I give you something?'

'She paid, don't worry,' James said. They smiled awkwardly and tightly.

'Sorry. You did warn me about Laurence. I didn't imagine he'd launch himself at Aggy.'

'Yeah, you and him – it was never going to end well.'

Anna frowned. 'The ice rink date? You think he had a grudge because I wouldn't see him again?'

'I thought you'd met up again recently?'

Anna was quizzical.

'No?'

James felt a stab of hopefulness that made him a little reckless.

'You haven't shagged him?' *Yeah, could've phrased that better, James.*

'Of course not. The last contact I had with Laurence was some grimy email blaming the Mock Rock plot entirely on you. He said he knew how I felt cos he'd once had a sales presentation "go banana shaped". I told him to get bent. Thanks for telling him who I am, by the way.'

James stuttered. 'God … sorry. Loz sent me a text message saying something about Italy … joining the war …'

Anna shifted her weight to her other foot.

'From one vague text message, you assume that?'

'Ah. Uhm. Mea culpa,' James said.

'Your meter's running,' Anna said, shivering. She turned back and followed Aggy into the flat.

As James climbed back into the taxi, his white knight's black chariot, he figured it out. That text had referred to Aggy, not Anna.

No doubt when Laurence had finally given up on Anna, he'd turned to his second choice. It wasn't an accident that Laurence had created this confusion – he wanted to see if James reacted angrily, to prove his theory that James was after Anna.

So much for earning brownie points, anyway. After a lavish gesture that ought to have gone some way to restoring his tattered reputation with Anna, James had done a great job of plucking defeat from the jaws of victory by offending her with that presumption. He ought to be cursing himself.

But, it turned out she *hadn't* fooled around with Laurence?

James didn't expect that knowledge to make him feel so chipper.

When the cab pulled up at his house and the driver asked him for an exorbitant total, James's reflection in the rear view mirror revealed that without realising it, he'd been smiling.

60

'And so it's all sorted? It's going to be in Italy?' Michelle said.

'It's in Italy and you're both invited. My sister's largesse is still large enough for you.'

Aggy's squealy excitement over her nuptials had previously seen her invite the butcher, the baker and the candlestick maker, but her impulse to include Michelle and Daniel was quite sincere. Aggy loved Michelle as Anna's best friend and thought of Daniel and his girlfriend as part of the Anna package.

'Nice one. I need a holiday,' Michelle said, sorting cards with her e-fag wedged in the mouth, like a proper card sharp.

'It's Princess Di, Queen of Hearts! Queen of Hearts, ladies and gents,' called a sing-song voice, over a microphone.

Michelle turned a card over. She was trialling a new head chef and had a rare weeknight off. She demanded Anna and Daniel join her for a game of Sticky 13 at an old men's pub in Islington.

'Yep,' Anna said, aligning her cards in colour co-ordinated rows. 'My sister's event planning skills kicked in. She was like a UN diplomat in Uggs. I took Chris for a drink while she hammered through Italian websites, with my dad on the phone, translating. Chris and I agreed that for the good of their relationship, we should collude behind Aggy's back more. It turned out he'd had serious doubts about the bills and she'd told him I was overlooking her financial management to put his mind at rest! Luckily Chris has enough for a much more modest wedding while Aggy's sorting repayments on the card bill. And the Maldives honeymoon has been swapped for staying on in Tuscany.'

Anna sipped her drink.

'My parents are overjoyed with the new location because it means all my dad's older relatives can go. And everyone who's met Aunty Bev is overjoyed that she's said she's boycotting because she hates foreign food and budget airlines. If it wasn't for Aggy's debt I'd say I'm glad it happened. And thanks for saying you'd host the hen night!'

'Total pleasure,' Michelle said. 'From what Aggy says of her friends, I'll make more from them thrashing the bar tab than I would from a full house on a Saturday anyway.' She leaned across Daniel. 'What kind of system is that?'

Daniel had his cards in a whirlpool on the table in front of him, with no care for colour, card value or suit.

'All makes sense to me,' he said.

'Three of Spades! Three of Spades, ladies and gents,' said the caller.

Daniel turned it over. 'See. Not missing anything.'

'God, I wish I hadn't had to ask for James Fraser's help.'

'You said he sorted it pretty well though?'

'Yeeeees,' Anna conceded. 'But between Patrick and Aggy I've had to eat two lots of humble pie with him. I could've really done without that. And it was completely out of order that he accused me of sleeping with Laurence!'

'Laurence is a bit of a lad though? He was probably boasting.'

'Yes, but. To think I'd do *that*.'

'Sex is a thing that sometimes happens, my love. Not much to me anymore, granted,' Michelle said.

'Jack of Clubs! Jack of Clubs, if you please!' called the compere. Michelle turned a card over. 'At last!'

As bickering over the game continued, Anna's mind drifted to James. She didn't quite know why him thinking she'd sleep with Laurence upset her. She'd gone on a date with Laurence, after all. She'd never explicitly ruled it out. Yet James believing that really did bother her. Had it bothered him, the idea of her and Laurence, in flagrante? He'd not been a fan of that ice rink trip, after all. She couldn't tell. He'd still done her the favour of acquiring Aggy, so it mustn't have bothered him that much. Unless it was a straight like-for-like payback after the Fi phonecall? That had been a strange one, hearing James's boss wax lyrical about how she thought Anna had a miraculous effect on him – 'We all noticed that he couldn't keep his eyes off you, that night at the bowling.'

Had that been true? Probably tracking her to make sure she didn't do anything to shame him, like a store security guard monitoring a possible shoplifter.

'Dan, I forgot to say that obviously your invite to Aggy's nuptials is a plus one with Penny,' Anna said, absently.

'Thank you. I don't think I can go,' Daniel said, shuffling his cards.

Michelle and Anna looked at each other.

'I can't leave The Pantry.'

'Don't be soft. There's plenty of cover.'

'I can't afford it,' Daniel said.

'It will be pricier than other weddings of course, what with the flights, but it's also a nice excuse for a holiday,' Anna said.

'Yeah. Penny's talking about doing an MA in conservation. So it's time to tighten our belts.'

'Isn't it time for her to tighten her belt?' Michelle asked.

'We support each other,' Daniel said.

'So she's going to work full time when you decide to do an MPhil?'

'Conservation, sounds interesting!' Anna interjected, nervously.

'This is no reason to miss this wedding,' Michelle said. 'I'm not having it. In fact, I'm giving you a raise.'

'Eh?' Daniel said.

'Michelle, you don't have to …' Anna began.

'It's sorted. You got a raise, you can come.'

Daniel blinked his big eyes. 'Easiest raise I ever got.'

'Two of Clubs!' cried the caller.

'Sticky 13!' Daniel said, doing a two-arm air punch. 'I've won!'

'Winner buys the round,' Michelle said.

Daniel ambled up to the bar.

'You are so generous,' Anna said to Michelle.

'Pffft, I was underpaying the stupid beardy-weirdy anyway. Loads of people want him. And do you know what he said to some woman who was being a cow about her moules marinières, last week? She announces: "Don't contradict me, I am a cancer survivor!" And he replies: "Then I'd have thought you can put the disappointment of these molluscs in their proper perspective, madam." I swear he should do stand up. A whole group nearby clapped. She's flamed me on Toptable of course,

356

but it was worth it.'

'Oh God, that's funny. Am I allowed to find that funny?' Anna said, hand over mouth.

'What's funnier is that she called them moules "marine air" throughout the attack on my attention to detail with saucing.'

Michelle put her e-fag down and took a swig of vodka tonic.

'It's not Dan I resent paying, it's her. *An MA in conservation,*' Michelle said to Anna. 'Penny's an expert in conserving her own energy, am I right?'

61

James was hurtling towards Highbury & Islington on the over-
ground when he had the epiphany. It arrived while he was
staring at a discarded *Metro* on the floor and listening to the
rattle-shake from the iPod of the person next to him. What
psychopath would listen to 'Gangnam Style' before nine in the
morning? All of a sudden, doing something about the heavy
pall that had settled in his stomach didn't seem an impossibility.
It was the only thing to do.

He bounded out of the train doors and up the stairs, pushing against the tide of commuters, through the ticket barriers
and out to the freedom of the fresh air.

He hit 'Work' on his phone. *Please be Lexie please be Lexie
please be Lexie please be Lexie* … Harris.

'Hi mate, I'm not going to be in today.' James thought as
he was pulling a sickie, he should try to be ingratiating. 'I've
puked up and I've got a feeling there's going to be a bad sequel.
Maybe two, like *The Matrix*. Could even go to *Pirates of the
Caribbean* numbers.'

There was a sceptical pause on the other end of the line.

'Where are you? It sounds noisy.'

'Highbury. I had to find a waste bin here, fast.'

'There aren't any waste bins at stations.'

'No, well done Inspector Wexford, that was in the street. Do you want me to go and take a phone pic of the evidence for you?'

'Nah. You've ruined my chorizo hash brown as it is. Is it anything contagious?'

'I think it's more likely last night's leftover rice from the Chinese than SARS, but thanks for your concern.'

James turned his phone off and worked out his route. He'd walk. He'd quite like to clear his head. If London's morning traffic fumes could help you clear anything.

Anna was walking across the lawn in front of the grand colonnades of the main building, her breath making ghosts in the freezing air.

Across the quad, she noticed a blurred figure striding purposefully towards her. She suddenly placed the black hair and dark blue coat, as the rest of the features came into focus.

Her heart jumped up to block her throat and she pushed it back down where it belonged and gritted her teeth. She was annoyed with him, not nervous. So why did she feel nervous?

James reached her. He looked apprehensive. It was a strange time of day to turn up. Uh oh. Was this going to be the 'it was a long time ago, we're all adults, let bygone be bygones . . .'? Anna came to a halt with some reluctance.

'Hi. Can I talk to you?'

'What about?'

'School. About what happened.'

'I've got nothing to say about that.'

'Will you listen while I talk, then?'

Anna shrugged.

'I want to say how sorry I am. It was awful and cruel and I can't imagine how badly it hurt you. All I can say is that I was an utter fucking fool when I was sixteen years old and I can only hope I've improved since then, if far too slowly.

'And I'm sorry I was an idiot when you confronted me with it, and used a horrible word. It was a lot to take in. I was in shock and blurted those things because you were angry with me and I was ashamed of how I'd behaved. I can't believe what I said. All I should've done is given you a grovelling apology, and it's shameful that I didn't manage even that.'

Pause.

'I've asked myself countless times since that night at yours, how I could have done what I did at school. The truth was, I blocked out the fact that you were another human being with feelings. I decided you brought it on yourself by being different. I played along with the group to be popular. I wish my character had been stronger, but it wasn't.'

'Done?' she asked.

'... In essence?' James looked quite fearful of her. *Good.* 'I wanted you to know how sorry I am.' He cleared his throat. 'From the bottom of my heart.'

'Is that a long way?' she said, unsmiling.

James managed a wan smile.

'Cheers. Thanks,' Anna said, and walked on.

James turned as she passed him.

'Is that it?' he said.

'What do you want me to say? Do you want forgiveness and absolution, so you can file this one away? Then I forgive you. Over.'

'I don't want forgiveness. I understand if you can't forgive me, or not yet.'

'Then what do you want?' Anna asked.

'To talk. To be friends again.'

Anna shook her head.

'I don't want to be friends.'

'We were getting on before I saw that picture. More than getting on. We had a laugh, we really clicked. What's changed?'

Anna even cringed at the words *that picture*. If he'd seen her in her surgical stirrups it'd have barely felt more exposing.

'I never meant to have anything to do with you. It was a working relationship, after the total shock horror of seeing you in that meeting. Then I went to your company do as a favour. I knew I shouldn't have even done that. The whole fight over the picture was a massive wake-up call. I don't want anything to do with you.'

'Because of school? You think I can't change?'

'I don't care if you've changed or not. Because I've changed. Because I don't let superficial dickheads get to me anymore.'

James grimaced.

'That's harsh, Anna.'

She was finally riled. She felt the kind of raging hurt that swelled behind the chest wall and travelled up the throat and out of the mouth in the form of ugly words.

'*That's* harsh?! Try five years of daily hell topped with a public demonstration that a whole school-full of people hate you, James. That they're laughing at you for your stupidity in ever thinking you could take part,' she spat. 'You haven't ever met harsh. You haven't been *near* it.'

'With the Mock Rock, there wasn't as much reason to it as that. It was dumb crowd mentality.'

'Oh, here we go – you think it'll help for *you* to tell *me* it wasn't that bad really? You think some "there there, dear" is going to do the job?'

'No, this is a policy of complete honesty.' James pulled his bag over his head and dropped it at his feet. 'Last time I saw you, you said something about me knowing you liked me at school. I didn't. What happened was …' He bit his lip. 'A month or so before, Laurence was doing one of his hugely mature "would you rather" conversations. When you were mentioned, I said you would look OK if …' James paused.

'… If?' Anna folded her arms.

'If you lost weight. And Laurence teased me relentlessly that I liked you. He put me up to the Mock Rock stunt. I did it to get him off my back. I had that teenage peer group head on where you go along with it, so it's somebody else instead of you. I was a craven arsehole who didn't want to be bullied either, I guess. If that's the word.'

'It's not the word.'

'I know.'

'No, you don't know. That's like telling someone who's lost an arm in a thresher that you had a paper cut that really smarted once. No one would've bullied you like they did me if you'd said no. People like you can never understand a person like me.'

'People like me?'

'People who float through this world, who are handed things easily, who are treated as special because their face fits.'

'Oh come on. I'm not for one second saying you haven't

been through the mill, but saying you're alone in knowing suffering is a bit much.'

'Did you ever get punched and hit, and your bag stolen and thrown in the bin for the crime of being fat and ugly, James? Did you sit through detentions for lost homework rather than reporting that someone had ripped it up, because reporting it meant more bullying? Did you ever have to tell your parents you got those bruises from P.E., whilst seeing the tortured look on your little sister's face because she knows exactly where they came from? Did you wake up every morning before the alarm went off, feeling sick at what you'd have to face? Did you count a good day as one where you were only viciously abused once every lesson?'

James put his hand out to touch her arm but she stepped back, out of his reach.

'What else? So much to choose from. Let's see … Did you get dressed up in your fat girl dress and dropped off at the leavers' do by your dad, wait until he was out of sight, then go and sit on your own in a park for hours, because you couldn't bring yourself to tell your parents you weren't welcome?'

James stared at her, then the ground.

'And best of all, did the most popular person in school make you, for one shining moment, think he might be unlike all the other bastards? Then put you in the stocks, get you pelted with food and call you an elephant? You know James, you were a tiny bit of happiness at school, for me. Just getting to look at you, thinking about you, writing stupid stuff in my diaries. You were only nice to me in my imagination, but that was enough. You didn't need to do anything. All I needed you to do was *nothing* to me. But you didn't let me even have that.'

James was stricken, and yet Anna couldn't hold back. It was like the floodgates had opened.

'... Every night I poured it all into my diary, great screeds of misery. I promised myself that one day I would get away. That the time would come when I'd never have to see any of you fuckers again. And by being friends with you, I'm betraying that girl. That's why I don't want to be friends. You didn't want to be friends back then. But you do now, now that the very sight of me isn't an embarrassment. Well, I don't want to know you. What did you call that, "harsh"? Why don't you try to pick up the shattered pieces of your life and limp on?'

It was quite a tirade and when James spoke, his voice sounded weakened by the onslaught.

'I want the chance to make it up to you, Anna.'

'You *can't*. That's what you're not grasping.'

Anna knew she'd finally done enough to make James walk away. It was a battle of wills, him pushing against a door to get into a room that she was determined not to let him into. Somewhere, deep down, it was possible she wanted him to try hard enough. But she was certain he wouldn't. There was no way he was winning this. In strength of feeling, she had the power of twenty men.

'I have to get back to work,' she said. 'Goodbye.'

62

Anna made it a few paces across the grass, bristling with a poisonous sense of triumph, before James tapped her on the shoulder again.

'You think I'm the last person you want around. What if I'm precisely the person you need?'

Anna eye-rolled him. 'Which movie poster did you whip that from?'

'I'm serious. You need to exorcise Rise Park. You need the person responsible, or one of them, to truly understand what they did. So you can let go of it.'

'I was living my life fine before you came along, thanks.'

'Despite you being a much better person than me, I don't accept we're as dissimilar as you say. We wouldn't make each other laugh so much if we were. You don't think we have anything in common?'

'No.'

'You said you liked me at school? You mean you had a crush on me?'

Anna lifted her chin in a terse nod.

'Why? We never had one conversation, until the Mock Rock.'

'I knew things about you. You know how it is with the cool kids and the no-marks. We watch from the sidelines while you're in the spotlight.'

'But we never interacted. You simply liked the way I looked.'

'So?' Anna shifted her weight and made a face that let him know his time was nearly up.

'You were judging purely on appearances.'

'Hah. Nice try. But that's a phony equivalence. It's hardly like I made your life worse. You didn't even know I was there.'

'My point stands. We both judged on appearances. I thought you weren't worth anything and you thought I was worth something. We were both wrong.'

James took her pause as encouragement.

'I can't begin to imagine what it's been like to be in your shoes, and to then have people treat you so differently once you're … well, obviously you're beautiful. It'd make most people deadly cynical. Yet you're not, and that's impressive.'

'You're beeyoodifull. Oh, please. *Not that hot and not your type*, was the real assessment, I recall.'

James went red. 'Come on, I apologised for that. I was trying to discourage Laurence. Of course I think you're beautiful, everyone does. Take a compliment.'

Anna shrugged with a nonchalance she didn't really feel. 'So would you want to be my friend if I still looked like Aureliana?'

James looked to the heavens in mock despair and back down.

'Yep. Nothing in our friendship was about looks. Wouldn't you agree? It was unusually pure, in that respect.'

'Mmmm. Are you finished? I do have work to do.'

'No. I'm not leaving things like this,' James said. 'I think your pride won't let me back in. So tell me what it needs me to do. I will do anything you ask of me to atone for this. But I won't simply go away. You've got to let it out. Punch me or something.'

She knew they were inching closer to her saying the thing she didn't want to. Her voice became tremulous.

'James. You have no idea how bad it was. This is not fixable with jokes, or token acts of play-fighting. You don't know what you're interfering in, here.'

'I was there. I have some idea. Tell me.'

'I don't want to.'

'Put it this way. Why do I deserve to be spared hearing it?'

Anna opened her mouth. Closed it. Checkmate. She had no answer for that.

'A month after the Mock Rock,' she said, her voice small and careful, 'I left a goodbye note on my bed, and took a ton of aspirin …'

James's mouth opened slightly and his eyes looked shiny. He put a hand to his mouth. Anna felt the stabbing pain in her jaw and the pressure in her ears that meant tears were coming, in a big way. She willed herself to keep speaking.

'And I tried not to think about who would find me. It was Aggy. She sensed something was up and doubled back and came home from school. My little sister, James. She saved my life. No fourteen-year-old should have to go through what she went through …'

The tears began and she wiped at her face with a freezing cold hand.

'I felt so, so guilty. But there was nothing about my life that made me want to continue it. *Nothing*. The Mock Rock proved to me I was simply a joke. A big, flabby, foreign, repulsive joke.

I'd finally left that school, but it had broken me. I realised that if adulthood was going to be more of the same, I couldn't take it. So tell me why I should stand here and make friends with one of the people who almost made sure I wasn't here?'

She and James stared at each other. Anna's chest rose and fell, and she knew her face would soon crumple.

'You did that? After the … what we did. Oh Jesus, Anna …'

James put an arm out and stepped towards her.

'Oh sure, give me a hug so you don't have to see me cry,' she said, half-kidding, with the last speech-noises her larynx could make.

'It's so you don't see me cry, you idiot,' James muttered thickly, and grabbed her so hard it nearly winded her.

She felt arms around her and a hand on the back of her head as the tears flowed in earnest. He only held more tightly as she cried, making it known that she wasn't expected to stop. She heard her own sobs as if they were coming from someone else. It was the kind of liberated ugly-crying you usually only allowed yourself as a child.

They stood like that for a while; Anna didn't know if it was five minutes or fifteen. Gradually, her breathing became more regular, and the weeping turned into weak hiccups.

James shushed her and mumbled something into her hair, a jumble of indistinct sounds she couldn't immediately form into words. She cried herself out, waterlogging and snotting his no doubt ridiculously expensive coat.

When they finally moved apart again, Anna knew she must look like a seasick Brian May, and she could honestly say she didn't care. Something had happened. Something had shifted.

'Don't feel guilty. You have no reason to feel guilty,' James said. He helped brush wet strands of her hair from her face. He looked slightly moist of eye himself. 'You were a victim and you did what you did because you felt you had to. It's the rest of us who should feel guilt.'

'I made the decision to take those pills, so I put Aggy through it,' Anna said, as she wiped at the corners of her eyes with a sleeve.

'You were forced to it.'

Some students passed them and they both sniffed and looked in opposite directions until they were gone. London's daytime traffic thundered past, a short distance away. James exhaled, heavily.

'What you said was right. No apology can possibly be enough for what I did to you. I'm not sure I can claim to be the friend you need. All I can say is that I'll carry this until I die. Please know that you're not alone in that anymore.'

'You were the straw on the camel's back, to be fair,' Anna said. 'You weren't a long-term tormentor who put the hours in. You can't steam in at the end of something and take the credit for the results of their hard work …'

Anna gave him a small smile. James shook his head in dismay.

And to her surprise, she found that her anger had left her. Her tears were cried out. James was still here, and she had to accept that he wanted to be here. It wasn't conscience-cleansing, it wasn't for show, it wasn't a whim. He wholeheartedly wanted to make amends. Everyone should be allowed to leave the past behind. Didn't she know that better than anyone?

James hoisted his bag back over his body. He looked at her, at a loss for what to say in parting.

'I should let you get back to work …' he said, vaguely. 'If

you ever need anything …'

He looked so sorry, genuinely sorry. Beaten up by it, even.

'I suppose we could *try* being friends,' Anna said, slowly. 'See where it gets us. I'm thinking that if you feel eternally guilty, I'll probably never have to stand my round.'

James smiled a small smile.

'Can I ask you something?' he said. 'Why would you lose your arm in an off-licence?'

'Eh?' Anna said.

'Lose your arm in a Thresher?'

'Threshing *machine*. Good God, you're a bimbo,' she smiled at James.

'Oh, man. I'm going to carry that till the day I die too.'

They stood grinning at each other like a pair of goons.

'I can't go back to work looking like this,' Anna said.

'Then don't,' James said. 'I'm playing truant. Play truant with me. I'll buy you lunch anywhere you like.'

'Why are you playing truant?'

'Duh. I wanted to come to someone else's workplace and be told I was an irredeemable dick today. A change is as good as a rest.' He smoothed her hair over her ear again and Anna felt an inner light switch on, despite herself.

'What do you say?'

'If it's your treat, how can I say no?'

They trudged in comfortable silence to the road, Anna angling her head down in case a student or colleague passed them. Luckily the Baltic temperature meant there were few dawdlers.

'Think big with lunch,' James said, as they crunched over the grass. 'Today is too momentous to waste on a Meatball

Marinara sub. Anywhere you like. On me.'

'Well, in that case, how about Bob Bob Ricard?' Anna asked.

James blanched.

'Fucking hell. Are you sure it was *that* bad at school?'

They laughed. Anna was pleased about the swift resumption of the affectionate teasing. This was normality. She didn't want to be treated like an invalid.

As James figured out the best route, some words he'd muttered earlier formed a sentence in her head.

I can't bear to think about it, Anna.

Yet for the first time, she could.

63

If that had been cathartic for Anna, she'd probably never know what it meant to James. There'd been something scratching at the other side of the cellar door for so long, and it turned out it was simply: *you can be better than this*. She'd helped him understand what it was, at last.

He had prized the wrong things for so long – false things – and wondered why life felt like a sham. Well, duh, he could hear his sister say.

James didn't know how to tell Anna she'd saved him from a life of all surface, no substance, or if he ever could. He didn't want her to think she was his street cat named Bob, a cute motor for his redemption.

It didn't come for free, obviously – thinking about her nearly topping herself, thanks in no small part to him, was abundantly grim.

'Anna,' he said, on the walk there, 'I know we're having a laugh now, but if you ever want to talk more about the … thing you told me.'

She smiled at him. 'I did a lot of talking with the counsellor I saw in the year afterwards, don't worry. I'm all talked out. But thanks.'

It was authentically terrifying to think you could do so much damage to another human being, and then mentally store it away in the attic. Imagine if he'd never met her again? If he ever had kids, they'd have a Don't Be Mean talk from him that'd involve a PowerPoint presentation.

But now he had a second chance to be the friend to her that she'd so badly needed half a lifetime ago. He could see her, as she used to be, in his mind's eye, on that stage. Portly in an orange dress, with a mad helmet hairdo, her eyes streaming. He longed for a time machine so he could go back and do it all differently.

Bob Bob Ricard was an excellent choice. On such an unusual day, the restaurant fitted perfectly: stepping through its entrance in the middle of Soho was like entering a portal to an *Alice in Wonderland* alternate universe. As if a white rabbit might scurry past, checking a pocket watch. The inside of the restaurant resembled an Orient Express car, via a Hollywood Hills bathroom, circa 1961. It was a crackpot opulent riot of golden brass fittings, marble, mirrors and an inlaid patterned tiled floor.

James remarked that the colour of the leather booths, like something from an Edwardian train, were 'cerulean blue', only to forget Anna knew much more stuff than him.

'It's a little deeper and richer than that. More lapis lazuli?'

James smiled. 'Airplane toilet flush blue, then?'

'Poetic.'

There was even a bell to 'press for champagne', James prodded it in the spirit of adventure. Two flutes arrived on a tray, carried by a white-gloved waiter in pink waistcoat, inside a minute.

'It's like being in an Agatha Christie!' Anna whispered.

They over-ordered ridiculously rich posh-Russian-meets-American-diner food: blinis and soufflés and lobster macaroni cheese and truffle mash. Then they declared anarchy over who chose what, shared everything and finished nothing.

James was aware that having a three-course lunch in the middle of the day with a woman he wasn't romantically involved with, could've felt deeply uncomfortable. But strangely, given all that had passed, their meal was one of the most comfortable ones he'd ever had. Conversation flowed as freely as the champagne, and would have done so, with or without the booze.

Every ban had been lifted, and there was no taboo left to trip over. James didn't censor himself, nor did he try to show off. When they touched on school memories, he told Anna about losing his virginity in a series of clumsy and shaming encounters with Rise Park diva Lindsay Bright in her dad's shed. 'More of a summer house,' he insisted. 'We did do it on a bag of compost though, and a pitchfork up the arse counts as one of the worst coitus interruptuses ever.' Anna laughed heartily.

'She was the girl we all wanted to be!' she sighed, twiddling the chain of her necklace.

'Wow. Are you kidding? She was bratty and appalling.'

'You went out with her!'

'Only in that "arranged marriage" way of school. Don't look to sixteen-year-old boys for taste and judgement. Don't look to them for anything until at least twenty-six, in fact.'

Anna insisted as the plates stacked up that they were going Dutch and he said, don't you dare, you have to let me get this, and she relented. James wouldn't have told her this but her enchantment at the surroundings was plenty payback.

Looking around, Anna sighed. 'I've always wanted to come

here and never found an excuse,' she said.

'Couldn't you do it on one of your millions of dates?'

'I didn't want to waste it on a duff one. It had to be special,' Anna replied. She was too busy filleting about in a venison steak tartare to realise what she'd said.

James beamed at the top of her head. Her sloppy jumper was slipping from the shoulders and he found himself gazing at her collarbones. There was something about a woman's collarbones, he'd always thought.

There was only one moment the mood dipped and she welled up, when discussing her departed confidante, the corpulent hamster, Chervil. God love her, but who cared about those things? Less a mammal, more a squeaky dog toy with longer batteries. Without even thinking, he put out his hand and gently grazed his knuckles against her cheekbone.

He wasn't usually the kind of man to go in for paternalistic patting and petting of women he wasn't seeing, or even those he was.

But she made him feel … there was an old-fashioned word for it. *Tender*. She made him feel tender towards her.

James couldn't have staggered on to dessert but Anna insisted on the 'Signature Chocolate Glory' that arrived as a gold leaf sphere that looked as if it was going to start vibrating and crack open.

'This was the best idea you've ever had, James Fraser,' Anna said thickly, through a mouthful of pudding, and suddenly James's heavy heart felt as light as a feather.

64

'Is it naughty?' the girl asked, cake slice poised above a sandy disc of salted caramel torte.

She had an amazing sleek whorl of a blonde bun, like a Danish pastry. It was the sort of do Anna tried to attempt, but had always found her hair too curly and unruly to hold the shape.

'It's patisserie, so it has no moral implications, my love,' Michelle said.

'Hee hee!' she said. 'How many calories though? Per slice, like so?' She made a 'V' with her hands.

Michelle sucked on her e-fag, ruminatively, wearing the expression of Gandalf with his wooden pipe surveying a fool of a Took.

'212. Point five. 212.5.'

Blonde bun girl put the cake slice down and got her iPhone out, tapping at the keypad with a French-manicured forefinger. 'My points app says I can!'

She teetered off in her precipitously high salmon-patent heels, grasping forty-five degrees of 212.5 calorie torte daintily in a white paper napkin.

'Was that true?' Anna asked Michelle.

Michelle swivelled sarcastic, swoopily eye-linered eyes towards her.

'Yes, while cooking the food, chilling the grog, sorting the playlist and doing the décor, I had a team of nutritionists analyse the approximate energy value of slices of my puddings, as a handy guide for neurotics,' Michelle said. 'Anyway, not as if it's going to do her any harm. I've never seen anyone so thin they make a peplum skirt look like a good idea before.'

'You've done magnificently here, Michelle,' Anna said. 'Thank you.'

The Pantry had been henned up for the evening in style. There were tiles of light scattered by a disco ball, more candles than a *Baywatch* hot tub scene, and an iPod dock as DJ, full of oestrogen-loaded songs on shuffle. The tables had been pushed back to create a dance floor space, with one covered in a white tablecloth, full of platters of food. Michelle had thoughtfully created an Anglo-Italian spread of things that were easy to juggle while holding a drink and dancing.

The area by the till was now a bar, with one of Michelle's staff serving the free drink on arrival: a ginger cordial and Prosecco creation of Aggy's she called a Ginger Stepchild. Anna was dubious about her sister's mixology skills, but it tasted great.

The hen herself was in a fearsomely tight, short, ruby tutu dress, a sash and a tiara. As Anna surveyed the room, she realised that Aggy's friends were like seeing flamingos up close: improbable legs and wild colours. The Pantry was awash with rivers of glossed hair, tiny dresses, St Tropez bronzed limbs and four-inch platform stilettos, caught in a cloud of Viktor & Rolf's Flowerbomb.

'Aggy! AGGY! Look, lol!' Aggy's curly-haired, hyperactive best friend Marianne squealed, producing handfuls of penis-shaped confetti from her pockets and strewing them around the table.

'Uh oh ...' Anna said, looking to Michelle, who merely waved.

'It's fine,' she said. 'No doubt they'll turn up in a sugar bowl when we have the Michelin inspectors in.'

'Hahahaha!' Marianne squealed, dumping a load of pink penis-shaped straws on the table and getting a blow-up inflatable penis out. When full size, it was roughly the size of a sausage dog. They started taking camera phone photos of each other astride it, shouting '*ride a cock horse to Banbury Cross*',

Anna was sincerely glad to have Michelle there.

'Do you ever understand the penis motif?' Anna said to Michelle. 'It's not as if many people getting married nowadays are about to sleep with their partner for the first time. Why all the "woo hoo, willies" like we're eight years old again?'

'Especially as willies, plural, is what you're giving up.'

'Thanks so much for this, Michelle,' Aggy said, tottering across to give Michelle a hug.

'You're welcome,' she said. 'I'm glad you're enjoying.'

'Such a good suggestion of James's,' Aggy said absently, sucking on her penis straw in a flute glass, and waving at her friend across the room. 'So was Italy. *And* he bought me my dress. I've invited him later by the way. Oh my God, tunnnnnnneeeee!'

Aggy was all ready to hit the dance floor, causing Anna to grab her arm to stall her.

'James got you your what?' Anna asked. 'And he's invited tonight?'

'Oh. Yeah. I said I couldn't afford it until my bonus. So he lent me the rest of the money I needed for my dress.' She put her head on one side. 'He's soooo sweet. I know you think he's a general helmet, but he's not anymore, I don't think.'

'Aggy,' Anna barked. 'You took *money* from James Fraser?'

'Argh, only for two months! For my dream dress!' she said, with an expression that said she knew she couldn't be too badly told off at her own hen party.

Aggy cantered off to do some obscene back-to-back ass-grinding. While Michelle went to the ladies, Anna whipped her phone out and fired off a question.

Her phone obligingly rippled with light a moment later.

Ah. Aggy wasn't supposed to tell you about that. Yeah I lent her some money, no big. Though she did use you as security on the loan. If she defaults, you're helping Parlez design the campaign for the Turkfurter account. They're turkey frankfurters. 'Nom' . Jx

Why was I not meant to know? Hen is good, apart from recurring penis motif. Ax

Can't beat a recurring penis motif. Because I prefer to perform my heroics anonymously, like Batman. You only know me in my Bruce Wayne playboy mode, it's just a clever facade. Jx

Anna laughed in disbelief. He'd put the phone down on her that evening that Aggy had disappeared, gone out, found them and sorted it. At considerable cost, both literal and metaphorical, it sounded like. He'd come up with the idea of The Pantry, and Italy? Anna had been startled at the speed of her sister's recovery from the loss of the Langham, and it looked as though

James was responsible for it.

Why had he done all this? Her heart whispered that he had done it for her.

Anna tried not to be too effusive, but the combination of the gratitude, alcohol and sheer surprise tipped her into gushing a thank you to him, and on behalf of her family, who, she pointed out, didn't know they owed James their younger daughter's salvation.

Aw! My pleasure to help with the planning, Alessi. Spoiler warning -> The police investigating a complaint about a disturbance will be strippers. Unless real police also respond to a complaint about a disturbance. Don't grab any nightsticks till you're sure. X

'He is joking about the strippers, isn't he? Didn't Marianne promise you there wouldn't be any?' Anna said, showing a passing Aggy her phone.

'Lol yes,' she said. 'We're being classy.'

Anna's eyes drifted to someone playing air guitar with an inflatable penis, and back down to her phone again.

Michelle studied her.

'Oh, hello.'

'What?'

'You're gazing at your texts with the expression of a mother looking at her newborn baby in an incubator. Who's the message from …?'

'James.'

'A-HAH.'

'What?'

'The artist formerly known as evil James Fraser?'

Anna had felt duty-bound to sketch in something of the UCL bloodletting to Michelle and Daniel. She'd managed to balance exoneration of James without going into fine detail. Something about the nature of that day made her want to keep it between the two of them. They had a high regard for Anna's opinion and were willing to accept that if she said he wasn't who he once was, he wasn't.

'We're friends now.'

'Friends who go for romantic meals with champagne and vibrating chocolate.'

'It wasn't romantic! And it wasn't actually vibrating.'

'And he's coming to a hen do? Which man comes to a hen do who isn't being paid by the hour?' Michelle asked.

Anna smiled. She didn't particularly want to stop Michelle.

'Alright, I'm blue skying this bullshit now,' Michelle said, topping Anna up from a bottle of Prosecco. 'He's hot. You're hot. You're both single. Where's the harm in some fumbling? It seems to me he's given you the signs you need to proceed to Commencement of Physical Phase.'

Anna shrugged, not knowing what her answer was.

'I'm not saying that special person who's perfectly right for you and makes sense of everything *isn't* going to turn up. But why not enjoy yourself until then?'

'Maybe I don't do casual very well,' Anna said. 'I'm too serious when it comes to relationships.'

'You don't want to turn an opportunity with a seriously fit man down and regret it. When I got to thirty, it hit me, this is going to end very soon. Imagine being in one of those shopping centre wheelchairs, burgundy legs swollen like balloon whisks, Scottie dog on your lap, thinking: all that nobbing I could've done?'

Anna laughed. James's rehabilitation was still recent. And she didn't like him *in that way*. Did she? He was gorgeous, sure. Did he like her in that way? Maybe this changed everything.

'What I'm saying is, don't save yourself for a rainy day. Unwrap your presents. Mix your drinks. Shag him and have some fun, for God's sake. Arancini ball?'

Anna smiled and accepted one from the heaped plate.

'Even if I did decide I wanted to do this, how the hell am I supposed to go about it?' she said, with a mouthful of fried risotto rice. 'I'm a useless flirt.'

'Oh it's easy. Be a bit tarty. Brazen it up. The secret of seduction is, ninety-seven per cent of it's done in holding eye contact. The male ego will do the rest. Trust me, you can practically see the moment when it dawns on them that they're going to get some action. Clunk.'

Anna remembered James's advice at the British Museum launch with Tim and it dawned that of course he was no novice.

How did you flirt subtly? Though from what Michelle said, subtlety wasn't the aim.

Anna felt a burst of interior sunshine at the prospect of seeing James. It was as if her back got a little straighter, her wits sharper, around him. She hoped the red dress she'd worn looked acceptable. Or even, better than acceptable.

She tapped a foot to the music and wondered if Michelle was right, if there was a chance she and James would be going home together. The idea intimidated her beyond words and yet, made her feel other things too. She wasn't going to say no. Michelle was right. It was time to start living.

65

When James slipped through the door he was nicely soundtracked by the opening bars of Daft Punk's 'Get Lucky', as if he brought his own music with him.

He put a palm up in greeting to Anna and she responded in turn as Aggy squealed, assailed him and chattered, arms around his waist.

James listened and politely tolerated the slightly over-familiar embrace. He was in a black cardigan and a thin, pale blue shirt that needed more attentive ironing to stop the collar curling up. He looked even more Clark Kent-ish than usual. Although, Anna couldn't help but wonder at seeing *another* James Fraser cardigan. How many did the man have?

The room's predatory mammals smelled man-blood, and soon he was surrounded by new friends, making surreptitious mock-panicked eyes to Anna.

She supposed she could grow to like the cardigan thing. Now that she cared about the person inside it. She had an urge to take Aggy's place and slide her arms around him and hold him very tightly. She tested thinking lascivious thoughts about unbuttoning cardigans, which didn't seem quite right.

Like a seduction scene involving unclasping dungarees, or rolling surgical stockings down. And then as he talked and made her sister laugh and the disco ball cast light-swirls of patterns across them, she realised her feelings went beyond wanting to take the clothes off.

She wanted to get under his skin. She wanted him to give her his heart.

'I'm going to say hello to your sister,' she heard James saying.

As he walked towards her, it felt as if her own heart turned inside out.

'Evening,' he said. He leaned to one side of her, then the other, checking her outfit. 'I see no recurring penis motifs. Or t-shirts saying *Aggy's Slag Squad*. Entirely tasteful. Well done, you churlish old bluestocking.'

Over his shoulder, Anna saw Michelle do two thumbs up at her. She tried to remember how she was with him before she'd felt this way.

She defaulted to further thanks for help with the Aggy crisis. As James talked about severing ties with Laurence, Anna noticed that having waited thirty-two years for the thunderbolt, she didn't feel the way she expected. She thought it'd feel like safety: knowing you were home, where you were meant to be. In fact it was more like being strapped to a chair and tipped at an angle over the edge of a cliff. Precipitous.

'You know, we never watched the Tim documentary,' James said, accepting a glass. 'Did you see it?'

'No ...' Anna had been so keen to see it too. However, she had associated it with their curtailed evening and hadn't worked up the courage to watch it yet. 'We could try again? Minus Mills & Boons, cosmetic surgery brochures and massive fights.'

Wait, Anna thought. Was this a flirting opportunity?

'That was when you offered to give me an independent norks assessment to reassure me it wasn't necessary,' Anna said.

'*Did* I?' James said. 'Past James was a rascally sod. Past James, I hardly knew ye.'

She laughed. This was flirting, this was good. This was the whole 'get him to imagine you naked' thing they talked about, right?

'I'm going to take you up on it,' Anna laughed. 'You can hold up a gold scorecard paddle with a number.'

'Oh God,' James rubbed an eye. 'Nooooo!'

'No? Don't boys usually like baps?' Anna said.

'Yeah, but. You're my friend. It'd be like seeing my sister.'

Ouch. *Ouch*. Anna felt the dulled impact while drunk, like being punched through a pillow. It'd hurt like hell when she remembered in the morning though. She realised she should come up with some distracting chatter but she couldn't muster any. Like a *sister*? She was a disaster at reading men, at romantic situations. She was too gutted to respond.

'Anna. Anna?' she heard James saying.

'Mmmm,' she said, pretending there was something going on in her glass that had momentarily fascinated her.

'*Anna.*'

He put his hand on her chin and tipped her face towards him.

'I didn't mean that. I was being flippant and trying to not sound like a letch. I don't want to because I'd feel giddy and unusual and improper towards you.'

'That's what I was hoping,' Anna said. The words had formed in her brain and left her mouth before she had consciously decided they'd be a good idea. Boom. Done. She'd said it. She'd said the thing.

James stared back at her with lips slightly parted as the music pounded and Anna tried to work out a way to amend or modify their meaning. None occurred to her. They teetered on the brink, with James's reply now defining everything between them from here on in. Anna felt like a gambler who'd pushed all their chips onto red, and was waiting for the roulette wheel to stop spinning. Were they going to kiss? Did she imagine James moved closer, their heads inclining …?

'I'm back with Eva,' he said, pulling back with a tone of slight shock, as if he hadn't known until this moment either.

Anna felt that dull punch again. But this time by someone who'd put more driving force into the elbow action. Despite the noise and hubbub around them, the silence between them in the ensuing seconds hung thick and heavy.

'Oh,' Anna said. She could hear the winded emptiness in her voice, even in that one syllable.

'Early days,' James cleared his throat. 'She came round yesterday. We're taking it slowly. She's not moved back in yet.'

'Right,' Anna said, dully.

'You can still come round?' James said.

Anna had experienced some moments of feeling small and stupid in her life. This was up with the best of them.

'Hah. No, I don't think so,' she said, shaking her head with a thin smile.

'Of course you can,' James said, not sounding as if he'd convinced himself. He looked perplexed, turning things over, wanting to ask more things of both Anna and himself that he couldn't find the right words for.

'I can't,' she said.

'When things have sorted themselves out, then,' he said, hopefully. She knew he wasn't listening to what he was saying.

'No …'

'You're always welcome …'

He made her sound like a maiden aunt who they'd get the Fox's Classic tin out for.

Anna smiled and summoned what little courage she had left.

'James. Please stop saying I can still come round. We both know I can't. I hope it goes well. Thanks again for all you've done for Aggy, I can't thank you enough. I'm going to get another drink.'

Anna went to the bar, in a decisive manner.

'James is leaving!' Aggy called, minutes later, and she saw him shrugging on his coat and waving.

Anna waved back with a broad smile and enough vigour to excuse her not crossing the room. She had no idea what she'd say to him. He must've understood she wouldn't want to because he slipped away quickly, no mean feat when a drunk Aggy was clinging to him like a koala bear.

'Nothing doing?' Michelle said, nearby, having witnessed his departure.

'Nah,' Anna said, with a leaden fake-lightness.

Michelle answered, 'Hmmm, this one's a puzzler.'

Anna could've solved the puzzle, but she wasn't ready yet. She needed to assimilate it in private first. She was glad the night was drawing to a close, as she no longer felt remotely partyish. Hah. For some mad reason, her old diary doodles floated back to her: JF 4EVA. For Eva. She'd even predicted it.

When she got in the door of her flat, her phone bleeped with a text.

I'm sorry. Jx

It took her half an hour to agonise over a reply that was also only two words long.

It's OK. Ax

66

He'd found her sheltering in the porch, the downpour having turned her longer hair into damp ropes and her eye make-up into punky, soot-sparkled smudges. Her duckling blondeness always looked darker when wet.

'Why didn't you call me?' he asked.

'It was spontaneous. I didn't want to make an appointment,' Eva said, and James knew what she was here to say.

She disappeared upstairs and came back down with her top half clad in only a bra and one of his cardigans, the material nearly wrapping twice round her slender hips.

They'd talked for an hour and a half, the rain beating a tattoo on the ground outside.

Eva had always been a wild free spirit before meeting James, she explained. She'd travelled and done things on a whim, and in the haze of being madly in love, she'd committed to things too fast. It had caused a kind of jet lag that outlasted the literal type from their honeymoon in Sri Lanka.

She'd never told him, but she'd had something like a panic attack the night before the wedding, going faint, heart palpitations. James would have thought she was having doubts about him, but that definitely wasn't it. It had just all been so fast, making the lifelong commitment. But maybe with hindsight she shouldn't have suppressed it, and told him. She wiped Man Ray-like perfect fat tears away at the memory.

James said: 'So what's changed?'

'I missed you too much. I missed *us*.' She curled her legs in tighter, looking tiny and vulnerable on the vastness of the giant pink couch.

Hmmm. Nice and vague. It couldn't be that he'd started getting flirtatious comments on Facebook from female friends, colleagues and even exes, could it? Or that the estate agent's photos had gone up and viewing requests had started? No. He told himself it couldn't be that.

'How's Finn taking it?'

Eva wiped at her nose with the cuff of his cardigan.

'I told him it was never going to work between us, long-term. He understands that.'

James wondered what she'd told Finn when she moved in with him. When he and Eva started dating, he recalled a friend of hers, Victoria, saying to him in a tone that was aiming for playful and fell slightly short: 'What you learn with Eva is, there's what she says and then there's what she does. If you don't expect the two to match up, you'll be fine.'

He'd told Eva this and she'd snorted that Victoria had a crush on him and she was 'a bit of a bore', but James couldn't recall Eva inviting her to anything after that. It struck James that when you're most in need of character references for the person you've met, everyone goes silent, or risks ex-communication.

But he mustn't let what had happened make him cynical. The whole point of learning from his recent experiences was to try to be less so. Eva was his wife and she wanted to try again. He wasn't Laurence. Love had to be selfless and forgiving sometimes.

Eva wasn't moving back in straight away. He'd take the house off the market, she'd stay at Sara's, and they'd meet and talk until they were ready for a full reconciliation.

And if she ever, *ever* messed him around, they would be over. She solemnly understood that. In some ways, James told himself, he was safer than many in terms of his wife cheating. She'd spent that credit already. She wouldn't dare do it again and imagine he'd take her back a second time.

Today she'd asked him to go for lunch at the Roebuck in Hampstead. Eva arrived with a bright green Cambridge satchel full of *Homes & Gardens*, largely ignoring her lunch in favour of rifling through the shiny pages. She was going for an androgynous look lately, with flat lace-up brogues and slim-fit trousers.

When James asked why the special interest in armoires and Persian rugs, Eva explained she had a budget to buy a piece of furniture from her parents.

'Isn't it strange to get you a "well done for going back to your husband" gift?' he said, uncurling a piece of crackling on his pork belly.

'That's not what it is. They know I've been through a rough time.'

'*You've* been through a rough time?' He screwed his face up.

'We both have. But I'm their little girl.'

After lunch, they went on to drift round the kind of shudderingly expensive interiors boutique where everything was glass, chalky dove grey or flaky yellowing-white. A phantom world where only items of exquisite paleness existed. It was lucky for Luther that he co-ordinated. But then, that's why he'd been chosen.

A small Baby Boden-clad boy in box-fresh Kickers, walking like a wind-up toy, bumbled past James, his Spanish-looking mother in close pursuit. He had her coal-black hair and olive skin. When Anna had kids they'd look Mediterranean. There was no way those Italian genes were buckling to the pasty British colourway.

Anna.

There had been so many things he'd wanted to share since he saw her last month. They were friends, weren't they? He thought: I'm allowed to contact her, surely? His sister was back home for a while and he so wanted her to meet Anna, for Anna to see he had some decent people in his life. And for him to have the satisfaction of seeing Grace hit it off with Anna. The thought made him so sappy he'd even gone as far as to open an email and type it, before hitting discard.

He almost persuaded himself she didn't mean the things she'd said at the hen do about it not being OK for them to see each other. She'd had a lot to drink, was grateful to him for helping her sister, and had then impulsively said something suggestive. But she'd never been attracted to him. Had she?

He didn't just miss her. He missed the James he became with her.

'Jay,' Eva said, softly, from across the shop floor. 'Jay?' A couple of men who'd been discreetly tracking Eva's progress glanced over, assessing the partner. James was used to being subjected to greater scrutiny when he was with her. He used to like it. In fact, he used to love it.

'How about this?' She was pressing a leaflet from the shop

against her mouth, lingering in front of a vast mirror.

'It's huge,' James said. It was the size of a table football with an ornate crest at the top and a distressed pearly frame, the edges of the glass speckled and puckered with tiny flaws.

'I'd love a floor mirror for the bedroom.'

'Hmmm. I'm not sure I want to see that much of myself in the morning.'

'Naw. You're looking ripped. The misery regime clearly suited you.'

James stared at her, stupefied.

'You have to be careful in these places, these days,' Eva continued under her breath, moving the brochure an inch away from her mouth. 'I love Gustavian, but the whole shabby chic thing has become so commoditised. Too many repro white French Antiques. You might as well just get Next homeware cushions and those coloured champagne goblets with Mr and Mrs on. For your maple Shaker-style B&Q kitchen.'

'Who cares where you've bought your cushions?' James said. For his answer he looked around the room, at all the smart good-looking polished thirty-something couples, acquiring more elegant clutter for their enviable lives. James fitted in so well.

'Haha, let's go to Argos and get a mirror with a stainless steel frame, then,' Eva laughed. 'And Ikea for a wiggly mirror and twisty bamboo.'

She turned to face their reflections again, leaning her head on his arm and putting her hand up to his chin.

'Is the beard here to stay? I've come round to it.'

67

Anna wasn't prepared for the way the hopeless quasi-adolescent yearning permeated all aspects of her existence. Every song on the radio spoke to her, every thought was two steps away from a connection to James. Every humdrum daily task hummed with reminders he was gone. How could an absence be so noisy? He was everywhere now he was nowhere.

Whenever her email or phone pinged she longed for it to be him.

Anna had plenty of time in recent weeks to dwell on the ironies and strangeness of her situation. The monster from her past returned, only to have an effect that was quite magical. Anna wasn't haunted by school anymore. It still hurt, it always would, but James's willingness to face up to his crime had performed some sort of vanquishing.

It sounded strange, but in forgiving him, she forgave herself. She hadn't realised she had always blamed herself for being bullied — a kind of self-loathing shame. That ex-boyfriend Mark who had continually picked fault with her at university, she realised now Mark hated himself too. That's why he encouraged hatred in Anna, to make her feel as bad as he did.

So it made sense – Anna's perfect tonic had to be someone who loved himself.

She so wished she could share this observation with James, hear his peal of laughter, his sarcastic comeback. How would she ever find someone who made her laugh like he did again?

Only now, when she had no chance of trying to encourage him to fall in love with her, did she consider how well James might've suited her. He was intelligent and he was a challenge. They had enough similarities to make things comfortable and enough differences to keep things interesting. He'd made efforts with her friends and family. He knew her whole history. That one fact set him apart from everyone at a stroke.

And obviously, she coveted him. That part had never really been in doubt, but her brain wouldn't permit her loins the freedom until now.

When she looked back over their tumultuous re-acquaintance, she now understood and trusted James's motives at every stage. He was decent, kind and honest when it mattered. He'd kept these solid basics buried under a lot of self-regard and foolish knitwear. Unlike Laurence, or even Patrick, James had wanted to know, and accepted, the real Anna, with no amorous agenda or wish to bed her. Although in the end, contrarily, she wished he had.

The pain of imagining him with Eva was almost too much. The thought of them in a frantic reunion coupling gave her a sensation like acid reflux. James wasn't Eva's kind of person. He seemed like he was, but he was Anna's kind of person really. Or was he? Had Anna just been an ideological holiday fling from heartless hipster world? If this plane went nose cone first into grey cold ocean, would James shed a tear at news of her death?

'Anna? Anna. Are you in there? Have you got locked-in syndrome?'

Michelle passed a hand over her face. In the intensity of her reverie, Anna felt as if she was being yanked from the warmth of a womb.

'Are you OK?' Michelle said. 'You've been a bit spacey, lately. You've been staring at cloud bank for a half hour.'

'Well . . .' Anna wriggled her spine back up her seat, 'there's only cloud out there.'

'Don't remind me.'

Michelle returned her hand to her arm rest, which she'd been gripping hard since take off. Michelle was an extremely nervous flier. She'd swallowed fistfuls of Kalms with two double gin and tonics and needed Anna and Daniel holding an arm each getting on, as if she was elderly.

The wedding party had all but taken over an Easyjet flight from Stansted to Pisa. Daniel had come without Penny in the end, who'd decided she was simply too skint. ('I half expected him to say that she was coming but he was staying at home,' Michelle had remarked.)

The plane bumped up, then down gently, and the fasten seatbelt light came on with a soft *ding*.

'What's going on? Why are they telling us to fasten our seatbelts?' Michelle barked. She'd never unfastened hers.

'We've probably hit some turbulence,' Anna said, as she clipped her belt. The plane dipped again, sharply, then bounced some more.

'Oh what fuckery is this?!' Michelle wailed. 'Why isn't the captain speaking? He's gone very quiet! And the cabin crew have all disappeared!'

'They have to sit down and strap in during turbulence too,' Daniel said, holding up a round tin full of icing sugar. 'Barley twist?'

'I don't want a bloody barley twist, I might need a cyanide capsule. They've all scattered because they don't want to look us in the dead doomed faces.'

'In that case, I will die sucking a sweet,' Anna said. She reached across Daniel to claim her barley twist and at that point the plane dropped, juddered and rattled and a few gasps were heard from non-nervous fliers.

'It's fine, Michelle,' Anna said, trying to pat her knee reassuringly but the movement in the cabin meant her hand missed.

'We're going to die, this is it, I knew it. I always knew it and that's why I wouldn't get on planes,' Michelle said, squeezing her eyes shut. 'I'll never do all the things I want to. I'll never see Sydney Opera House, or sleep with Guy.'

'Sleep with who?' Anna said.

'Guy. The posh bloke from Meat Cute, that new burger van down the road from The Pantry. He asked me out.' Michelle still didn't open her eyes.

'And yet I get told off for eating his beef!' Daniel said, peering at Anna round Michelle.

'Sydney is a long flight,' Anna added.

'Shutupshutupshutup. And I don't see why you two are so blasé, you've hardly made use of our short time.'

'Oh, here we go,' Daniel said.

'Anna, you need to stop moping about the past and have sex with all the men,' Michelle said.

'All of them?'

'And Dan, for God's sake, get rid of Penny. She's bloody awful.'

'I thought scared passengers were meant to gabble their *own* secrets?' Anna said, embarrassed for Daniel.

'I can't split up with Penny,' Daniel said, bracing his palms against the shaking seat in front.

'Yes you *can*!'

'I can't!'

'You can! You think you can't, that's fear talking!'

'It's logic talking. I've already split up with her.'

'What?' Michelle opened her eyes. 'When?'

'Before we came away.'

The turbulence abated and Anna said: 'I hope you're OK, Dan? I'm so sorry.'

'Are you?' Daniel said, with a small smile.

'For you,' she added.

'What happened?' Michelle asked.

Anna gave her a surreptitious squeeze to convey *do not say too much*.

'Remember the gig at the Star & Garter in Putney? She did another song about me.' Daniel sighed. 'And I thought, do you know? You're not *kind*. You can live without lots of things. You can't live without that.'

'That's very wise,' Anna said.

The seatbelt light went off with another ding.

'See, Michelle!' Anna said. 'We must be through it.'

She made to unfasten her seatbelt.

'No!' Michelle said. 'Don't trust it. They probably want to grant us the mercy of having free hands for prayers.'

The tannoy came on.

'Ladies and gentlemen, this is your captain speaking. You may have noticed we've been experiencing a pocket of turbulence …'

398

'Oh, thanks for nothing!' Michelle shouted. 'I'll give you a pocket of turbulence!'

Aggy had organised an off-duty school bus to ferry the wedding guests around over the weekend and its first charter was to the walled city of Lucca for dinner and drinks, at the foot of the mountain.

Lucca was the ideal introduction for those who hadn't been to the country before – unspoilt and yet still classically, picture postcard Tuscany: medieval architecture, red roofs, olive trees.

Aggy had booked a charming, inexpensive trattoria for the food, and afterwards they wandered through the square, along cobbled streets in the gathering dusk to a café bar. Anna didn't know how Italy did shabby chic so well. At home, peeling paint was peeling paint. Here, it was impossibly romantic.

Every few moments she saw or thought of something she wanted to share with James and touched the smooth oblong of her phone in her pocket. *Don't text him when you're piddled*, she thought.

The café ceiling was filled with bunches of plastic grapes, the doorways wound with fairy lights. The guests milled around, drinking Aperol Spritzes and picking at plates of crostini. Shabby chic and civilised boozing, yes, they were definitely abroad. Anna's dad was propping up the bar, relishing the chance to speak his native tongue to the barman. As with all displaced countrymen, his accent had got three times more pronounced as soon as they'd landed at Pisa.

Anna looked round the room and thought that you'd never know this excursion was a shove-by replacement for a different wedding. She had to hand it to Aggy, she really was an event planner extraordinaire. No wonder her fairly silly sister was paid fairly silly money. If not quite silly enough for Aggy's liking. She remembered Aggy was in hock to James for thousands and winced. She understood why James had kept it from her. Knowing what he'd done made her feel uncomfortable.

'I'm circulating,' Aggy said, wafting up to Anna, Michelle and Daniel's table with a giant glass of red. 'I'm on holiday with all my family and friends, when am I ever going to do that again? I don't want to miss a thing. Also, I'm letting you know that Chris and I have a surprise for you all tomorrow.'

'Oh God no,' Anna groaned. 'It better not involve audience participation.'

'Wait and see,' Aggy said, primly, and Anna clapped a palm over her eyes.

'I hate surprises,' Anna said. 'I like predictable things.'

'Boo to boring big sister. Now, what were you talking about? Wait— ' Aggy squealed, not waiting for an answer. 'You didn't tell me James Fraser had got back with his wife!'

Anna's stomach puckered in on itself like a deflated football.

'How do you know that?' she asked.

'Selfish of him, don't you think? Right when we'd earmarked him to give Anna a good seeing to,' Michelle said.

'I friended him on Facebook. His wife posted some love poem to his wall the other day. Loads of people were commenting on it,' Aggy said. 'I saw it when I checked my phone was working earlier. I was worried we wouldn't get a signal up here.'

'I can imagine you standing at the top of the mountain trying to touch a wire coat hanger to lightning if we couldn't,' Daniel said.

Anna writhed at this unexpected confirmation of the renewal of James's vows. *Posted a love poem to his wall.* Anna was biased, but Eva sounded a terrible person. She roiled with jealousy and misery like the water in a boiling kettle, fiddling with the stem of her glass.

'The wife's so gorge. They're going to have amazing babies.'

'Aggy, stop being such a snoop!' Anna snapped. 'You're not even a proper friend of his!'

'Yes I am!' she said, stung. 'I sent James an invite to the wedding but he had a work thing.'

'Aggy!' Anna squawked, shrilly.

'What? He's been really nice to me.'

'You should've asked me first.'

'Would you have said no?' Aggy said.

'Yes.'

'Why?' she asked.

Uhm …

'Because of the wife.'

'Is she that bad?' Aggy asked. 'I didn't think you knew her.' Michelle was appraising her, curious.

Anna had an image of herself in a large hole, furiously turfing earth over her shoulder with a shovel. Nobody at the table could quite read Anna's reaction, but they collectively sensed something was not right. Anna's instinct was always to absorb and conceal things that hurt her. She didn't want to do that anymore. They became weights that dragged you down.

'Sorry. It's not your fault, Aggy. It wouldn't be wrong. The thing was,' Anna drew breath, 'I accidentally, not intending to, sort of unhelpfully … ' – Anna was going to use a word she'd not tried out loud yet – '…fell in love with James Fraser. And right when I made a move, I found out he'd got back with Eva.'

Michelle and Aggy gasped.

'Do you know what, actually I'm not surprised,' Aggy said.

'You gasped!' Anna said.

'Yeah but it was a kind of "Wow,"' Aggy mimed a stunned look and then a nod. 'Not a "whaaaaat?!"' She put a palm up and shook her head. 'I totally knew. Once you were friends and had made up, I knew.'

'How did you know?'

'Number one, who *wouldn't* fancy him? I know you're my stupid sister but you're not that stupid. Two, you talked about him all the time.'

'This is true,' Michelle agreed, nipping the straw in her drink between her teeth. 'There has always been a lot of Can You Believe What James Said! Terrible, awful, infuriating, unacceptably sexual James.'

'So you knew before me? I wonder if he did too. God, that's a grim thought.'

'Did you tell him?' Daniel asked.

'That I was in love with him? Not in so many words. Well, not in any words in fact. I said something overtly flirty at the hen do, he looked mortified and announced he was back with Eva. *Awkward.*'

'Maybe you should have told him anyway,' Daniel said.

'Wouldn't that have made my humiliation greater, for no reason?'

'Yeah, but if he doesn't know, he can't do anything about it.'

'I don't think telling him will make his feelings for his wife go away,' Anna said.

She recalled their conversation about Eva when they were

on the London Eye. He'd seemed evasive about her. At the time, she'd half-thought it might be the words of a vain man, not admitting the strength of his affections in case his bid to win his wife back failed. Now she had every reason to hope he genuinely was undecided about her.

At that moment in time, Anna wished life was like one of Patrick's video games, with a chance to select an option, get machine-gunned for your stupidity and then reboot and choose another.

'Anyway, it would never have worked,' Anna said, in that tone of voice where you pretend to be resigned to something very raw. 'You all couldn't stand him.'

'We didn't like what he did back then,' Michelle poked ice cubes with her straw, 'but by the hen do I liked him. He'd made things right with you. He was a laugh. I could see him as a Mr Anna, sure.'

Aggy nodded.

'I was mad at him for not saying sorry to you but I could tell when I saw him at The Zetter that he was really sorry. If he'd treat you well now, that's what matters, and I think he would.'

'Oh,' Anna said, not sure whether to be pleased or not.

'And he has made a total mistake. You two are meant for each other,' Aggy said. 'You have the same hair colour. And the wife's Facebook photos are full of bathroom mirror selfies. Totally up herself. I don't know what James sees in her.'

'Apart from the startling looks,' Anna said.

'If he's chosen Eva over you then he wasn't good enough for you,' Aggy concluded, staunchly. 'No one good enough would rather have her than you.'

Anna smiled.

'Thanks. I can see why he can be good enough *and* pick her though. They're married, they have a house together, and a history, and a grumpy cat. It was never a fair fight. The weight of gravity is very much on her side.'

Everyone nodded politely and didn't query the binding nature of a grumpy cat.

'You know what Aggy's Facebook thing about posting the poem reminds me of though?' Anna said.

'Facebook is to stupid what jam is to wasps?' Michelle said.

'You can't get rid of anyone anymore. We are now in an age of digital eternity. Whenever I have a weak moment, I'll be able to see what James is doing. His profile picture will change to a sonogram, and then it'll be him with a kid, then another. I mean, literally, you can stalk people hourly nowadays. It'll be "James Junior is on the potty lol".'

'That's going to sting,' Michelle nodded.

Aggy sighed.

'Well, if this was a film, James would've done a dash to the airport to tell you he felt the same way before the plane took off,' she said.

'Not helpful, Agata!' Michelle said. 'And that airport dash is the bullshittiest of the clichés, I reckon. Most people go straight through passport control to get to the Duty Free, don't they? So are these loverboys buying a ticket just to make their speech? I do not think so.'

Aggy put her hand on her chin. 'Yeah …'

Anna wondered: was Daniel right? Should she have told James how she felt? She was ninety-nine per cent sure he was wrong and it would be a futile move. The remaining one per cent was enough to make her act though.

As the chatter continued around her, Anna opened an email. She felt as if she was limbering up for a feat of exertion. She began to type.

Dear James. I am in Italy, full of wine and pasta. The wine's more relevant in respect to what's to follow. All I can think about is how you brought this wedding about. You could probably shorten that to: all I can think about is you. I'm sorry that we can't be friends anymore, but that doesn't stop me wishing nothing but good things for you. I'll never regret that you came back into my life and changed it forever, for the better. I can't blame you for the fact I fell suddenly, unexpectedly, but it seems persistently, in love with you. I REALLY can't blame you, as you spent most of your time being rude to me. Anyway, guessing this is all a bit Mills & Boon for your tastes. I still remember your jokes about those. Take care of yourself. And Luther. And remember me fondly, like I will you. Anna xxx

Was it too much? In drink, at a distance and in emo-mood, it was so hard to tell. Sod it, she already knew she was going to send it. She clicked and cringed. She checked it was in her sent items. She sighed.

They left the restaurant and climbed on board the coach. As the bus steadily wound up the mountain to Barga, Anna checked her phone about seventeen times.

'All OK?' Michelle said, as they bumped up the road, over the volume of Aggy's singalong to Kelly Clarkson.

Anna admitted what she'd done.

'I know it doesn't stop you regretting him, but if he's thrown himself away on this icy Hitchcock blonde then he wasn't right for you.'

They rested heads on each other for the rest of the journey.

In the seats behind, Anna could hear Daniel deep in conversation with a PR girl who was explaining 'friend zoning' to him. Anna smiled. She was sort of sad, but she was happy-sad. She'd done all she could; whatever would be, would be.

As Anna was turning out the light in their room in the spartan-but-pretty B&B, she accepted the probability that the email had been read was very high, and that meant the chance of a reply was now very low.

She could picture the scene when James received it, far, far away, entwined with the feline Eva on the pink couch, Luther next to them.

'Who's that?' Eva would say. *Oh. No one.*

The lack of light pollution meant the room had the kind of thick velvet blackness where you could hardly see your hand in front of your face. Yet she could see James's face, clear as if he was right in front of her.

As she was falling asleep, her phone pinged with a message alert. She started awake and scrambled for it, the phone casting an eerie moonglow on the nightstand. *Please have said something nice … something I can hold on to while I wait for the wanting to go away.*

She grabbed the handset and opened her mail.

Anna! Long time no talk! I notice you've gone quiet on the dating front. Ready for a second attempt at chasing that incredibly elusive 'spark' yet? ☺ Neil x

68

Anna feared her sister might be a whirling dervish on her wedding day, and well, a little unbearable. But as the day dawned, Aggy became regally serene and calm. It was as if now that all her plans had come to fruition, she could now simply ride it, like a noblewoman in a sedan chair. At a late breakfasting hour, she sat sipping a peach bellini in the B&B's largest bedroom, while the hairdresser threaded small pearls on fine wire into her up-do and her dress hung against a large rosewood wardrobe, their mother having done an inch-by-inch inspection to make sure its splendour was unsullied by horny-handed airport staff. When satisfied, she then took over the 'unbearable' duties, clucking, fretting, fussing and shrieking all morning long.

By midday, Anna couldn't stand it any longer and said something chiding-yet-mild about the importance of keeping Aggy on an even keel so she didn't get over-wound. Her mother replied: 'But this might be the only time I'm ever a mother of the bride!'

Anna said it was a good job she wasn't all that bothered about getting wed or that *might* be construed as hurtful, but Judy had already moved on to bleating about some other aspect of the arrangements.

The bridesmaid was into her full costume in well under an hour, hair and make-up finished, an outsize white silk rose affixed to the side of her head, peacefully reading a book about medieval Italy.

'Aureliana, how can you read a book on your sister's wedding day?!' her mother wailed.

'She's only having her hair done. I won't be reading it during the ceremony.'

Her mother tutted in horror. Anna padded over to the window, with its deep sill, and opened the latch. The scenery beyond was majestic – they were so high up that low-hanging cloud wreathed the hills in frothy, smoky wisps. The air was full of the scent of soil and vegetation, the warmth of the weak, wintery sun heating the earth.

Being among her family and friends, surrounded by loved ones, was the best thing for Anna's spirit. When Aggy had finished being froufed, as Anna hoped her father had practised calling it, she stood up, one hand on her skirts. A lace-edged veil spilled down her back.

'Well?' Aggy said.

'Astonishing!' Anna said, surprising herself as a tear rolled down her face. Her little sister, who she used to fight over the TV remote with in Superted pyjamas, was now a vision of black glossy hair and snowy tulle.

Their mother sank to the bed in her spring green Phase Eight shift dress and had to be handed the full packet of Kleenex scented tissues while she whimpered. She left them, reluctantly, with Anna offering gentle encouragement that the guests needed her more than they did, now that Aggy was in her finery.

'So. Ready to get married?' Anna said, once they were alone.

Aggy's false-eyelashed eyes widened. 'Shit. I'm getting married!'

'You are,' Anna said. 'To Chris. I love him almost as much as you do. You did good, Aggy.'

'Oh, Anna!' Aggy said, putting her arms round her. 'You're the best sister. There's someone out there for you who's going to love you as much as we all do. I know there is. I *promise* you. And this will be you one day.'

'That would be nice, but I honestly don't need him. And I'm going to enjoy your wedding just as much as I would mine. Probably more. I have everyone I need here. You know I've always needed you the most. More than anyone.'

'Oh … that's so lovely …' Aggy's face crumpled. 'Sometimes I think about how I nearly … we nearly lost you …'

'No! Don't think that! Oh, Aggy…'

They whimpered at each other with heavily panda-ed eyes and realised the potential make-up catastrophe that was coming their way.

'No crying!' Anna barked, hoarse with emotion. 'Mum will kill us if our mascara runs!'

'Woah woah woah,' Aggy and Anna had to dance a Zulu dance in small circles trying to get the tears to stall, flapping their hands at their faces.

'Think of something un-emotional!' Anna urged her. 'Hang on, drink! Throw it past the lipstick.' She pushed the dregs of a bellini into Aggy's hand and swigged the remainder of her mother's.

'Better? Under control?' Anna said.

Aggy nodded.

'Let's go, before we well up again.'

Clasping tightly-packed bouquets of white roses, the sisters walked from the B&B to the building for the civil ceremony, Aggy holding her gown an inch from the ground, with Anna following close behind her. They made stately, elegant progress due to the height of their heels and the steepness of the narrow, stone-flagged streets that wound between the washed-out vanilla colours of the villas. Everyone who saw them stopped, clapped and occasionally wolf-whistled as they passed.

Elderly Italian villagers stood in doorways calling, 'Bella! Bella!' When they said 'thank you', a man on a rickety bicycle shouted, in accented English, 'Marry me! Marry me!' to more laughter and applause.

Aggy wouldn't have had this in London, Anna thought. It felt so much more special than sitting in a white Rolls in traffic. The town was spontaneously coming to a standstill for them, and had the special, peculiar charm that only unplanned elements can bring. Anna felt as if she was in a film, or a very high-budget advert for Mastercard.

'This is the best wedding ever,' Anna said over her shoulder, 'and it hasn't even started yet.'

It had only just turned from morning to afternoon. Anna loved the freshness of the air up here, you could smell the chestnut trees that covered the mountains beyond. It was autumnally brisk but not cold, and out of season, the town was peaceful. No expensive hotel could compete with this sort of beauty — terracotta tiles, geranium-filled window boxes, the dusty lemons, corals and greys of the paintwork, the shutters painted a deep grass-green. In the distance, a vista of rolling hills could be seen, filled with clusters of cypress tree spindles.

'You definitely know the way?' Anna said, to the back of her sister's head.

'Oh yeah. I checked it like a hundred times,' Aggy said.

'Good. We don't want to arrive with our phones out, looking at Google Maps. Are you nervous?'

'I was before I got in my dress. But now I don't want to waste a moment not enjoying being in my dress.'

As they reached the top of the incline, their father stood waiting for them.

'*Mie bellissime figlie!*'

He kissed Anna on the cheek and held out the crook of his arm for Aggy. They all beamed at each other, saying nothing, sharing this small moment before a big moment.

'Veil down?' Anna said, gesturing at it.

'Oh yeah. Dad, can you…?' Aggy turned.

Their father obliged with fumbling hands and Anna suddenly felt choked. It was weird how you didn't think you were into things like proper white weddings, then on the day you had your heart split apart by it. She wanted to burst into the room and tell everyone she loved them, although they would probably spot the influence of a bellini.

Anna took a deep breath as the shuttered doors were opened and she stepped into the room. She paced herself walking the aisle, holding the bouquet in front of her. Behind her, the wedding march struck up and she could hear the ripple of reaction as Aggy followed.

The registrar at the Palazzo Comunale wore a sash in the colours of the il Tricolore flag and Chris looked endearingly nervous and unusually brushed up and neat in his cravat and tails.

He winked at Anna. She was so glad Aggy was marrying someone who truly loved her.

The service went smoothly, and everyone politely tittered at Aggy's vows and possibly found humour where none was quite intended. While Chris's were about the things he truly loved about Aggy: her concern for other people, her sweet nature, and the way she always bounced back tirelessly from adversity. There were some knowing smiles at that. And then, a kiss, applause, and Anna's sister was a wife; one with a husband that Anna was very pleased to have as a brother.

The mothers dabbed their eyes while the painter-decorators and Hornsey contingent whooped and wolf-whistled. People had always praised Anna as a good influence on Aggy, the properly grown-up elder sister who took care of her. But at that moment, Anna thought how well her sister took care of her. Anna needed someone around with Aggy's joie de vivre and jump-in-feet-first attitude to life. Someone who'd once literally yanked her right back into the land of the living.

Outside the ceremony, a loud cheer went up as they threw handfuls of rose petals at the happy couple. And they were happy, they really were. Anna had seen her younger sister over-excited too many times to count, but this was the glow of real lasting contentment.

They streamed back down through the streets and piled into the bus which would take them to the restaurant where the reception was to be held, half an hour's drive away.

The restaurant, Da Serena, was a vast, barn-like space, run by generations of a local family. The rows of tables were set with paper tablecloths, pots of breadsticks and platters of bruschetta. Anna was wearing a tube slip under her dress that looked and felt like it had been designed by the aeronautics industry, and hoped she was going to be able to do the many courses justice.

At one end of the room there was a stage where a band was setting up. The room was so cavernous there'd be no need for 'turning it around' between day and night. For the umpteenth time, Anna thought how much nicer the atmosphere was than a crucifyingly expensive venue with rules, regulations and fiddly food.

As they took their places for the meal, Anna realised she was sitting opposite a raffishly gorgeous Italian man with a kind of curly mop top. He looked as if he should be draped across a Vespa on the cover of *GQ Italia*.

'Aureliana?' he said, in that beautiful accent. 'Primo.'

Oh good grief, yes, Primo. She'd forgotten about him. *Thanks Aggy, even at your wedding breakfast, I'm on a blind date.* No wonder she was so vehement there was a man in the pipeline for Anna. That said, getting off with a stupendous Tuscan architect tonight wasn't the worst way to deal with her existential pain. Plus, he was eyeing her the way a stray dog looks at a chop.

In some situations Anna might've minded, but right now she'd take the boost. She fluttered her not-all-natural eyelashes and as the meal got underway, happily accepted regular refills of vino rosso.

Primo had very good English, but conversation felt stilted all the same.

'You work very hard?' he said, over the prosciutto and salami.

'I suppose I work quite hard. But I love it,' Anna said to Primo.

'You are so beautiful,' Primo said, in a sudden lurch in topic, as if he was remarking on the weather.

'Wow thanks. You can stay,' Anna said, feeling distinctly more British than Italian in the face of a compliment. He held her gaze and she heard a line of Michelle's come back to her: *you can see the moment it dawns on them that they're going to get it.* It had dawned on Anna and she thought: should I? On the one hand, it would be making meaningless fun, not love. On the other. Rrrrrr, Primo.

After more food than Anna thought it was possible to eat in one sitting, and speeches, they were all ushered towards the stage for what Anna assumed would be the first dance.

The band struck up and Aggy appeared, holding a microphone. She launched into a stately a cappella version of a song that Anna didn't instantly recognise.

'Shakira, "Underneath Your Clothes",' Michelle helpfully supplied.

'Oh no. A song about your man with his kit off?' Anna whispered back. 'Only my sister . . .'

'Bold choice,' Michelle said. 'The oldies seem to be coping with the frisson though.'

Anna looked towards her parents and the Barking contingent. They were all looking vaguely baffled, apart from her mother, who was swaying with a look of intense pride. The Italian family seemed similarly nonplussed but generally positive.

At the other side of the stage, Chris walked on with a microphone and started singing over Aggy. The tempo sped up and her song segued into Cee Lo Green's 'Forget You'. The lyrics about money and needing to be rich to be with Aggy were amusingly appropriate, if a little near the knuckle.

They could both hold a tune, more or less. But more importantly, Anna thought, it must surely end soon.

Oh, no. Marianne led a gang of PR girls onto the stage behind Aggy and they started singing 'You Know I'm No Good'.

Anna turned to Michelle.

'Infidelity now. What next? "The Drugs Don't Work"?'

Michelle was shoulder-dancing: 'The tune works quite well though.'

Anna looked across the room and her mum and Aunty Carol were bopping about doing mum-dancing to the words '*carpet burn*'.

Chris's brother and best man Dave and the ushers piled onto the stage behind him and 'You Know I'm No Good' became Rod Stewart's 'Do Ya Think I'm Sexy' in a back-and-forth *West Side Story* gang sing-a-thon.

'Is it me, or is this arseing mental?' Anna said to Michelle, weak with laughter.

Aggy disembarked from the stage as the dance floor filled and passing Anna, skirts gathered in one hand, squealed: 'What did you think? A riff off! Like in *Pitch Perfect*! I hope Uncle Riccardo got that taped. I'm putting it online when we get home. No one's ever had that before!'

'For … a reason?' Anna said, but Aggy wasn't listening.

Michelle had been grabbed and whisked onto the dance floor by an elderly Italian uncle whose gaze was split between Michelle's face and chest. Meanwhile, Daniel was deep in conversation with the PR crowd. Who'd have thought he'd find such kindred spirits among the *Grazia* girls? They'd been schooling him in their Recovery Rules after a break-up. Anna doubted Dan needed to watch *The Notebook* that many times though.

Primo found Anna amid the crowd.

'Smoke?' he said, doing a putting-cigarette-to-mouth-and-taking-it-away gesture. 'Outside?'

Anna wasn't well practised in the arts of woo but she recognised that a smoke probably wasn't all Primo was intending.

'Yeah. Why not?' she said.

69

They walked through the gardens outside, crunching out onto the gravel stones of the wide car park. The edge of it fell away into the mountains, the scenery plunging into blackness. The only light burned from the building behind and the vehicles that winked as they dipped in and out of sight, winding round the mountain.

'It's so fresh somehow, up here,' Anna said, shivering, looking up at the low-hanging moon. It was cold but they were glowing with booze-warmth. 'Like you don't realise how choked you are down in the cities. All that ... pollution.'

It was quite difficult working out what to say to someone when you thought they might try to stick their tongue down your throat at any moment.

Primo put his hand inside his suit pocket and produced cigarettes and a silver lighter. Handing a cigarette to Anna, he clicked it alight in one smooth move.

She sucked smoke down into her lungs with the cold air and started coughing violently.

'I don't – smoke – ' she said, as she hacked.

'You don't smoke?' Primo said, white eyes and teeth sparkling.

Anna shook her head, spluttering, whilst waving her hand in front of her mouth.

'Ah, no,' Primo said, laughing, putting a hand lightly on her back.

Anna barely had any time to get her breath back before Primo had put his arm round her, with one hand right on her backside. Goodness, Italians didn't muck about.

'Aureliana,' he said, and it was lovely to hear her name in the appropriate accent. She thought about succumbing. But she didn't want this. She wanted someone else. All of a sudden, after a day of enjoying so much company, she badly needed to be alone. She drew back.

'Primo,' she said. 'Can I have a moment?'

She wasn't sure if he understood her.

'Just me,' she added. 'And my first cigarette.' She waved it. 'And the moon. La luna!'

'I'll see you inside?' he said, nonplussed, obviously thinking British girls drank as much as he'd heard.

'Definitely.'

Primo turned and left her and Anna stood with her smouldering cigarette, shivering, staring at the mountains beyond. She wasn't the same person to the one who went to that reunion, she thought.

She wasn't sure she was going to go back to internet dating. Single Anna was whole Anna. Not finding someone wasn't a failure, it was just a fact. If others chose to draw conclusions from it, then let them. There were lots of other facts about her. She loved her job, she loved her friends and family. She'd had a crap time at school and she'd tell anyone who asked her about it – but it was time she stopped feeling defined by it.

Oh yes, and her idea to end the awkwardness between her and Patrick by finding him in World of Warcraft, where he was a panda and she was an Undead Warlock? *That* was a good idea. Well, she hoped. They were chatting easily again. Though Patrick was trying to get her to go on raiding missions, whatever they were.

Anna put the cigarette to her mouth again and practised the angle as she took a drag. Anna, she thought, you will never be cool. And you don't need to be.

There came a light crunch of gravel underfoot and a male voice, somewhere behind her.

'I didn't know you smoked?'

She turned to see James standing in front of her, clean shaven in a dark suit and white shirt.

Anna stared and stared, and then stared some more.

'I don't,' she said.

Despite the fact that James looked, as Aggy would put it, 'ZOMGs', it wasn't his handsome man-ness but his best friend-ness that struck her, right in the solar plexus. He was one of her very best friends. He was here.

She dropped the cigarette, ground it under her heel, pelted towards him and grabbed him hard round the middle, with both arms.

'It's so good to see you,' she said, squeezing him, feeling the crush of material and the smell of a new shirt and his solidity underneath as he hugged her back.

The miracle of James Fraser suddenly being in a car park, up a mountain in Italy? Whatever he had come to say, she knew a prayer had been answered.

'Thanks for your message,' James said, as she disentangled

and stepped back.

'You got it! I wasn't sure about … network coverage.'

'I got it,' he said, looking at her steadily, and Anna's insides went a little liquid.

'I maybe shouldn't have sent it to a married man.'

'Separated. Divorcing.'

'Oh.'

James cleared his throat.

'You said you remember my stupid jokes? Well, I remember things you say too. You said you liked it when a man made a big declaration of his feelings. This could be quite embarrassing, but shall I have a go?'

James grinned and Anna nodded.

'OK. So. The thing was, when I met you again, I realise now I was pretty lost. I've never been very good at picking the right path. Then there you were, and you changed everything. All my stupid nonsense, it had worked with other people but I knew, almost straight away, you were different. To be around you, I had to drop that and be better. And before I knew it, I was falling in love with you.'

Suddenly, Anna no longer felt the cold.

'You think school is some sort of shame, but it's not, or not for you. The way you came through it proved what an extraordinary person you are. That's what I want to tell you, and it's more important than saying I'm madly in love with you, because being in love with you is easy, Anna. But what you've done is difficult. You are extraordinary.'

He paused for breath and Anna burst out, 'James, it's so nice you think I'm an admirable person, but you need to actually fancy me. You said you thought of me as a sister … and you said yourself I'm not your type …'

'Oh for God's sake, I was lying to try to seem cool,' James said. 'If I didn't fancy you, would I kiss you like this?'

He stepped forward and leaned down, his hand on her face.

Anna may have burned her teenage diaries, but if she had one left, she'd open it write in the margin to tell her past self that her premonition was true.

One day, James Fraser would kiss her so passionately that she'd forget anything else had ever mattered.

70

James broke away from her for the second time with some self-discipline, and adjusted the drooping rose on the side of her head.

She was always beautiful, but tonight she looked ridiculously lovely.

'We should go inside,' he said, quietly.

'Can't we run off, just the two of us?' Anna said, putting her arms round his middle again. The outline of her body against his made him feel slightly stomach-turbulent.

'Hmmm, we could. I think your sister's wedding is unmissable, though.'

He gripped her hand in his as they walked down the path.

'How did you find us?!' Anna said.

'A combination of Aggy's wedding invite and then a very arsey taxi driver. I texted her to tell her I was coming and to keep it secret. Do you know your sister's answering texts on her wedding day?'

'Nothing surprises me less.'

'Do you want to introduce me to your parents?' James said.

'Yes. Who should I say you are?'

'Laszlo Biro, inventor of the ballpoint pen? Or, how about James?'

'I mean, as my boyfriend?'

'I know what you meant.'

They bumped into the Alessis almost as soon as they were in the doorway of the venue.

'Mum, Dad, this is James. My … boyfriend,' Anna said, gripping his hand more tightly.

They looked understandably startled to learn of a boyfriend at the same time as meeting him, but went with it.

'Anna's never said a word!' her mother exclaimed.

'I think she wanted it to be a surprise?' James said.

'You're certainly that,' she said, and Anna rolled her eyes.

'You were delayed?' her dad said.

'Ah yes. By one thing or another,' James said. 'I'm very glad to be here now though.'

'Consider this place if you two ever marry,' her dad said.

'Dad!' Anna cried.

'Very reasonable, quality fare and all that outdoor space if you choose spring or summer. Put a tent up, have a barbecue. Anything you like. And Italians aren't like the British with their drink. No vomiting.'

'It couldn't be nicer here, Mr Alessi. Zero vomiting. You must be very proud.'

Her dad reached out and patted James's shoulder.

'You take care of my daughter. This one's my favourite.'

James laughed while Anna's mum tutted.

They waved hello to Anna's friends across the room who looked suitably amazed, her friend Michelle then making a 'get in' pumping arm gesture.

'Dance with me?' James said.

James led Anna onto the dance floor and held her waist. He could feel the tight layer of material girdling her beneath the rough texture of the lace of her dress. He felt so incredibly lucky that she was his and he was here.

'So. No Eva?' Anna asked.

'I came to my senses there. Sorry it took so long. Slow learner. She didn't move back in. However, I warn you that in the terms of the separation, I'm losing the house but keeping Luther. Don't take me on if you don't want him; we're a package deal.'

Anna smiled broadly.

'Seeing Eva again made me realise it was you I had to have. All I could think about was you.'

James's mind returned to the strangeness of the previous evening, Eva walking from kitchen to front room, barefoot, with a bottle of Chablis with an Alessi corkscrew wedged in it, and him staring at it and realising tonight was the night she would expect to stay over. Everything had suddenly come into sharp focus, with a millimetre twist of the camera lens.

He didn't want her to stay. He wanted someone else. Someone he didn't realise he absolutely couldn't live without anymore until he was required to live without her. He'd simply blurted he'd met someone else. Eva had been stunned, then shouted and wailed about his lack of emotional honesty. Somehow, his falling in love with Anna got very unfavourably compared to Eva falling in lust with Finn, which he didn't quite follow. The fact he and Anna hadn't slept together also made it worse, even more confusingly.

It was as if Eva was behind toughened glass, and they were

only speaking on those telephone handsets. *I'm so sorry*, he kept saying. *I didn't know until now. I didn't expect it either.*

Eva left and James spent two hours going back and forth over whether the evidence suggested Anna wanted a lovesick divorcee offering her his heart or just a shag on the spur of a moment. Then his phone received a message.

He'd nearly called her on a steep international rate and stormed about saying florid, half-cut and over-the-top things about how she never need worry about anyone letting her down again. But then he dwelt on the generosity of the gesture she'd made.

She had no reason to bare her soul, or reassure him he'd done her good rather than harm. Or to say such a warm farewell. Her only motive was care for him. A gesture like that deserved another.

'How did we take so long to work this out, then?' James said to Anna. 'It's probably been glaringly obvious to anyone but us for a while. I mean, we fooled everyone in my office without even trying. That should've been a sign, perhaps?'

'I didn't properly know how I felt until the hen do,' Anna said. 'And you can't have known, then?'

'I had some idea. I was like a slow-wit with a jigsaw of Big Ben and one last piece he was refusing to put in, saying he still couldn't see the picture. So it was the hen do?' he said, squeezing her gently, with a smile. 'Interesting. That was why you made that disgustingly brash play for me?'

'You cheeky sod! I was trying to be enticing.'

'"Come round and rate my rack sometime." What it lacked in mystery it certainly made up for in earthy appeal.'

They laughed and James said: 'I've missed that laugh. In all honesty I might have tried my luck earlier but I never thought you liked me *that way*.'

'Oh, well. I don't really. I'm just closing my eyes and concentrating on your bubbly personality.'

George Michael yodelled 'A Different Corner' and she put her head on his chest.

Aggy and her husband were further away on the dance floor and she waved a hello at James, whilst he raised a palm in return.

He was in a foreign country at a wedding surrounded by people he didn't know, and yet he felt more at home than he ever had.

A word came into his head, about his feelings for Anna. It wasn't a word that he ever used, but it was the right one: adore.

He adored her.

71

His dark gaze slid over the swell of her bosom in the silken negligee. He ran a hand across his stubbled jaw as he feasted on the sight of her.

'Mi carina!' he exclaimed, in gruff approval. It was no longer merely a term of endearment but an urgent demand. He required nothing less than the complete surrender of her unsullied womanhood to his power.

She wilted under the determined intensity of his stare as the rosy bloom of innocence washed her cheeks.

'You have toyed with me long enough, *inamorata*,' he said, his breath becoming ragged, taking a lock of her flaxen hair between finger and thumb.

'N-n-no!' she cried. 'Think of your responsibilities, Luca! You cannot inherit the estate of the De Vici family if you marry a woman who the family has not chosen for you. And you must not use me as a—' her voice trembled and lashes fluttered at the indelicacy, 'passing fancy.'

A curse in his native tongue escaped his lips and his cobalt eyes flashed. 'Duty be damned! I must possess you!' He was poised, ready to devour her, to dominate her as the hungry lion with its prey, as . . .

'Sorry, have you got a menu?'

'Oh! Thanks,' Anna said, looking up from her Kindle at the waiter in the spotted neckerchief, who was proffering two textured sheets of paper.

In the fourteen minutes she'd been sat at the table in Morito in Clerkenwell, the Italian Count had been working up to a serious dicking, and she'd forgotten all about the necessity of choosing tapas dishes.

'Would you like to order drinks?'

She scanned down.

'Two of the tinto de veranos, thanks.'

'I'm not late, am I?' James said, appearing beside her. He leant across to give her a quick kiss before flinging his bag down, cold skin pressed against her warmer face.

'A little, but I'll let you off,' Anna said, her face lighting up.

The chill made his pale skin look as if he'd been hewn from marble, by a sculptor who could really do cheekbones. Had anyone else ever looked as beautiful while shrugging their coat off and muttering: '*Harris outdid himself in ludicrous titfers today, he's got a canary-yellow top hat. I feel like I'm working in the Wonka factory*'?

Anna doubted it.

'I was kept company by the Italian Count, anyway,' she said, holding her Kindle up.

The drinks were placed in front of them.

'What's this?' James said, tipping the glass.

'Tinto de verano. Faffed-with red wine. It's nice.'

James clinked his glass to hers and sipped. 'Lovely.'

Anna beamed.

'Right, let's see some of the Italian Count's action.' He held his hand out for the Kindle. 'If you're admiring some other man's prowess, I want to compare notes.'

Anna passed it over, with a broad smile.

Bar snacks arrived with the drinks and Anna popped an almond into her mouth.

'*He was poised, ready to devour her, to dominate her as the hungry lion with its prey, as she quivered with ecstatic need …*' James read aloud.

'The woolly thinking really lets it down. Lion's prey? What, hyenas? Warthogs? So what he's about to do is make love to her like a predator chewing the windpipe out of a flailing warthog?'

Anna started gurgling with laughter.

'You're ruining it!'

'No, I think it's the poor choice of metaphor that's ruining it.'

Anna looked at him as he read on and thought about how much she had enjoyed the space he now occupied in her bed, and her life, even if Luther's litter tray really wasn't the charm in her kitchen. And she wouldn't be telling James this, but the shouty Count really had nothing on him. Especially as James had made sure she knew how very attractive he found her, both in words and actions. Her pupils dilated at the thought.

James clicked to turn the page. 'Something something "*became near-demented with arousal and uttered words they barely heard … she shattered into a million pieces*"? Uh?'

He looked up at Anna.

'That's her … that's the end result of the Count's hard Count-ing. They always shatter or explode.'

'Ohhh …' James said, 'I see.'

429

'… She thinks maybe he's infatuated with her but it'll wear off and he won't marry her. But guess what? He will.'

Anna sipped her drink and James handed her Kindle back.

'What happens after they boff, then? Do they transfer this level of intensity to the Sainsbury's run? Is Count thingy trying to scan bags of pre-washed salad, storming: "Yield to me!" at the self-service till?'

'No, once they do it, it's over. They get married and maybe there's a hint of kids but, that's it.'

'Why all the emphasis on marriage?'

'Mills & Boon heroines don't usually do string-free bonks. There's always a wedding at the end.'

'Seems sexist.'

'Well, yes. It is an old-fashioned fantasy.'

'Working men's clubs are sexist but you wouldn't fantasise about them.'

'Are you seriously surprised that some modern, independent women still like weddings? You came to my sister's, so you can't be in any doubt about that.'

James laughed. 'I'm trying to work out the appeal of these archaic attitudes. It's so irrelevant now. I mean, are *you* really into the idea of getting wed, in the first flush of a new relationship?'

'Uh …' Anna ate another almond to stall for time. 'I'm not sure. It'd be nice, I suppose. Ask me again when I find the man I want to marry.' She grinned.

'Oof.'

'I used to do this thing, on internet dates. I'd imagine that what happened during the date might end up in a best man's speech,' Anna continued.

'You were on a first date, imagining the wedding speeches?

Woah.'

'This makes me sound mental but it's not really. Couples who meet naturally don't know they're meeting for the first time, right? On a date, you do know. And how you met always comes up in the wedding speeches.'

'Keep talking, I'm just calculating the weight of the waiter who's blocking the doorway,' James said.

'You've got no worries, I don't do this with *you*. I'm guessing you don't want to, anyway. Again, I mean,' Anna said, trying for an air of affectless easiness, and missing, slightly.

'Oooh boy.' James reached for another olive. '"My intentions."'

'No! Let's drop this.'

'This *is* our first proper date though. That's the one which always comes up in the speeches, isn't it?'

'Usually. Or how you met.'

'Hmmm. Can you pass me that napkin?'

Anna handed over a paper napkin, as James found a pen inside his coat pocket and clicked the nib.

Anna gazed at his tangle of blue-black hair as he dragged the biro across the tissue. He handed the napkin back to her. She unfolded it.

I WOULD MARRY THE HELL OUT OF YOU.

Amid the crush and clatter of the restaurant, Anna was perfectly still, and smiling.

'There, we're future-proofed now,' James said, clicking the pen. 'The speech won't have to be about me being an idiot when we were sixteen, or "James took the mickey out of The

Italian Count's Potato Croquette on Anna's Kindle."'

Anna felt as if her heart was full to brimming.

They looked down at the menus, James reaching for Anna's hand across the table.

'You're rehearsing the wording with the napkin in it, aren't you?' James said, glancing up after a minute.

'No!' Anna looked up, having not taken in a word of tonight's specials. 'I'm thinking about the … cheese balls.'

'There aren't any cheese balls.'

'That was what I was thinking.'

They laughed, loudly enough that the couple at the next table looked over.

The waiter appeared at their side, pen poised.

'Ready?' he said.

They looked at each other and nodded.

So for those of you here today who don't know, James and Anna met at school…

THE END

LOVE WHAT YOU'VE READ?

Keep an eye out for Mhairi's next book which will hit the shelves in winter 2014.

And if you've got any smarts at all, you'll follow Mhairi on Twitter @MhairiMcF and visit www.mhairimcfarlane.com to keep up to date with more of her brilliant writing.

Rachel and Ben. Ben and Rachel.
It was them against the world.
Until it all fell apart ...

Hilarious, heartbreaking and everything in between, you'll
be hooked from their first 'hello'.

Get the number one bestselling novel from Mhairi
McFarlane in all good book stores now.

Follow Avon on
Twitter@AvonBooksUK
and
Facebook@AvonBooksUK
For news, giveaways and
exclusive author extras